The Tides That Reign
Book 1

DESIGN OF DARKNESS

By RD Pires

This is a work of fiction. Names, characters, places, and incidents either are the product of the author's imagination or are used fictitiously. Any resemblance to actual persons, living or dead, events, or locales is entirely coincidental.

DESIGN OF DARKNESS. Copyright 2024 © R.D.PIRES. All rights reserved. No part of this book may be used or reproduced in any manner whatsoever without written permission except in the case of brief quotations embodied in critical articles and reviews. For more information visit www.midnightmeadowpublishing.com.

Cover design by Elizabeth Jeannel

ISBN 978-1-956037-38-8 (hardcover)

ISBN 978-1-956037-37-1 (paperback)

ISBN 978-1-956037-36-4 (eBook)

First Edition

First Edition: June 2024

This eBook edition first published in 2024

Published by Midnight Meadow Publishing

www.midnightmeadowpublishing.com

Midnight Meadow Publishing

Contents

CHAPTER ONE ... 1
- Mariana ... 1
- Kaori ... 27
- Mariana ... 49
- Emilio ... 68

CHAPTER TWO ... 78
- Kaori ... 78
- Helena ... 94
- Arsenio ... 101
- Kaori ... 115

CHAPTER THREE ... 125
- Arsenio ... 125
- Helena ... 135
- Emilio ... 144
- Mariana ... 158

CHAPTER FOUR ... 171
- Arsenio ... 171
- Kaori ... 183
- Emilio ... 198
- Arsenio ... 204
- Queen Yiscel ... 214

CHAPTER FIVE ... 227
- Helena ... 227
- Mariana ... 240
- Kaori ... 264
- Ira ... 274
- Queen Yiscel ... 286

CHAPTER SIX ... 292

Kaori	292
Emilio	306
Mariana	313
Kaori	322
CHAPTER SEVEN	**338**
Ira	338
Arsenio	346
Emilio	358
Arsenio	369
CHAPTER EIGHT	**380**
Taigen	380
Mariana	391
Queen Yiscel	400
Ira	410
Kaori	417
ACKNOWLEDGEMENTS	427
About the Author	429

TAISCHON

NOKARA

Taischon Channel

Jishian River
· Xialiao
Keepers Village
· Nanwida · Black Tide Cove
· Maigoda
Taiganji · Genjiko

Lake Hiroshi
Daimon Straight

· Hado
Shondai ·

Lake Okoda

Komorebi ·

Masaka ·

THE
SERT
EA

N W E S

KAILON

BANGUET

ASTER

Banguet City

SAMPAGUITA

Pauwe

Singober

MEDINILLA

MAUHELE

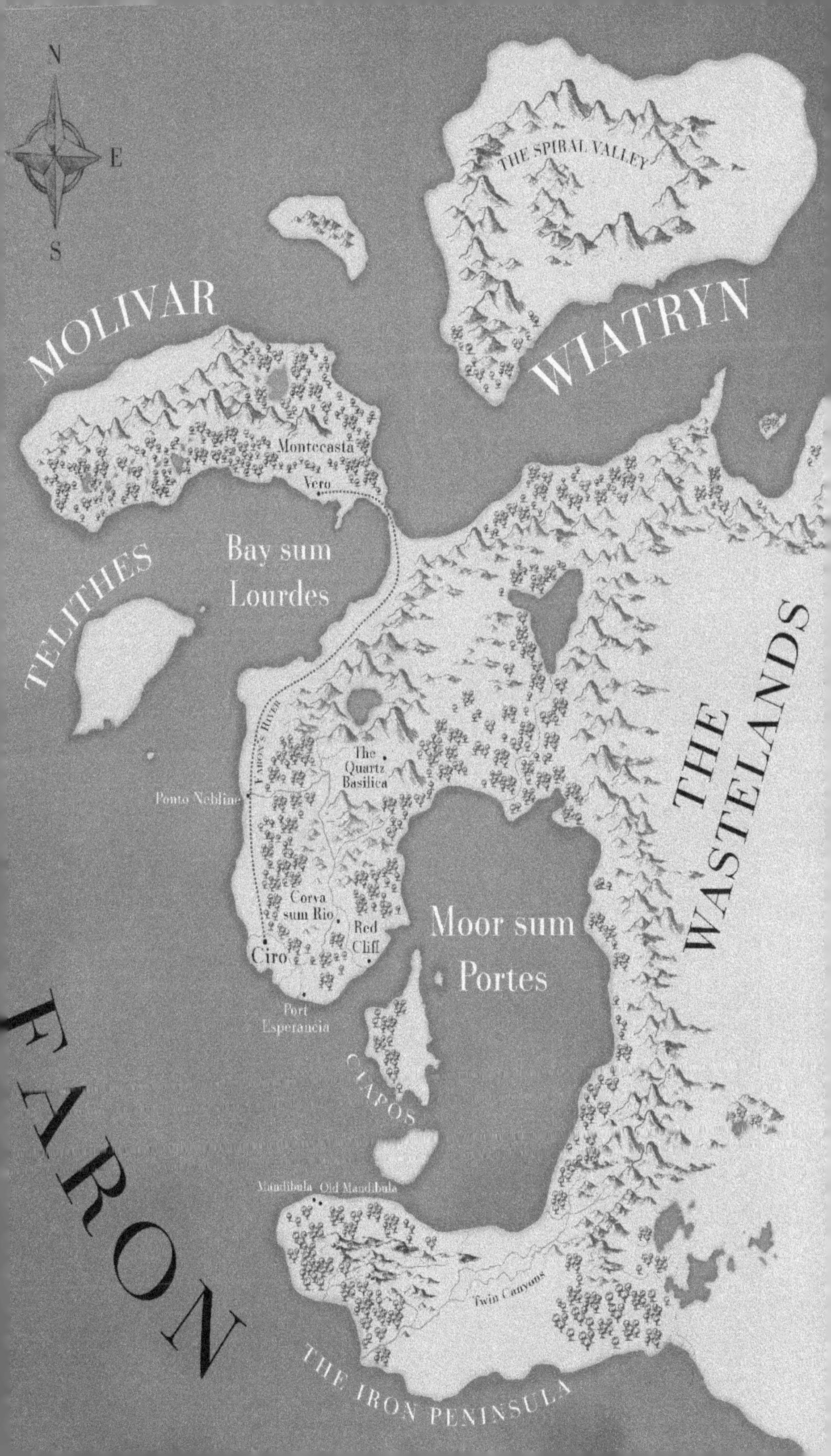
N
E
S
MOLIVAR
WIATRYN
THE SPIRAL VALLEY
Montecasta
Vero
TELITHES
Bay sum
Lourdes
FARON'S RIVER
The
Quartz
Basilica
Ponto Nebline
Corva
sum Rio
Red
Cliff
Ciro
Port
Esperancia
Moor sum
Portes
CIAPOS
THE
WASTELANDS
FARON
Mandibula
Old Mandibula
Twin Canyons
THE IRON PENINSULA

For Alex

Manuscripts change, but my love for you does not.

CHAPTER ONE
FROM THE FIRE

Mariana

Red light bled through the cracks in the shutters. Outside, panicked voices shouted to one another. Windows and doors slammed. Feet pounded the dirt like drums. She stared, unable to move until the crescendo of noise and thrashing of her heart became too much to ignore.

Mariana flew to the window and threw open the shutters.

A flickering, orange glow painted the buildings. Though a chill clung to the winter night, waves of heat emanated from fire to the north. Below her window, the villagers fled, some still in their bedclothes, others struggling to dress. Mariana traced their path upstream until she was looking into the heart of the flames, the brightness growing steadily.

She darted away from the window to the armoire. Her field trousers and shirt from that day lay haphazardly inside. Grabbing them both, she shoved them on over her sleepwear. Then, she dived to the floor, reaching an arm beneath the bed to grab her best boots. The second she had them on, the door flew open.

"Mari!" Helena tumbled through. Her eyes were wide with panic as she fell to her hands and knees, chest heaving.

Mariana hurried forward and helped her younger sister stand. "What's happening?"

"I don't know! It must be a raid."

Together, they fled the room. As they passed an open door in the hallway, Mariana skidded to a halt. "Find Mamãe and Papai," she shouted to her sister.

Backtracking to the doorway, she found Arsenio struggling to get his arms through a black leather vest. He wore only one boot and his hair stood up straight. He must have been the last to wake.

"Brother!" Mariana called, beckoning him with a flapping hand.

"One second," Arsenio replied through gritted teeth. He nearly ripped the vest in two before his other arm slid through the hole. Then, he sank onto the bed, his foot high in the air while he shoved the second boot into place. He looked around the room, again muttering, "One second."

"We don't have another second!" Mariana pleaded.

Lunging forward, he snatched a black pouch from the bookshelf. As he followed his sister out of the bedroom, he grabbed a burgundy sash which hung by the door. Mariana tried not to roll her eyes at him as she led him down the stairs. Even in a crisis, her twin was never one for impropriety.

Helena stood in the kitchen with their parents.

"—people are trapped," their papai, Severino, was saying.

"My children," said their mamãe, Luzia, noticing Mariana and Arsenio arrive. She pulled all three of the siblings into a firm embrace. Mariana felt her mother's heart racing through her shirt.

"Are they the Benevolent Leader's men?" Mariana asked.

"It appears so," Severino replied.

"Two days before we leave?" Arsenio said, eyes wide and fearful. He looked to both of their parents. "Do you think he knows?"

"We can't be certain," Papai said.

"Are we—"

"There's no time," Luzia said. "Corva sum Rio is burning. We'll be safest at the outpost."

She turned and threw open the back door.

In the street, the pandemonium had escalated. The low rumble of footfalls and the crackling of the flames underscored the screams of fleeing villagers. Mariana caught glimpses of people she knew, people she'd grown up with. Sabina Coelho dragged her kid brother behind her. Renato Freitas carried a sobbing old woman on his back. None of them paid her any mind as her mamãe ushered her and her siblings across the threshold.

Beyond the back door, a strange mixture of cold and hot air intensified.

"Come now, quickly," her papai said.

The five made to join the fleeing throngs, but at the last moment, Luzia held back.

"Severino," she said, suddenly distraught. "Galina had watch tonight."

For a moment, Mariana's father looked like he might dismiss his wife's last-minute concern, but her insistent expression made clear she was unwilling to let it go. Mariana watched her parents' unspoken exchange with confusion. If Galina had been at the outpost on watch tonight, didn't that mean she was already safe?

"It may be too late, love," Severino said in a low voice.

"We can't know that," Mamãe replied. "I will go to her house. Take our children to the Wild Wood, to the outpost."

"Luzia, I—"

"There's no time," she said firmly.

Helena frowned, grabbing their mother's arm. "You are not coming with us?"

"I'll be right behind you," Luzia said, pressing a hand to her daughter's face. Beside them, a scream rose as an older woman fell in the street. Those behind her did what they could to dart out of the way, but with the crowd's momentum, some couldn't avoid trampling her.

Luzia removed her daughter's grip. "Go. Now! All of you!"

She turned and began fighting her way against the tide. Confusion and anger mixed inside Mariana, squashing her sense of fear.

"Wait!" she cried. "Where are you—"

"Come," her father said, taking her wrist. "We must get to safety."

He began dragging the siblings down the gentle slope of the village, away from the fire. Stunned, she let him lead her for a few paces before coming to her senses.

She can't go alone.

"No," Mariana said firmly. She planted her foot and wrenched her wrist from her papai's grasp. He let out a grunt of surprise, but before he could say anything, she chased after her mamãe.

Mariana slid through the throngs with less agility than Luzia, though she managed to keep her in view. Once, she glanced back to see if Papai had come after her, but found, with relief, that he was nowhere in sight. He must have decided he couldn't leave both Arsenio and Helena into danger just to give chase. That was fine with Mariana. She was the most capable of her siblings.

Everywhere she looked, fires licked the black sky like angered demons. The farther into the fray she followed Luzia, the more terrifying the flames became. Walls crumbled, windows shattered, and a building collapsed. Although her mamãe moved with purpose, Luzia paused multiple times. First, to help an old man who had fallen, and again to coax a child from her hiding place beneath a stairwell. Each time she slowed her pace to help someone, Mariana was able to close the gap a little more.

"Mamãe! Wait for me!" she cried, though she knew Luzia couldn't hear her.

Down another street she followed, hands raised to block the heat from her face. Perspiration beaded on her lip, and her eyes stung from the smoke. Still, she ran, trying desperately to catch up. This far into town, the streets had emptied. Luzia no longer searched the doorways and windows for stragglers. She raced through the roads and alleys before halting on a wide street near the very edge of the village. The fire burned hottest here. Flames reached out from every window, acrid smoke curling upward in thick pillars.

"Mamãe!" Mariana called, then devolved into a fit of coughs. What was she doing? There couldn't possibly be anyone left in this part of the town. And if there was, they were beyond help.

Her mamãe began calling out, hands raised to her mouth, but the words were lost to the roar.

Mariana shouted, but it was no use.

Luzia darted forth, angling her shoulder to ram the front door. Before she could, it swung open, emitting a plume of black smoke. Luzia stumbled to a halt and, thirty paces behind her, Mariana did the same. A trio of shadowed figures emerged from the house like demons born from the fires of Vaspoena.

Silhouetted by the orange glow, all that could be seen of them was the thick armor they wore as though prepared for battle.

Her mamãe turned to run, but one of the figures lunged forward and grabbed her by the hair. They yanked her back, exposing her neck to the light of the flames. In her last moments, she locked eyes with Mariana, surprise replacing the fear on her face.

Run, she mouthed, just before the armored figure slit her throat.

Mariana didn't have time to scream. She was no longer herself. No longer the girl standing amid a forest of flame. Where she might have expected pain or anger, there was only a hollow chasm widening in her chest. As the other two dark figures advanced on her, she at last had the presence of mind to do as her mother bade. She turned and fled back the way she'd come—back to where they'd left the fleeing citizens of Corva sum Rio behind, where the world was not yet consumed by fire.

Papai. Arsenio. Helena.

She would grieve, she knew would come later. Once the danger had passed. Once there was nothing else to occupy her mind. Once feeling returned.

Through the buildings she dashed, leaving behind the advancing flames that ate away the town. She passed her home, standing dormant among the others waiting patiently to be consumed. Hers was the only window open, shutters swinging in the breeze. The orange glow behind her faded the further she ran from the fires, until the only light came from the odd lamp hanging beside a front door. She found herself among people again—stragglers who had only just mobilized after realizing the danger and those who couldn't move any faster. She darted between them, pushing aside anyone who stumbled into her path. Only when she'd come to the edge of town where the rest of the villagers crowded, where the houses gave way to fields and forest, did Mariana slow.

She had to find her family.

Coming to a stop, she raked the mob with her eyes. Though she recognized people here and there, she caught no sign of her papai, brother, or sister. Faces melded together, some tear-streaked, others burnt and bloodied. She kept her gaze from lingering too long on any one countenance, afraid that if she registered their emotions, the dam keeping her own thoughts at bay would break. Panicked and out of breath, Mariana began fighting across the current.

Her conflicting trajectory was met by angry calls above the din of confusion. Mariana ignored them, pushing her way through despite the resistance.

"Papai! Arsenio!" she bellowed, sliding between a middle-aged couple who, for the briefest of moments, had looked like her parents. She jumped, allowing herself to be carried back a few steps in exchange for a few brief seconds of an elevated vantage. She knew her papai. He wouldn't have entered the Wild Wood without her. He'd have waited at the tree line.

"Helena!" she called. This time someone shoved her hard. Mariana felt the wind leave her lungs. There were too many people. Before tonight, Corva sum Rio had always seemed small enough that no matter where she went, she either knew or knew of every villager, but plunged into chaos, the populace became overwhelming.

Mariana dug her toes into the gravel and fought the current again. Progress was slow, but the onslaught thinned as the villagers dispersed.

She saw the burgundy sash about his waist first, and a spark of relief cut through the dark chaos in her mind. She was not alone, her brother—her twin—was still here.

"Arsenio!" Mariana called again. Correcting course, she made for him, cutting across a half-dozen rows of people. "Arsenio!"

This time, he heard her and spun around. Their eyes met.

"Where's Helena? Papai?" she asked. Her brother shook his head. She saw then that his face was streaked with dirt and blood. He had a cut above his left eyebrow. Grabbing her hand, he pulled her off to the side.

Mariana swallowed hard, her jaw tight. She tried again, "Helena—"

Arsenio looked away, but not before she caught the shine in his eyes.

"We were fine for a while," he said in a distant voice. "Where the streets merged, there was no room for the crowds. Everyone kept shoving us out of their way. They tore us apart. Then one of the buildings collapsed." Puffs of vapor curled from his lips. His voice had gone hoarse.

"I tried my best to hold onto her," Arsenio continued. "She was by my side the whole time until the building fell. And then she wasn't."

Mariana's heart tore in half. "Helena," she breathed, suddenly dizzy.

Not her too. How could that be?

"And Papai?" she asked.

"He didn't see what happened. When I told him, he went back to look for her body."

He must be mistaken. Mariana made to fight the crowd again. "We have to help him. You should have—"

Her twin shook his head. "You didn't see it happen, Mari. She was crushed. The blood..."

Mariana heard an involuntary cry of anger escape her throat. She wanted to hit him. She wanted to grab him by the shoulders and shake some sense into his head. Only minutes ago, Helena had been alive and well. As her older brother, Arsenio was responsible for her well-being. He shouldn't have left until he'd dug her out of the rubble—even if all that remained was a bloodied body.

"We have to go back for her," Mariana demanded.

"We have to get out of here," Arsenio said.

"No! She needs us."

"Papai said he would meet us at the outpost."

"But—"

"Mari." Arsenio held her by the arms, his eyes spilling over. "He made me promise not to let you go back."

She bristled at the statement. "Yes, well, you also promised to keep Helena safe."

Her twin stared back at her with wide-eyed hurt. She felt a twinge of guilt, knowing he must already blame himself, but their sister was dead and now was not the time for coddled emotions. Mariana's throat felt constricted. This was all a deranged nightmare. She didn't want to agree to his plan—she didn't care about her own safety. But the words wouldn't find her. There was too much noise. Too much destruction. Too much loss all at once.

"Where is Mamãe?" Arsenio asked, dragging his sleeve across his eyes.

"She—she's dead too," Mariana said, her voice lifeless. The exodus of villagers began to thin. She didn't like how vulnerable this made her feel. Regardless of what they did next, they couldn't stay out in the open.

"How did it happen?" Arsenio asked.

"It doesn't matter. She's gone," Mariana replied brusquely.

Another crash rose up from the village. People ran past with fresh terror on their faces; wide bloody gashes marred their arms and growing stains of deep red patterned their clothes. One man stumbled by with an arrow sticking out of his back. Mariana recognized him as Laurenço Nunes, a carpenter.

"I don't believe it," Arsenio whispered. "Mamãe..."

"Whether you believe it or not, it's true," she said in a voice angrier than she felt. She turned her face away, craning her neck to see over the crowd as if her papai might come stumbling into view. *Was I responsible for keeping Mamãe alive?* Of course not. Luzia was the parent. "If we're going to the outpost, we'd better leave."

Arsenio nodded stiffly. "To the Wild Wood, then," he muttered.

Turning his back on the village, he led the way into the mass of trees. Shadows clung to the fluted trunks as thickly as the branches overhead. Most villagers had chosen to flee down the road that eventually led to the villages in the foothills, but Mariana could see others dispersing into the foliage around her. Clustered groups headed out to face better odds of surviving the night. The further in they went, the safer she felt.

Mariana fought the encroaching tendrils of despair. Every time the face of her mamãe arose in her mind, she blinked the image away, swallowing the lump that formed in her throat. She did the same for her Helena. They were ghosts now. She banished the memories, which materialized in the darkness, her jaw drawing tighter with each dissipated specter. Grief was still something she could not afford.

Mariana had never seen so much blood. She had never seen so much fire.

~

They had been to the outpost twice before, both times in the dead of night. She'd paid careful attention to the journey—their parents had made sure of it—but they'd never tread the route alone, nor without a light. The added layer of loss and peril chipped at Mariana's confidence. It was as if the darkness had rearranged the landmarks, morphed the trees into unrecognizable facsimiles of themselves. Muttering the directions beneath her breath, she glanced up at the moon and stars as often as the forest canopy allowed.

When they first entered the Wild Wood, Mariana could see at least one group or another trudging through the shadows in any given direction. But as time went on, this occurred with less frequency, until she and Arsenio were left very much alone. She dreaded this isolation. It reminded her that Papai was not with them.

Eventually, the quiet became too much for Arsenio.

"Do you think the Benevolent Leader attacked because he knew of our mission?" he asked, reiterating his concern from before they'd left their house. "This is too aggressive for a common raid."

"I know less now than I did when the fires began," Mariana said, unable to keep the acidity from her voice. In strenuous times, talking calmed her brother—even if it was just conversation for the sake of conversation. By contrast, she had no desire for words.

"Why weren't there more killings then?"

"Mamãe and Helena might beg to differ."

Her twin was silent for a long pensive minute, but it was too much to ask that he remain that way. "Helena's was an accident," he said in a low, small voice. "They allowed most everyone else to flee Corva sum Rio."

Mariana sighed. She wasn't in the mood to postulate. "The king can't rule over a pile of bones."

"He has little to gain from people with nothing."

"He has little to fear from them either." Mariana bent down and grabbed a fallen branch. After sizing it up, she decided it would suffice and began using it as a walking stick. She'd grabbed no weapons and, from what she could tell, neither had her brother. Inwardly, she admonished herself. That should have been her first instinct. A knife, at least. "And you needn't refer to him as the *Benevolent Leader* when nobody else is around. He's a tyrant. There's no reason to refer to him as anything but."

"If I use his preferred title all the time, I'm less likely to slip up when there's company."

"Then at least call him the king."

"Do you think our house is gone?"

"Yes, I do," Mariana said, wishing he would shut his mouth. She looked over at him. He'd pulled a black pouch from his pocket, the one she'd seen him grab before leaving his room. He used two fingers to open the drawstring and turned it upside down. Out slid a necklace, a silver chain with a black stone pendant. On the pendant were carved a tetrahedron, a sun, a serpent, and a diamond. Symbols of the Holy Order. Mariana frowned.

"What is that?"

"Mamãe gave it to me just this morning. Or—yesterday morning, I suppose," he said, slipping it around his neck. "It's not real—the stone, I mean. Just common rock. But even so, she told me to wear it as protection."

"I didn't think she was so superstitious."

Arsenio shrugged. "Neither did I. But our Benevolent Leader claims to be religious, so maybe she thought it might help in a tight situation."

Mariana had the urge to snatch the necklace from him and stomp it into the ground. He was stupid to wear it. The pendant was a useless artifact that would do nothing to help them. But she fought her anger. He probably found comfort in wearing it.

Maybe it would be best to stop wandering for the night and rest. Exhaustion was only aggravating her tempestuous mood. They hadn't yet reached the outpost, but dawn couldn't be more than a few hours away. Once light arrived, they'd be more vulnerable.

Exhausted and vulnerable was a bad combination.

The suggestion was on the tip of her tongue when she saw the flicker of orange light ahead.

Not more fires, she thought. But this one was small. Controlled and welcoming. Meant to bring warmth to a frigid night. Mariana could make out hushed voices: a group of at least a dozen individuals if not more. From the rushed phrasing and clipped tones, she guessed they were hastily organized. The outpost at last. She and Arsenio reached the edge of a clearing and slowed to a halt.

Fire burned bright in the center of a stone circle, healthy and untended. Crates littered the surrounding area, some covered in rough spun blankets, others open while people sifted through their contents. Mariana spotted piles of bags filled with what she could only guess was food. A triangular stack of barrels stood on the far side of the clearing. At least two dozen people hurried about to take stock of the items.

Nearest to them were a woman and a man conversing in barely more than whispers.

"Barros just arrived, but he said he hasn't seen the Silvas since he had dinner with them earlier this evening," the woman said, gesticulating severely. Mariana recognized her as the leader of their chapter of Afonso's Light; Galina. "And Gaspar and Lorena are nowhere to be found."

The last bit of news made the man frown. "They lived the closest. They should've been out first."

"I can only think they were with Luzia and Severino."

Mariana and Arsenio both stiffened at their parents' names. They locked eyes with one another before Arsenio stepped forward, announcing himself with the clearing of his throat.

Galina turned their way, revealing a red, glistening burn down the left side of her neck that encroached on her throat. Mariana gasped at the sight of the fresh wound. The woman was still up and about directing the members of Afonso's Light when she should be receiving medical attention.

"The Avilla twins," Galina said, and dismissed the man beside her with a stern nod. "Where is the rest of your household?"

Mariana forced herself to take a deep breath. "Our mother is dead."

"Helena was trapped beneath a collapsed building," Arsenio explained. "Our papai went back to try and dig her out."

A flicker of pity flashed across Galina's face, but Mariana knew her to be a proud leader who rarely showed any emotion beyond strict determination. The pity was gone in the next instant, though she spoke in a softer voice. "I am sorry for your losses."

"Papai will return," Mariana said, wincing at her own childish resolve.

Galina pursed her lips and nodded. She reached out a hand to beckon them both forward. "Come into the warmth of the fire," she said. "You look like icicles out there."

Mariana did not need telling twice. She and her twin traipsed between the stacks of crates, following the woman to the fire, around which were arranged several logs. As they sat, various busy members of the rebellion looked them over. Mariana recognized several faces, but didn't have the energy to recall their names before they disappeared into the shadows. She hadn't realized how much her feet hurt until she'd taken her weight off them. Beside her, Arsenio rested his elbows on his knees. Galina chose the next log over, thankfully hiding the sight of her glistening wound from view. The fire turned her brown eyes orange and gold.

"I'm sorry to hear of Luzia's passing," she said. Her tone was blunt, almost angry. The aggravation in her voice was surprising, though it somehow didn't detract from the sincerity of her words. "Do you know how it happened?"

Mariana could feel her brother staring at her. The cold sank through her clothes like water, saturating her skin and dragging her heart from its place in her chest. Her lips opened, but she found no words.

"Did you see it?" Galina asked.

Mariana nodded.

"Was it the Tyrant's men?" Galina didn't often refer to the Benevolent Leader by his preferred title.

"Yes," Mariana said. "When we saw the flames, we headed here, but Mamãe—she said something about you being on watch tonight and ran toward the fires instead."

She searched Galina's expression for some sign of surprise or confusion, but the woman's face was a blank mask.

"I followed, not wanting to leave her on her own, while our papai led Arsenio and Helena to the Wild Wood. My assumption was she led me to your house—"

"She did?" Galina said in a harsh whisper. "You must have arrived before me. Did you see anyone with her?"

"No. I—It was burning by the time we arrived," Mariana said. "I couldn't see or hear much. The heat of the flames made it hard to breathe. She meant to run inside, but these three figures emerged—"

"The Omens," Galina muttered.

Was that who they'd been? The Omens were the king's three favored military commanders, infamous for their brutality and their inhuman nature. Mariana swallowed hard. If Galina's assumption was true, she hadn't realized just how close she'd come to death.

"They slit my mother's throat and—" Mariana's words faltered, a knot forming in her throat. She finished in a whisper. "And spilled her blood across the cobblestones."

The admission left her tongue and was carried away on the gentle breeze sweeping through the woods. Around them, the other members of Afonso's Light continued their chaotic dance about the outpost. Organizing supplies, packing crates, treating injuries—a flurry of footsteps filling the silence. Within the hemisphere of firelight, the trio sat still. Galina stared past the flames into the shadowed woods. She almost seemed to have forgotten the twins, her mind elsewhere.

Mariana looked at her brother. Silent tears streaked his face.

"Galina?" she asked. "What did my mamãe hope to find at your house?"

"I assume she was looking for me."

"But she knew you were on watch tonight."

"Then I haven't a clue." The woman sighed under the weight of exhaustion and too much loss. It was the first sign of vulnerability Mariana had seen her show. "Your sister—"

"Do you think the king knew about our plans to send for help?" Mariana asked. She lowered her voice so that it barely eclipsed the crackling of the fire. At this, Galina finally broke her distant stare, locking eyes with Mariana.

"No. He can't have," Galina said. "Only those involved knew of the plan: myself, your household, the Silvas, Barros.... We kept all others in the dark. I believe if he'd had that much information, he would've attacked this outpost."

Instead, he burned our village to the ground.

Mariana's hands clenched into fists. She struggled to quell her urge to scream into the night sky, to tell all these scrambling strangers to be still for one moment so she could think without distraction.

"I fear the tally of lives lost," Galina said. "Many were members of the rebellion. As if we had the numbers to sacrifice."

Mariana could feel the woman's emotions burning like the fire before them. Passion, intensity, and rage. But there was something else beneath the surface. Perhaps the most powerful emotion of all, and the one she struggled to mask the most: grief. Who had she lost tonight? Mariana hadn't seen much of Galina outside meetings with the rebellion. Occasionally, they'd encountered one another in the market but, not wanting to raise suspicion, they hadn't talked much. You never knew who was loyal to the crown. But Galina had always been alone on those occasions. Mariana assumed she had no family.

That does not render her immune to tonight's tragedy.

No matter who had died, every resident of Corva sum Rio would grieve.

It was then the face of her mamãe broke through her mental dam with unstoppable force. What was Mariana to do now that she was gone? She hadn't lived a single day without her mamãe. She was always there in the mornings and when Mariana came home after the workday. The same was true of Helena, who had slept just across the hallway every evening. And though Mariana had known a day would come when this was no longer the case—perhaps when she had married and moved out of the Avilla house—she'd never imagined it would arrive in such a fashion.

What now?

"What's all this?" Arsenio mumbled, waving a hand at the general commotion around them.

Galina cleared her throat, breaking out of her stillness.

"We have to move the outpost," she said. "We can only assume the Tyrant will learn that we weren't keeping our supplies within the village. We must honor the sacrifice of those we've lost, but Afonso's Light cannot rest. There is much to accomplish and no time to do so."

What will I do now?

"I'll be sending sparrows come daytime. We have to know if he discovered only our chapter, or if there were other casualties." She sighed as the prospect of further loss weighed heavy on her. "Then, eventually, I suppose we'll have to return to the village and see what's left of it."

"Much to accomplish?" Mariana frowned as she registered the woman's words. "You can't be serious. Corva sum Rio is—is nothing but ash and stone. We've lost, Galina. I'm sorry to say it, but the truth can't be ignored. And if he's found the other outposts—" she stammered, fighting her way through incredulity and frustration, "—then Afonso's Light is dead as well. We don't stand a chance."

Galina faced both Avilla twins, the scarring tissue on her neck visible once more. Her prominent cheekbones cast dark shadows across her face in the firelight. They made her look gaunt, hollow. And perhaps that was how she felt. "I expected better from you, Mari. I thought your youth, at the very least, would give you more resilience than a scrap of paper in a storm. Do you remember meeting me for the first time? The night your parents first brought you and your brother to this clearing? You looked me in the eye and told me you would spit in the face of our Benevolent Leader if ever you saw him. I knew the words were the boastful parading of an adolescent, but I'd thought I saw a fire in you.

"Afonso's Light will not simply dissolve because of one defeat. Who knows how many died tonight—how many have yet to die because of tonight's events. But so long as there is one soul with an eye turned toward freedom, the Light has not been extinguished." She pursed her lips, mulling over her next words before voicing them aloud. "I had hoped you would carry out your mission as intended."

The siblings stared wordlessly back at her. A strong part of Mariana wanted to scoff at the idea, to wisecrack at such a ridiculous suggestion. Another part of her wanted to flee back into the Wild Wood and give herself time to process this relentless evening. And yet a final, smaller part of her thought maybe it wasn't such an absurd notion. Despite that sense of loss simmering beneath the surface, Galina still appeared to be as devoted as ever to the rebellion. Why shouldn't Mariana do the same?

Because I've lost my mother. My sister too.

And her papai was still nowhere to be found.

"Perhaps it's best if both of you get some sleep," Galina said. "Give yourselves time to consider your futures."

This was the best suggestion she'd made thus far, though Mariana wondered if sleep was possible. Her body ached with exhaustion, but the emptiness inside her was even more discomforting. She didn't imagine sleep could remedy that. Still, she followed the woman to a corner of the clearing where wool blankets lay folded in a pile. She and her brother each took one and lay out behind a stack of crates, away from the firelight, where the autumn leaves gave some cushion to the forest floor. Neither sibling spoke. As she had feared, Mariana's mind raced, churning over what lay ahead and what was the right thing to do. The choice, it seemed, was impossible to make; and as she dwelled in her emptiness, listening to her brother crying quietly beside her, Mariana drifted off into a deep, dark sleep.

~

When she awoke, the sky was a bright blanket of gray clouds, and yet it was early enough that the morning stillness lay undisturbed. Arsenio sat beside her on the ground with his arms resting over his knees, the blanket rolled up at his feet. Much of Mariana's exhaustion remained—they couldn't have slept for more than a few hours—but resting any longer felt wasteful. Instead, she rolled up her blanket as well, smoothing her auburn hair away from her face.

"I can't remember the last thing I said to Helena," Arsenio muttered. His tangled mess of curls was the same color as her own. Bits of leaves had caught in the strands overnight.

Mariana swallowed, her eyes falling to the forest floor. "It was probably something kind. You two were never mean to one another."

"Maybe." He shook his head. "But everything was in such chaos last night. I might've yelled at her."

This wasn't like him, dazed and listless. He was usually so punctilious, sometimes annoyingly so. She disliked seeing him this way.

Beyond the crates that shielded them, Mariana heard lively movement in the camp. There were voices again, louder than they'd been in the hours after the attack. More of them, too. Leaning forward, she put her hands over her brother's arms, squeezing in a manner more comforting than she felt.

Footsteps came to a halt beside them.

Mariana lifted her gaze to see her papai looking haggard and morose. Judging by the dark rings beneath his eyes, he hadn't slept a wink. The three remaining Avillas were silent for a long minute, letting the sounds of the camp and the waking forest wash over them. Mariana searched for words, so full of questions and afraid of every answer.

"Did you find her?" she asked.

"I...." He hesitated, holding his breath as if he could keep the pain of his words from his remaining children. "I reached the site of the collapse. There were a few others digging through the rubble with me, calling out to loved ones."

He hadn't looked at either twin, staring over their heads with a flat expression. Mariana didn't need to hear his story, his explanation. She already knew where it ended. Helena was not here with them; any other details were superfluous. Yet, she said nothing to stop him, her grip on her brother's arms tightening.

"We dug out a few bodies, all of them dead. By then, the fires were too close. Too much smoke in the air. Then King Fogosombre's soldiers appeared, firing arrows at us." He gingerly placed a hand atop the crate that separated the trio from the rest of the camp. His hands had always felt so strong to Mariana, so powerful. Now they appeared shaky and timid.

"She was under that rubble," Arsenio said. "I saw it."

"Then she has departed this life," Severino said.

"She's *dead*," Mariana said.

"If stating it so makes it easier for you."

"It doesn't matter what words we use. Their meaning is the same." Mariana stood, brushing her clothes off. She'd known her sister was likely gone, but that didn't make the sting of hearing her father confirm it any softer. His insistence on coating the young girl's death in sugary language only aggravated her. Euphemisms felt gaudy.

"Galina told me about Mamãe," he said.

"Then we're all caught up, aren't we?"

"Mari." He took a step toward her, but she angled away from him.

"So, what are we going to do now?"

Arsenio stood, his dazed expression gaining some focus. "What we pledged to do before."

Mariana shot him an incredulous stare. "You can't be serious. Arsenio, our mother *and* our sister are dead."

"Yes, by the Benevolent Leader," he said. "What more reason is there to remove him from power?"

"Oh, well, yes, when you say it like that it's so simple!" She couldn't help the acidity leaking back into her voice. "Have you forgotten that we also don't have any food or clothing either?"

"You heard Galina last night. The rebellion doesn't die because of an attack."

"Papai, are you listening to this?" Mariana asked, turning to their father and hoping he might talk some sense into Arsenio.

"I am," Severino said, his stoicism turning pensive. "If your brother's first instinct is to continue the fight, I'll admit he's a better man than me. That doesn't make him wrong."

Mariana's frown deepened. "You're not telling me you agree with him?"

"In the course of one evening, I lost two of the people I loved most in this life. The best revenge I can exact will be upon the man responsible." Her papai looked each of his children in the eye, searching their faces for something, though Mariana could not decide what. She was certain all he would find in her countenance was anger and bewilderment. He and her brother simply expected her to leave Mamãe and Helena behind as if nothing had happened? That was unlike them. It went against Faroni rites of passing—which included burial and periods of mourning, gathering together friends and family to memorialize those lost. But of course, this was an unprecedented situation. Few whom she'd known in Corva sum Rio were left to memorialize anyone. And who knew how many more souls required burial and mourning.

Severino sighed. "But this is not a decision I can make for you, my children. I will not force you to leave behind everything you have ever known in this world if you don't wish to go. And I will not leave you if you choose to stay."

Then the choice fell on her. Mariana already knew how her brother felt. His conscience told him to carry out their original plans, and so he would follow through unless told otherwise. Her anger and confusion—and the lingering sadness that hummed beneath it all—were tainted by guilt. How could she give up on the cause now when she was faced with the very facets of King Fogosombre's regime that made rebellion necessary?

She saw the last moments of her mamãe's life once more. The fearful look in her eyes as she realized her eldest daughter had followed her into the flames. How she begged for Mariana to *run*. It was a memory too painful to visit for long, but one that would stick with Mariana for the rest of her life.

"Alright," she said, unable to parse through her warring emotions. Even amid her uncertainty, she knew it was the only response that would feel right in the end. "Alright. Let's not waste more time."

~

The camp was a hub of movement. As the morning progressed, more villagers had assembled, hustling back and forth across the clearing. Mariana noticed some of the inventory missing; there were fewer crates than yesterday, and almost all the sacks of food were gone. The more she watched folk scampering every which way, the more purposeful the chaos seemed to be. Even if that was an illusion, it left her feeling peripheral.

"Galina," Papai called out as the leader passed them.

"Severino." She muttered something to the woman by her side, then backtracked to the Avillas.

"Has there been any word?" Mariana asked. "From the other outposts?"

"Not from the sparrows I sent, but it's only been a few hours," Galina said. "We did hear that the Twin Canyons have been attacked, same as we were, so I'm not hopeful."

"That's terrible," Arsenio said. The inadequacy of his sentiment stung.

Galina offered no response.

"Perhaps it would be wise to accelerate our plans," Papai said.

Galina raised an eyebrow. It was clear she'd expected the Avillas to withdraw from Afonso's Light, given their recent loss and Mariana's attitude the previous night. Following through with their mission showed true dedication, something she valued. She gave a single nod. This form of approval was the closest thing to a smile Mariana had seen on her face, though that wasn't surprising. There wasn't much to smile about at the moment.

"You understand, of course, what you are volunteering to do?"

"It's become more and more clear that we cannot win this fight on our own," Severino said, the sturdiness in his voice returned. "Many in the kingdom of Faron are brave and willing to risk their lives for their freedom, but many more are not. They fear retaliation, they fear for their families—for their children."

He wrapped one arm around Mariana and the other around her twin, drawing them in close. It was brief, but Mariana noticed a flicker of sadness cross Galina's face before her mask of stoicism reclaimed her.

"The people have seen the damage the Tyrant can cause," Severino continued, "I cannot blame them for being afraid, but neither can we make them rise against him. And with as many as we lost last night—here, and in the Twin Canyons, and in any of the places from which we've yet to receive word—our numbers are insufficient."

Mariana felt her uncertainty fade at her papai's words. Yes, she wanted space to grieve. Yes, she wanted to stay. But he was right.

"We are ready to sail across the Great Ocean," he said. "To reach the shores of Nokara. We will plead with the empress there and convince her to aid in our liberation. In doing so, we will honor the lives lost in Corva sum Rio."

Galina pursed her lips. "Barros is the only other volunteer who remains," she said, as if testing their resolve. "I cannot spare much attention for your mission. Right now, I need to focus on gathering the scattered people of our village."

"The details for our journey have already been set," Papai said. "We don't need much from you."

"You wouldn't rather postpone?"

"If the king is attacking outposts, then there may not be much time."

"We can do this," Arsenio said. "Mari and I are both eighteen, past the age of majority. We are not children. Let us do what was asked of us."

"You've changed your mind then?" Galina said, turning her gaze toward Mariana. *You wouldn't rather rest?* Her eyes seemed to say. *You wouldn't rather stay?*

"I'm going with them," Mariana confirmed. "My tomb will be my refuge."

She could tell Galina weighed their proposition with interest. Mariana knew she wanted to get as many of the villagers to safety as quickly as possible, to find them shelter and stability. It would take many members of Afonso's Light to round up their scattered people, but she wouldn't necessarily need the Avillas.

"May Deus judge you mercifully," she said. "Let's find Barros."

~

Barros was a hulking man with deep-set black eyes and a wide, flat nose. He spoke in gruff tones and always sounded displeased but, like the Avillas, he knew the plan for their journey across the Great Ocean. That was worth more than amiability. While he and Papai tied hefty axes and swords to their belts, the twins were each given modest sabers and a pack with food to last them several days. After that ran out, they would have to procure sustenance on their own.

"By the time you arrive in Nokara," Galina said, "we'll have set up new headquarters in Red Cliff. Send a sparrow to me there and another when you've convinced the empress to aid in our cause."

Mariana longed for a few more days in the company of Afonso's Light, some time to prepare herself for a journey far beyond anything she'd experienced before, but they couldn't afford to wait. The sooner she, Arsenio, Papai, and Barros left, the better. Heart heavy with loss, she and her companions draped their packs over their shoulders and set off into the Wild Wood once again.

Kaori

Drummers beat the steady, doleful rhythm of passing from the lookout towers above the palace walls. Though the dark sky promised a storm, the rains held off. Perhaps in respect for the late empress of Nokara, in whom it was well known that the gods held favor. Even the winds calmed, the great ocean waves dispersing before they entered Black Tide Cove.

Kaori stood among the ranks of the Palace Academy students, his hands clasped respectfully behind his back. Adorned in perfectly manicured red uniforms, the two hundred or so students lined the path between the palace steps and the gates. Beyond, citizens gathered to along the city's main road to view the procession. Countless distraught faces looked on in mourning—the delicate dabbing of an eye with a handkerchief, others unable to look entirely. Children who didn't yet understand the gravity were held at bay, placated with admonishing looks from their parents.

How they loved Empress Mai. How they flocked to show grief for their wise leader who had ruled with a fair hand for more than fifty years and finally succumbed to age, passing silently in the night. For most, she'd been the only leader they'd ever known—Kaori included.

When the drums ceased, he turned away from the crowd and looked instead up the palace steps. So loved was their empress that foreign leadership attended her funeral as well. Queen Yiscel Baquiran from the Kailon Islands stood on the grand balcony of Kingfisher Palace, overlooking the gathered Nokari people. The friendship between the two leaders was legendary. Together, they'd successfully ended decades of tense relations between the adjacent realms, producing an era of unprecedented peace. And now, the island queen was here to mourn the passing of her friend.

The double doors opened. Two rows of the empress's maidens descended the stairs, spreading fuchsia petals across the steps. Their vibrant dresses stood in contrast to the obstinately monochrome clouds, but the joyful palette of their garments was intentional. After all, the great empress was passing into the immortal realm. They should celebrate her death. Surely, she was with the gods now.

After the maidens came the coffin. Six sturdy guards carried it down the steps. Kaori had heard rumors that Empress Mai opted not to be placed in the Halls of Heritage, and so her body would be purified in flame and released to the winds of the cove. Whereas many leaders chose to adorn their coffins with depictions of their great deeds, Kaori was surprised to see that Empress Mai had chosen a design without any carvings at all. Instead, strips of various woods interlocked with one another along the length and width of the box. Kaori found this selection rather fitting. She had built her legacy upon the harmony woven between people of different regions. A cohesive Nokara, inside and out, was the prevalent theme of her leadership. Many rulers were known for the blood they'd shed; Mai would be remembered for the wounds she'd healed.

He admired her for that. As a student of the Palace Academy, he'd met with her several times throughout his education. On those occasions, Empress Mai had been cheery, engaged, and genuinely interested in his development toward the potential vocations his future promised. "A great leader," she'd once said to him, "must be ready to serve the people in the ways they are asked to."

Trailing the coffin were a handful of musicians, some playing the flute-like shinobue and others who carried the eight-stringed kotodori—an instrument Kaori himself was familiar with. The haunting melody they played seemed to descend from the heavens to grace the congregation, wringing more tears from the people. Kaori had to resist the temptation to wipe at his own eyes, knowing he could risk damaging the pristine costume. That would earn him an admonishment. Instead, he closed his eyes and listened to the music in darkness.

He didn't open them again until the procession had passed through the palace gates and faded. The citizens were allowed to follow the empress through the city to the Temple of the Four Winds where her body would be cremated, but the students were beckoned around the side of the palace toward the academy buildings. Even though this was a special occasion, it was not market day and the students were therefore not allowed outside the palace walls.

Tonight, all of Black Tide Cove would mourn. Plenty of cups would be raised in the name of Empress Mai. Plenty of speeches would memorialize her achievements. As the heavens breathed in her ashes, her followers would rest easy knowing she had transcended the limits of mortality.

Tomorrow, the twenty members of the Elliptic Council would begin the process of electing Nokara's next leader. And when they did, for the first time in five decades, the country would know someone new to the golden throne, someone other than Empress Mai.

And heaven help anyone chosen to follow in her footsteps.

~

Taigen pulled off his robes and slunk beneath his bed sheet.

"No matter how many times you ask the gods," he said, "Mitsu will not agree to bed you."

Kaori finished muttering Yuuka's Methods of Deliberation, then stood from his spot by the window, smiling at his friend. "You are the crudest human being I've ever met. I was completing my recitations. Though I wouldn't expect you to recognize those, since you've probably never read them."

"Of course, I've read them," Taigen said, propping himself up on his elbow. "Once. I don't understand why you're always muttering those methods under your breath, though. They never test us on that gibberish."

"Something needn't be on a test to be worth remembering."

Taigen rolled his eyes. "When you're made lord of a thirty-person town, I'm sure they'll all be grateful that you can recite the Methods of Constipation. Then they'll go back to farming and you can focus on your bowels."

"Very funny," Kaori said. "Maybe when that happens, you'll have stopped thinking like a child."

Taigen launched his pillow at Kaori, who caught it and added it to his own bed.

"And maybe you'll learn not to carelessly throw away your sources of comfort," Kaori added.

"Thief!" Taigen declared, aghast.

"I'm no criminal. You threw it at me."

Taigen was the only person Kaori felt comfortable teasing. Mostly, that was because they'd shared sleeping quarters since they were five-years-old. If the students at the Academy were allowed familial relations, Kaori would've considered him a brother.

"Well, give it back."

"I don't know," Kaori said. "One pillow is nice, but two sounds luxurious. I've never had *two* pillows to sleep on before."

"You ass. Give it back, Kaori."

"You can't ask for a gift back, Taigen. That's rude."

Taigen sat up. "Okay, *ha-ha*, you've made your point. You can recite your stupid lessons to your heart's content and I won't say anything more about it. Now, give it here."

"And?"

Taigen rolled his eyes again. "And you're much smarter than I am, which is why you always win our arguments even though I could knock you out in two punches."

"And?"

"*And* some people might find you slightly more appealing, even though I'm the better fighter?"

"And?"

"And..." Taigen had run out of responses. "What else is there?"

Kaori laughed. "I'm not sure, I just wanted to see how many responses I could wring from you."

"You're insufferable, did you know?"

Kaori picked up Taigen's pillow and took it back to its owner. "I know."

Then he swept to the lantern and blew out the flame, plunging them into darkness. With the moon covered by thick, rolling clouds, little light made it through their octagonal window.

Kaori quickly undressed and slid under his own sheet. Though every room of the palace proper had beautiful ceilings painted in vibrant colors and adorned with precious jewels, the rooms of the Palace Academy were as plain as could be. He'd always taken this to be a method of teaching humility to the students—the handpicked individuals from whom the leaders of the country were selected. They might have opulence one day, but until then they would familiarize themselves with minimalism.

"How many days do you think it'll take the Elliptic Council to choose?" Taigen asked, his voice wafting out of the dark.

"I don't know. Historically, it takes at least three," Kaori said.

"I'll bet it's someone young this time. An eighteen-year-old."

"Not a chance. They always pick someone who's less than a year from Last Vocation—twenty, at the youngest."

"But I think they'll do something different," Taigen said. "And it's going to be a boy this time."

Kaori let out a barking laugh and had to slap a hand over his mouth, hoping the sound hadn't carried too far beyond their door. When they could be sure nobody was coming to admonish them, Taigen whispered, "What's so funny?"

"They're not going to pick you."

"What makes you so sure?" Taigen hissed, though his smile could be heard.

"There are over two hundred students to choose from," Kaori said. "They're not going to elect some halfwit whose only interests include his meals and his cock."

His words were welcomed by complete and utter silence. For a moment, Kaori thought maybe he'd gone too far. Then he and Taigen erupted into uncontrollable laughter that had them clutching at their stomachs. Taigen even rolled out of bed, falling to his hands and knees on the floor.

It was only when a sharp rap sounded against the door that the both of them clamped their hands over their mouths and struggled against their mirth. Taigen appeared at Kaori's bedside.

"When I am made emperor," he whispered, the dam of hilarity threatening to break open again, "I'm not choosing you as one of my advisors."

Kaori nodded. "Alright. I can handle that."

And without another word, Taigen crawled back to his own mat and slid beneath the sheet once more. Still smiling, Kaori stared up at the ceiling and wondered just how possible it was that his friend would be chosen. Nokara would be in for quite the shock, going from wise and noble Empress Mai to crass and childish Taigen—though he *was* undeniably charismatic and could be level-headed when he put in the effort. Of course, the council had been keeping track of the students for their entire enrollment at the Palace Academy and would never in their right minds elect a leader such as he. Still, the possibility was irresistible to consider. The elected was given no choice in the matter, but Taigen would have little problem accepting the role. Any reason to boast was good enough.

And despite the promise his friend had just made him, Kaori was certain Taigen would include him in his inner circle. The thought of them together in the throne room was too entertaining.

~

Three days later, the drums sounded again.

Kaori was in class, trying desperately to ignore distractions from Taigen, who was making grotesque facial expressions each time Kumo Amaya turned her back to them. Immediately, everyone looked up toward the windows. Contrary to the slow, mournful rhythm of the funeral, these drums were lively and joyous, celebrating a new era in Nokara's history.

"We'll continue this lesson tomorrow," Kumo Amaya said as the students stood and headed for the door.

"All but one of us," Taigen muttered.

"Well—" Kaori began, but Taigen had already left. Technically, his statement wasn't true. If nobody from this class had been chosen, they'd all be coming back, but that was neither here nor there, he supposed. Kaori stood.

"You haven't sprinted away with the others," Kumo Amaya said with a smile.

Kaori shrugged. "No matter where you stand, the answer will be the same."

"Walk with me?" Kumo Amaya asked.

Although Kaori would've preferred walking by himself, or with Taigen if that had been an option, he consented. He waited for the kumo to draw level with him before heading toward the palace. Of all his teachers, he felt most comfortable around Amaya. She taught practical ethics of moral leadership. Most students wrote her off as dull, though this was only because they found her subject dull. But from interactions outside the classroom, Kaori had discovered Amaya's subtle humor sprinkled throughout her anecdotes. She was also incredibly kind toward him, probably because he was one of the few students who'd bothered to have conversations with her. For instance, he knew she had never married or had children, and that these were personal choices she'd never once regretted in her sixty-seven years. Her vocation was to teach at the palace, and she committed herself wholeheartedly.

"You don't seem especially excited," Amaya observed. "Unlike your peers, you've continued to pay attention to me the past three days. Though, I suppose, that's not completely out of the ordinary."

They broke out into the light of the overcast day. Outside, the beating drums grew louder, echoing across the palace grounds. The breeze coming in from the coast carried the slightest hint of seawater, though the red outer walls blocked any view of the Endless Ocean.

"I am excited," Kaori said, "but I'm also concerned."

"Concerned?"

"Empress Mai was so highly regarded. I'm worried whoever follows will have a hard time living up to her name."

Amaya smiled again and even chuckled a bit. "A great leader need never live up to their predecessor. True greatness is not decided by how well you fit the mold of *past* greatness."

"Widespread respect for her meant peace. If the new leader isn't similarly adored, that peace could end."

"Then hopefully the Elliptic Council has chosen wisely."

They mounted the steps of the palace's west entrance, the chorus of drums following them still. Many of the palace hands roamed the grounds, hard at work, though they did so with one eye on the students and teachers flocking indoors. Only the members of the Elliptic Council, and the students and kumo of the Academy, were invited to the announcement.

"You're close with some of the council members," Kaori said. "Have they—"

"Oh no." Amaya waved her hand jovially. "This is too large an issue for them to discuss openly. A vote for empress or emperor is a secret affair that should not receive outside influence. That's why they lock themselves in that chamber while they decide."

"You mean they don't leave at all?"

"Yes. I believe food is delivered by dumbwaiter. As for bathing, well…"

Kaori was shocked. He'd assumed they left each night. If they'd been up there this whole time, then each of the twenty council members had gone three days without leaving that room—the inside of which he'd probably never see.

Finally, they reached the inner ceremonial chamber on the first floor. Servants held open the cypress doors, waiting for all the students and teachers to enter. Kaori nodded his thanks as they passed.

Inside, the floor slanted gently toward the far wall, where the members of the Elliptic Council stood on a raised dais. Great wooden columns supported the high ceiling, on which were painted murals depicting the stories of the gods. This was the only assembly chamber that could fit the entirety of the Academy's staff and students. As such, Kaori had only been in this room a handful of times, and his eyes immediately gravitated toward his favorite mural: a picture of Otokida descending Kaeramu—the mountain of clouds—to start the first human settlement on Nokara.

The assembly was arranged in two large groups in a semicircle around the dais. A column of teachers lined the center aisle with students arranged outward from there, eldest to youngest, ending with the children who had joined the academy last waning season to the far left and right. A last column of teachers capped either end.

Amaya took her place on the aisle and Kaori moved along the row until he reached an appropriate space for his age. He looked around for Taigen, but his friend was nowhere to be seen.

The cypress doors closed with a resounding thud.

A bald man, whom Kaori recognized as Hinata, came forward. He'd been a member of the Elliptic Council before

Empress Mai's former chief advisor had passed away several years ago, and she'd chosen him as the replacement.

"Thank you all for assembling so quickly," Hinata said as he surveilled the audience, who quieted down immediately. "As you know, this is a rare time for our community. A time for both joy and mourning. A time to reflect upon what has been and look toward what is to come. I'd like us to take a moment to honor Empress Mai, who is no doubt among the gods, looking down upon us now."

Hinata looked around again as everyone stood in silence. Kaori imagined a painted version of the late empress sitting among the murals overhead.

"But we cannot dwell for too long. Nokara awaits their new leader." Hinata spread his arms, gesturing to all the assembly. "As per tradition, Empress Mai selected the crown for the next individual to sit upon the Golden Throne."

He turned just as a member of the council came forward with an open box. Hinata reached in and from it produced a thin metal circlet. From this distance, and because the floor wasn't angled enough to grant him a clear view, Kaori could not make out any details. The empress or emperor never wore too elaborate a head piece, but the designs were generally elegant nonetheless.

"Behold, the Crown of Mai, adornment of the new leader," Hinata said, and held the piece aloft for a moment as if in offering. The crowns were chosen and named this way as a reminder that the new leader would ascend the throne carrying the weight of their predecessor's decisions. Kaori thought the tradition poetic. "And now, after three days of intense deliberation, the Elliptic Council has agreed upon whose head it shall rest."

The assembly held its collective breath. Kaori felt the silent prayers of a couple dozen hopefuls rising in the air like thermal winds. Though they'd had grace and humility pounded into their skulls since the day they arrived at the palace, he knew there would be dashed spirits tonight. Never in their lives had such an important appointment been made, and no matter who you were, it was impossible not to feel at least a twinge of hope that the unimaginable possibilities would fall upon you.

"Kuze Kaori. Please come forward."

Though there was no physical change, and though not a single disciplined head in the room turned, phantom eyes searched the crowd.

Kaori stood frozen in place, all prior thought dissipating instantly. His body seemed to have lost the ability to regulate itself, for though his blood had turned to ice, he couldn't help perspiring. His first instinct was to remain still—if he didn't move, then maybe he could ignore the name echoing repeatedly around his skull, his own name. However, the rest of the congregation didn't seem to abide by the rules he was trying to enforce.

He felt a hand gently nudge at his back and then another.

"Kaori? Please, come forward," Hinata repeated.

He had no choice but to comply. Stiff-legged, Kaori edged toward the aisle. Every student in his row backed away a step, allowing him to pass. Now that he'd moved, every eye turned, every head swiveled. He couldn't read their expressions; blank stares fell on him. And all the while he kept thinking to himself, *This cannot be. They always choose someone older. It has to be someone else.*

Kumo Amaya stood at the end of the row, and she smiled at him, moving so he could walk by her.

And then he stood alone in the center aisle. Necks craned to get a better look. Far below, on the dais, Hinata held the crown aloft with a knowing glint in his eye.

The Crown of Mai.

Kaori was no longer in control of his feet. They dragged him down the aisle, his posture composed due only to muscle memory. His heart hammered louder than his footfalls. He was suddenly aware of the awkward swinging of his arms, how overly large his hands felt. Twenty-one faces waited for him at the end of this slope. All but one of them had sat in a room for three days, and at the end of that arduous deliberation, had chosen to elect *him* as Emperor of Nokara.

The title hit Kaori square in the chest and he nearly collapsed. What came out instead was a sort of gasp.

He reached the foot of the dais and, at last, lifted his leg to step up beside Hinata.

The bald man was beaming now.

"Honor has befallen you, my boy," he whispered.

The crown he held was wrought from black metal, the circlet made of thin, twisting strands like vines. At the front were welded two feathers that crossed midway, the work of a skilled hand and designed with subtle artistry. Kaori knew immediately why Empress Mai had chosen this one.

His crown.

Hinata lifted the circlet in one swift motion and set it down on Kaori's head. He felt the weight of it: light, but conspicuous. No points pinched or prodded. And it fit perfectly so that the crossed feathers sat just above his forehead.

With a gentle hand, Hinata spun Kaori around to face his peers and his teachers.

"I present to you all, Kaori, Emperor of Nokara."

Kaori stared in wonder, speechless, at the hundreds of faces peering back at him. Before he knew it, Hinata had bent to the floor beside him. Behind Hinata, the members of the council dropped to their knees, bowing their heads in reverence. Then all around him, the assembly followed suit. Teachers of mathematics, literature, and philosophy. Students aged five to twenty. A rumble filled the room as one by one they all bowed, and he was the only one left standing.

He, the new emperor.

~

That afternoon, Kaori was presented to the city in the Temple of the Four Winds. Amid an unending sea of people with heads bowed his way, he felt his life truly change. The sight shook him to his core, and then he was swept away again. As the day quickly progressed, what frustrated Kaori most was that he never received the opportunity to privately react to his own sudden thrust into power. Used to isolated contemplation, the constant company discomforted him. The rest of the day was spent being passed from person to person, many of whose purposes he had barely the time to figure out. New robes had to be fitted, new fabrics sent in from villages across the empire. An artist would be commissioned to paint his portrait and another to repaint the mural in the palace entrance hall to commemorate his inauguration.

A festival for the city would have to be planned. People would travel from all over to see him and pay their respects. His curriculum would change. His daily routine would change. He needed to learn proper behavior.

He would also need to choose his advisors.

This worried Kaori a great deal. The empress, or in this case the emperor, chose a group of up to five close advisors. He could designate a specialty for each depending on their strengths, but they could also refuse the position if they didn't want it.

At least they have that option, Kaori thought. Like a doll, he allowed his arm to be raised while a tailor measured from his neck to his wrist.

The advisors didn't all have to be chosen at once, which was a relief, but sooner rather than later was best. Especially since he was going to have to start making decisions soon. He had one person in mind and sent for her in the interest of time. Preferably, he would've sought her out himself, but he hadn't had a moment to wander off since the crowning.

Kaori jumped as the tailor wrapped tape around his middle to measure his waist. He hadn't been paying attention.

"Jumpy, are we?" the man said. "Not to worry. That's completely natural, Your Majesty."

Your Majesty. He didn't know how long it would take to get used to that. Maybe fifty years.

The door opened, and a palace guard entered with Kumo Amaya at her heels. The teacher looked around before spotting him and smiled. She was not in her teaching garments. An elegant black robe draped her long frame to her ankles. Neither was her hair in its usual tight bun. It fell to her waist like a cascading black waterfall, blending seamlessly into the fabric.

Kaori had no idea what time it was, but he assumed it was late enough that she'd no longer been at the palace.

"I'm sorry," Kaori said. The tailor finished his measurements and scurried away, allowing Kaori to step down off the stool. "I've been in constant movement all day. I didn't realize you'd gone home."

"That's quite alright, Your Highness," Amaya said. "I happened to be lounging in formalwear." She bowed her head slightly, though not before giving a sly wink.

"Please, you may still call me Kaori."

"I'm afraid that would be disrespectful of me."

Kaori thought about stressing his point but decided it wasn't worth the effort at this time. He could argue more about what she called him later. Clearing his throat, he continued.

"I thank you for your prompt arrival," he said. "I've summoned you to ask a favor. A great favor. And I'm hoping you'll oblige."

"I will do my best."

"I'd like to make you my head advisor."

Amaya bowed her head again. "Emperor Kaori, you flatter me with this request. I'd wish nothing more than to serve the throne in this capacity, but I have to wonder. Are you certain I'm the person you wish to choose?"

"Yes, very."

"Then it would be an honor to serve at your side." Her smile widened, and Kaori had to wonder if she'd been expecting the request.

"Thank you very much," Kaori said, flooded with relief. After a day's worth of holding tension, he marveled that every tendon in his body hadn't snapped. Maybe his first evening as emperor demanded an herbal soak. He'd never had one before, but several stalls in the market hawked soaking tablets that the merchants swore would rejuvenate any soul. He'd bet the empress had her own baths and now he could put whatever he wanted in them.

Amaya cleared her throat, reminding Kaori that she was still in the room.

"Oh, yes of course," Kaori said apologetically. "That's all."

"If I may, Your Highness."

"Kaori, please."

She persisted without acknowledging the request. "Shall I move into the palace tonight, or wait until tomorrow?"

He'd forgotten the circle of advisors lived in the palace with the empress—emperor. He didn't much care if Amaya moved tonight or tomorrow or the next week, but as he assumed it was getting late, he reasoned there was no need for her to make the transition immediately. "Tomorrow is fine."

She left, and for the first time since that morning, Kaori was alone.

It lasted for all of ten seconds.

A door behind him opened and a young woman, perhaps only a few years older than he, stepped inside. She bowed her head. "Emperor Kaori, your rooms are ready."

Rooms?

The empress's chambers! Of course, he'd be living in the palace proper now. With so many other activities hurled his way, he'd completely overlooked this fact. Did this mean he'd finished the day's relentless stream of activity? Perhaps he'd be allowed to sleep now. Kaori eagerly followed the woman.

She led him down a long corridor that was partially exposed to the outdoors. The left-hand wall was a wooden lattice made of interlocking geometric shapes. Cool air blew against his face, its chill refreshing. Night had arrived, and through the holes in the design, he saw orange pinpricks that had to be the lanterns of the palace grounds and the city beyond. He hadn't realized how high above ground level the antechamber was.

Halfway along the corridor, they entered a set of double doors guarded by two armored men, which led to a wide staircase. He followed the woman to the top.

The emperor's living quarters were larger than any single residence Kaori had ever seen. They were essentially one grand room divided into three sections by a mixture of columns, furniture, and folding partitions. In one section was a dining area with an ornate table surrounded by high-backed seats. Another housed lounge chairs arranged among brass and gold statues with a smattering of bookshelves. In the center of the final section was a massive four-poster bed piled high with a mountain of pillows that looked to Kaori like a silk cloud. Along one side of the sleeping area, sliding doors of the same geometric lattice-work as the corridor below had been pulled back to reveal an unobstructed view of Black Tide Cove.

When he saw this, Kaori gasped.

"It's most impressive, Your Majesty," the woman agreed shyly, though a smirk flashed across her face.

Kaori nodded.

"I don't think Empress Mai ever closed those doors. Even in the waning season."

"I can see why," Kaori muttered.

"Before I go, Your Majesty, there is one more thing."

"Yes?"

"A visitor came to see you. He said you'd agree to have him. His name is Taigen, Your Majesty."

A grin washed over Kaori's features. He should have known. "Yes, I will see him. Is he downstairs?"

She nodded. "I will send him up."

"Thank you," Kaori said. "May I have your name?"

"Izumi, Your Majesty."

"Thank you, Izumi," he said and she left to fetch his friend.

The moment she was gone, Kaori ran forth and threw himself on the bed. As he'd imagined, the pillows engulfed him with ease. If he hadn't known his friend was on the way, Kaori might have fallen asleep then and there. Forget baths or undressing. That the bed was so far off the ground didn't bother him either—the mattress sat on a wooden platform, whereas his mats had only ever lain on the floor—though part of him did wonder what would happen if he fell off. He sat up, his gaze taken again by the panoramic view. Sliding off the silken sheets, Kaori made his way over to the balcony.

As soon as he crossed the threshold from the interior to the exterior, some form of magic—real or imagined—took place. The breeze off the cove touched him, and he smelled the faint aroma of the salty seawater. Below him, the many rooftops of the palace wings unfolded, as if he were looking down the slopes of a tiled mountain. He could see stone statuary he'd never noticed from the ground, eaves where resourceful birds had made their nests. Below that, the treetops shielded the gardens from full view, while the gabled roofs of the student and servant residences stretched above them. Beyond the palace walls were the curving streets of the city, buildings that piled on top of one another like trees competing for sunlight. If he stared hard, he could make out the peaked tower of the Temple of the Four Winds in the distance. Just beyond the inland side of the city, the towering forest and mountains faded into blue.

If he'd had the option to live out the rest of his life on this balcony, he might have taken it.

"Well, it doesn't get much better than this."

Kaori's head snapped around. Taigen was leaning against one of the columns, his arms crossed over his chest. Kaori couldn't read his expression. His friend looked past him at the view.

"No, I don't believe it does," Kaori said.

They made eye contact and, for a moment, did nothing but stare. Kaori held his breath, not sure what came next.

Then Taigen broke into a wide smile and began laughing. His big, bellowing guffaws filled the space until Kaori couldn't help but join in. They laughed until they couldn't hold themselves up, Taigen clinging to the column and Kaori to the sliding doors.

"You slimy, fucking bastard," Taigen said, giving up and dropping cross-legged onto the floor. He shook his head while wiping tears from his eyes. "I can't believe they made you emperor. You! Fucking emperor!"

"I'm just as bewildered," Kaori said. He tiptoed to the four-poster and hopped up onto the mattress. "Do you want to lie in a cloud?"

"Do I." Taigen stood in a flash and hopped up onto the bed with him, throwing himself back into the pillows the same way Kaori had minutes earlier. "No one will walk in on you servicing yourself here."

"Taigen!"

"Oh, right! You'll have people who can do that for you."

Kaori slapped Taigen across the shoulder. Taigen sat up and made to punch him back but froze.

"Dammit. I can't punch the emperor."

Kaori raised an eyebrow. "You have permission to punch the emperor. Please, everyone has tiptoed around me this whole day, like I might strike them down at any moment. I keep telling them to refer to me by name, but it's *Your Royal Highness* this and *Your Majesty* that."

Taigen chuckled again. "Well, you *are* the one wearing the crown."

"I'm well aware. It's completely mind-bending."

"Our country's done for, really."

"I asked Kumo Amaya to be my head advisor," Kaori said. A knot twisted in his stomach at the thought of his new duties and the decisions he had coming.

"I knew you would," Taigen said. "She's the only teacher you've said more than three sentences to outside of class. She's like you."

"She is not like me."

"I mean that in the best way! She's patient, deliberate. She never says anything without thinking it over first; that's what made her lessons so *boring*." Taigen grabbed a pillow and hugged it to his chest. "Plus—and I say this as someone who finds it endearing—I don't think anyone's ever described her as 'intimidating' before."

"Well, that's not what I want to hear," Kaori said. "A ruler has to be intimidating sometimes."

"I'm sure they'll teach you how to do that," Taigen said. "But what she has that you don't have is wisdom. So as soon as your name was called, I knew you were going to pick her. Honestly, I think it was a good decision."

"I want you to be my second," Kaori said, squeezing the words out before he could overthink them.

Taigen stared at him over the top of the overstuffed pillow, forehead wrinkled in surprise. Kaori might've laughed again if his heart weren't pounding so. Even though this was his best friend that he was talking to—his roommate since the day they'd both been chosen for the Academy—the gravitas of the request made him anxious. Uncertain.

After a minute, Taigen placed the pillow aside and slid himself over so that he was sitting right beside Kaori, their shoulders bumping in the process. Their legs dangled over the side of the bed, a strangely infantilizing sensation. They were just two boys sitting together, Kaori realized, but one was being made to rule the realm and the other asked to serve by his side.

"You want me to be one of your advisors?" Taigen asked.

Kaori nodded. He tried to smile but it manifested as more of a grimace.

"Are you sure?"

Kaori stumbled over his words. "Yes, very. Your communication skills are much better than mine, and you read people in ways I can't—I mean, really *read* them. That's an invaluable skill. Also, you're enough of an ass that I know you'll be honest with me at all times. I could benefit from your service."

Taigen grinned. It was the most authentic expression of excitement Kaori had ever seen him wear. Gone were any traces of the usual wise-cracking jokester. In their place was pride.

"Of course," Taigen said. He threw an arm around Kaori's shoulders and squeezed. "Of course, I will."

The journey ahead would be arduous and winding, and Kaori knew it would be a long time before any of this made sense, or until he was comfortable with it. But as far as endings went, this day had a better one than he would've hoped for.

Mariana

Ciro, Faron's capital city, was the best place to go if one wished to acquire passage across the Great Ocean. The easiest way to get there from Corva sum Rio was by sailing down the Urse River. Walking was out of the question, as it would take them at least a fortnight on foot, and without beasts to ride, they had no other choice.

"Gaspar's boat is docked in the wide bend," Barros said in a gruff voice.

Mariana knew the wide bend he spoke of. It was a particularly open section of the Urse River outside of town, where the water was deep and slow. She and her siblings swam there during many a warm season, splashing on the shallow banks with their friends to combat the dry heat.

"How long does it take to get to Ciro once you're on the river?" Arsenio asked.

"Three days," Severino said, "assuming we don't stop anywhere for long."

"Do you think the boat is still there?" Mariana asked, thinking about how pervasive the flames had been. She was surprised the Wild Wood itself hadn't caught.

"That'll depend on how thorough the tyrant's folk were," Barros said.

"And if it's gone?"

"Then we'll be out of luck, won't we?" Papai said, turning to look at her. "We'll have to walk."

Mariana sincerely hoped the boat was still at the bend.

"So we get to Ciro," Arsenio said. He and Mariana had discussed the journey in hushed voices while their father, Barros, and Galina had put together their supplies. The details of their plan had been left to the adults, with little input from the Avilla children. But given that travel was imminent, it was time to make those details known. "What happens then?"

"We have to buy passage across the Great Ocean," Severino said.

"You mean you haven't already secured passage aboard a ship?" Mariana asked. She'd assumed everything had been prearranged.

"The thing about secret, treasonous organizations is they have to operate in secrecy," Barros said. Mariana rolled her eyes at his sardonic reply. "We can't have some sea captain waiting around for us to show up."

"My apologies," Mariana retorted. "This is my first time overthrowing a regime."

Severino chuckled. "There's not much travel between Faron and the Nokari Empire. Our best bet would be on a non-Faroni trade ship, one conveniently in need of a new flag. According to those who've visited Ciro, the best place to find such a ship is at an inn called *The Severed Tongue*."

Arsenio repeated the name with a scrunched face. "That doesn't sound like a place I'd want to stay."

Barros laughed. "It's a salty tavern on Cava Rua, west of the wolf fountain. Favored by sailors while ashore. If you want to do anything without being noticed, that's the place to go. Nobody who goes there wants to know anything about anybody."

"And then we sail to Nokara?" Arsenio asked.

"Then we sail to Nokara." Severino stared off into the trees, one hand gripping the handle of the sword slung over his shoulder, the other swinging at his side. He was quiet then, a silence that widened the space between the four of them, accentuating the emptiness of the Wild Wood. Mariana spotted the cloud of smoke rising into the air in the near distance, emanating from the ashen remains of Corva sum Rio. The travelers fell silent, treading softly on the ground. Who knew whether the king's folk had moved on or lingered in the wake of their destruction.

Once again, Mariana saw her mamãe's last moments. The desperate look on her face as she urged Mariana to flee. The harsh, orange light of the flames on mamãe's skin. The dark blood as it spilled from her neck. Mariana's heart ached, but she ground her teeth and forced her mind away from the horrific memory.

"This isn't going to work," she said.

"Mari, keep your voice down," her papai whispered.

"What are you saying?" Barros hissed, impatient.

Mariana huffed, but responded in a lowered tone. "I mean to say we will not succeed unless we are honest with one another. Completely. We are traveling to places very few from Faron have gone before. We cannot have secrets if we mean to survive."

She glanced at her papai as she said this, but he was squinting through the trees ahead of them at the approaching edge of the Wild Wood. All morning, she'd been attempting to address a pestering curiosity that'd been tugging at the back of her mind since her papai had appeared at the outpost; something she hadn't considered amid the chaos but bothered her now.

"I have no secrets," Barros said. Mariana rolled her eyes.

"The boat!" Arsenio whispered, pointing.

As they came out of the woods on the eastern side of Corva sum Rio, the wide bend in the Urse River came into view. Water flowed from the northeast and passed languidly around the bend before turning sharply west and cutting around the village.

Mariana felt her heart begin to race. She eyed the columns of smoke again. Though the village was still hidden from view by foliage, the acrid smell of cinders and charred remains permeated the air.

There will be nothing left, she thought, her stomach sinking.

Where the bend narrowed, a wooden bridge arched over the river. The four darted across, then doubled back along the opposite shore to the dock where the small boat bobbed on the surface. It was such an unassuming thing, built for one fisherman and barely large enough to hold them all comfortably. Mariana wondered how they'd been expected to sail in it together with the full group intact.

"Quickly now," her papai instructed in a low voice.

Mariana handed her satchel of food to Barros, who set about arranging their provisions beneath the seats. The oars lay on the bottom of the boat and he removed them one by one, handing them out as he went.

"Papai," Mariana whispered.

"Yes, Mari?"

"What I said about no secrets."

"Of course, there can be no secrecy among us." His voice was distracted as his eyes darted from Barros to the tree line and back again.

"Then tell me why Mamãe ran to Galina's house? What was so important she couldn't stay with us, her *family*?" Though she tried her best to keep a neutral tone, Mariana couldn't stop her questions from sounding accusatory.

"Now is not the time for such things," he replied. "Suffice to say, her cause was just."

"Enough to abandon us?"

"Things are far more complicated than you realize, my dear."

"If I'm to take part in this mission, you *cannot* continue treating me like a child," she hissed.

"I'm not—"

"No secrets."

"I'm not trying to keep things from you," he said. "We don't have all the answers. We're not really sure what we know."

"Tell me what you suspect."

Finally, her papai met her gaze. She was surprised to find sadness there. The realization, perhaps, that she was *not* a child any longer. She was a member of Afonso's Light. His companion on a journey that would invariably lead them through danger. She had every right to know all that he knew. He sighed.

As Severino opened his mouth to explain, an arrowhead ripped through the front of his throat. A gurgle of blood replaced his words. Mariana felt the warm spray of her papai's blood on her face. She gasped, paralyzed by shock, and realized only a moment too late that he was tipping forward. Before she could dive out of the way or brace herself, she collapsed beneath his weight. Her head cracked against the wooden dock and stars danced before her eyes.

There came a splash.

"Barros!" her brother shouted from the water.

"Get in the boat," the hulking man commanded.

"Fuck," Mariana shrieked as her vision swam. A metallic taste coated her tongue, and the stench of blood filled her nostrils. Papai's crumpled form pinned her to the dock. She tried to move, but her mind refused to cooperate, gripped by fear and confusion. Then she realized Papai was still alive—barely, but he stared down at her with wide, terrified eyes. His mouth moved, whispering something she couldn't hear.

"What?" she asked, barely able to draw breath herself.

"The Severed Tongue," Papai growled. Then, with a cry of agony, he pushed himself up just enough that Mariana managed to wriggle free. The moment she'd slid out from under him, he collapsed again, scarlet blood dripping through the gaps in the boards.

Voices shouted, followed by the thunder of footsteps.

"Into the boat!" Mariana cried as Arsenio pulled himself back onto the dock.

Arrows flew overhead, missing them by a hair's breadth as the twins dived into the rowboat. Mariana fumbled to untether the rope.

"Barros!" Arsenio shouted. "We need to go!"

Uniformed figures rushed out of the trees, their weapons drawn. Barros stood at the end of the dock, roaring at them like some untamed animal as he swung his axes wildly.

"The rope!" Arsenio shouted.

"I'm trying!" Mariana yelled, eyes flicking between the knot in her hands and the fight unfolding in the shore. "*Fuck*."

"Barros!"

"Away with you," he howled at the twins He sank an axe into the first soldier to reach him and wrenched it back with a spray of blood.

"Come on!" Arsenio pleaded.

"Leave now, you cunting children." As soon as the words left his mouth, an arrow pierced his side. Barros roared again.

"Mari, the tether!"

"I know!"

The knot came loose. Immediately, Mariana sat up. She shoved against the dock with all her might, desperate to put distance between her and the attackers. The movement brought her face to face with Papai. The life had gone from his eyes and he stared blankly at the water's surface, surrounded by a halo of his own blood.

Not you too.

Barros howled in anguish. He sank to his knees, an arrow through his thigh. In the next instant, his head had been cut clean from his shoulders and bounced along the ground. Gore spewed from his open neck. His decapitated body sank to the ground with a harsh thud.

Arsenio began rowing madly, his teeth clenched. As they picked up speed, Mariana watched the first of their pursuers running out onto the dock, standing over Papai's corpse. She wondered if he might jump into the river and swim after them, but instead he knelt beside her father to search the body. The others gathered at the water's edge. One stood apart from the rest, a deep maroon cape pinned to the shoulders of his armor. He raised his bow to nock an arrow just as the twins passed beneath the bridge. Before he released, they rounded the corner at the end of the wide bend and disappeared from sight.

~

"Mariana." Arsenio repeated her name over and over as he rowed, maybe even unaware that he was moving his arms. Mariana stared at the river behind them, certain at any moment she'd see their pursuers giving chase. "Papai was just talking—he was talking to us! He was fine and then—Deus above, they shot him. Damn their rotted souls to the pits of Vaspoena. I—I can't believe he's dead. We're going to be next, Mari. What do we do?"

"Shut it!" Mariana snapped, spinning in her seat to face him. "You're going to shut it, that's what you're going to do."

"But he's dead, Mari! Papai is dead!"

"I know," she snarled, and realized with exasperation that her face was wet. She'd been unaware of the tears leaking from her eyes. Hurriedly she wiped at the moisture and her hands came away red. She was still covered in her papai's blood. "So are Mamãe and Helena, and Barros too. Half our village is dead!"

"We have to go back," Arsenio mumbled. Then, louder, "We have to go back and tell Galina. We have to join up with the rest of Afonso's Light and—"

"And what? Lead Fogosombre's people right to the rebellion?"

Arsenio shut his mouth, eyes wide with fear.

"We can't go back," Mariana said. She gave up wiping away her tears and let them fall freely.

Arsenio stopped rowing, letting the current carry them instead. Her words seemed to have stunned him, his gaze fixed on the depths of the river. He was still drenched from head to toe from having fallen in, his hair darkened and plastered to his forehead. She realized the rowing had given him something to placate his mind. Now that he'd stopped, Mariana could see panic building behind his eyes as he grappled with their situation.

"What we need to do is keep moving forward," she said firmly, bringing him back to the present.

"But Papai is—"

"*I know.* Papai is dead." She looked down and realized his blood had splattered over her shirt as well. Mariana's stomach clenched, but she willed herself to be calm. One of them had to remain in control. They wouldn't survive otherwise. "He—he told us the plan. He told us where we're supposed to go. I think we have to follow through."

"But—"

"We don't have much of a choice, Arsenio. I know it's shit, but weren't you the one convincing me to follow through on this grand plan this morning?"

"That was when Papai was alive."

"Our willingness to fight can't hinge on who's with us," Mariana said softly. "We don't have that luxury."

On either bank, the Wild Wood pressed in. Thick trees huddled over the water as if waiting to reach down and pluck them out of the boat. With each passing second, Mariana and her brother found themselves farther from their home than they'd ever been. The twins sat in silence, letting the boat carry them downstream, and listened to the world as it passed by. Mariana found it remarkable how completely her life had changed in less than a day and yet nature went on as if nothing had happened—so indifferent to her woes.

When he'd calmed, Arsenio spoke at last.

"You're right," he said. "Of course. We have no other choice. It's the right thing."

Mariana nodded. "We can do it, you know. We just have to get to Ciro, find The Severed Tongue—"

"On Cava Rua, west of the wolf fountain—"

"—secure passage across the Great Ocean, and convince the Empress of Nokara to aid us in our cause."

Spoken aloud, their plan sounded far more impossible than it had in her head. Mariana wiped at her face—intentionally this time. In doing so, she attempted to wipe her mind clean. She'd stopped crying, though her heart felt heavier than ever before. She couldn't afford to give thought to anything but their mission. Not grief. Not loss. Just their path forward along the winding Urse River.

~

The twins let the current carry them, using the oars mainly to steer whenever they drifted too far toward either bank. They drank the river water and ate the provisions they'd gathered at the outpost. In the evenings, they searched for a calm bank on which to beach the boat for the night and took turns keeping watch while the other slept. Mariana feared these long nights the most, for though she could distract herself with travel during the day, there was nothing at night to stop her seeing the faces of her lost family members. She stared into the darkness, listened to the rushing river, and wondered at how quickly it had all changed. Though the risks of their involvement with Afonso's Light had always lingered beneath the surface, they'd lived a relatively quiet existence in their humble village. Now, suddenly, she and her brother were outrunning the king's soldiers on their way to a realm across the Great Ocean.

True to Papai's estimation, they reached the capital on their third day.

The boat rounded a bend in the river and the first signs of Ciro appeared. Small buildings stood at the outskirts, standing sentinel along the banks. Quickly, the buildings grew taller and wider, transitioning from wood to stone. Roads filled with people appeared. They shouted at each other, gesticulating with flailing hands. Children caked with dirt darted between legs, carrying sticks to whack each other whenever the mood struck. So crowded was the canal that Mariana and Arsenio seemed perpetually in the way of other boats.

Mariana clung to the sack over her shoulder, wary of every person she saw.

Perhaps the poorest parts of the city are along this riverbank, she tried to tell herself, but she couldn't come up with a convincing reason why that might be. Was this really the great city travelers spoke of, the proud capital of the kingdom?

Regardless, it did little to quell her anxieties.

The sun had begun to set when they reached a particularly wide section of the river where several wooden docks stretched out into the water. If they went any farther, they'd find themselves sailing their little rowboat into the harbor. Mariana didn't want any part of that. She and Arsenio chose the least busy-looking dock and brought the boat up there. By that time, the sky was nearly dark.

"So this is Ciro," Arsenio said, breaking their silence. He climbed up onto the thick wooden planks, then held out a hand for her to take. Realizing how big of a height difference it was from the boat to the dock, Mariana accepted his help. He pulled her up beside him. "It's so much larger than Corva sum Rio."

"That's not saying much," Mariana said.

"Docking fee," said a voice from behind them.

The siblings turned in unison to face a disgruntled woman with a soggy-looking hat shoved over her curling, dark hair. She held a leather-bound booklet under one arm, and held out an expectant hand toward them.

"How much—" Mariana began, then let her sentence drop. The pouch of money had been tied to Papai's waist. Neither she nor her brother had much, if anything, to offer this woman. Did it normally cost money to leave a boat at a dock? That struck her as an odd request. This one was normally just tied up at the wide bend. Nobody had ever paid anyone for it as far as she knew. "We don't have money for the fee."

"Then you can't leave it here," the woman said, frowning.

"Oh, but we're not going to use it," Arsenio explained.

At this, the woman cocked her head, narrowing her eyes at the two of them. "What are you playing at, exactly?"

"We're not staying here," Mariana said, decidedly less friendly than her brother. If there was one detail that had been driven into her head by folk who had been to Ciro over the years, it was that you had to stand up to people in the capital. "Why would we need to pay?"

"Are you a daft bitch?" the woman asked, choking out a phlegmy scoff. "There's plenty of folk who'd like this spot for their boats. Ye can't simply claim it without paying the fee, or I'll give the spot to someones who *can* pay. Now hurry up, your vessels about to make a break for it."

She was right. After being confronted, Arsenio hadn't managed to tie their boat to the dock yet. He held the rope loosely in one hand, and the length was seconds away from pulling taut.

Mariana leaned her head toward him. "Let it go," she said in a low voice.

"But the boat—"

"We won't need it. Not if we're leaving. By the time we return, I'm sure we can find some other means of getting back to Corva sum Rio." Would they go back? There was nothing left for them of the village in the forest. Nothing but ash and memories.

Arsenio looked like he might argue, staring down at the little rowboat as if it were their only connection to their former lives. He nodded. Gently, he tossed the rope into the bottom of the boat. The current dragged it slowly away from the dock, twisting into the middle of the river. The woman let out a squawk like an injured gull.

"Now what'd you do that for?"

"No fee," Mariana said.

"I coulda used that boat! I coulda sold it for something if you brats weren't going to use it!" She continued on, gripping her soggy hat with one hand as the empty rowboat floated away. Mariana wasn't listening anymore. She and Arsenio trod along the wooden planks toward the city.

"Which way is Cava Rua?" Arsenio asked.

"Your guess is as good as mine."

Once they'd left the docks and were walking up a wide lane. A pair of lamplighters ahead of them went about with ladders, lighting the oil lamps.

"This place is strange," Arsenio said. "I never really realized places could be more than just trees and roads and buildings."

"What's that supposed to mean?"

"They carry feelings too. A heartbeat." He scanned the windows of the houses around them. On this street, the homes stood shoulder to shoulder, butted up against the paved road to either side. They were taller than the buildings back in Corva sum Rio, and the extra height felt imposing. "Do you think we'd have really done it? The whole family, I mean?"

Mariana looked over at her brother, shocked. "Of course. Afonso's Light asked it of us. Our parents would've followed through."

"Yes, but they'd never left our village. None of us had. This is no small trip. We would've all been uprooted and dragged to the ends of the world."

"Maybe dying was their way out of it," Mariana said dryly. She let this statement linger, regretting her icy tone. She'd been so comfortable in their village, and had thought the same of the rest of her family. The only family member who'd ever shown a desire to explore new places was Helena. She'd never expressed any doubts about the journey.

"That's not funny," Arsenio said.

"I know."

They reached a fountain with four wolf heads protruding from a central column pouring water from their open maws. Turning left, they continued onto Cava Rua. The new street was noticeably darker, the lamps spread thinner, some of them unlit or broken. Down here, many of the buildings were wooden instead of stone. Mariana noticed hazy, darkly windowed shops: an apothecary, a store of oddities, and one lively place she had a sneaking suspicion was a brothel.

Out of the gathering dusk emerged a bright light that spilled onto the cobblestones through open windows. Music filtered through the air, lively strings and an accordion with brazen singing to match. Just below this was the roar of chatter, a cacophony of voices competing for dominance. Every so often, an exclamation would rise above the rest. "You think I'm a fuckin' idiot?" and "That's right, Gabriel. Pour a girl a proper drink!"

Mariana and Arsenio exchanged glances, but it was clear from the wooden sign that they'd reached the right place. *The Severed Tongue* stood out in red letters with a long, forked tongue curling around the side. The sign swung in the gentle evening breeze.

"I guess we'd better go inside," Arsenio said.

Holding their packs tighter, the siblings entered the establishment.

If the outside was loud, it was nothing compared to the roar inside. The tavern was packed wall to wall with patrons in varied states of intoxication. Some sat in chairs, some sat on tables, and some stumbled around sloshing ale down their fronts—and down the backs of others, much to their chagrin. In the corner opposite the bar, a trio played their instruments while those nearest them joined in a rousing chorus, slapping the tables with open palms to keep rhythm. A harried-looking boy wove between the patrons holding a platter stacked high with empty mugs. Although the oblivious guests made for challenging obstacles, he dived and dodged expertly.

"We're meant to ask one of them?" Arsenio said, nodding at the room in general.

"This is going to be impossible," Mariana said.

"Shall we split up? Cover more ground?"

Mariana nodded. "Best of luck to you."

They began on opposite sides of the room. Their papai had made finding passage sound easier than it was. She tapped on many shoulders, asking if people were on a ship preparing to sail overseas. One drunken man thought it funny to point out that "We aren't on no ship, miss. This is a tavern!" before breaking into uncontrollable laughter. Most people gave her a suspicious look, ignored her completely, or answered her question with a witless innuendo.

One woman looked Mariana square in the face with a sneer plastered on her lips. "Who's asking?"

"It's just me and my brother," Mariana said. "We're trying to get to—"

"Aren't no ships here, *meu bem*. But the pretty boy with the sash can take a dip in my seas if he's lookin' for his first taste of fish. Bring me a tall glass, eh?" The woman devolved into cackles and clinked glasses with the smarmy woman next to her. Mariana grimaced and moved on with no intention of passing along the invitation.

Growing more and more desperate, Mariana took to inquiring about the status of every patron, even the ones who didn't look like sailors. This earned her aggravated grunts and threats of beatings if she didn't leave well enough alone. Before she knew it, she was standing in the center of the pub with her brother beside her looking just as dejected.

"No luck?" Mariana asked.

"None."

They moved to a small round table beside the stairs at the back of the room. A steady stream of people kept running up and down the steps in various states of dress, shouting to each other over the din.

"Nobody will talk to us," Mariana said, slouching into a chair. With so many people packed into the room, the air was stifling. She wiped her hair away from her forehead.

Arsenio sat silently, continuing to stare at the drunken patrons. A large, sturdy woman behind the bar talked sternly to a pair of frightened-looking gentlemen. Mariana guessed she was the owner.

"There has to be at least a dozen people here planning to board a ship," Arsenio said in a low tone. "Only, none of them want to admit that to us."

"Probably to do with our Benevolent Leader. I doubt he likes folks coming and going as they please," Mariana said. "Do we not look trustworthy?"

"I think we look a little *too* trustworthy."

The fiddler tipped over and came crashing to the floor to the cheers of onlookers. Mariana smirked.

"I suppose I could knock out a few of my teeth and soak my hair in wine. Then maybe I wouldn't look so suspicious."

A loud thud from behind them made both siblings jump.

"Mind yer fuckin' step, you blasted dew-beater!" a woman hissed at her companion who, by the looks of it, had fallen down the stairs while carrying the front end of their wooden chest. The sprawled man gained no sympathy from the woman, who cracked open their weather-worn cargo for a quick look inside.

"It ain't my fault, Jocaste! The damn steps are slick with liquor."

"That'd better be the only thing slick with liquor. If *any* of this is damaged before we've reached the cove, Captain will have your innards strung behind the ship for the kaicats."

Mariana and Arsenio exchanged glances. The woman, Jocaste, had clearly said she and this man were headed for *the cove*. Could that be Black Tide Cove, the Nokaran city Galina had instructed them to find? This would be a fortuitous turn of events if Mariana believed they had a chance of convincing this pair to bring them aboard. But judging by the woman's harsh glare, she didn't exactly have a soft heart.

Mariana nodded at her brother. As the two travelers regained their composure and slipped out the back door, the Avilla twins stood and did the same. They were greeted immediately by a dark, cold night. The door led into a back alley, which sloped downward toward the left. Keeping to the shadows, the two followed the man and the woman, careful not to make any sounds. Along the path they crept, Mariana both thankful for and cursing the lack of light. She stepped in something that squelched under her boot and gave off a faint aroma of excrement, but didn't stop to check. Up ahead, she could barely make out the forms of their unwitting guides, moving much faster in the open air.

Before she knew it, they'd reached the docks. As she and Arsenio ducked behind a stack of chained-together crates, she allowed herself to marvel at the Great Ocean. The world disappeared beyond the shore, stretching out into a black nothingness that ended only where the starry sky dipped down to meet the sea. She had never been afraid of water before, but the boundless darkness held so many foreboding possibilities that she felt her heart hitch just thinking about it.

The man and the woman lumbered down to the second dock on their left, hauling their cargo up the ramp to the ship's deck. Mariana wondered how such a large vessel could remain afloat. Three masts reached up into the night, lit from below by flickering lanterns. The ship rocked back and forth on the gentle waves like a giant breathing while it slumbered. On the front of the ship was carved a large merman reaching into the air before him, his wooden body a paragon of musculature.

Another pair of sailors brushed suddenly by their hiding place. Mariana nearly let out a yelp. She ducked down again, watching as they passed, each carrying a much smaller chest than their predecessors' and guffawing over some unknown subject. Mariana spun to check behind them. For the time being, the path was abandoned.

"It's now or never," she whispered to Arsenio. "We can get on the ship and find someplace to hide."

"I don't know if this is a good idea," he whispered in reply.

"What would *you* suggest?"

"We can go back in and keep asking—"

"Nobody wanted anything to do with us."

"But stowing away?"

"We don't have much choice, dear brother."

"We don't even know if they're going to the right place."

"It'll have to do," Mariana said. "I'm not staying in Ciro with the king so close by."

Arsenio's eyes darted between his sister and the ship. "Why can't we ask them?"

"What makes you think their answer will be different? It's just as likely they'll deny they've a ship while shouting to us from the deck."

"Alright," he said. "Do you think they'll throw us overboard if they catch us though? Because eventually, we will have to eat and—"

"I don't know. Go!"

Both of them stood and crept toward the dock, trying hard not to make any noise. Their hurried footsteps thudded softly on the wooden planks, but this was masked by the sailors' boisterous conversation. Beneath them, the waves lapped at the dock supports. As the two men reached the top of the ramp, Mariana scurried up after them with her brother in tow. The ship creaked, rocking gently back toward them and moving the wooden ramp ever so slightly. Mariana had to put out her hands to keep from falling into the water.

On the ship's deck, she felt terribly exposed. The lanterns bathed most of the area in a dim yellow light, which she avoided. Instead, she and Arsenio ducked below a set of stairs that lead to an upper deck. A trio of barrels stood against the wall beneath a canvas. Careful not to make any noise, the twins slid the barrels away from the corner and tucked themselves behind. Thin as the canvas was, it still plunged them into complete darkness, leaving only the sound and smell of the rolling waves and creaking ship as company.

"Now, we just have to keep quiet," Mariana whispered. In the black, she found her brother's hand and gripped it tightly.

"And hope they don't need whatever's in these barrels," he replied.

She shrugged, though she knew he couldn't see. Their fate was in the hands of Deus.

Emilio

The light blinded him even through his closed lids.

Emilio opened his eyes. He was lying on a hillside among vibrant grass. The sky above was wide and as blue as could be. He noticed the silence first. Not even the breeze made a noise. Just to be sure he hadn't gone deaf, Emilio clicked his teeth together. No, he could still hear. He sat up, bits and pieces of memory coming back to him. This was the field near his home. Judging by the position of the sun, it couldn't be past midmorning. He'd taken a nap, though his chores weren't yet completed.

The last bit could get him in trouble.

Emilio stood and scanned the field. All across the clearing, green grass flourished from recent rains. Stalks of wildflowers popped up in groups, and insects dipped and dived over them as they pollinated.

He turned and ran home.

What had he already done this morning?

He remembered feeding the chickens and the pigs. The old sow had snorted at him, unhappy with his offering while her offspring squealed in delight. She'd never taken to Emilio even though, more often than not, he was the one who fed her. She preferred Mamãe.

Then he'd gone to fetch water, but... he couldn't remember if he'd actually done it or not. The spigot came to mind, but that was probably because he went to it nearly half a dozen times a day. Knowing himself, he'd gotten distracted by something and wandered off. A bird maybe, or a dragonfly. Mesmerizing; the way they kept themselves aloft on nothing but air. That was just like Emilio. Papai always said that his focus was as tenuous as a spider's thread.

The houses came into view. A portrait of modesty. Gray stone with wood-shingle roofs and shuttered windows. By each front door hung a single lamp. Leaving the trees behind, he wandered to his family residence and entered.

Davi was in the living room, playing stacks where he sat on the floor beside the hearth. With his back to the front door, he didn't see Emilio enter, too engrossed in his game even hear him. The rocks in front of him stood eleven levels high—enough to threaten Emilio's record of thirteen. Davi breathed slow, patient breaths. His hands steadily judged the remaining rocks for the best contender. With uninterrupted time and concentration, he stood a chance at defeating his older brother.

Smiling, Emilio crept up behind him and bent over until his lips were right beside Davi's ear.

"You're doing great."

Davi gasped. His hand twitched and knocked over a column of rocks just as he was placing the next level.

"Emilio!"

Emilio laughed, collapsing into the rocking chair.

Davi looked from the ruined game to his brother and back again. He stood, hands on his hips. "I was about to beat you!"

Emilio shook his head. "No, you weren't. You were close, I'll give you that, but the next one would've fallen no matter if I'd scared you or not."

"Not so," Davi said. "And you didn't scare me. You startled me. There's a difference."

Emilio shrugged. "I suppose. If you think you're right, you can try your same strategy next time."

"Fine then. What was I doing wrong?"

"You're looking at the individual rocks, not the stack itself. You think too much; you go too slowly. The trick is just to stack."

Davi rolled his eyes. "I don't believe you."

Emilio raised his palms in surrender. "You're only talking to the reigning champion."

Davi seemed to consider this for a moment before lowering his hands. He brushed the rocks aside with his foot. "They're just stupid rocks anyway."

Feeling a twinge of guilt now that he'd successfully overruled his younger brother, Emilio backtracked. "You're getting better at it, don't worry. You were almost going to beat my record. *Almost.* You might've gotten twelve levels."

Davi shrugged off his attempt at levity.

"When I'm done with my chores," Emilio said, "would you want to go for a walk?"

This made the boy perk up just a bit. "We can go now. I finished them for you already."

"You did?"

"Yes. Well, you were gone, and I figured it could be my early name day present to you." Davi smiled.

"Right," Emilio said, feeling guiltier now than before. *I had to go and be an ass, just because he was about to best me at something.* Emilio stood, the rocking chair swinging back behind him. "Thanks for doing that. I'll just let Mamãe and Papai know, then."

He jogged to the next room, where his mother and father stood hovering over something on the dining table. A map of some sort. Emilio cleared his throat.

"Davi and I are going out for a walk," he said. "We'll be back."

"Alright, well, return before supper," Papai replied.

The brothers whisked out the door in the next minute.

"Where shall we go?" Davi asked. "I hear Nadia Alba's got these new stretchy candies that'll glue your mouth shut for hours. Gracia swears she had one last week and had to skip lunch *and* supper because she couldn't get her jaws open."

Emilio laughed. "As appealing as that sounds, I wasn't heading for town."

"No? Where then?"

"To the shore?" Emilio suggested. They didn't often walk down to the gravel beach. It was a longer path, one that required a bit of climbing for which he'd been scolded after tearing holes in several pairs of trousers. At his own suggestion, Emilio felt a strange sense of melancholy. This perplexed him. He enjoyed the beach, but it wasn't as sacred to him as, say, the meadow. The emotion came off misplaced, as if it wasn't really his.

Still, the shore seemed right. When they reached the olive tree with the curling branch, the Sagrado brothers turned left onto a seldom-traveled path. Through the limping stalks of silvergrass they trod until, in a burst of sudden energy, Davi shoved Emilio and took off running with a mischievous cackle.

"Hey!" Emilio called. "That wasn't fair."

"Neither was knocking over my game!"

Emilio darted after him. The silvergrass whipped at his trouser legs and he ducked beneath several low-hanging olive tree branches, the light playing over his face in broken rays. The terrain was uneven, but he ran with little care, hopping over rocks and brush in his pursuit. They ran by Moss-Crusted Boulder, then around Mosquito Pond, and over the twin hills Camilo Rios had once told him looked like breasts—an image Emilio had never been able to shake.

After the stretch of grasslands came the short bluffs leading down onto the gravel shore. Still sprinting, Davi was headed for the edge. Emilio had the sudden realization that his younger brother might not remember the drop was there.

"Davi!" Emilio called out. Urgency flooded him, but it was too late. The boy went over the edge. "*No!*"

He pushed harder, puffing great, heaving breaths. The sandy soil granted less traction to his boots. Davi shouldn't have been playing around in these fields; Emilio shouldn't have run after him. That only encouraged the boy. He didn't want to think that his brother was hurt, but the silence, devoid of screams, didn't bode well.

As he neared the bluffs, Emilio slowed and threw himself into a slide so that he came to a stop just as his feet went over the edge. He slid himself until his legs dangled, then his waist. And when he'd lowered himself enough that he was holding to the rocky cliff with only his fingers, he let go.

The gravel scrambled underfoot to accommodate his impact. Emilio whipped around, eyes darting as he scanned the area. His brother should've landed somewhere beside him, but the ground was empty.

"Davi!" Emilio shouted. Maybe the boy had rolled further down the beach. He looked out toward the Great Ocean, but there were no bodies along the shore. He lifted his hands to his mouth and called again, "Davi!"

Behind him, someone burst into a fit of giggles.

Emilio spun and looked up.

Davi was draped over a barren shrub growing out of the cliff face, completely unharmed. He continued to giggle as he looked down on his older brother, his face an expression of triumph. Obviously, he'd known the branch was there.

"You little trickster," Emilio said, shaking his head. "And to think, I was worried about you."

"You should've seen the look on your face."

"You should see yours once I get my hands on you."

"Papai will skin you alive if you hurt me!"

"I'll tell him you fell off the bluffs because you were running too fast. Who's he going to believe?"

They argued in this way until Emilio convinced Davi to come down, promising not to injure him. Reluctantly beholden to his agreement, Emilio didn't touch his brother, but reminded him all bets were off on his name day the following morning.

"All I wanted was a calm walk on the beach," Emilio mused once the threats had been made. "Instead, I'm bargaining with a demon."

Davi smiled proudly, strutting with more arrogance than warranted. They walked along the beach, stopping here and there to toss stones into the receding waves. Emilio stared out into the sea, wondering if his surge of melancholy had been a product of his approaching name day. Whenever he came out here—which was usually alone—he would inevitably find himself pondering the vastness of the world. He'd been to other parts of Faron besides Mandibula, but never to other realms or kingdoms. He'd heard several priests and elders talk about the land west of the sea. Lands with creatures so foreign you'd never guess they were real, jungles with foliage to ignite the imagination, and climates that were alternatingly unbearable and heavenly.

Some unexplainable part of him longed for these places, even felt attached to them, as if they informed some aspect of him. This was impossible, of course—he'd never been overseas—but that was how he felt. And as tomorrow was his name day, that part of him ached more strongly. This beach was as close as he could get.

"The house is going to be different when you're gone," Davi said.

Emilio turned to him, wondering if perhaps he'd been thinking aloud. "What do you mean? Where am I going?"

"Well, it's your last name day before you reach majority," Davi said. "You'll start a career soon and marry some girl from Old Town. And then you'll move out."

Emilio shook his head. "What are you talking about?"

"I saw what Mamãe and Papai got you for your present. It's an *elder's* gift."

Chuckling, Emilio turned back to the water. He bent to pick up a few stones and tossed them one by one into the ebbing tide, wondering what his parents could have possibly gotten him that would cause this reaction in Davi. Never before had the boy expressed concerns that Emilio was going to leave him. If anything, they spent more time butting heads than showing affection. Perhaps this was a sign that his brother, too, was getting older. "You don't need to worry, Davi. I'm not leaving any time soon."

~

Only two name days in Faron received much flourish: when one entered adulthood at age seventeen and when one surpassed a half century. One hundred years was also celebrated, but very few were lucky to achieve such a thing.

In this way, it was forgivable that Davi confused the significance of Emilio's sixteenth name day if he'd seen their parents preparing a remarkable gift. This confused Emilio too; he was certain his parents knew he had another year to go before such things were expected.

So, from the moment he awoke on his name day, Emilio pondered what he was going to find in the wrapped package conspicuously placed on the dining table. It was small enough to fit in his palm and had almost no bulk. If he were confident enough to touch it and think that nobody would notice, he could have checked its weight or the sounds it made when jostled. His mamãe's powers of observation were faultless though, so he knew she'd notice a crinkled edge.

He'd have to wait.

That morning, Emilio completed all his chores without distraction and was outwardly kinder to his brother than he might've normally been—to which Davi took suspicion. Mamãe and Papai greeted him enthusiastically with traditional well wishes of "a hundred years on your name day." However, several times throughout the day, he caught them watching him with a mystified awe, almost as if he *was* leaving and they wanted as much time as they could get to memorize his features before he disappeared. This was an alarming way to feel, given he was unprepared for any significant life changes.

By the time they finally sat down to supper—Papai had cooked Emilio's favorite caldeirada—Emilio was dying to open the gift. The fish stew tasted sumptuous as always, but Emilio was so fixated on the package lying in the center of the table, he didn't realize he'd finished his bowl until his spoon came up empty.

He joined in the conversation until the rest of his family members had finished their own meals.

Finally, his papai stood.

"Well now. It wouldn't be a proper name day without a gift," Papai said, looking across the table at Emilio. "This is something that has been in our family for generations. Maybe we should have waited until next year, but your mamãe and I thought now was the right time."

Papai lifted the package and handed it to Emilio.

Emilio's heart accelerated, a flurry of excitement rushing through his body. Something that had been in their family for generations? He wasn't aware of any long-standing family heirlooms, but perhaps it was one they didn't display the way other families touted their pottery or precious gems. If that was the case, there could be no doubting its value. His fingers fumbled to undo the brown paper.

The rest of the family watched for his reaction. So many layers encompassed the gift that Emilio couldn't feel what was inside—or, for that matter, if anything was inside. Over and over the parcel flipped in his palm until he clawed at the paper like a ripcord.

And out fell a stone.

Or, more precisely, a necklace *with* a stone: a large, pure-black gem shaped, oddly enough, like a bear's canine. The top of the stone was wrapped in copper wire to hold it in place, dangling at the end of a copper chain. Emilio held it up in his palm, examining the gift with curiosity. Although the necklace was surely beautiful—and he'd never been given jewelry of any kind before—he couldn't help but feel a little disappointed. His brother's sentiment regarding the present had seeded his imagination, and this necklace looked... well, rather ordinary.

"That's pure obsidian," his papai said, staring intently at the black stone.

That changed things.

Obsidian was considered sacred in Faron and was extraordinarily rare in its pure form. Though the gem still paled in comparison to the imagined treasures Emilio's mind had conjured, the necklace was nothing to turn his nose up at. He appreciated how special a gift like this was. Especially given his family's modest circumstances.

"Thank you," Emilio said. "It's magnificent."

"Cherish it," Papai said.

"Make certain you don't lose it," Mamãe said.

"I won't," Emilio responded. He knew just where it would go. When they'd finished dessert—a moist berry cake which exemplified the best of his papai's talents—he crept into the room he shared with his brother, to his chest of drawers. On top, he kept a roughhewn box he'd carved out of a soft white stone found by the shore. Many years ago, Emilio had picked this stone off the beach and carried it all the way home, where he spent weeks and weeks carving away at it with a granite arrowhead. In the end, he'd made something he called a box, though its form was closer to a bowl, for which he'd created a lid using a tin plate. Inside, Emilio kept various treasures, objects of sentimental value. A petrified rose bud, a shell from the Great Ocean, a wooden boat a friend had carved for him when he was younger. To these, he added the obsidian necklace.

The stone glinted in the candlelight, dark and beautiful. He admonished himself for feeling disappointment at receiving something so meaningful. Who knew how many generations it had passed through. Trust his imagination to mar the experience.

Emilio replaced the lid, feeling important as he trod back into the living room where his family sat around the hearth.

CHAPTER TWO
THE DAGGER STRIKES

Kaori

Kaori called for the next visitor.

A woman entered the throne room. She genuflected on the mats before him.

"Greetings," Kaori said.

The woman nodded, then stood. "Greetings, Your Majesty."

"What may I call you?"

"I am Naomi."

"Welcome to Kingfisher Palace, Naomi. Please speak."

The woman took a deep breath. Her nervousness disturbed Kaori, who struggled to keep his expression light. Holding court felt strange to him, least of all because every citizen who presented themselves was older than he, but mostly because he still felt unqualified to advise anyone or decide how to handle their issues. Every day, Kumo Amaya assured him his unease would pass once he became accustomed to his role—but that seemed about as likely as spontaneously sprouting wings and taking flight.

"I'll do my best to be brief. As I'm certain His Highness has noticed, this has been an exceptionally dry waning season. I come from Maigoda, one of the empire's major farmlands. Unless the rains pick up, I'm afraid we'll be unable to provide the bountiful harvest the empire expects from us." Naomi looked him in the eye as she said this, her gaze steady. He could tell she'd rehearsed this speech many times with whoever had accompanied her to Black Tide Cove.

"That is a problem," Kaori agreed.

"If I may, Your Majesty."

"Continue."

"We'd like to build more wells. We wouldn't need to borrow anyone from the capital—our people are willing—but we request additional supplies," Naomi said. "An underground river runs by our lands. We access it for use in our village, but if we could build wells closer to the farmlands, we may be able to alleviate the worst of our conditions."

Her plan seemed practical, and she undoubtedly knew more about how to improve their circumstances than he. As usual, Kaori was tempted to immediately grant her request, but he'd learned to pause and look to Amaya and Taigen before jumping to a conclusion. Taigen shrugged, but Amaya spoke to him in an undertone.

"The palace stores for stone, brick, and concrete are currently well stocked," she said." There are forty carts available at last count."

Kaori turned back to Naomi. "Your concerns have been heard. Maigoda will be provided six carts and oxen with materials for the wells. A member of my staff will accompany you and see that the carts and oxen are returned. Is this pleasing?"

Naomi bowed low. He glimpsed her smile of relief and relaxed. "Yes, Your Highness, you are most generous."

"Are you in need of anything else?" Kaori asked.

"Nothing else, thank you." And with that, Naomi left.

Immediately, Taigen slouched in his chair. "Great gods, this goes on forever. I'd rather have a rogue tiger claw my face than listen to another *concern*. I thought Empress Mai had left the country in good shape." He rubbed his temples.

"No empire is ever devoid of needs," Amaya said. "Emperor Kaori is doing well. That was an appropriate amount of material to grant the people of Maigoda."

"Thank you," Kaori said. He turned to Taigen. "I told you advising wouldn't be wholly enjoyable."

"I know, I know." Taigen rolled his eyes. "Honestly, though, if it weren't for the privileges of my title—I told you about those companions...."

He drifted off once he caught Amaya's disapproving look. Taigen *had* told Kaori about the companions, and he blushed now, remembering the detailed descriptions Taigen used. He'd never employed such vibrant imagery in any of their writing classes.

A woman passed through the doors unannounced. She wore a blue sash over one shoulder: a messenger. Kaori refocused his attention, glad for a change of subject. The woman crossed the throne room at a quick pace and bowed once she reached the mats.

"A letter, Your Grace."

"Approach the throne," Amaya said.

Taigen stood and, as the messenger stepped toward the dais, he came to meet her. She held in her hand a small, rolled-up slip of paper: a letter sent by sparrow. Holding the roll between his index finger and his thumb, Taigen brought it to Kaori.

"Who is this from?" Kaori asked.

"It comes from Queen Yiscel Baquiran of the Kailon Islands."

"Ah," Amaya said, "the Bamboo Throne recognizes the new leadership."

Kaori remembered the regal woman who'd sat in the palace porticoes watching the funeral procession. He knew there'd been a bond between the two leaders; this had been one of the many ways in which Empress Mai's reign brought peace to the realm. He unraveled the small scroll. Although he'd been taught to read and write Wikang, he was grateful to see the message in Nokaran.

Emperor Kaori,

Congratulations on your appointment. Your empire and my kingdom have a long and troubled history, one your predecessor and I elected to overlook in the interest of a mutually beneficial accord. It is my belief, and hopefully yours, that we can continue this relationship.

Queen Yiscel Baquiran of Kailon

Kaori breathed a sigh of relief. He didn't expect the island queen to declare war by any means, but as a new leader, the respect of foreign powers was something he knew he couldn't take for granted. Of course, the letter didn't mean that she respected him, merely that she respected the throne, but it was a start.

When Amaya finished reading the letter, she had a similar reaction. "This is good news. Some regions have become quite dependent on trade with Kailon."

"Well, she doesn't have much of a say in our elections," Taigen said, finishing too. He rolled the paper back up. "She couldn't really have done anything about Kaori's appointment."

"That is not true," Amaya countered. "If she was unhappy, she could have stopped the trade."

"But it's not as though the Elliptic Council could remove me and appoint another emperor," Kaori said, almost hopeful. "Elections are final."

"That they are, but all the same, she could have shown disapproval by withdrawing her support."

"And inciting unrest again," Taigen finished. Amaya shrugged. The whims of powerful individuals could halt progress in an instant.

"Emperor Kaori," a guard said, standing at the door to the throne room. "You have one more visitor."

Kaori sat up straight, as did Taigen beside him. He pulled at a crease in his robe. "Please, send them in."

"Gods in heaven," Taigen muttered. "If it's one more—"

A tall, thin man swept into the room. His affinity for the elegant was immediately apparent. The visitor's peacock robe brushed gently along the floor, parting at his black, polished boots. He wore several rings of orange gold, while his beard and mustache were both immaculately shaped. In addition to refined vestments, the man gave off the aura of shrewd intelligence, evidenced by his haughty expression. He observed Kaori and his two advisors before bowing deeply.

"Greetings, Your Majesty," the man said. He stood again and smiled, the corners of his eyes wrinkling.

"Akedi Kento," Amaya said. Taigen and Kaori looked to her in surprise. "It's a pleasure to see you again."

"Indeed, Akedi Amaya, I feel much the same." The man called Kento nodded to Kaori's head advisor.

"You've met?" Kaori asked.

"Yes," Amaya said. "We were both kumo once, before Kento was promoted to Empress Mai's circle of advisors."

"Indeed," Kento confirmed. "I advised the late empress faithfully for twelve years. I may not have been as visible as Hinata, but I can assure you I did everything in my power to best serve the Golden Throne. Empress Mai never found reason to speak ill of my abilities, and I would have gladly given the rest of my days to her service—*Anaguro, mitsuane.* Your pain, my sadness. I would have come to you sooner, Your Majesty, but I've been distraught these past weeks after our loss. Empress Mai was a dear friend of mine."

"No apologies needed," Kaori said. He relaxed, knowing Amaya and this man were acquainted. "What brings you to the throne room?"

"A plea," Kento said. As someone Kaori guessed was not used to pleading for anything, he knelt awkwardly on the mats and clasped his ringed hands together. Kaori frowned, unsure what a man of his respectability and obvious fortune could want. "At the end of an empress's time, her surviving advisors either return to their former occupations or otherwise retire. I will not waste your time with anecdotes or asides. Put simply, I am not inclined to choose either of these paths. I wish to continue serving the empire in the same capacity."

"This is a highly irregular request," Amaya said.

"I am aware," Kento said. He moved further onto the mat, his eyes wide now. "But I served admirably as Empress Mai's Sage of Histories and Strategies. I helped her bring prosperity and peace to the nation. My actions have been nothing but advantageous for Nokara. Could your circle of advisors not benefit from my inclusion?"

Kaori hadn't expected the request. Reasonably, Kento didn't look old enough to retire, but was he so against returning to teach at the Academy? From what Kaori understood, the kumo life was not extravagant, to be certain, but it was comfortable—more so than many of the other professions found in Black Tide Cove.

Or perhaps Kento had truly found his calling as part of the royal committee. Without being present during any of Empress Mai's decision-making, Kaori had no way of knowing who had counseled for or against what actions. Therefore, he couldn't judge whether Kento had caused Nokara more harm or good. Yet, Kento's pleas felt honest enough. Kaori couldn't deny that another experienced hand would be invaluable. He turned to Amaya, who looked deep in thought with her fingers templed against her forehead.

"If you will excuse us a moment," Kaori said. Then he whispered to Amaya, "What do you think?"

Amaya hesitated before answering. "Kento was always friendly toward me when we both taught at the Academy. He was a favorite among the students, who praised his cunning and his assuredness. I never heard Empress Mai speak ill of him after the appointment."

Kaori turned to Taigen. "And you?"

"He seems honest enough, if a bit self-assured," Taigen said. "Advisors can always be removed too, if they prove incompatible. It might not hurt to have someone already experienced with the throne."

Kaori agreed.

"On the other hand," Amaya interjected, "our traditions don't include retaining advisors. Although it's not strictly forbidden, perhaps a decision like this warrants more time for thought? The decision, as always, is yours, my emperor."

Kaori turned back to Kento, who was still kneeling with a hopeful gleam in his eye. Suddenly overcome by the hours of deliberation he'd already undergone, Kaori couldn't find an answer. He longed to spend some time alone, to visit Kuriku Garden, which he hadn't had the chance to do since his crowning. So much of his position required being poised and engaged at all times that he found the mental strain taxing.

Amaya's last suggestion appealed to him most.

"I'll consider your request, Kento," Kaori said. A part of him lamented the disappointed look which spread across the man's face, but Kaori had had enough of sitting in the throne room. "You will receive an answer soon."

Kento bowed and stood, backing away until he was nearly at the doors before turning to leave.

"There is no reason to rush the decision," Amaya said. "This way, you can deliberate without him present."

Kaori stood. "I will do that, but I think I wish to do so alone."

As he made to leave the room, a pair of guards came to stand on either side of him. Kaori faced them.

"I'm just going to the gardens," he said. "I don't need escorts."

"Your Majesty," Amaya said, standing as well. She wore an apologetic smile. "I'm sorry, but unless you are in your chambers, you aren't allowed to be without protection."

"Even within the palace grounds?"

"Even within the palace grounds."

Kaori's heart sank. Officially denied his desire for solitude, he succumbed to frustration. With a sigh, he turned again and continued out the door, wondering if he could find some semblance of peace in Kuriku if he tried ignoring the guards. Somehow, he didn't think so.

~

Tides rose and fell under the moon as it shrank to a sliver of ghostly white. Kaori fulfilled his duties, and when he wasn't, he attended lessons from select kumo whose tasks were to instruct him on how to be a decent emperor. He learned how to sit, how to dine, how to address those around him with confidence, what to expect from his guard, what to expect from the Elliptic Council, and various histories about past rulers deemed too specialized for general education at the Palace Academy.

He'd had lessons in sword fighting before, but now his training became more intense, focused on keeping the mind calm and level so he could make prudent decisions even in the heat of battle. The soldiers were there to fight; the emperor—should he take up the sword alongside his general—was there to lead. As an average swordsman, Kaori found these lessons physically taxing. They were not his favorite.

His lessons in geography also became more detailed. He'd been taught the names of the regions and their major cities before, but now he memorized the names of smaller cities and their contributions to the empire. These lessons he didn't mind as much; he'd always been a good bookish student.

In the midst of the additional workload, Kaori found a new sanctuary: Empress Mai's hidden garden.

He'd been there once before, many years ago, during one of his periodic meetings with the empress—meetings he would eventually have to host between himself and each of the Academy students. That day, he'd arrived at the anteroom of the royal quarters, only to be guided to another chamber at the back of the palace instead, this one with unassuming black doors. Along one wall was a set of panels painted with a beautiful pond-side jungle scene. Light filtered through the painting as if the sun were really there, reflecting off the green water.

The young Kaori was about to touch the painting to see how much of the vision was real when it split down the center. Empress Mai waited for him on the other side in a lush garden. She introduced him to her sanctuary, which she'd commissioned on a piece of land that rose up to meet the back of the palace. The garden was closed in by rocky cliffs jutting up into the sky on either side, with a sheer cliff down to the ocean along the back edge.

"The gods left this land for me to build my sanctuary," she'd said.

That's when a massive Nokari tiger had strode out of the foliage, startling Kaori out of his seat. The empress giggled and introduced Ajira as her friend. The giant cat stood more than a meter tall and over two meters long. It was not uncommon to house tigers in Nokara and many people used them as a means of transport; but Kaori, who'd never been so close to one, was amazed. When Empress Mai encouraged him to touch Ajira, he'd marveled at the softness of her fur and the gentle strength he sensed in her body.

Piko the sloth had joined them shortly thereafter, examining Kaori with curiosity. Empress Mai explained that he expected new visitors to come with a treat. When Piko realized Kaori had nothing to offer, he disappeared slowly back into the greenery.

The empress had offered Kaori tea next, and they sat in the shade amidst her beautiful creation.

"Ajira and Piko are my friends," Empress Mai had said, "but they are also my reminders of what a true leader should be. Ajira is strong but reserved. She is kind but, at a moment's notice, can rear her mighty claws to pacify threats to her safety. Piko is curious and deliberate, but he is wise enough to know that patience is often the key to good decisions. Together, they can teach us all we need to know about leadership."

Kaori had thought the empress slightly peculiar at the time, but he sat in awe of her safe haven. Only once he'd endured weeks of training did he remember the existence of the garden and convince himself that it wasn't a dream. He sought it out and after insisting that the guards had once let Empress Mai out there on her own, he was granted the same privacy.

Despite the hard work, he'd begun to adjust to the changes.

Kento was allowed to remain in the palace and at times join the meetings with Kaori's advisors—a probationary period of sorts. Kaori had to admit that Kento's knowledge was useful. He added a certainty that the group lacked, and his familiarity with the politics of the lords and ladies of the regions could prove useful in the future. Together with Amaya and Taigen, Kaori determined that Kento would become his third advisor.

Then Amaya came to him one morning with an unforeseen challenge.

Kaori had just finished dressing when Amaya ascended the stairs. She greeted him with a guilty stare, unable to mask her discomfort.

"What troubles you?" Kaori asked, sitting in one of the armchairs. Amaya sat across from him and pulled a book out from under her arm.

"It has been brought to my attention, Your Grace—"

"Kaori."

Amaya abruptly readjusted. "*Kaori*. The Elliptic Council has brought to my attention an issue we should address right away. Now that you've been made emperor, tradition dictates that you marry."

Kaori realized he'd been absentmindedly fiddling with a miniature gonryo trinket as it dropped from his hand. Quickly, he snatched it up off the floor again, checking that the figurine of the plump, flightless bird hadn't cracked. "M-marry?"

"Yes," Amaya said. She flipped through the book to a marked page and ran her finger down until she found what she was looking for. "They are correct. As soon as possible after the crowning, the newly seated ruler must take a partner."

"But Empress Mai was unmarried."

"She'd been married before, but her husband passed away when you were quite young. There is no law that the ruler must re-marry in that instance, but she did initially take a spouse."

Kaori stammered, trying to find another argument to make. The room had become unbearably warm, and he removed the coat he'd put on only minutes before. "How do I do that? How am I supposed to find someone to wed?"

Amaya consulted the book. "I believe that's up to you. When Empress Mai was elected, she'd already fallen in love with her husband. Before her, I think the empresses usually sent out invitations for available suitors."

"And they met with *all* of them?"

"You could employ a screening process."

Kaori couldn't imagine there were enough hours in a day to meet with so many people in addition to his daily tasks. *Choosing a suitor?* How had that slipped everyone's mind for this long? He wasn't prepared for this. He'd never even kissed anyone before. Perhaps he should talk to Taigen. As soon as that thought entered his mind, Kaori brushed it away. Taigen's advice on the matter would be carnal and inappropriate. He knew lust, not love.

But maybe his friend would have some interesting pointers.

"Kaori?" Amaya asked.

Kaori shook himself into awareness. "You're certain this has to be?"

"Yes, quite."

He sighed. "Why do the trials continue to pile up? Alright, well, I suppose you can send out an invitation, but... maybe only to residents of the capital. We—we can start there."

"As you wish." Amaya stood and bowed before dismissing herself. "I will have a scribe draft an announcement requesting the presence of all available maidens in Black Tide Cove."

Kaori was beginning to see why rulers weren't allowed to refuse the throne once elected. If any of his predecessors had experienced as much frustration as he did with all the tasks thrust upon him, there'd be nobody left to accept it.

~

The sky was still black when the hand covered his mouth. Kaori awoke with a start. He twisted beneath the sheets, trying to distance himself from whoever sat over him. At the sight of Taigen, Kaori calmed somewhat, though the look on his friend's face was alarming.

Taigen raised a finger to his lips. "You have to come with me, Kaori."

"What's going on?" Kaori asked, but Taigen shook his head.

"There's no time," he said and held out his hand.

Kaori took it and allowed himself to be helped off the bed. His shoes had been placed on the floor beside the four-poster and he slid them on, his mind racing. Taigen hadn't made any of his usual jokes or lewd comments. Kaori had never seen his friend so serious before. The worst scenarios came to mind: they were under attack; the city had caught fire. But from what he could see out the window, neither of these scenarios was true.

Then a pair of armed sentries pulled him toward the stairs. They descended in a run, joined in the latticed hallway by more guards. Nobody spoke. Nobody looked at him.

They jogged through the palace, past the chambers where he had his lessons and the private halls where he met with lords and ladies. More guards gathered as they went until they reached a hidden interior room. Bursting through the door, he found himself in a plain, candlelit chamber made of dark stone. Inside, Amaya and Kento sat at a long table, while a handful of other guards stood sentinel around the perimeter. Amaya turned to him, frightened and relieved. Kento simply stared into space, shocked.

The door shut.

"What's happening?" Kaori asked.

"There's been an attack," Amaya said.

"Hinata has been assassinated." Taigen placed his hand on Kaori's shoulder.

The late empress's head advisor? The man who had crowned Kaori only weeks ago? Kaori rested his hands on the table. Every part of his body clenched.

"What?" he asked, flummoxed. "But he'd resumed duty as deputy headmaster of the Academy. Wasn't he living—"

"On the palace grounds? Yes. He was in his quarters, as a matter of fact." Amaya folded her hands. "That's why we're here."

"The assassin breached the walls?" Kaori asked.

"I'm afraid so."

"Could they get inside the palace?"

"It's not beyond the realm of possibility at this point, though the palace itself has more security than the grounds," Amaya said. "Even so, this is more of a precaution. We cannot take chances."

"Why did they kill Hinata?"

"We're not sure yet," Taigen said, "but it had to have been someone highly trained. How else would they get past the patrols and into the deputy headmaster's quarters?"

"Is he the only one?"

"It would seem so. The remainder of the staff are taking attendance of the students, but none of the other kumo live within the palace."

Kaori sank into one of the seats. He'd stood beside Hinata's encouraging presence so recently. The man had passed along Mai's blessing. Now he was dead.

"Do we know anything about the assassin?" Kaori asked.

"We—"

"It was the Jade Dagger," Kento said, speaking for the first time. His face had drained of color as he looked around the table at the rest of them.

"What?" Taigen asked. "Who's that?"

"A partial myth," Amaya said, her brow creased. "The Jade Dagger is the deadliest assassin of our time, rumored to be responsible for the death of Hatazori Gwang Baekje of Shondai and Harada Tokikage of Hado. Rarely seen, and only then a shadow, their skills are said to rival the gods… but that is all greatly exaggerated, of course."

"They got past the guards," Kaori observed.

"How can you tell it was them?" Taigen asked.

"The Jade Dagger's trademark is that they always take a souvenir," Kento said, palms spread on the tabletop. "*Always*. But it's only ever one item. Hinata was missing Skyswell, the sapphire ring he wore on his right hand. It was a treasured gift from Empress Mai—he'd never have taken it off. I was there when she presented it! Any other thief would've taken all his jewelry. The orange-gold necklace he wore was worth three times what Skyswell would fetch on the black market. Mark my words: it was the Jade Dagger."

When Kento fell into silent contemplation, Amaya turned to face Kaori. "I'm afraid I don't disagree with him. Someone with this level of training, who left with only this one trinket, aligns with the methods of the Jade Dagger—as exaggerated as the myths may be."

"What do we do then?" Kaori asked. His gaze flitted between the three of them, waiting for someone to speak up, but Amaya pursed her lips, Taigen seemed at a loss, and Kento's gaze bored holes into the wall across from him. What was the proper course of action when an assassin who'd murdered someone behind the palace walls had been compared to a shadow? He'd had lessons about attacks on the city or civil unrest, but nothing of this sort.

"Perhaps we should investigate who hired the killer," Taigen suggested finally. "If the assassin is so impossible to catch, perhaps going after the source is wiser?"

Amaya nodded. "Yes, I agree that seems like a more attainable investigation. A hired hand has no motive or connection to the victim, but by tracing other information, we can at least find who paid for the attack."

Kaori considered this. It made the most sense to him. "Alright," he said, clearing his throat. "Send a section of guards to sort this out. Find who hired the Jade Dagger and bring them in. Send another group to pursue the assassin on the off-chance they can find something."

"For the time being, I think you should remain in this room," Amaya said. "Who knows if the job is done."

Reluctantly, Kaori agreed. Perhaps the killer had come to take only one life—after all, why would they start with Hinata if their other target was the emperor?—but he didn't relish the idea of walking around tonight even if it was inside the palace.

Kaori sighed and sank further into his chair. It would seem the surprises never ceased.

Helena

She floated in and out of the waking world. At times, her consciousness was no more than a throbbing headache. At others, she felt herself trying to wake up, listening to muffled sounds like distant thunder around her and unable to respond. Did she imagine opening her eyes once? Did she imagine glimpsing the stars through a ring of barren treetops while she rocked rhythmically?

She couldn't say how long this state lasted, nor when any one day transformed into another. There were no dreams—at least, none that she could remember afterward. There was only shadowy darkness.

Then, quite suddenly, she was aware.

Helena felt the cold bristle the hairs on her arms. She smelled aged wood and stale air. For a moment, skepticism refused to let her believe that she was truly awake, but the wave of soreness following her consciousness confirmed this was real.

A door closed only meters away and Helena's eyes fluttered open.

She lay in a cot, a rough-spun blanket pulled up beneath her arms. Beside her, a candle cast shadows as it flickered from a square table. The cramped room comprised plain stone walls and a ceiling she could probably reach if she stood on her toes. Other than her cot and the table, there was only a simple wardrobe against the opposite wall and a mat laid out on the floor.

Helena looked around with painful difficulty, terribly confused. This was not her home, nor did it even resemble anything in Corva sum Rio. The people in her village used wood to build their houses, not these large, cut blocks of stone.

The events of that night came back to her: the fires, the chaos in the streets, running with Arsenio and their papai, and then darkness. Had someone attacked them? Was her family alright? She tried to call out to them, but her voice died in her coarse, dry throat.

Instead, she noticed that the door, though it had been pulled closed, hadn't latched and it had swung back until it was ajar. Through the gap, she could just make out a woman's back, standing as if to block entry to the room. Voices came next.

"I *knew* it," someone else was saying, another woman. She hissed with barely controlled anger. "I knew you were hiding something. What is she doing here, Engana?"

"She was alone in the Wild Wood," the woman blocking the door said. She paused, then in a lower voice muttered, "Just outside Corva sum Rio."

The other woman didn't respond right away. "You brought her along?"

"I—I couldn't leave her, Jacinta," Engana said. "She's been injured. I went down there. I saw what happened. You were the one who told me that to eliminate my doubts. I needed to take action."

"I didn't mean for you to bring one of them *here*." Helena imagined the other woman shaking her head in quiet frustration. She sounded quite a bit like Andreia Ferro, the older woman who ran the bakery on Estrada Lubo. "Do you understand how dangerous that could prove? What are you going to do with her? What exactly is your plan?"

"Feed her, bandage her wounds, get her health back."

"That's all very well, but—"

"She could be inconspicuous. A servant. I'm sure she knows how to clean. We can start there."

"You brought her all this way to clean?" Jacinta's tone was icy.

"Nobody saw me bring her in. You need not worry."

A frustrated grunt followed this reassurance, then, "My tomb will be my refuge."

"What would you have me do?"

Silence. Helena strained her hearing, hoping not to miss a word. It would seem her fate rested in the hands of this Jacinta. What that fate might mean, she still couldn't say. Who exactly were these women, and where had Engana taken her? She searched her surroundings, hoping to find something that might give her location away, but the room lacked identifying features. Nothing but stone and wood.

Helena let her gaze fall. As she strained to dissect her surroundings, memories rushed back to her. Flames rippling in the air. Hundreds of fleeing people. She was supposed to meet the rest of her family in the Wild Wood, out of harm's way. But her memory blacked out at the same moment every time: the moment she'd been torn away from her brother. Helena could only hope that the rest of her family had found each other. Were they here too?

When she looked up, Engana stood in the doorway. She was a young woman with thick eyebrows, a pointed face, and hollowed cheeks. Her dark brown hair was plaited down her back, and she wore a loose-fitting white robe that cascaded all the way to her feet. Seeing Helena awake, her expression turned wary.

"How do you feel?" Engana asked.

Helena opened her mouth. Her voice was weak and clumsy from disuse. "I...I..." was all she could manage.

"What's your name?"

Helena swallowed, feeling what little saliva she could muster trickle down her throat. "Helena."

The woman nodded, as if this confirmed something. Behind her, Jacinta appeared in the doorway. Helena had been right; the woman was at least thirty years Engana's senior. Her dark hair was streaked with gray and pulled back in a bun. Whereas Engana's robes were plain and white, Jacinta's dress was the deepest blue with faint, elegant patterns about the skirt.

"Have you lived your entire life in Corva sum Rio?" Engana asked.

Helena swallowed more of her own saliva, moisture returning slowly to her mouth. "Yes."

"And your parents? Your family? They all lived there too?"

"Yes," Helena said.

Jacinta closed her eyes, her brow creasing down the middle.

"What's happened to them?" Helena asked.

Engana sighed and stepped further into the room. As she did so, Jacinta followed and shut the door behind her.

"There was an attack on your village," Engana began.

"I was there! It was—"

Helena meant to blame the king, but remembered at the last moment that this could prove a disastrous folly depending on who heard. Engana held up a finger at that exact moment to silence her.

"Your village was completely destroyed," she said solemnly. "The entire village burned into rubble and ash. Many, *many* people were killed. I'm afraid there's a good chance that includes your family."

"No," Helena said, shaking her head as best she could. This woman didn't know what she was talking about. She didn't know Helena's family. They were members of Afonso's Light. Her siblings were clever and quick, her parents resourceful and intelligent. They'd fled the fires; they wouldn't have been caught or killed. In fact, if Engana hadn't found them, then they were probably roaming the Wild Wood right now, looking for her. She needed to leave. She needed to find them. Maybe her village had burned down, but not her family. Certainly not her family.

Helena made to sit up, but as she did so, her head throbbed and pain shot through the right side of her body. She flinched.

"You need to continue resting," Engana said. "You've been asleep for four days."

Four days? Helena's eyes widened. She'd been separated from her family for four days? If she didn't find them soon, they were going to think she was dead. The urge to flee became a desperation, and her eyes flickered to the door.

"I have to go."

"You can't. Not now, you're too weak." As she said this, Engana turned to look at Jacinta, whose expression remained impassive.

"You don't understand, my family—"

"Helena—"

"I have to let them know I'm okay!"

"There is nobody left!" Engana said, raising her voice to match Helena's distressed tone. Helena opened her mouth to argue, but Engana pressed on. "When I departed, when I found you, I'd searched the area. The abandoned streets, the Wild Wood. Everything. All the villagers had either died or fled. I'm sorry, but they're all gone."

Helena was taken aback, unable to place the widening chasm inside her chest. She couldn't fathom what this woman had said, but the desperation in her eyes spoke of truth. And yet, it still didn't make sense to Helena. Her family would never have left her behind, not unless they thought her dead—or, unless they themselves had perished.

"She's right," Jacinta said. They looked to her, Engana relieved and Helena worried. "You shouldn't go. Especially not now. Not when there's nothing for you to return to."

Helena looked back and forth between the two women, her chest heaving. Her body was tired and aching, bruised in more places than she could count. Still, something about the older woman's expression, something about her finality, made it clear to Helena that leaving was not a possibility. No matter how her heart ached for her lost home and loved ones, she had no choice but to stay.

"Who are you?" Helena asked finally, voice shaking. She still needed something to drink. "Where have you brought me?"

Jacinta stepped around Engana so that she stood between her and Helena.

"My dear," she said. "You are in the Quartz Basilica."

Helena had opened her mouth, preparing a retort. But the words caught on her tongue. The Quartz Basilica was an ancient, holy site tucked far from Corva sum Rio in the Urse Mountains. The site could not be visited by simply anybody. To enter, to live inside, you had to be an important member of the Holy Order. A Magistrata.

"You're priestesses, then," Helena said. Suddenly, the dresses made more sense. She looked down at the blanket covering her, wondering if she lay beneath something blessed.

"It's just a blanket," Engana said, as if aware of her thoughts. "And yes, we are."

"But how can I be here? How can you have taken me inside? I—I'm only a commoner. Unholy. My family hasn't made a pilgrimage to a temple in years."

Engana hushed her. "Be still. A Magistrata can bring in whomever they please."

Helena didn't know what she'd done to deserve such protection, but no person of ill will would dare harm her in the basilica. It went against every church teaching. Though she hadn't asked to be taken to the remote holy site, she certainly understood why Engana's decision to bring her here posed such a dilemma to her superior—and why it would be unwise for Helena to leave, especially as she recovered.

She nodded, her lips held tight by sheer will alone.

"Rest here in Engana's room for one more night," Jacinta said. "Tomorrow, we'll find you a space in the servants' quarters. Please, stick to me at all times and to no one else. As your face becomes familiar, people will be less inclined to ask questions."

Helena lay slack-jawed, unable to discern quite how she felt. But having been carried this far from her destroyed home, she was in no condition to refuse shelter. The more she observed, the more Helena realized that her initial judgment of Jacinta's severity was incorrect. If anything, she looked tired and worried rather than harassed. Full of concern for the guest she'd unwittingly received.

Helena grimaced against the pain in her body as she turned to face the Magistrata. "Thank you," she said. "I won't be a bother, I promise. I—"

"Give her bolo de serta and water," Jacinta commanded, turning to leave. "I will be back again tomorrow."

Arsenio

He'd never felt so cramped before.

Arsenio and his sister sat huddled behind the barrels for three days, emerging only to scavenge food and drink, and to relieve themselves when they could be sure the crew was asleep. Each night, unraveling was a painstaking process. His joints and his back ached from sitting in the same curled position all day and he'd never felt more disgusting in his life. But he told himself that this pain was better than the alternative. There was little mercy for a captured stowaway.

Still, by the fourth night, he and Mariana had taken just about all they could handle. When they emerged, they went on a search of the ship, seeking out a new hiding place. They avoided the crews' cabins and the kitchen, spending a tense moment frozen on the stairs when they heard muttered conversation.

Eventually, they settled on the lowermost deck, where the many chests they'd seen the crew lugging onboard were stored. As soon as they'd shut the hatch, both twins breathed a sigh of relief. Arsenio stretched out on a mound of netting, excited not to be spending another day huddled in a dark corner.

It was here they remained for the entirety of the next day, free to roam about the cabin so long as they kept an ear out for approaching footsteps.

Several times, they ducked for cover, but it wasn't until the fourth instance that someone actually entered their hiding place among the cargo. Arsenio and Mariana dived beneath a pile of canvas. No sooner had they done so than the hatch was yanked open and two crew members descended onto the lowermost deck.

"Captain will be happy to see them," a man said, the first to dismount the steps. Through a gap in the canvas, Arsenio could see him looking about the dark space, a lantern held high. "Reckon he might reward us."

The second was a woman. "Wouldn't that be a nice change? I'd fancy some special treatment, like. So, we'll want to find 'em quick."

The pair went straight to the nearest set of wooden chests, peering around the sides without unlatching any of them. Neither Arsenio nor Mariana had attempted to open anything since establishing their new residence. As such, Arsenio couldn't guess whether the item the sailors sought would bring them close to him and his sister.

As the two made their way around the inventory, Arsenio lost sight of the crew members and had to resort to listening for their location. Their muttering back and forth became too difficult to understand, lost beneath the creaks of the cabin before disappearing altogether. But he imagined if they found what they were looking for the reaction would be loud and obvious. Subtlety was not abundant aboard this ship.

He held his breath, wondering suddenly if maybe something else was afoot.

Then the canvas was torn aside. Arsenio and Mariana scrambled to get away, but it was too late. The man had grabbed ahold of Arsenio and wrapped a thick, sweaty arm around his throat, growling in Arsenio's ear as he did so. Likewise, the woman had Mariana restrained in a matter of seconds. The pair of sailors grinned wickedly, their features elongated by the light of the lantern.

"I knew I'd heard someones creeping about the stairs," the man said, tightening his grip and blocking Arsenio's airflow. "Looks like we've got ourselves a pair o' stowaways."

The woman shrieked delightedly in response.

In the roughest way possible, their swords were confiscated and Arsenio and Mariana were hauled from the ballast deck. The other crew members took notice, pausing from their daily tasks to gawk at the stowaways as they were marched by. Some jeered, some laughed with delight, others looked disapprovingly then went back to their work, unfazed. Arsenio struggled against his captor, but found he wasn't strong enough to break the man's hold. He was powerless as they climbed the steps to the main deck and the open air.

The frigid wind whipped at his face. In the distance, an orange sun set on the water. For the briefest of moments, Arsenio was treated to the sight of endless sea. As far as he could tell, their ship was the only semblance of land anywhere, surrounded on all sides by rolling waves of topaz.

They climbed to the upper deck outside the captain's quarters. The sailor holding him burst through the double doors and Arsenio and his sister were thrown unceremoniously to the floor.

The captain stood inside, his back to them. He wore a brown leather coat that fell to his calves, beneath which Arsenio spied boots that had seen their fair share of the world. The man stood staring down at a desk. As they watched, he turned on the spot, calm as could be.

The captain observed the siblings, his expression unreadable, then looked up at his crew members.

"We's found stowaways," said the sailor who'd manhandled Arsenio. He pointed down at the prisoners.

"Tell me," the captain replied in a deep, rumbling voice that Arsenio felt in his chest, "when it was I granted ye permission to enter, Lionel."

"Them's stowaways though," the woman interjected.

"Tell me," the captain repeated, louder this time. The pair stopped their sputtering.

"I don't believe you did, sir," Lionel said.

"Tha's right. I didn't." He stepped *over* Arsenio, approaching the two sailors, who cowered suddenly. "And we're all aware how the captain doesn't like disturbing, does he?"

"No, sir."

"Then ye best go, hadn't ye?"

Without another word, the two slunk from the room like scolded dogs. Through his fear, Arsenio felt some semblance of satisfaction that instead of the praise they'd hoped to gain, the sailors had received admonishment instead. The captain shut the doors and slid the locks up into the doorframe to prevent further interruption. He spun to face the siblings on the floor.

Arsenio had expected an older man, but the captain couldn't have surpassed his thirty-fifth name day. He had bright yellow hair that fell beneath the brim of his hat in twisted strands. Sandy stubble lined his jaw and chin. A bright pink scar marred the left side of his face from ear to cheekbone and his round eyes were a pale blue. Arsenio hadn't known eyes could be such a color—like ice in the dead of winter. Even while he knelt on the ground, he could tell the captain was easily one of the tallest men he'd ever met, his stature lean and powerful.

Then the captain did something completely unexpected—he began to laugh. Arsenio exchanged a worried glance with his sister.

"Welcome aboard the *Flaming Virtue*," the captain said, spreading his hands.

"That was ridiculous treatment," Mariana said, rising from her knees. Arsenio could tell she was trying to put on an air of confidence, hoping they might gain control of their situation. It didn't work.

"Ye be the ones fool enough to stow away aboard my ship!" the captain roared. "I'll take no sass from you, miss."

Mariana stepped back, startled. The man smiled.

"Call me Captain Elwin Simmerhorn Hadleigh," he said, bowing politely. "Come now, we mustn't act poorly. Up, boy."

Arsenio did as he was told, standing beside his sister in the center of the room. Captain Elwin paused, his eyes lingering uncomfortably long on Arsenio's face. Then he circled around the two, returning to his desk where he leaned back against the tabletop, smiling still. He was a handsome man, though any charm was sacrificed to the threat of being tossed overboard—or worse. Arsenio eyed the black handle of the sword that hung at the captain's hip.

"Now, what good fortune brings the pair of ye aboard my beloved vessel?"

"We were just—"

"And don't go spoutin' tales. I can tell a lie when I hear one—been around them all my life, what with this lot."

Arsenio swallowed. Without the opportunity to confer with his sister, he couldn't gauge how much of their story to convey. He imagined Mariana struggled with the same concern, but neither dared turn away from the captain.

Elwin chuckled. "Come now, just a moment ago you were rarin' to tell me what for. Now the pair of ye have gone mute? It's me presentation, isn't it?" he asked, outlining a curvy figure in the air with a wink of those strangely colored eyes. "Or maybe the scar's got ye rattled. Fine then. Let's start with names. I've gone first."

"Ar—Arsenio. Avilla."

"And I'm his sister, Mariana."

"From where do ye hail?"

"We come from Corva sum Rio."

"I'm afraid I'm not familiar," Captain Elwin said.

"It's a village upriver from Ciro," Mariana explained.

"Our people have suffered under the leadership of King Fogosombre Marchosias," Arsenio said. "You must know of him."

"Aye, him I know."

"He sent troops who burned our village to the ground. Our family, our friends, everyone we knew either fled…or died," Arsenio said. He paused, thinking of their parents and their sister. "The latest in a string of hostilities against our people. This, in addition to the harsh taxes, routine violence, and constant fear Fogosombre uses to oppress Faron. The only ones who benefit are those who support his regime and perpetuate its transgressions."

"Whoa there!" Captain Elwin burst into a round of hearty laughter again. "I may speak the common tongue, but there's a host of words I can't follow, boy. What you mean to say is, he's a bad man. But what has this to do with the pair of ye stowin' away upon my ship?"

"We've gone to seek help," Mariana said. "There are other nations out there. If we can't overthrow the Tyrant on our own, perhaps we can find others who will help us."

Elwin's laughs stopped immediately. "Ah, now we have cause. Now we have reason. Ye knows our headin'. Ye seeks passage to Nokara."

"You mustn't throw us overboard," Mariana said. "We can be useful. We're hard workers and we learn quick."

Captain Elwin smiled again; it was more charming each time. Light glinted off his canines, which were capped with gold. "I'm generally not keen to treat stowaways with mercy," he said, running a hand along his stubble. "Especially those doling out commands as if they've some power. Cut many a man down his middle, I have, and sent him to the depths for the bakusawa to nibble. Others I've soaked in their own blood, tied 'em to barrels, and let them float 'til the sharks came. Such savage, *savage* acts, but not one wink a sleep have I lost. What makes ye think I'll show ye mercy?"

"Please," Arsenio pleaded, "we only wish to help our people. Once we're in Nokara, you'll never have to see us again."

"That still leaves the trouble of me hospitality being taken advantage of."

"We'll do anything."

"Anything, you say?" The captain considered their words, his left hand resting on the hilt of his blade. Arsenio found himself unable to breathe, listening to his rabid pulse and fearing that each beat might be the last. He and his sister had never been so far away from home, and to make it this far, only to be killed, felt like such a waste. Galina would never know how far they'd made it—though she hadn't shown much faith in them to begin with.

"Me mood don't favor spilling blood tonight. Count yourselves lucky I'm in rare form. If we hadn't just lost Tegine and if I hadn't just seen Damios puncture that awful wart…" The captain shuddered. "But if you're part of the crew, then ye best behave the part. There'll be no second chance if I regret me decision."

"Thank you, Captain," Mariana said, and Arsenio hoped Elwin couldn't hear the slight sarcasm that laced her words. He repeated the sentiment in earnest, unwilling to believe their fortune.

"You're dismissed, Mariana," Elwin said, and Arsenio froze. Beside him, his sister was reluctant to leave.

"But—"

"I believe I dismissed you, Mariana. Ye need not worry, love. I've no intention of harmin' your precious kin." The captain stood straight, grinning at Mariana expectantly. "I wish only a word."

Mariana's eyes shifted between the two of them, and Arsenio wanted desperately to plead that she stay, but the captain shooed her onward. She whispered, "I'll be right outside," to Arsenio before turning to go. In a matter of five steps, she was gone, leaving only him and Elwin Hadleigh in the room.

"*Arsenio*, was it?" Elwin asked. He almost sang the name.

"Yes."

"A handsome name if ever I've heard one."

"My parents gave it to me." Arsenio didn't know what else to say.

"Ye might be asking yourself why it is I've not skewered ye and your sister," the captain said, then clicked his tongue against the roof of his mouth. "I've spent many a year crossing tides. Seen corners of the world ye'd never imagine, I have. And I've learned spilling pretty blood can be a cursed gamble, and regretful to boot. Tegine was me cabin boy. What a waste."

Elwin clicked his tongue again and crossed his arms, looking away from Arsenio for the first time in many long, tense minutes.

"I hope ye'll understand, *Arsenio*. Being captain of such a glorious vessel as my beloved *Flaming Virtue* requires much from a man. I've me crew to think about. Their hungers, their desires, their payments." He rubbed imaginary coins between his fingers.

"I understand," Arsenio said, confused as to why he was being treated to this lecture. Despite the bluntness with which he could turn to threats, the captain now seemed to be dancing around the issue at hand.

"What I mean to say is, I hope ye won't think ill of me. I can't show kindness to every soul what stows away upon me ship." He stepped closer. Though Arsenio had been among the tallest boys his age in Corva sum Rio, his eyes only came level with the man's shoulder. Elwin lifted a hand to brush away a strand of hair at Arsenio's temple. When he spoke again, it was soft, almost gentle—when the worst of a storm has blown through and all that's left is the retreating thunder. "But I am a reasonable man."

Arsenio looked up at him. Captain Elwin's entire face had transformed. There was something else to him which had breached the rough exterior. A sadness. A longing. Arsenio was no longer afraid, but neither was he comfortable.

"A reasonable man," the captain repeated. "A lonely man."

"Aren't I a little old to be cabin boy?"

"Ye misunderstand me so."

"What are you asking of me?"

"Would ye make me say it?" He tried a laugh, but it came out hollow. Arsenio turned away, feeling his face go hot as he realized what Captain Elwin meant. "There be room for ye here. Beside me."

He placed the lingering hand on Arsenio's shoulder. Reflexively, Arsenio twisted away. "I'm sorry," he said.

"Think hard on it, boy," Elwin said gruffly, his grip stiffening.

Arsenio struggled, trying to create distance between him and the captain, but Elwin's other hand gripped the back of his head. Long, rough fingers intertwined themselves with his hair.

"Stop," Arsenio gasped.

"Start slow, we can. Bear you not me burden with chaste cloth between us. A night in company is shorter than a night alone."

"Please!" Arsenio beat a fist against the man's chest. Fear choked him, a lump rising in his throat.

"But the feel of another might entice us so," the captain continued, his voice heavy with lust, "the warmth. Isn't that better than icy solitude?"

"I don't want to!"

"Ye said 'anything' before!"

Arsenio expected a hand across his face, for the captain to explode in rage or to take back his promise of safe passage. He expected to be grabbed by his collar and dragged out onto the deck to be thrown overboard. He expected anger.

Instead, the captain looked down at Arsenio, his features stern but controlled. The longing never left his eyes. Elwin released him, backed away to the desk where he'd been before the interruption. "Seems ye didn't mean that," he muttered.

Arsenio's heart pounded as he backed out of arm's reach.

"Ye are dismissed," Captain Elwin said gruffly. "Join your sister."

~

Though neither sibling had been on a ship before nor had they even seen the Great Ocean, the twins were put to task same as any other lowly member of the crew. They scrubbed the decks and cleaned the kitchen. If they were tasked with something for which they'd neither experience nor frame of reference, they received loud, angry words and perhaps the back of an aggravated hand. The crew took pleasure in hurling insults Arsenio's way, which paralyzed him with frustration. Several of the crew had been given monikers far more familiar than their birthnames; Arsenio's only hope was that "mast-licker" wouldn't become his.

Mariana had a significantly easier time adjusting. The first day after they'd been discovered, she was the subject of howls and hollers from a handful of the male crew members—the same ones whose colorful slurs followed Arsenio—but Mariana's scowl greeted each remark and when one unlucky fellow tried to pass off a hand's brush with her backside as an accident to the cheers of his friends, she hit him across the face with the handle of a mop and that was the end of her hounding. The crew treated her with more respect following the incident, whereas the man and his peach-sized black eye became the subject of mockery.

Each evening, as the sun dipped down into the water, the crew gathered on deck for supper. These mealtimes weren't complete without a rousing round of tall tales where crew members took turns regaling them all in their most glorious feats of courage. The vast majority of these stories were laden with garish exaggeration and, when boiled down to their basics, might have been decent tales of bravery had they been delivered in a less fantastical manner.

One evening, Damios, the first mate, recounted his defeat of a gluttonous one-eyed giant who'd been stealing children from his hometown, taking them up into the hills, and flaying them alive to feed to his rabid dogs. While fighting the giant, Damios had stabbed him through his remaining eye and tricked him off a cliff into the Moor sum Portes. But as his tale progressed, he went from being one of three rescuers to the sole hero, and the giant went from three meters tall to four and eventually four and a half. At the end of his triumphant tale, Damios received a chorus of cheers and laughter as he sat back down, rosy-cheeked and triumphant.

"Who shall we hear from next?" called Jocaste, one of the pair who'd discovered Arsenio and his sister.

Her question was met by an indecipherable cacophony of bellowed nominations. She cackled at the chaos, her blackened teeth bared. Arsenio glanced around the room and noticed Captain Elwin had snuck in. He sat midway up the steps to the aft deck, drinking from a tin cup, his smile glinting in the lamplight.

It wasn't until Jocaste raised her hands that everyone calmed down.

"I've heard nothing but swill from the lot of ye, and I shan't mar me honest reputation with lies about wanting to hear more." This was met with raucous laughter. "There's but one sailor from whom I've gleaned nary a whisper. And I think I'd like to change that now. Miss Redthumb."

The crew cheered louder than ever for a woman who Arsenio hadn't spoken a word to but had seen several times running about the main deck. She had dark, freckled skin with lips that were almost black, and most of the time, she wore an unimpressed scowl on her face. At first Redthumb refused, shaking her hands at the crew who encouraged her boisterously, but after a minute of playful hollering, she stood and adjusted the tattered skirt around her narrow waist.

"Aye," she said with a thick accent and a husky voice. "Ye think after all this time I'll tell me tale then?"

The crew cheered, slamming their hands repeatedly whatever surface was within reach.

"Fine." She looked at each person in turn with a haughty grin on her face, pearly teeth shining bold. "Born in a poor village, I was, on the hottest day o' summer. Me folks don' have nothin' to they name. So what does me papa do? Soon as I'm old enough that there is me beauty shone through, him sells me off to a white devil come to take me. Pays me papa in gold, this pale man does. Them's good fortune for me folks, bad fortune for me.

"Where does the white devil take me? Him had a master, no doubt. A man go by Lord Fausten." Silence gripped the cabin at this point. Arsenio guessed that nobody had managed to get Redthumb to tell her tale before and tonight, her divulgatory mood had enraptured them all. Even the usual creaks of the ship had gone quiet. "What does Lord Fausten want, you might say? Him have gold and food and servants. *Quat je duvelne*. I tell you. Him wants a beauty to speak his name right. *Whip*. Him wants a beauty to wear dresses and stand proper. *Whip*. Him wants a beauty to fondle his fat pink prick. *Whip!*

"So what choices had I? Learned how to touch his cock, I did. Wore all the frilly dresses them put on me. And me learned to say *Lord Fausten* all pretty like so him not hit me." She curtseyed, her harsh smile sweeping the crowd again. Then she stood straight, eyes solemn again. "On me sixteenth name day, gave meself a gift. Him asked me for the touchin', an' I squeeze the dangling sack on him 'til him balls pop like plums in me palm. *Pop!* And I slit him throat using me own thumbnail."

She dragged the infamous digit across her own neck and the nearest row of crew members withdrew as if avoiding the spray of gore. When she was finished, Redthumb stood straight, a barely detectable smile on her lips. Arsenio could tell she enjoyed the shocked silence, relished it even. "Would've hunted me down, them folk. Would've cut me up, kil't me. But them's not fast enough, no. I run away from that place, run far into the land where the sun set. I never look back. I never will."

No shouts nor laughter followed her story, only the continued silence. Not every tale of bravery was one to cheer over. With one hand, Redthumb brushed her hair behind her shoulder. No crew member stood to speak next.

Arsenio looked around at the stairs, but the captain had left.

Kaori

When the session ended for the day, Kaori stood, grateful that once again he'd survived without incident. Kento congratulated him on his diplomatic responses as he had every day since Kaori had appointed him to his group of advisors. Taigen, however, chided him for being the conciliatory emperor who upset no one. His services no longer needed, Taigen fled the throne room, muttering something about alcohol and female companionship.

In perhaps a more conspicuous manner than he meant to, Kaori avoided looking in Kumo Amaya's direction by busying himself with his robes while he stepped down off the dais.

He had roughly two hours before sword lessons with Gen and he longed for a moment of peace and solitude. Yet even as he stepped out onto the portico, his favored teacher didn't leave his side. An expectant silence hung between them, which he couldn't ignore. He knew Amaya was waiting for him to ask what business she had to discuss—her rigid observation of hierarchy never bent—but both of them were fully aware of what she was going to say, and how reluctant Kaori's participation would be.

Eventually, Kaori felt bad enough that he relented.

"You have another issue to address, Amaya?" he asked.

"I do, Your Majesty," she said, bowing her head.

"Tell me, then."

"I am pleased to inform you that the council has elected Hinata's replacement. A young woman named Chiyoko. She was a year above you."

"Excellent," Kaori said, hoping his sigh of relief was not too obvious. "If that's all you've come to tell me—"

"I also have another suitor who seeks your audience," Amaya said. Before Kaori could express any sort of refusal, she pressed on. "This one is quite intelligent and beautiful. She was known to be extraordinarily prudent in her district. In fact, she taught herself how to read and write by studying the stone inscriptions in the temple. Though I would hazard a guess that the joshen lent her paper to practice writing on, otherwise I don't see how—"

"Is she here already?" Kaori asked.

"Yes," Amaya said. "She's waiting in Tatsu Garden."

Kaori sighed. If she was waiting within the palace walls already, he couldn't very well delay meeting her. He didn't want to be rude.

Still, the idea of meeting with another hopeful young woman pained him. He knew what the traditions stated, but Amaya's determination to find him a wife had proven more aggressive than he'd been prepared for. Two days prior, she'd arranged four meetings for him, none of which had yielded anything promising—though he had ingested an over-abundance of food as a result. Yesterday, another three women had been brought to his attention, though he stuck to tea that time around.

The problem wasn't with the women Amaya had found; they were all perfectly nice and polite with interesting personalities. He just wasn't comfortable with any of them. Their interactions felt forced—which, of course, they were—and that only added to his inability to relax in their presence. He stumbled over simple topics, and often found himself relying on the women to keep the conversation flowing.

Inevitably, every meeting ended with Kaori expressing his gratitude and letting them know how nice it was to meet them. Then they were escorted away by a servant while his eager advisors approached. He would shrug and shake his head, sad to disappoint them but unable to feign interest. This was, after all, someone he was expected to spend his life with.

Taigen thought Kaori should be much more relaxed about the entire ordeal and not hold the potential relationship to such a high standard. In his view, the people just wanted the emperor married—if he wanted to *indulge* in other intimate forays, that was ultimately his business. In that regard, Black Tide Cove had plenty to choose from. Beyond the palace walls were several locales worthy of Kaori's discretionary patronage.

"Your problem," Taigen had informed him the previous night, "is your inexperience. It's making you nervous—that's why you aren't making a connection. That last girl was absolutely gorgeous. You really shouldn't have turned her away."

"She was beautiful," Kaori agreed.

"If you can't talk to them, let me take you into town tonight. We'll find you a companion and you can let her lead the way. After she's bounced around on your cock for a few minutes, you'll be much more comfortable." Kaori felt this plan was more for Taigen's benefit than his.

"I can explain things to you if you'd prefer," Taigen said with a wink, "but hands-on experience is the best teacher."

Kaori had blushed. "I am already aware how it works, thank you."

At least Kumo Amaya's intentions were pure.

Kaori sighed again. Turning to Amaya, he said, "Alright, what's her name?"

"Sugi Kanamori," Amaya said.

Kaori followed her down to the palace gardens.

Kingfisher Palace was widely regarded throughout the empire as an unparalleled triumph in architecture, but Kaori had always thought the true beauty lay in the many gardens scattered throughout the grounds. Though his preference was Kuriku, most students of the Academy frequented the gardens closer to the palace. Tatsu Garden was the obvious favorite: a grid of modeki trees which, during the rising season, sprouted cottony white flowers that formed a canopy of clouds over the benches and stone paths. Taigen had often made Kaori study there with him so he could flirt with the girls, but Kaori avoided Tatsu Garden otherwise. It was loud, almost as crowded as the market sometimes on a particularly beautiful day. In addition to the students, the palace staff would come down during the afternoon to mingle before heading home to their families. There would be overlapping conversations competing in volume, hormonal teenagers vying for each other's attention, and barely anywhere to sit.

However, the crowds of Tatsu had thankfully thinned when he arrived. Conspiratorially, Kaori wondered if the vacancy was engineered. Amaya walked with him until they spotted Sugi sitting on a bench beneath one of the barren modeki trees. Then Amaya backed away without a word and left Kaori to his fate.

Among the seven women Kaori had recently met, he'd noticed a common thread: despite their differing personalities, they were all attractive in a conventional way, following the current Nokari standards of beauty. Walking up to Sugi, Kaori noticed that this time around, Amaya had chosen someone of a different mold. Her silken black hair was cut short at her shoulders, and she wore it down instead of in an elaborate style. She had a round face with a small mouth. Thick eyebrows emboldened her dark eyes. She sat not as though she were waiting for someone, but as if she had come here to think and appreciate her surroundings. Indeed, when he came within a few yards of her and cleared his throat, Sugi almost seemed surprised to meet him there.

She stood.

"Are you Sugi Kanamori?" Kaori asked.

She smiled. The expression was genuine and friendly. "I am. I don't need to ask; you are Emperor Kaori."

Kaori nodded and she bowed, her hair swinging freely.

"May I join you?" Kaori asked.

"Yes, please do."

They sat again and Kaori looked around. He'd been wrong; the modeki tree above them was not bare—one clump of brown leaves still clung to a branch, braving the winds of change admirably.

"I have never seen a modeki tree before," Sugi said. "I wish I could have seen them during the rising season."

"You've never seen them?" Kaori asked, surprised. He'd spent most of his life in the palace. The presence of the tiny white flowers was a common sight to him when the weather grew warm. He hadn't considered that the trees didn't grow throughout the city. "Are they really considered legendary?"

"Second only in fame to snowdrift vines of Taischon," she said. "My friends and I would sometimes try to catch glimpses of them by climbing trees on the other side of the walls. Just there, I believe."

She pointed to a stretch of the solid red wall in the distance.

"I can't imagine the guards liked that."

Sugi giggled. "No, they didn't. I think one time they even threatened to arrest my friend, Bo. We knew we could run away faster than they could come after us though, so we didn't pay them much attention."

Kaori imagined a bunch of kids taunting the palace sentries. Within the Academy, nobody dared bother the guards because they knew word would get back to their guardians. Punishment could be severe.

"I'm sorry you weren't invited at a better time."

"You've nothing to apologize for," Sugi said, staring up at the resilient clump of leaves above them. "I have often found that my imagination is more satisfying than reality."

This struck Kaori as quite sad. Although he avoided Tatsu, he always agreed that the white modeki canopy was delightful. He couldn't say it would eclipse her mental image, but he wished he could show Sugi that the blossoms *were* majestic.

"Do you spend much time here?" Sugi asked when they had been silent for a few moments.

"I live in the palace. I haven't had much time to leave—"

"I meant here in this garden."

"Oh." Kaori blushed, but Sugi only laughed. "Of course, you knew that. In Tatsu? No, not particularly. I don't spend much time anywhere in the gardens lately, not since I was crowned. These days, I'm in the throne room or at lessons. But even before all that, I never came out here much. This place is usually crowded with students, teachers, and the palace staff. I've rarely seen it so empty."

"Perhaps because you and I are here," Sugi said. "Where would you normally be then?"

Kaori hesitated. "My favorite place on the palace grounds was Kuriku Garden."

"Then why don't we go there?"

Kaori could think of no argument. With a nod, he stood and led Sugi across the grounds. She walked beside him, unashamed as she scoured the landscape with her gaze. She seemed to drink in the features of the palace, assessing every ornament and bit of foliage to measure it against her expectations. The other suitors had rarely looked away from Kaori, fixating on his personage with an eerie and uncomfortable focus. Sugi seemed to be more interested in what the palace grounds looked like. He was grateful not to be the center of her attention.

They walked until they came to the arch over the garden entrance. Kaori gestured for his guest to enter first and she complied, drinking in the details with the same studied gaze. Kuriku featured a path alongside and crossing an artificial creek by means of several arched wooden bridges. Walking the trail took only fifteen minutes, if taken at a constant pace, but Kaori rarely wandered the garden without stopping to sit on one or two of the bridges and swing his feet above the water.

"This is more beautiful," Sugi said, her gaze following one of the lazy catfish drifting down the creek. She sat at the water's edge and tucked her legs beneath her. "Serene."

"I agree," Kaori said. He crossed the nearest bridge to the other side of the creek and sat down on the opposite bank so that he faced her. He felt the distinct urge to initiate further conversation, not in the obligatory way he had with the other women—scrambling madly for any topic of discussion—but because he wanted to keep talking. She didn't seem to ask him any more than she cared to know and didn't read off a mental list of rehearsed questions.

"People talk about how young you are," Sugi said, lifting a hand to tuck her hair behind her ear. She continued to stare down at the floating fish.

Kaori felt his stomach tense. "Do they?"

"Yes. It's what most people bring up when they discuss the new emperor."

So he was right to believe that those who came to him with such adoration and praise did not represent the true sentiment of the people. Nobody had bothered to inform him of the public's opinion. Now, that information was coming from an unexpected source.

"Are they upset?"

Her willingness to speak truthfully was refreshing. "No. At least, not most of them. They are willing to give you a chance to grow into your role. After all, even Empress Mai took some time to become the ruler she was by the end."

"How very kind of them."

"They would like to see you married soon." At these words, Sugi looked up at him, her dark eyes searching. Kaori stopped himself from retreating, holding her stare for as long as he could before turning away. "You don't wish to marry."

"I have no problems marrying. I just don't enjoy being obliged."

"I see," Sugi said, and he believed that she understood. She spotted another catfish coming back their way and smiled. "If I touch one, will it swim away?"

"No. But they may think your hand is a fish and try to bite you," Kaori said. He had stuck his hands in the creek to pet the fish before. Sugi laughed.

Kaori sighed inwardly, trying to convince himself that the unusual comfort he felt around his guest was a sign of attraction.

She was kind and honest, not to mention beautiful. He could see Taigen pursuing her should he turn Sugi away—the way he'd done with a few of Kaori's previous suitors. She lay propped on her elbow, staring down at the aquatic life in a purposeful way that made him think she was giving him permission to observe her. He resisted at first, his propriety in control, but then he remembered the pleading way Amaya looked at him each time she spoke about his romantic imminence. Even Taigen's crass bedroom talk echoed in his ear. So, Kaori looked.

Sugi's skin held a layered sheen to it, a softness he associated with clouds. Her face, her neck, her collar—all her exposed skin was so smooth. Undamaged by even the harshest heat Nokara had to offer. Her shoulders were round, her arms toned and long. Her breasts were modest but shapely, and the way she slimmed at the waist gave her that curvature he knew to be desirable to men.

Kaori couldn't shake his own awareness of his purposeful stare. He stopped, looking down instead at his hands. Sensing that he was finished, Sugi sat up. If she was disappointed, she showed no signs. Rising to her feet, she leapt deftly across the water to his side. Kaori stood to meet her.

"You may be young," she said, "but not so young as they say you are. I think you will make a fine leader of the empire."

Kaori blushed. "Thank you."

"If I may?" she asked, and when he nodded, she leaned forward to embrace him. Her forehead came up just to the height of his nose. After a moment of surprise, Kaori returned the gesture.

When they parted, Kaori said, "I should… return to my lessons."

"Learn all there is to know," Sugi said, "and you can't be doubted."

"I would like to see you again," Kaori said, though he wondered if he should have phrased the request another way. He didn't want to see her in the same capacity that his advisors wanted him to see her—try as he might, he felt no romantic stirrings—but he wished to see her again, if only for her company. She was the first person he'd met since ascending to the throne with whom he'd felt comfortable almost instantly. And maybe some part of him was hoping this meant he might feel something more for her with time.

Sugi smiled. "I would like that."

He walked with her out of Kuriku Garden and back through the palace grounds toward the gates. As she left, she looked back and bowed low, following the sign of respect with an eager wave. Kaori bowed as well, then watched her retreating form until the guards had closed the gates.

CHAPTER THREE
CLIFFS AND CLIMBERS

Arsenio

Morning came on the sun's rays and brought with it land.

Alerted by the lookout, every crew member took notice, pausing as they ascended the main deck to look out across the water.

From what Arsenio could see, it was an island. The wide stretch of yellows, greens, and browns emerged from the sea like the ridged back of the lizards he'd see on the banks of the Urse River. Overjoyed as he was to see land again, however, he was also confused. He'd imagined Nokara to be a vast continent, not an island. He walked along the deck until he found his sister.

Mariana had her hair tied back to keep it out of her eyes. The green head scarf had been given to her by Jocaste, the very woman who'd tried to get them thrown off the ship. Despite their tense introduction, Mariana had gained a semblance of mutual respect with the woman—as she had with most of the crew—and the gift had cemented their truce.

Arsenio had received no such gifts.

"Is that Nokara?" Arsenio asked.

"I've no idea," his sister replied. She turned and tapped a sailor as he walked past. The man looked at her. "Danilo, are we headed into Black Tide Cove?"

The sailor squinted at the mountainous island and wiped the sweat from his brow with his forearm. "No, Mari, them's Medinilla."

The siblings exchanged a glance.

"Medinilla," Danilo repeated with more emphasis, as if that might jog their memory. "You know, one of the Kailon Islands."

"Sorry, we're unfamiliar," Arsenio said. "I thought we were headed to Black Tide Cove."

"Aye, we are, but ne'er the captain sails to Nokara without a kip in Kailon," said the man. "They's a trades-well. Most all ships pass through, so they've some of every type of thing ye never knew ye needed. Not to mention they make damn good pogtat, and ye've not had a *true* drink until ye've had pogtat."

"Puh… pugta?" Arsenio asked.

"Coconut liquor," Danilo said, slapping him on the shoulder. "If ye can handle that sort of thing, pretty boy."

Arsenio frowned at the jab.

Danilo continued, "We'll be on our way in a day or so."

He wandered off. Arsenio was still frowning when he turned back to his sister.

"If you want them to stop, you've got to *make* them stop," Mariana said unhelpfully.

He returned to his duties as more crew members scrambled about the decks, gathering things to take ashore: empty crates to fill with supplies, sealed crates he assumed were for trade. Captain Elwin led the effort, barking orders while twirling his telescope like a baton. When he spotted Arsenio watching, he winked, sun glistening on his bare shoulders and arms. The heat had continued to swell the longer they were out at sea, until Arsenio felt like he was in summer back home; only, this heat brought with it a humidity he'd never experienced. Most of the crew had shed their outer layers, resorting to vests instead.

"Alright there, lad?" Elwin called.

Arsenio picked up his bucket and walked over to the captain. "I'm doing fine, Captain. Yourself?"

"I've a swamp brewin' where the sun don't shine, but elsewise I'm peachy." He roared with laughter, gold teeth glinting in the hot sun.

"If you don't mind me pointing out, sir, I don't see a port."

"Ah." Captain Elwin tapped a finger to his temple and then flamboyantly wrapped an arm over Arsenio's shoulders. "There's a good question. See, the *Flaming Virtue* don't make port in Kailon, not for six winters now."

"Why's that?" Arsenio asked. He meant to turn his head to look at the captain, but instead his cheek collided with the man's sweaty bicep. Arsenio grimaced at the slickness left on his face.

"Oh, I used to do good trade in Kailon. Passed through each season, and they'd keep a weather eye on the horizon for these sails. Me pockets swelled with the treasures I brought: spices and jewels from your country, fabrics and art from Nokara. But trading hands are fickle friends. They decried a mark on me honor. Seemed to think I'd robbed them somehow."

"Had you?" Arsenio almost felt like he didn't need to ask.

"Mayhaps I'd filled a barrel or a dozen half with stones! I knew what me services were worth. They weren't paying me fair what I was owed for those goods." He laughed, lost in a fond memory. "I was a day out to sea before the sparrow'd tapped me window. Couldn't do nothing about it then, could I?"

Arsenio wanted to point out that he could've turned the ship around and sailed back, owned up to the sleight he'd pulled. He couldn't see how Elwin was in the right. With the captain's sizable arm around him, however, he had no choice but to stand there until the man's great guffaws had died down.

"Well, needless to say, the tides changed. No longer was my beloved ship allowed in the ports of Kailon," Elwin said in a voice that mourned the past. "Relegated to the black market now, so I am. Can only make trade where the flags of the monarchy fly out of sight."

"You use the longboats, then?" Arsenio asked.

"Aye. We go to shore in groups, do our trading, and return." Captain Elwin retrieved his arm from around Arsenio's shoulders, leaving a strip of sweat across the back of his shirt.

The longboats could comfortably carry groups of five at a time with an additional member to row them back to the ship. The *Flaming Virtue* had two such boats, but with one in desperate need of repairs, their transportation was limited. The crew lined up while the captain moved down the row, selecting which individuals would be the first to land. Every sailor did their best to catch his eye, shouting their accomplishments as leverage. The first to land would be the first to have fresh water that hadn't sat stagnant in barrels. They'd also be the first to find pogtat, and the first to bed an escort if the urges were calling—which they almost certainly were. But the captain made clear his selections weren't based on merit alone. He emphasized a need for shrewd bargaining. A nationwide festival approached, and the locals would be looking to add flair to their celebrations. Whatever that meant.

Arsenio watched as the captain made his selections, knowing it was very unlikely that he'd be chosen. Elwin wanted those who were quick and personable, who could set up trades before the goods had even been brought ashore. Arsenio had shown neither of these qualities. If Elwin wanted someone who could ramble pointlessly, then maybe he'd have a chance.

Damios would go as the guide to paddle the boat back for the second group. Redthumb was first and nobody protested her selection. She stepped out of line and stood off to the side by the longboat. Next was Lionel, who sneered in triumph at the rest of them. His appointment was loudly contested, but the captain held up a hand to silence them. The next two were people Arsenio hadn't spoken much with: a woman named Lenora with crimson hair pulled back in a knot and a stout man named Bhaskar whose legs seemed perpetually bowed.

Finally, Captain Elwin reached the end of the line and turned on his heel to face them all again. He stuck out an arm, pointing.

"You," he said, staring straight at Mariana.

Arsenio's sister looked as surprised as he felt. She placed a hand on her chest as if to question whether or not Elwin truly meant her. He nodded affirmatively, and she stepped out of line.

Arsenio's mouth opened. Mariana hadn't protested, but he would.

As the rest of the sailors grumbled among each other, he ambled up to the captain, enraged.

"You can't send her without me," he said.

The captain smirked. "And I suppose ye plans to stop me?"

"Yes, I do." He tried to ignore how hollow his threat felt as he stared up into Elwin's face.

"A fine addition to the crew, she's been. The lass is quick, bold, *and* a proven fighter." Elwin glanced over at the man who'd taken the bad end of her mop handle.

"But she and I stick together. Where she goes, I go."

Elwin chuckled. "Unless you mean to boot someone off the longboat…"

He trailed off, eyebrows raised. Arsenio faltered. He'd meant to keep Mariana from going in the first group, not challenge someone for their place. He didn't stand a chance against any of the captain's *first choices*. When he hadn't responded after a few seconds, Elwin Hadleigh laughed again.

"I thought as much, boyo." He grabbed Arsenio's shoulder and spun him around to face the landing party. "Besides which, your sister doesn't seem to share your concern."

Mariana stood by the railing, prepared to climb down into the boat. She didn't look like she meant to say anything to him before departing. Arsenio felt a pang of betrayal, though he tried not to let it show. Perhaps she'd taken too well to life onboard the ship.

"Fine," Arsenio said, spinning back around. "Fine. But I want to be in the second group then."

Captain Elwin shrugged, grinning mischievously. "Be that your wish, Mister Avilla. When Damios returns, ye may have a place on the longboat."

The woman with the crimson bun was the last to climb down before his sister. Arsenio went to Mariana, gazing down at the watercraft below, which looked so small compared to the ship. It bobbed on the waves like a toy.

"Before you go, Mari, take this," Arsenio said. He pulled their mother's necklace over his head and held it out for her. Mariana snorted.

"Why?" she asked.

"It's from our parents."

"Ah yes. Their residual love is certain to protect me."

"You don't mean that," Arsenio said, and indeed Mari looked as though she regretted the harshness of her sarcasm. He grabbed her hand and shoved the necklace into her palm. "It can't hurt though, can it?"

"I'm docking with others. You'll be along soon enough."

"I know, but just in case."

She eyed him incredulously, but in the end, she humored him and slipped the necklace over her head. The dull silver chain glinted against her sand-colored skin as the black pendant disappeared down the front of her shirt. With a half-smile, she swung a leg over the side of the ship and began her climb down to the longboat.

"I'll see you on land," she said.

Arsenio clenched his jaw.

Mariana descended until she sat among the other crew members, and as he watched, she looked up at him. They'd deployed different strategies along their journey, he and his twin. She integrated with those around her to make their journey bearable. Arsenio kept everyone at an arm's length; the ship was a means to an end. Now, he could see those disparate strategies distancing them.

The boat sailed across the blue-green waters toward the shore, casting a widening wake behind it. Mariana raised a hand to wave at him, and he did the same, anxious for Damios's return. Every moment away from his sister's side felt tense and vulnerable.

~

When the passengers had been dropped ashore and the longboat headed back, the crew gathered around the captain again for the second pick. This time, the chosen were Jocaste, Danilo, and two other crew members whom Arsenio couldn't name. As per his request, Arsenio was selected as the last of the bunch, to the jeers of his crewmates. He ignored the snide comments, returning instead to his post by the railing to watch Damios's progress.

Arsenio wished he could swim like the swarms of fish roaming about the clear water below the ship. Then he wouldn't have to rely on a boat to get across. Back in Corva sum Rio, he would jump in the river with his sisters, but the bend where they'd play was never too deep to stand in, with a docile current that did little more than usher you gently downstream.

Among the fish, a larger body came into view. At first, he thought it was a large cat, but that couldn't be possible. Cats didn't have fishtails, and cats weren't *blue*. He leaned in closer, narrowing his eyes. The animal surfaced enough for him to see black spots along its body, but then it dived out of sight again.

"Captain!" the lookout shouted from above. Arsenio broke his stare to turn and tilt his eyes skyward. Jocaste was on duty, and she gripped the rail of the crows nest with one, white-knuckled hand. The other pointed out over the bay. "Gold sails!"

Elwin leapt onto the banister, hand tight to the rigging, and bellowed orders. "Weigh anchor and hoist the mizzen! Miss Santos, prepare the hooks—I want that longboat brought aboard with me first mate intact!"

The ship devolved into organized chaos. Arsenio sputtered, trying desperately to figure out what was happening. Sailors fled across the deck, returning to their posts as if preparing to sail.

"Cap—"

"What be our heading?" someone interrupted Arsenio.

"Out of these waters! Off this blasted reef! There be no heading at the moment!" The captain bolted for helm. Arsenio charged after him.

"Captain!" he shouted.

"Give me the short of it, boy," Elwin replied, mounting the stairs.

"It's just...it looks like we're leaving," Arsenio said. Beneath him, a pair of sailors lowered the hooks to hoist Damios and the longboat back aboard.

"That'd be correct."

Arsenio's legs turned to lead. The captain swept between him and the view to take hold of the helm.

"But why?"

"Gold sails, Mister Avilla! Gold sails! The queen's fleet. They be after my ship and his crew."

Arsenio fought the urge to wrestle the wheel from the captain. "You coward!" he shouted. "My sister is still on land—your crew is out there!"

"If they prize their skins, the lot'll deny affiliation."

"We can't leave them!"

"It don't sit well with me neither, what needs doin'," Elwin roared, "but it be a need and not a want. Better to leave five ashore than to've sailed our last day!"

"But Mariana—"

"Brave the blue if ye think ye can take the swim! Be my guest!" The growl in his last words let Arsenio know the captain wouldn't bat an eye if he dove overboard. Elwin spun the wheel. Arsenio stumbled as the ship lurched beneath his feet, changing course for the southern tip of the island. Below, the crew heaved the longboat over the gunwale, cheering once before half of them scattered to their posts and the other half took to securing it. Damios leapt out, lucky to have made it back in time.

Arsenio opened and closed his mouth, but nothing came out. Before he realized what he was doing, he'd darted forward. Grabbing the hilt of the captain's sword, he tugged. The sword made to slide from its sheath, and Elwin gave an enraged cry. In the next instant Arsenio staggered back, stars bursting before his eyes.

"Try that again, boyo, and you'll be attempting the swim whether ye means to or not."

Arsenio's world spun. He shook his head, steadying himself, then stumbled to the starboard side. Desperately, he gripped the banister.

"Mari!" he shouted, though he was too far for his sister to hear him. For a moment, he contemplated flinging himself off the ship. He could feel the wind whipping past him, his stomach sailing into his throat before he crashed into the salty blue-green water. But he couldn't dive. If he survived the fall, then he'd either be swept out to sea or wrangled in by the Kailonese warship. He'd never make it to shore. His gaze lingered on the ship in question coming toward them, the golden sails like a spiny fin sticking up into the sky. From the mast flew a gold flag with the black outline of a blossoming flower in the center.

Arsenio combed the coast with his eyes, but he was too far to discern any of the figures on the short docks. Mariana was out there somewhere, a moving dot among many, marooned on a foreign land alone and watching him sail away.

Helena

Jacinta brought Helena out into the living quarters one evening. Sparse groups milled about the halls, chatting in quiet tones. Helena could tell which were Magistrata by their long, monochrome robes. The attendants all wore beige tunics. Everyone they passed greeted Jacinta, who replied pleasantly but never stopped long enough to field questions.

Then she led Helena to a simple dwelling: four stone walls with an oil lamp and a bedside table. From what Helena could tell, this was one of the few single-occupant rooms. When Jacinta told Helena it was for her, she questioned why she should have this privilege, but her concerns were waved away.

Jacinta informed her she would return with food and drink for the girl, and that she was allowed one last full day's rest.

As soon as Jacinta had left, Helena lowered herself onto the cot and fell into a heavy sleep. Though most of her injuries had healed and she could move about independently now, her abilities had yet to return to what they'd been at full health. As usual, her sleep was restless and full of muddled dreams. It was only when she awoke in the middle of the night, soft light spilling through the cracked doorway, that she noticed Jacinta had left her water and bread on the nightstand. She ate it then and there, listening to the sounds of the sleeping dormitories.

The next day, she tried to take advantage of her last hours of sanctioned rest. She slept away the morning, her bones aching every time she moved. Again, Jacinta brought her food and drink, but as the day wore on, Helena became conscious of the voices passing by outside her door, discussing her laziness.

Not one to take criticisms lying down, Helena left her room to seek out Jacinta.

She found her in one of the chapels of the basilica, kneeling in silent adoration before the statue of a menacing-looking woman. For a moment, Helena contemplated the statue's harsh features. They felt overdrawn. No *real* woman could've possibly looked so harassed. But Helena understood why someone might pray to this figure: she inspired fear.

The Magistrata turned to face her.

"Helena, I thought you were resting?" she said, her mouth a straight line.

"I'm feeling better," Helena said, though this was only a partial truth.

"I underestimate the restlessness of youth." Rising from her knees, Jacinta made her way to the door. "Follow me."

And so, Helena's life as a servant to the Holy Order commenced.

Jacinta took her outside first. Though the air was icy up in the mountains, Helena welcomed the chill. She hadn't seen the outside world in days, bedridden by command in Engana's tiny room. She'd almost forgotten how fresh the air could taste. How much sweeter it was than within the damp, old walls.

Jacinta led her down stone steps onto a gravel road. The holy site was situated in a large basin, with black rocks jutting out of the ground haphazardly on either side of the path. They walked until their road met up with another, one that circled the lip of the basin. Helena imagined that somewhere along the perimeter, a road broke away which wound down the mountainside and disappeared into the woods. That would be the way back home—if she still had a home and a family to return to.

Helena turned around and her breath was taken away.

Doubtlessly, the basilica had been stunning when in pristine condition; however, years of weathering had given it an incomparable magnificence—an aged beauty composed in equal parts brilliant construction and cultural significance.

Almost the entire structure was comprised of great white stone slabs, some as thick as she was tall. Four expansive wings extended in each cardinal direction, forming a massive cross jutting out of the earth. These were topped by pitched roofs of brown tile. Each wing ended in a tower topped with a symbol of the Holy Order: a tetrahedron, a sun, a serpent, and a diamond. Like the rest of the ancient walls, the brass symbols were tarnished by encroaching black dirt that somehow only made them more elegant.

The basilica proper made up the southern wing, whose stained glass windows stretched ten meters high or more. The living quarters were in the east; the kitchens, common areas, and archives in the west. Jacinta didn't speak of the north, though Helena stared at it with curiosity. Its windowless tower stood far taller than the others, rising thin and long into the air like a needle.

At the center of the cross, a great dome gleamed in the dying light. Helena reckoned that if the tallest tree in Corva sum Rio stood beneath it, she could climb to the highest limb and still not reach the dome's underside The translucent nature of the quartz meant that when the sun hit the dome as it rose and fell, the white stone glowed as if it were a beacon of Deus, radiating its own light.

Next, they toured the interior. Jacinta kept a steady pace, her pauses few and far between. While Helena felt herself tiring, she didn't let her struggle show. She didn't want the Magistrata to think her weak, even if she was still recovering.

Each corridor beheld the same grandeur as the outside. Arched ceilings pointed up toward the heavens, and where the light was dim, some of these pinnacles disappeared into blackness. In every one of the many recesses was some statue or display honoring prominent figures in the church's history. Great stone faces stared down at her as she hustled past, their eyes laden with sorrow or awe. One such statue sat in an outdoor passage where birds had made use of its many perches. Helena had to turn away, certain it was blasphemy to laugh at a holy figure covered in excrement.

Other displays were more impressive, including a four-meter-tall painting flanked by intricate hanging tapestries. Helena wished she could stay a moment to figure out who the woman in the image was, but her guide hastened away and she had no choice but to follow.

After she'd been familiarized with the basilica, her work began. Her first task was cleaning the wooden floors, of which there seemed to be an unlimited supply. She lugged around buckets of soapy water and a mop, sliding back and forth across the rooms until the ground was somewhat glossier than it'd been before. The ancient wood wore its age fondly though, and often she had to decipher when she'd scrubbed enough and what things would never come off no matter how many times she mopped them. Over the course of the next week, she progressed through the wings of the complex: first the east, then the basilica itself in the south, and finally the west. She did not mop the floors of the north wing, nor did she step foot beyond its entryway. She was told sternly that the North Wing was off limits until she was given express permission to enter.

While members of the Holy Order congregated every morning for prayer services, Helena and the other servants were only required to do so every other day. Shortly after the sun rose, bells would ring all around the grounds, signaling their summons. She'd drop whatever she was doing to take her place in the rows of wooden pews. She was not enthusiastic about these grave sessions, which could last upwards of an hour depending on who led the ceremonies, but she found them to be less arduous than she would have expected, due mainly to the sheer magnificence of the Quartz Basilica.

The dome rose high into the air, so that the apex seemed to sit in the heavens themselves. Carved all along the inside of the curving stone were winged beings who stared down at the congregation. When lit by the sun outside, the beings danced, their eyes alight with glory. Great arches supported the dome from beneath, their columns as wide in diameter as Helena was tall. Each was carved by a different artist, with some so intricate she couldn't imagine how long they must've taken to create.

As she was told, Helena didn't attempt to make friends with the other Magistrata or attendants. She kept to herself, waiting to bathe when the others weren't around or eat her meals when they'd finished. Some people were pleasant toward her, smiling as they passed in the corridors or nodding her way in the morning. Others leered at her when they thought she wasn't looking, making snide comments behind her back insinuating that she thought herself above them just because she'd been given her own room. If Jacinta wanted her to go unnoticed, this perhaps hadn't been the best strategy. Helena told her guide as much, but Jacinta merely smiled and encouraged the girl to keep her head down.

Engana no longer showed interest in Helena. And on the rare occasion they encountered each other, she barely acknowledged her presence. Not surprisingly then, Helena's only acquaintance became Jacinta, who spent the evenings with her after her chores were done.

Jacinta taught her to sew when she realized the girl had never learned. She brought out spools of thread and silver needles, and they sat in the arcade outside the west wing, looking out over the horse pasture. Unused to such precise and methodical tasks, Helena struggled to master the craft, but after a week's worth of evenings, she found she could carry on a conversation while mending a tattered robe at the same time.

In the same way, when Jacinta discovered Helena also couldn't read Luzanti—the ancient alphabet in which the Scriptures were written—she began bringing out books and scrolls with feather pens. She seemed delighted to have the chance to teach the girl.

"But why should I learn?" Helena asked the first time the Magistrata handed her the writing utensils. "I know how to read and write the common tongue. Nobody uses Luzanti anymore."

But Jacinta couldn't be dissuaded. It was imperative that Helena learn. She'd go on and on about the importance of literacy in the old tongue and the power of words on paper. Helena agreed that only the wealthy or powerful were taught such things as reading and writing in multiple languages, but also thought Jacinta oversold the influence of ancient literacy just a bit. After all, what good was your ability to read the Scriptures if someone ran you through with a sword?

When she told Jacinta this, the Magistrata simply shook her head with a skeptical smile on her face and pointed Helena back to the place on the page where she'd left off.

~

A fortnight into her stay, Helena again found herself sitting under the portico with the older woman. A sheet of paper lay on the stone beside her, fresh ink drying in the open air. The last tendrils of pink sun painted the undersides of the clouds, dripping warm hues onto the stony landscape.

"How did you find yourself on solid ground again?" Jacinta asked, having just heard the tale of ten-year-old Helena's attempt to climb the tallest tree in her village. She'd disobeyed the express orders of her mother, who wasn't keen on the idea of her climbing anything. Rebellious to a fault, Helena climbed the tree anyway, with the intent of tying a ribbon about the top bough to mark her achievement. Three-quarters of the way up, however, she'd made the mistake of glimpsing how far away the ground was and sat paralyzed by fear until the sun had waned and her siblings stood below, begging for her to descend.

"I fell most of the way," Helena said, staring down at the letters she'd created.

Jacinta gasped. "No!"

"Got caught on another limb and broke my arm. My mother was the only one who managed to climb up high enough to come get me." In her mind, Helena could see her mamãe pulling herself up onto the branch beside her. They'd sat together while Mamãe convinced Helena to follow her down. "She told me to put my feet wherever she put hers, and to hold tight with my good hand the way she did. It was painful with a broken arm, but I made it. In my memory, getting back down took all night, but I'm sure that's not true."

"It worked though, did it?"

"Yeah, but I've been terrified of heights ever since."

Jacinta chuckled, a rapid emission of *hoo hoo hoo*s that made Helena laugh.

"Fear does its best to keep us from dying," Jacinta said. "But so do mothers."

"Sometimes they're one and the same."

This made Jacinta chuckle harder, which made Helena laugh harder as well.

"I'd wager you never did it again though," Jacinta said.

"Climbed trees? Not so much. I stuck mainly to the ground."

"As it happens, I suffer from the same fear as you," Jacinta confessed.

"Do you?" Helena asked. She couldn't imagine this woman being afraid of anything. She seemed so... *put together.*

"Oh yes. It's something I've never been able to master," Jacinta said, folding her hands in her lap. "There was this group of insolent boys in my village growing up. They liked to terrorize other children—make them eat the heads of toads they'd killed or threw their clothes in the mud. That sort of thing.

"They chased me up a cliff one day, had me cornered on the very edge with the rocky outcroppings and thrashing waves of the Great Ocean far below. They pressed in, jabbing me with sticks and taunting me. I knew I was going to die. I just cried, staring down from that menacing height."

"What happened?" Helena asked, horrified.

"My mother saved me, chased them off; but by then, the damage was done. I kept dreaming of that cliff afterward. Nightmares of being pushed off the ledge, tumbling forever, and then dying on the rocks below." She stared out into the evening, her face a mask of solemnity. Helena wondered if the nightmares still came now and then.

Light spilled out into the gathering dark. Helena and Jacinta both turned to look. A door had opened beneath the tower of the west wing. In the light that bathed the landscape, Helena saw a horse and rider appear towing a small wooden cart with a pile of blankets on top.

A group of Magistrata descended the steps, their robes furling around their ankles. The rider halted and the group converged to lift the load of blankets between the four of them. Immediately, the rider and the horse and trotted away.

Helena's brow dipped in concentration. She'd seen brief glimpses of such processions before: groups of Magistrata transporting objects in a similar manner. They always headed for the north wing. Whenever she saw them, she did her best to remain inconspicuous, hoping to see what they carried.

When the Magistrata turned to mount the steps, the pile shifted as an arm slipped from under the blankets, falling over the side of the wooden board.

Helena gasped.

One of the Magistrata hurriedly moved the arm back onto the stretcher and flung the blanket over it, but the image of the arm could not be erased. Helena turned to her friend, who stared, not at the scene before them, but back at her with a somber expression on her face. What they'd witnessed was no surprise to Jacinta. If anything, it seemed she'd been waiting for it to happen. Jacinta knew what she'd done—she'd intentionally let Helena witness the exchange.

"What happens in the north wing?" Helena asked.

"I will show you," Jacinta said. "But not tonight."

Emilio

The soft rapping of knuckles on the door woke him. Emilio's mother stood at the threshold. She wore a traveler's cloak about her shoulders, her long brown hair tucked into her hat.

"G'morning, Emilio," she said.

"Mamãe."

"I need to go into town," she said in a hushed tone. "Come with me?"

Emilio looked over at his sleeping brother. "Should I wake him?"

"No need," Mamãe said. "You and I will be fine."

Emilio slid his feet onto the floor, and the cold wood sent a shockwave through his body. He rubbed the sleep from his eyes, then peered out through the gaps in the shutters at the pale sky.

"I'll wait for you by the door," his mother said, and then she was gone.

As Emilio dressed, he wondered what it was his mother wanted to do in town. Making the trip wasn't so odd—they did it on a fairly regular basis—but this morning, she seemed different somehow. Secretive. Had he imagined it, or were her eyes shifting back and forth as she asked him to join her? Maybe these observations were merely remnants of sleep.

Pulling on his shoes, he tiptoed over to whisper a goodbye to his brother's sleeping form. Davi always slept like he was mid-adventure, arms and legs akimbo. In one hand, he clutched a pair of gloves.

Emilio rolled his eyes. Davi was *also* always getting into his belongings.

He took the gloves, placed them back in their proper drawer, and left the bedroom.

As Emilio skipped down the stairs, he spied his mother holding the front door open. She wore a pensive expression, staring outside as if watching a storm approach.

"Headed off then?" Papai's voice startled him. He hadn't seen his father at the foot of the steps.

"Yeah," Emilio said, coming to halt beside him. A cool draft blew in from outside. "Mamãe and I are going into town. Are you coming too?"

His father shook his head. "I'm going to stay with Davi." He held Emilio by the shoulders and looked his son up and down. Again, Emilio's suspicions were piqued. "Listen to Mamãe, eh? She knows what's good for you."

With that, he let go of his son and trudged off toward the kitchen. The floorboards creaked beneath each step. Emilio frowned, unsure what to make of the words. His father had almost seemed sad, nostalgic for something Emilio couldn't place. Regardless of what his mother had said, he no longer believed they were going into town—at least, not for anything typical.

At first, they walked in silence, listening to the sounds of the morning animals. Birds and insects sang from perches unseen, filling the motionless landscape with life that would otherwise be missing in this stillness. The gravel crunched underfoot, and Emilio could smell the rain from the day before.

Until they reached the trees, not a word was said, to the point where Emilio wondered if he'd been paranoid for no reason at all. Surely if they were out here to discuss something important, his mother would have spoken already. Perhaps he should relax and enjoy the morning walk with Mamãe, something he hadn't had the chance to do much in recent years. Not alone, at least. Not since Davi was old enough to join them. He used to spot badgers foraging in the foliage and stop to watch them. Mamãe would come back for him, laughing because she'd continued to speak without realizing he was no longer beside her.

When the shade of the trees covered them, his mother spoke. "You look more like a man and less like my little boy with each passing day. Sometimes, I see you and I wonder where my son went."

Emilio smiled.

"I know many good things will come from you as you get older," she continued, "but age has its own price."

The smile fell from his face. What did she mean by that?

Their path ended at an intersection with a wide road that marked by countless wheels, hooves, and boots. To the left was Port Mandibula, a bustling coastal settlement at the tip of the Iron Peninsula where travelers could easily find passage to the capital city, Ciro. To the right, the road led to Old Mandibula, what his family referred to as "town."

"I know your papai and I—"

She froze suddenly, cocking an ear up-road. Emilio halted beside her.

"Hooves," she said.

She grabbed him by the upper arm and dragged him off the road just as a trio of horses appeared in the distance. They slunk into the bushes, ducking down beneath the cover of the foliage.

Mamãe shoved him into a dense shrub of white blossoms, where she gestured for him to stay put. When she turned to watch the road, Emilio shifted so that he too had a view through the leaves.

For a while, nothing happened, though the steady gait of horses grew louder. His heart hammered, growing more raucous as the voices of men became apparent above the clip-clopping hoofbeats.

The men were nobles. Emilio could tell by their speech, which was punctuated and proper. They chatted idly about a woman Emilio hoped had never encountered them in person. Each comment was met with boastful laughter and another lewd response.

Emilio didn't need to ask why his mother had pushed him off the road. It was common knowledge in all parts of Mandibula that it was better not to cross paths with anyone who supported the king. This included nobles, who bankrolled his endeavors in exchange for immunity from the shadowed hand of discipline. The favor of the Benevolent Leader empowered them to commit spontaneous acts of cruelty at whim, without threat of consequence. What judge would side with a commoner over a noble? It was better to avoid the possibility of confrontation. Especially on an empty road in the middle of the forest.

When the men had passed, disappearing around the bend toward Port Mandibula, Mamãe looked back at Emilio, her expression fraught with concern. They stood again and continued on their way, careful to check behind them in case the trio had reversed course.

"You were saying, Mamãe?" Emilio asked.

His mother wrapped her cloak more tightly around herself and nodded. "The roads have always been dangerous, but it used to be thieves we feared most. Do you know the name of the king?"

Emilio frowned. "Of course. Fogosombre Marchosias."

"Never forget that name, my son. He is the enemy to all of us. He is the dark shadow over our nation's history. Every day, the world grows more dangerous as his reach extends."

Emilio had never heard his mother speak like this out in the open. In the secrecy of their home, both his parents decried the Benevolent Leader. But in public spaces, Mamãe always smiled and said the things you were supposed to say about Fogosombre—or *Fogo* as the villagers referred to him. Shortening his name was the closest they came to public defamation without possible recourse. The gravel road might appear empty, but you never knew what ears hid in the foliage.

His mother sighed. "This is why things must change."

Within the past year, Emilio had eclipsed his mother in height. She still felt just as strong and knowledgeable as she had when he was a small boy, but on the day he'd realized he'd grown taller than her, she became human to him. Suddenly, she was mortal. Even now, Emilio continued to grapple with this change in perspective.

"Your father and I have decided to fight back," she said.

Emilio stopped walking. Without missing a step, his mother hooked her free arm through his and pulled him forward so that they kept pace. His falter was barely noticeable, though his mind was in a frenzy.

"What do you mean?" he whispered.

"I mean that we've joined Afonso's Light," she said. "We can't keep living like this—the *people* of Faron can't keep living like this. Children are taken away and forced into labor or other unimaginable services, villages are regularly subjected to raids, anyone who doesn't demonstrate complete submission is arrested or worse, and Fogo hoards wealth as his subjects toil in poverty."

"Where are we going?" Emilio asked. A knot had formed in his chest. The more Mamãe spoke, the tighter it became. His eyes darted around the woods, scouring every shadow for listening ears. Fear tugged at him to turn back and run for home, but his mother's arm kept him striding forward.

"As I said, we're going to Old Town," she replied. "We are going to visit a friend."

~

Three times his mother knocked, then they shrank back into the shadows, watching the people who passed by for signs of suspicion. Since Mamãe first mentioned the rebellion, the tension inside Emilio had yet to come loose. Every eye that looked his way from beneath a shopfront awning knew what he was thinking. Every departing figure fled into the maze of cobblestone alleys to warn the nearest guard that he and his mother were plotting against the king. He had the impulse to call after them, to reassert his loyalty to the throne, but he knew that would only make matters worse.

The door to the house cracked wide enough for an eye to peer out. It was green as emerald. They must have been from the north.

"Whatever it is you're selling, I'm not interested," a raspy voice stated.

"The tides that reign ebb and flow," Mamãe said firmly.

"The will of the people stays strong," the voice replied

The door swung cautiously the rest of the way, and they were ushered inside by a large man with short silver hair. Once he'd gotten a proper look at him, Emilio realized that the startlingly green gaze was not the only feature of note. Half the man's left ear was missing, as if it had been sliced clean off by a sharp blade. Although Emilio was only a few inches taller, the man's bulk emphasized his presence. The stranger could have crushed Emilio with a simple embrace.

They entered a dim dwelling. Floorboards sagged beneath the weight of several decades, dust coated the edges of the windows so that the glass was nearly opaque, and the air smelled stale. Emilio surmised that this had never been a grand home, but the lack of effort put into maintaining it felt almost purposeful.

"This is my son," Mamãe said, without wasting time. "Emilio, this is Vittorio Angelino."

The man stuck out his hand, which Emilio shook. Vittorio had thick fingers and a swollen palm, and his grip was so firm that Emilio nearly winced in pain, but he was too wary to show weakness to this stranger. He gritted his teeth and waited for the man to release his grasp first. Afterward, Emilio's fingers throbbed.

"Another Sagrado," Vittorio said with an approving grunt.

"Vittorio is our leader," Mamãe explained.

"So, she has told you?" Vittorio said. He put another massive hand on Emilio's shoulder.

"Felipe and I discussed it," Mamãe said "Given the circumstances, he should know. He's old enough now."

"Tell me, boy, do you wish to overthrow Fogosombre?" Vittorio guided Emilio to a chair at a wooden table. He sat down more out of obligation than anything else. Here at last was the first sign that anyone lived in the house—a used teacup with the last dregs at the bottom. The large man sat across from him. Emilio studied the power in Vittorio's movements—almost lumbering, slowed by the amount of force it took to move each limb. This man had fought before; the scars on him proved as much. Meanwhile, Emilio was just an adolescent not yet ushered into the age of majority. He'd done little in his life besides the humble tasks of country living. His mother should have thought of this before presenting him to this warrior. How could he claim to want to fight beside this man? And yet, how could he deny them now, sitting there facing him?

"Of course," Emilio said, hoping to mask his fear, "more than anything."

"You must have questions," Vittorio said.

"How many?" Emilio asked before thinking. He rephrased, "How many of you are there?"

"Not enough, I'm afraid," Vittorio said, looking morosely at Mamãe. "But our numbers grow each day."

"Do you have weapons?"

"We're gathering supplies," Vittorio said. Perhaps he avoided specifics because Emilio was still an uncertainty. "It is a slow process, and we cannot arouse suspicion."

Emilio wanted to ask where, but he knew he probably wouldn't receive more than a vague response. Besides, it didn't matter in the end. The more he considered what was being asked of him, the more unlikely it seemed he'd be of any help. He wasn't focused enough to strategize. He wasn't brave enough to face down an enemy. He'd never had to push himself beyond his limits. That's what Vittorio didn't understand about him.

"I don't know anything about fighting. I can't use a sword."

"Fighting is nothing more than the marriage of skill and willpower. We can teach you how to use a weapon, but it's up to you to give it purpose." Vittorio crossed his arms over his sizable chest. "If you join the rebellion, we have places to train you."

Emilio and his mother stayed with Vittorio for most of the day, breaking fast and sipping tea with him while discussing the role of the rebellion in Emilio's life. Although he was skeptical, Vittorio and Mamãe managed to convince him that everyone could find a place in the ranks. Much of what he would initially be asked to do was look after his brother while his parents faced more important tasks. He wasn't opposed to this idea, though he was expressly told that he could not inform Davi of the true nature of their activities. As of yet, Davi was still too young. Not mature enough to handle such information appropriately. And if anything were to be discovered, his mother didn't want Davi targeted for information.

By the end of their lengthy conversation, Emilio felt as if a considerable weight had been lowered onto his shoulders. His gaze flicked between his mother and Vittorio, his brain thoroughly saturated with information and emotion.

"To help your people in this way is a great honor," Vittorio said. "Many have died in the name of this cause."

Emilio wished to say that the statement did nothing to assuage his anxieties.

"If the burden you bear now seems inconsequential, it will only grow in importance the more you prove yourself. We have a long voyage ahead of us, and every step along the road counts."

With that, Emilio and his mother stood. They shook hands again with Vittorio—Emilio prepared this time with his jaw clenched—and left through the back door, slipping seamlessly into a stream of unwary folk.

~

From the time they left Signor Angelino's home until the road changed from cobblestone to gravel again, Emilio did nothing to combat the chaos in his head. In a way, he desired the cacophony. He could lose himself in it. The questions and concerns sailed by, drawing fleeting attention to themselves before fading into the background noise.

Once Old Town disappeared behind them and they were alone in the forest, Emilio turned to his mother.

"How long have you and Papai been a part of this?" he asked.

Mamãe furrowed her brow. "A little more than two years. We joined when that fire claimed Jordão and Estela Nogueira. You remember them."

"Of course," Emilio said. Jordão and Estela had been family friends. Before the fire, their home sat nestled along the route to Port Mandibula, not far from where Emilio and his mother would turn to head home. They'd sold tea leaves to travelers. Both had died in the fire and the mention of their names made his stomach churn. "That fire wasn't an accident."

Mamãe shook her head. "Fogosombre's people asked them to report the activities of travelers along the road. Their home burned not long after they refused."

Emilio hung his head. In his mind, he could see the house as it stood now: black and decrepit, half reclaimed by wilderness. It had only been two years since the incident and already, young children spread myths about the ruins. They'd dare each other to enter at night, convinced the crumbling floors and soot-streaked walls were haunted. Of course, their parents, who had known the Nogueiras, forbade these disrespectful rituals, but they hadn't the power to eradicate them completely.

"You didn't worry about mine and Davi's safety?"

"We did—and still do, which is why we hadn't told you," Mamãe said. "We felt confident that Fogosombre's people would not seek you out because you had no information to offer."

"But what if they used us to force your hand?"

Mamãe sighed. "That's a reality Papai and I were reluctant to consider, but it was a risk we had to accept if we hoped to bring about a better world. We all have a responsibility to the people around us: our family, friends, the community. We could hide ourselves away, live in secrecy, and pretend the bad things don't happen. But that would be a selfish life."

Emilio nodded silently, the thoughts screaming inside him again. He knew that at sixteen, he was close to the age of majority, but he still felt like a child in many ways. He shouldn't be asked to take on the responsibility of his community. He didn't have the power to change things.

"Don't you worry, though?" he asked. "Aren't you afraid?"

"I am afraid every time I step outside my door. I worry whenever you are not nearby," she said. "But we cannot let fear stop us from doing what's right."

Emilio stared down the route ahead of them. The path was clear, though he could only see as far as the next bend in the road. Beyond that was always the possibility of danger. The trio of nobles might be on their way back, but he couldn't tell. He couldn't see anything.

"What do you do? You and Papai?"

She hesitated. "We gather resources, things Afonso's Light can use, and we store them in a safe location."

"Where?"

"You will know in time."

"What sort of things?"

"Weapons, so we can fight. Food, in case there are people who need to go into hiding," Mamãe said. "Vittorio sends word of large shipments coming into the port, and we siphon just enough that we aren't noticed."

"You steal?"

"Only from the nobility and the Crown."

Emilio frowned. His initial reaction was one of incredulity; that wasn't how she'd taught him to act. But he knew that wasn't fair.

"You don't want to be a part of the rebellion," Mamãe said. She didn't sound angry. Contemplative, perhaps.

"I just… I don't see how I can be of any help," Emilio said.

"A single stone can shatter a thousand windows."

They walked in silence the rest of the way. He wondered how he would talk to his parents now, how he could possibly keep from saying anything to his younger brother. He wasn't a great liar. If he wasn't careful, the boy would notice something had changed. Before long, their home appeared, and Emilio couldn't remember a time when he'd felt more relieved to see it. With the sun setting, its long shadow stretched across the path.

His mother's hand was at his chest, bringing him to an abrupt halt.

His first thought was the riders again. Emilio looked to Mamãe, who had a terrifying determination on her face. Her mouth drew into a thin line, her eyes dark.

"Mamãe—" he began, but she tapped his chest with her hand and he stopped.

Instead, Emilio followed her gaze to the house.

Grass grew around the edges as always, a war he relentlessly fought as one of his chores. The shutters on the windows sat opened or closed at random, signs of which rooms had recently been used and which had not. The eaves hung undamaged, the roof neatly-tiled as it should be; they'd only recently repaired it this past autumn, before the expected winter rains. And the front door… sat open.

This was not entirely unusual—after all, he sometimes left the door open if he was running to the well to draw water—but there was no sign of his family around. In fact, the door swung a bit on its hinges as the breeze swept up groups of fallen leaves and carried them across the threshold.

"Stay here," Mamãe muttered, then trod slowly forward. She reached down into her right boot and pulled out a short knife.

Emilio couldn't breathe. He combed the open windows for signs of life inside. Silence hovered over him like a shadow, clearing even the melee of thoughts that had been present only moments ago. Where was Papai to complain about the mess blowing in through the door? Why wasn't Davi waiting at the window for their return?

Mamãe entered the house, her knife arm outstretched. Alone outside, Emilio took a few involuntary, stilted steps after her. He twisted his head side to side, searching the world around him for approaching figures or spying eyes. But even the neighbors' homes lay still. Indifferent. Instead, he felt the weight of his solitude pressing in on him. He hated being so exposed.

"Wait," he breathed. Running now, he stumbled up to the door and rested a hand on the frame. There were no signs of forced entry. No signs of struggle at all. The door was simply open. He entered and shut it.

Indoors, the house creaked in the wind. His mother was nowhere in sight. He wanted to call after her, but inside the sound would feel too conspicuous. He didn't want to be the only voice in the stillness.

There were no signs of his brother or his father. If there'd been an attack, perhaps Papai had had the foresight to flee, taking his younger son with him into the woods to hide. He would know where to go, how to escape. If Papai had sensed danger, he would have removed himself from harm's way.

Emilio took a step toward the common room.

A guttural cry resounded through the house, chilling his blood. Emilio spun on the spot. Mamãe! Her stifled sobs barreled into his eardrums. Down the hall he fled, toward the dining room. His boots pounded against the floorboards, resounded loudly through the house, reverberating off the walls.

"Stay back!" she shrieked before he could enter. Emilio faltered. "Don't come in here, Emilio. Please!"

But he knew that no matter what lay inside, he couldn't stay away. He couldn't hide out in the hallway. He had to know. He had to see with his own eyes.

Mamãe knelt on the floor, her hands painted crimson. Before her lay a corpse in a puddle of blood. Several feet away lay another, this one's back to him, though there was no mistaking the slight stature, the familiar chestnut vest.

Emilio was on the floor, crawling across the wood with tears spilling down his face. He couldn't see, and yet he'd already seen too much. No longer thundering, his heart felt heavy, each beat excruciating. This couldn't be real. None of it. He clutched at the thin body, holding the lifeless boy in his arms. Wishing beyond hope to feel him breathe. To feel him move.

But the truth couldn't be undone. As Emilio sat there, cradling Davi in his arms, he knew inside that his father and his brother were dead. Somehow, though he had no room to contemplate the reasons, they were gone.

Mariana

The foliage whipped at Mariana's face as she ran after Redthumb. The woman's fleeing form bobbed in and out of view. After a few minutes, they burst through the line of trees, coming to the edge of a village. This far inland, more buildings were constructed with wood than mud, though the roofs were still grass.

"Arsenio—" Mariana said.

Redthumb shushed her. "Don't say nothing. Keep your voice down."

"But my brother!" Mariana said, struggling to calm herself. Her breathing came heavy, sweat dripping from her forehead. *I must get ahold of myself.* "Didn't you see they grabbed Lionel?"

"What did I just say, Mari?" Her companion looked like she might strike her, eyes narrowed in warning.

"But—"

"Shut it before I shut it for you."

The woman named Lenora drew level with them, scanning their surroundings with a wary gaze. "Easy, ladies," she said in an even tone.

Mariana willed herself to breathe. Around her, the villagers went about their daily lives as if a host of coastal traders hadn't come stumbling out of the jungle in a panic. She forced herself to focus on the geometric patterns incorporated all over the village's modest buildings: sharp diamonds with angled additions coming off the corners, squared spirals of various sizes. They were like fingerprints for the low houses—no two the same—adding character in the way some were dirty or fresh, sun-faded or crisp, small or large, made of paint or wood. She asked what the round wooden stalks used everywhere were called, to which Redthumb responded, "Bamboo."

"Why aren't we hiding anymore?" Mariana whispered.

"Because now that we've gotten away from the shore, anyone trying to hide is suspicious," Lenora explained.

Mariana tried to observe the villagers without moving her head. She couldn't understand their language, but the voices sounded agitated. Some carried on loudly, laughing and bantering, but beneath their show of normalcy, others whispered. For the first time in her memory, Mariana couldn't understand what was being discussed.

"I presume the topic is unpleasant," she said, locking eyes with Redthumb.

"Them say the merman ship come to harbor," Redthumb muttered. "Someone seen it coming, told the datu. She sent the boats. Disrupt the whole trade today."

Mariana hadn't expected the reaction to the Flaming Virtue's arrival to be so visceral, but then again, she'd only been with the crew a couple weeks. She didn't know the extent of the villagers' relationship with Captain Elwin. She'd also never heard the term datu before, but she could guess it was someone of power. Perhaps Medinilla's governess.

"Them say one of the thieves onboard was captured. Him in captivity." Redthumb's mouth was a straight line.

"What are they going to do to him?" Mariana asked. She wasn't particularly fond of Lionel, but that didn't mean she wished him ill. Not to mention, what happened to him was likely to happen to them too if they were discovered by the guard.

"None has said."

She hadn't seen what had happened to Bhaskar, the last member of the boat sent ashore, so, they continued walking until they reached the far edge of the village. Chancing the residents' amenable fealty to the government, Lenora traded a bracelet from her wrist for a trio of colorful fruits they could share. The mangoes, as Mariana learned they were called, were sweet and juicy. She had to work to keep the liquid from running down her chin, and when the fruit was gone, she immediately wished for more. But they had left the village behind and were surrounded now by dense jungle.

"We have to go back to the shore," Mariana said once they were out of earshot of the village.

"I think not," Lenora said.

"But isn't Captain Elwin going to come back?" Mariana asked. "Once the gold sails are gone, of course."

Lenora laughed. It wasn't cruel, but neither was it kind. "You don't understand how this works."

Mariana didn't appreciate being made to feel stupid. "Enlighten me, then."

"People like us, people who roam the seas like Captain Elwin, do what needs doing to survive. In Elwin Hadleigh's case, that means leaving us behind. He's not going to chance coming back even for his own crew—not at the risk of losing the *Flaming Virtue* or the treasures onboard."

"So it's money, then, that matters most," Mariana said with a sneer.

"Wait on the shore, Mari. Go ahead," Redthumb said. "Him come back the next moon, maybe."

Mariana didn't respond, following her companions in silence as they continued their trek. She had a sour taste in her mouth and a knot in her stomach.

In the shade of the trees, the heat didn't wane as she'd expected, though it lost some of its edge. The humidity, however, seemed to condense. It settled on her chest like a weight and made breathing difficult. Before long, Mariana had taken off her overshirt and wrapped it around her head to keep her soaked hair from sticking to her face. She'd lost the green headscarf somewhere in the chaos. Lenora did the same, but Redthumb didn't seem bothered by the conditions. Furthermore, her knowledge of their environment shone through. When they'd walked for several hours, she led them to a tree of large pink flowers, which when tilted poured water they could drink.

They rested for a short while before continuing on, burying themselves deeper into the island. Mariana didn't ask where they were headed, though she guessed by Redthumb's deliberate pace that they were, indeed, headed somewhere. As natural conversation waned, Mariana worried over her brother. Deus knew where the ship was pointed now—though she hoped Captain Elwin would continue on to Nokara. What distressed her more was that her last remaining family member had been ripped from her side. She'd only recently begun to realize how large the world was, and the reality that she might never see him again gnawed at her insides. She'd been harsh toward him the last time they spoke, chiding him for thinking that something bad might happen. His worries had been warranted, apparently. She regretted that now and found her hand wrapped around the necklace he'd given her. Arsenio could take care of himself—

though he had trouble adapting to new environments, he was resourceful—but she wished she could be there with him.

~

"Who rules Kailon?" Mariana asked the following morning.

Redthumb glanced over her shoulder. "A queen. Why asks you this?"

"And where does the queen live? Where is the capital?"

"She live in Banguet City on the largest island."

Mariana wondered how far apart the islands were. The warships that had come after the *Flaming Virtue* looked seaworthy, but she remembered the smaller boats parked on the docks, the ones she assumed were for travel between islands. Those had small sails and could only fit about a dozen people, by her reckoning. If that were the case, then the islands couldn't be too spread out.

"I want to go there," Mariana said. Both of her companions looked at her in disbelief.

"Why would you want to do that?" Lenora asked.

Mariana took a deep breath. She and Arsenio hadn't told anyone on the ship where they'd come from. It wasn't that they'd thought anyone aboard might support Fogosombre, but more that, they'd feared their intentions wouldn't sit well with the rest of the crew. They were traders walking the line of legality, after all; anything of a *political* sort seemed to repel them.

"My brother and I were trying to get to Nokara for a reason," Mariana said. "We weren't stowed away on the Virtue just to leave Faron."

"And what's in Nokara for the both of you?"

"We were going to convince the Nokari leader to help us overthrow King Fogosombre."

With that statement, the trio stopped walking completely. Redthumb turned to face her. "Ye damn yourself. Fool's errand, that is—ye speak fucking lunacy."

"Yeah," Lenora agreed. "There's no way you'll succeed."

"And why's that?" Mariana asked, irked by their immediate rejection.

"Made deals with devils, Fogosombre has. Him done dark deeds."

Lenora nodded. "Not to mention he has the whole of Faron's army behind him. And all the money. And all the resources at his disposal."

"But—"

"Besides, Nokara's army is large, I'll give you that, but you'll never get them to help," Lenora said. "Why should they? Who are you? Why would they listen to a thing you've got to say?"

"Ye plan to storm into Kingfisher demanding them go to war for ye? They'll laugh ye out of Black Tide Cove."

"What would you know?" Mariana said, indignant.

"Nokara's too proud," Lenora said. "They don't like normal outsiders, let alone nameless stowaways from merchant ships."

"I have a name."

"A worthless thing they'll not deign to utter."

"I may not be powerful, but that does not make me worthless," Mariana countered. "Minds change. If I can get an audience with the crown and plead my case—"

"I'm just as like to burst into flame."

Aggravated, Mariana folded her arms over her chest, though this did little more than make her warmer. She waved a hand at Redthumb, muttering an angry, "Well, let's go," before they resumed walking. Silence enfolded them once more, now wrought with tension. Mariana fumed, but refused to keep trying to convince the two cowardly, honorless *bandits* at her side. What did they know? They didn't have a people to protect. They were wanderers, tied to no lands, feeling no pride or sentiment about *anywhere* they went.

"The question still stand, Mari," Redthumb said, breaking the silence. "Why seeks you Banguet City."

Mariana briefly considered whether or not she wanted to answer. "Because maybe if Nokara won't help us, Kailon will."

Neither of her companions responded immediately, though she saw Lenora purse her lips. What did it matter to them why she wanted to go, anyway? Now that they were stranded on Medinilla, it wasn't as though they had any other purpose. Redthumb and Lenora could look for another merchant ship to join in the capital city.

"We can go, but once we reach that city, you're on your own," Redthumb said. "I'll not take part of your fool's errand. It'd stain me reputation to get killed."

~

Another day passed before they caught sight of the next village. By then, the grumbling in Mariana's stomach had emptied into a painful void. They drank every time they came across the pink flowers, but all Redthumb could find them to eat were handfuls of berries and tough orange fruit. She wasn't sure they could consume anything else without negative effects, including the insects. They tried hunting, but they came across few animals large enough to provide real sustenance.

Needless to say, when the first buildings came into view, Mariana was overjoyed. They emerged from the foliage in a larger village than the one they'd left behind. The architecture differed, as if the farther north you went, the more sophisticated the builders—or, more likely, the less impoverished. There were no grass roofs here, only wood and ceramic tiles. For the first time since arriving on Medinilla, Mariana noticed metal wares. Several villagers stood outside their homes, cooking over fires in large iron pots.

As they passed, the travelers were greeted several times by warm smiles. Recognized as outsiders, they were invited to sit down and enjoy some food. Mariana was even tempted to try one of the offerings before Redthumb informed her that the woman was asking for her clothes in return. She reconsidered.

Redthumb led them to an inn along the main road. Mariana had no idea what food she smelled, but the aroma made her aching stomach groan. Whatever it was, she wanted to stuff her face full.

A stout man waddled out from behind the bar to greet them. He spoke fast, his hands extended outward in enthusiasm. Lenora and Mariana looked to Redthumb, who said something back to the man in his native tongue. To their surprise, he broke out into bright laughter.

"My friends, you have luck. I am only innkeeper in greater Pauwe who can speak the eastern tongue."

Mariana was delighted that they'd finally met someone she could understand.

"I am Ramil. Welcome to my inn," the man said. He gestured at the room around them. A few of the patrons looked up from their food to eye the newcomers, but lost interest quickly.

"Thank the gods," Redthumb said. "Has you room for us?"

Ramil shook as he chuckled again. "Of course, of course."

"But I would like to eat first," Mariana blurted out, unable to control herself. This made the rotund innkeeper chuckle again.

"Before we do any of that," Lenora said, throwing out a hand to block Mariana from leaping forward, "we need to let this man know we haven't got much to pay with."

The shipmates exchanged worried glances.

Ramil looked them over, a finger to his lips. Though his smile was gone, he still appeared just as jovial. "What have you?" he asked.

Mariana's hand went to cover the necklace which hung down her chest beneath her shirt. Lenora had traded a bracelet for the mangoes. She still had more adornments to trade away, but it seemed unfair to have her part with all her possessions without offering some of her own. Besides, a room at an inn with food was bound to cost more than another bracelet or ring alone. From the way Lenora reluctantly fingered the metal bands on her wrist, it appeared she felt the same. Before either of them could say anything though, Redthumb stepped forward. She had a golden bead in her hand. Mari wondered where it'd come from—she certainly didn't have it when they'd left the coastal village.

"This be the sum of it," she said, placing the item in Ramil's palm. He eyed the bead, weighing it.

"A piloncito," Ramil said. "I'm being generous, but this could cover the room for tonight."

"No food?" Mariana asked, terror in her voice.

"I'm afraid not," Ramil said.

"What if we clean up the pub tonight?" Lenora pleaded. She must have been just as hungry as Mariana.

Ramil considered this offer.

"Please," Mariana begged. "We haven't had a proper meal in three days."

The man smiled. "Okay, okay." He shrugged. "Last pogtat is served when the moon has crested the sky. If the dining room and kitchen are left spotless, then you are paid. Please, have a seat, friends. I tell Ina to fix you something special."

With that, he laughed loudly and walked off toward the kitchen.

The trio slumped into chairs around a small table offset from the others. They said nothing to each other, waiting impatiently for their food to arrive. When it did, Mariana could barely hold herself back long enough to examine what she was eating: crispy rolled packets like dried reeds, and clear noodles mixed with vegetables. She stuffed both in her mouth and let the burst of flavor satiate her famished body. As if knowing how hungry they were, the kitchen had served them portions impossible to finish, but each woman did her best. By the time they were finished, an admirable chunk of each plate had been consumed.

Mariana sat back, her stomach full. Maybe in the future, she'd ask for the dishes' names but for now, it was enough to know that the food had been delicious and ended her involuntary fast. Aware that a bed awaited her upstairs, Mariana wanted nothing more than to crawl to her lodgings and sleep, but she hadn't yet earned that privilege.

Before she could stop herself, she let out a low belch. The din of the dining room drowned it out, but Lenora laughed. "A job well done," she said, eyeing their plates.

"I never want to not eat again," Mariana said. "The next time we need to go on a three-day walk, let's bring something with us."

"I'll try to keep that in mind."

"Redthumb, where did you get that bead?" Mariana asked.

A wry smile broke over her companion's face. "Them what has much to lose, don't notice when small things disappear."

"You mean you stole it?" Mariana asked.

"The Fates willed it upon me, is all," Redthumb responded. The three of them erupted into uproarious laughter, clutching their sides to keep from splitting. Mariana had never seen Redthumb truly smile before, let alone laugh. She did so from deep within, a pure and uncontrolled thing so unpracticed on her lips.

Between gasps of mirth, Lenora asked, "The Fates couldn't will upon you a second bead so I could rest a bit earlier tonight?"

"Take not more than will be missed," Redthumb said, raising her index finger to tap roughly at her temple.

Lenora raised her hands in surrender. "Alright. You're the mastermind."

The three women waited, and waited, and waited for the pub to empty. The trickle of exiting patrons moved at a painstakingly slow rate. More than once, each of the shipmates found their eyes closed and their heads bobbing. Then, finally, the room was empty.

Ramil came out to meet them.

"My friends," he said, arms wide again. "My staff have gone home and my wife sleeps, but I have decided to stay and help you."

"More likely to supervise," Mariana mused. Their host laughed.

While they worked, Ramil asked questions about their travels and their purpose in Medinilla. It was obvious they were not from around Pauwe, and not solely because they didn't all speak Wikang. Mariana didn't trust herself not to say more than was needed, so she left most of the personal questions to her shipmates. With Redthumb back to her stoic nature, this meant Lenora did most of the talking. To Mariana's surprise, she let

Ramil know they sought to meet with the queen, though every time he asked what for, she skillfully dodged a response.

"If you seek the queen, you have luck," the man said, supervising Mariana as she mopped the floor of the kitchen. He pointed to a spot she'd missed. "The Flower Festival is less than a fortnight away."

"The queen attends the Flower Festival?" Lenora asked.

"She does in Banguet City. They throw big event, unmatched anywhere else. With games, music, competitions with lavish prizes, and great displays from gardeners all over the islands. It is like nothing you've ever experienced, I assure you."

"I'm surprised you have your festival in winter," Mariana said.

"What is winter?"

"You know, the cold season?"

Ramil chuckled. "The temperatures do not change much in Kailon, I don't know if you've noticed. Our blooms come year-round."

Mariana reflected on what a stupid thing she'd said, given that she hadn't stopped perspiring since stepping foot on land.

"Do many celebrate?" Lenora asked.

"Oh, yes. All of Kailon! There are smaller festivals everywhere. Port Pauwe will host one too, but it will be less grand."

"Have you gone to the one in Banguet City before?"

"Yes, many moons ago. But the inn keeps me busy, you see."

"That's a shame," Mariana said. Ramil pointed to another spot she'd missed.

"It is, it is. But, my friends, do not weep for me. I had my share of celebrations. Besides, my brother travels to the capital every year now to attend this great festival. And he brings me back stories of its beauty."

"Your brother?" Mariana asked. "Will he be going again this year?"

"Of course! He would not miss it," Ramil scoffed. "Nohea visits a friend tonight, but you will see him tomorrow."

Mariana's heart leapt in her chest. "Would Nohea be opposed to taking us with him?" she asked.

Ramil pondered this, his finger to his lips. "We can ask him. My brother is not as friendly as me, but he is a good man. If he took our larger boat, then he could fit the three of you, no troubles. But of course, it would not be a free ride. You understand?"

Mariana feared that would be the case. She looked around the kitchen at the heavy iron pots with burnt remnants caked onto the inner surfaces and the sooty hearths, wondering how else they would earn the journey to capitol.

"You will be staying here, yes?" Ramil asked. Then, without waiting for their response, "I insist. I will have it no other way. Ina will be so pleased. No cleaning duties for a fortnight!"

CHAPTER FOUR
A STRANGER IN THE FOREST

Arsenio

Arsenio stood paralyzed on the quarterdeck until the Kailon Islands were nothing but a memory. If life aboard the ship had felt uncomfortable before, now it was outright hostile. Now shorthanded, the crew sneered at Arsenio as they worked around him. It wouldn't be long before the harassment resumed.

Mariana was gone. Just like that, his twin, whose side he had never left for more than a few hours, was out of reach. The distance that separated them built by the second. First Helena, then his parents, and now Mari. Sweat rolled down his forehead and his back, collecting at the base of his spine. The heat caused his world to spin. The sea rolled, taunting him.

He whirled around and fled, running to the captain's quarters. Grabbing both handles, he flung the doors wide so that they bounced back on their hinges. Captain Elwin was standing by the desk, his head bent low, but as Arsenio stormed in, he spun with an angry cry.

"Agh! Didja not hear me command ye knock first?" Elwin bellowed, drawing a knife from his belt. He slammed it down, point first, so that it stuck in the table at the center of the room, wobbling. "I've taken men's heads off for less, I have!"

Arsenio recoiled but kept his composure. "Take me back."

If Elwin was surprised by the demand, he didn't show it, though his flare of anger dissipated some. "And by what malady of the mind would I do that?"

"You left my sister on that shore! And some of your own people!"

"The ship can sail without them."

"They trusted you. You're their captain."

"Aye, and each of them knew the risks ye take boardin' a ship like mine. If ye seek a sail bound by legalities, by all means, board a merchant vessel and be done with it."

"You can't do that."

"I think you'll find I have, Mister Avilla, *and* I will continue to do so."

"There were only two ships," Arsenio said, exasperated. Drawing closer to Elwin, he placed both palms on the table. The captain eyed them, affronted by the invasion of his sacred space. "You could have taken them. I know it."

"And what'd be the purpose of vanquishin' a pair of the queen's fleet, eh? Bring a war upon meself and me crew? Instead of reparations demanded, it'd be hangings." Elwin yanked the knife out of the table. He examined the blade, then shoved it back in its sheath. Hands on his hips, he looked down upon Arsenio. "I do what's best for the whole and not the one. No cargo was lost. We sail on to Black Tide Cove. Isn't that what interested ye in the first place?"

Arsenio frowned. "Yes, but with Mariana beside me."

He stared Elwin Hadleigh in the eyes, searching for something that might give. Around them, the ship groaned against the shifting sea. The open doors swung as the boat rocked, and beyond, the raucous chatter of the crew carried on. Though he knew they must have taken notice of the confrontation inside, nobody came to bother them. After all, the captain could take care of himself, especially against the weakling stowaway.

Recognizing his assertions had gained him no ground, Arsenio gritted his teeth. He would have to change tactics. Whether he liked it or not, he could think of only one hand he had left to play.

Sliding his hands off the table, he turned toward the exit. Instead of leaving, he shut the doors gently and slid the latches into place. He would do what needed to be done in order to reunite with his twin. *This is in the best interest for the both of us.*

When he looked back at the captain, Elwin had moved a hand to his knife again, confused and cautious. He was undoubtedly a handsome man. His pronounced jawline stood out in the dim light through the curtains, covered in a blanket of sandy stubble. Arsenio tried not to think about where the scar on the captain's cheek had come from. No, he focused instead on the blue eyes.

"I'd not try anything hasty, lad," Elwin said. "I've not lost a fight in many a tide, and believe me, the next time I do it won't be at your hand." He chuckled, though Arsenio noticed the nervous waver.

"I'm not trying to hurt you," Arsenio said, raising his empty palms. He stepped away from the doors, the heels of his boots clicking audibly in the enclosed space. "I simply think that maybe we aren't understanding each other."

The captain's tense stance didn't relax. If anything, he seemed more on guard.

Arsenio hesitated.

Experience suggested to him that he was attractive, but he'd never actively tried to *appear* attractive to anyone before. His sisters teased him because of the attention he often got from the village girls. And whereas the appealing features of his peers etched confidence into their personalities, the attention he'd received had only ever crippled him. Anytime women remarked upon his looks, Arsenio's face grew hot and he did his best to ignore the comments or extricate himself from the conversation. Now, he attempted to emphasize his allure—an altogether more awkward and ridiculous task. Already, his face warmed and he knew the flush would appear soon enough.

"I wonder, Captain, if your offer still stands," Arsenio said. His hands trembled. This wasn't working. How did one seduce a man? Sabina Coelho, one of Mariana's friends, came to mind. He'd observed her in the village tavern before as she chatted with the men who inevitably gathered around her—how she balanced interacting with each of them. They bought her drinks, hung on her every word—

"What offer be ye referring to?" Elwin asked.

Another step toward the captain; another skipped heartbeat. "The offer you made me the night I was discovered aboard your ship," Arsenio said. Seizing inspiration, he lifted a finger and loosened the lacing at his collar. It helped with the sweltering heat anyway.

Now, Elwin most certainly knew what Arsenio was proposing. His yellow eyebrows shot up toward his hairline and he inhaled a sharp, shallow breath. The captain's eyes flicked between Arsenio and the doors behind him. No doubt checking whether or not Arsenio had latched them correctly.

"Ye speak coy, Mister Avilla," Elwin said. "Forgive me if I'm slow to catch yer meanin'."

"Suddenly you're a gentleman?" Stomach knotted, Arsenio slid between the captain and the table. He was close enough now that he had to tilt his head back to look into the man's eyes, and he felt the heat radiating from his body in the tropical humidity. The floor dipped as the ship crested a particularly rough wave and the sudden movement caused Arsenio to brush momentarily against Elwin. The captain's excitement pressed against his abdomen, his warm breath brushing across his forehead.

Prepared to recoil, Arsenio instead experienced a fluttering in his stomach. A strange urge to feel the prickling of fresh hair on another man's jaw. To drape Elwin's wide shoulders across his. Perhaps the captain felt the same way, for he stood over Arsenio, blue gaze fixated in an eye contact Arsenio wasn't sure he could hold.

"Ah, I remember me offer now," Elwin muttered. He wound his hand into Arsenio's hair, cupping the back of his head. In an instant, they pressed together, the sweat of their skin mixing in the tropical heat. Torso to torso, hip to hip. And Elwin tightened his grip and tugged, gently exposing Arsenio's neck.

Why didn't Arsenio want to pull away? He stared across the empty cabin without seeing, his mind an unfettered cacophony as the captain pressed his lips against Arsenio's throat, then the knot of his throat, and again at the base of his jaw.

Finally, Elwin brought his mouth tantalizingly close to Arsenio's ear, his breath warm as he whispered, "Ye declined."

He stood straight, one daring eyebrow raised. The spell broke, returning him to the captain's quarters. Fear overwhelmed him, and the sudden urge to cry. He stuttered, hoping Elwin hadn't perceived how completely his defenses had dissolved. There was no mistaking the desire in the Captain's eyes, but so too was there satisfaction. "I—I've reconsidered."

"Have ye now?"

"I have," Arsenio said. The flush was returning. "You've convinced me."

For a long while, they stood between the desk and the square table, swaying as the *Flaming Virtue* rocked, inches apart. Despite his sudden unease, Arsenio was sure his seduction had succeeded on some level. Whether or not that would be enough to bargain the captain into turning the ship around, he couldn't tell. He awaited Elwin's reaction, knowing that he couldn't be the one to speak next. All the while, confusion built up like a storm cloud within him, swirling around the unknown—that brief moment of longing he could not describe with words. Yet, every time he came close to an answer, Arsenio felt it slip away again.

"You're a pretty beast," Elwin said. "The nerve of ye making me wait so long."

Arsenio couldn't answer; his mouth had gone dry.

"But you'll find I can be a man of mercy."

"That's what I'm hoping," Arsenio whispered.

"Aye. So seldom do the winds change at our whims, be it in the sails of your heart or that of my ship." The captain exhaled a long, slow breath. Then an ironic smile crossed his lips. "You should know the wind keeps us true toward the shores of Nokara, lad."

Arsenio bristled, a shiver of frustration running through him. He sidestepped out of their close quarters. "You selfish, cocky—"

"Listen, boy," the captain said. "Lesser men than me'd rape ye and think nothing of it. Tread carefully. I'll not be turning back. That be me final take. The ones ashore are shrewd—some more than others, granted—but so long as they've not bared their britches, they'll be safe."

Arsenio had lost after all. His embarrassment inflamed his contempt—made more pungent by the confusion he suppressed within. Turning on his heel, he headed for the doors again, this time with the intent to storm out.

"Arsenio!"

He had every right to keep going, but at the risk of one last tendril of hope, Arsenio paused long enough to look back at Elwin. The captain looked rightfully offset, his smirk gone, his gaze desirous.

"I can offer you the return," he said. "We make port in Black Tide Cove as planned and on the route to Faron, we visit Medinilla. That be all I can offer."

Elwin looked on hopefully, his hands spread. But Arsenio took pleasure in denying the man that hope. Return after they'd gone to Nokara? They would be too late. Mariana's fate would have long since been decided. It might have *already* been decided. This was no compromise.

Shaking his head, Arsenio left the cabin and pulled the doors closed behind him. This much had been made clear: he couldn't trust the captain nor his crew. Not with promises nor with his safety. The lot of them were thieves and conmen who sought their own interests first and would sooner leave him for the wolves than defend him loyally.

He decided then he would raise no fuss. He would play his part, performing his duties without interaction. And when they reached the capital city of Nokara, he would slip away the first opportunity he got.

~

Arsenio did as he'd promised himself and the days passed slowly. The usual barrage of snide comments and name calling resumed, but with Arsenio's newfound focus, the attacks landed less effectively than before. More often than not, he just glowered silently at the perpetrator or ignored them completely. Much to his delight, this indifference decreased the frequency of harassment. Though a few crew members continued to refer to him as "bush-burrow," they did so without vindictiveness, as if it were just his name. As annoying as he may have found this, Arsenio refused to retaliate. Once they'd landed, he'd be rid of them all anyway.

When it came to the captain, Arsenio found that the functionality of their interactions had shattered. Elwin always seemed to be on the verge of saying something more to him. Each time he spoke, the end of his sentence hung in the air as if begging to continue, though he never did. Arsenio never asked him to. He had no interest in what Elwin Hadleigh had to say to him.

And given that he'd made a resolution not to speak to anyone else, Arsenio found that he had ample time to reflect. Most often, he thought about his family. About how only weeks ago they'd all been together and now they'd all gone—most of them dead. Perhaps everything had happened so fast that this crucial fact was only now sinking in, but a deep, overwhelming sadness subsumed his anger. By the fourth day, he woke regularly to find tears on his face. And sometimes, while consumed by a mindless chore, he would have to stop what he was doing and distract himself to escape a spiral of negative thoughts. He would never see his parents or Helena again. Not in this life, at least. He could help avenge their deaths. That seemed to be the only thing left within his power. Whenever the weight of his thoughts in on him, he repeated his plan to himself, either in his mind or whispered softly under his breath. *Land in Black Tide Cove. Leave the ship. Get help. Find a way back.*

At long last, the weather cooled. Though it was still warmer than Corva sum Rio this time of year, the crew donned the layers they'd shed in the tropics. On the ninth day, as the sun began its descent, the lookout proclaimed, "Land ho!" from the crow's nest. Everyone, including Arsenio, hastened to get a peek at the approaching shore, part of a continent which stretched beyond what the eye could see.

By the time the clouds were tinged pink, they'd entered the cove. Arsenio could see where the port had gotten its name. A wide circular bay sat within a ring of jagged cliffs that almost came full circle save for an open, hundred-meter channel. The shore all along the inside of the ring was composed of beaches with sand as dark as the night sky. Across the bay from the inlet was their port. A dozen wooden staircases scaled the black cliffs from the beach to the streets above.

When Arsenio looked up at the city of Black Tide Cove, his mouth fell open. Never had he seen such diverse architecture in such close proximity. Each building was a different color, and they were stacked so close together they might have all been connected. What amazed him most was the palace at the north end. It rose above all else, wider and taller than the houses, trees, and rocks around it. The walls were painted a vibrant teal that shimmered the more he looked at them. Black wood framed the doors, comprised the many archways, and supported the eaves.

And scattered everywhere were painted gold details that brought life to the magnificent structure. He'd never before seen a building whose design was more than simply functional. It expressed emotion, an intent to mystify the viewer.

That was where he had to go. That was where the Nokari Empress would be, the one with the power to help him.

The ship docked and in no time, the crew set about unloading their cargo. Arsenio helped someone carry a crate ashore, and when they turned back to board the *Flaming Virtue* again, he took one last look at the ship with the merman at its bow and took off for the stairs.

~

Ciro had impressed Arsenio with its grand scale; Black Tide Cove impressed him in both scale and splendor. At the top of the steps—he counted more than two hundred and fifty, though his numbers may have gotten muddled—he emerged on an avenue rife with movement. He ducked beneath a pair of women carrying a massive ceramic bowl, then dodged around another person as they swung a heavy canvas sack over their shoulder.

The alley joined a bustling thoroughfare. Everywhere he looked, people passed in clothing of vibrant colors. Bursts of steam erupted into the air out of the kitchens of food vendors, and shopfronts crammed with innumerable goods fought for the crowd's attention. The conversations of a thousand people filled his ears, and he inhaled new smells that made his mouth water. Arsenio understood nothing; not the symbols on the hanging signs, nor the language on the people's tongues. Yet the novel chaos enticed and overwhelmed him.

Until he caught the sound of voices speaking Luso.

"Oy there!" said one.

"Thought ye'd leave without goodbyes, skin-sheath?" said another.

Arsenio glanced back into the alley and spotted three crew members of the *Flaming Virtue* coming after him. Among them was Jocaste, whose plastered sneer betrayed her ill intentions. He hadn't imagined he was important enough to chase, but apparently he'd underestimated their animosity toward him.

Arsenio scanned his surroundings. He had no clue which direction to go, what paths led to dead ends, or if he could find somewhere to hide. But unless he planned to stay here and face the trio, he'd have to make a judgment call. Gritting his teeth, Arsenio spun and took off.

Threading through Black Tide Cove was harder than he could have guessed. Every time he rounded a corner, there was a cart in his way, and every side street had about a hundred new individuals crowding the path. He ducked beneath hanging towels, jumped over loose animals, and slid between merchants with their arms outstretched, full of glittering jewelry.

Even when it seemed that he'd lost his pursuers, Arsenio kept running. The weeks spent aboard Elwin's ship had suppressed a need for open spaces, and now that dormant instinct seized control. He ran until he left the city behind for tall, verdant forestry and a dirt road. At the sound of rushing water, he paused.

Breathing heavily, Arsenio bent and rested his hands on his knees. The sounds, the trees, the cool air. He was struck by memories of his homeland. Even though the trees were not the same, the smell of the forest was sweeter than that of the Wild Wood, he couldn't help but stagger at the familiarity, given how far away he was from the little village where he'd grown up. The last place he'd felt safe.

"Naught but by the gods' will could ye break from us, boyo." Jocaste's voice emerged from the trees like fog.

"What do you want?" Arsenio asked. In seconds, they formed a triangle around him and converged. He had nowhere to go.

"We wants nothing more than for ye to pay your dues," Jocaste said.

"Yeah, your dues," said the one to Arsenio's left. "No more bumming with the captain for light duties, no more whining, no more freeloading."

"I didn't—"

"No sister to protect you here, neither," said the third.

Jocaste was standing directly before him now, looking him straight in the eye as she grabbed him by his shirtfront. "You're not but a stowaway to us, Mister Avilla. We don't like stowaways."

And then she threw the first punch.

Kaori

He frowned, scanning the board once more before moving his piece. The game was not going well for him. As if in response to this thought, Sugi made her next move with confidence and finality.

"I win," she said, giggling. "That makes three in a row."

Kaori waved his hand in disgust.

"Shall we play again?" his friend asked.

"Haven't I suffered enough?" Kaori sat back on the sofa. "I was never very good at Igo."

"One more round," Sugi pleaded. She was enjoying this far too much.

"Please, no. I think I need to retire while I still have some semblance of dignity."

Sugi sighed, relenting. "Alright," she said.

They began packing up the game.

"I think the problem is that you don't settle on a strategy."

Kaori lined the pieces up on the floor of the wooden box and set the board neatly atop. He'd lost every round they'd played, but despite their amiable exchanges, the losses stung. With tabletop games, he was always too competitive. A flaw, given that he wasn't very good at them. Kumo Amaya had once watched him lose at Igo to Taigen, and when they'd finished, she'd remarked that she'd have bet on his victory if she didn't know him better. Kaori had sulked for a whole day after that.

"That's ridiculous. I have a strategy," he said.

Sugi closed the lid and placed the wooden box back on one of the shelves.

"You spend so much time looking at *every* option that you never form a real plan. You're left reacting to my moves instead."

"But you have to consider all your options."

"Consider them, yes, but don't drown in them."

She may have beene right, but that didn't help him change. Kaori sighed. "Another time then."

Sugi stood and stretched. Beyond his open balcony, the shadows of the city elongated, painting every wall and rooftop with the mixed hues of day and night.

"I should return home," Sugi said. "Night is falling."

They bowed to each other as the door into the emperor's quarters opened.

"Your tea, sir." Izumi appeared, holding a tray with a tea kettle and two cups. Kaori stepped out of the way to let her place the items on the table.

Taigen followed Izumi at a moderate distance, his gaze noticeably lowered. As she bent to serve the drink, he lingered, leaning against one of the columns, eyes alight. He might not have even noticed anyone else was in the room.

"Hello, Taigen," Kaori said, stepping between his friend and the servant, a broad and purposeful smile on his face. Taigen shot him a sly grin.

"*Your Majesty*," he said.

"Will that be all, Your Grace?" Izumi asked, thankfully standing straight again.

"Yes."

She left.

"Why do you have to spoil my fun?" Taigen asked.

"Because someone has to stop you from lusting after every woman you see," Kaori said. "Especially when we have guests."

Surprised, Taigen looked around the room and spotted Sugi for the first time. His face went through a sequence of emotions: shock, then mild embarrassment, and finally intrigue. Kaori rolled his eyes; he should have known.

"My apologies, miss," Taigen said, pulling his robe straight and puffing out his impressive chest. "I didn't see you there. How rude of me."

He held out a hand. Sugi gave him a look that said she suffered from no delusions about his character. Kaori could have laughed, but he held his tongue, wanting to see how the interaction unfolded. Sugi placed her hand in Taigen's, who bent low and kissed it.

"Kaori, who is this exquisite flower you're hiding in your bedroom?"

"My name is Sugi Kanamori."

"And what a beautiful name," Taigen said, releasing his hold. "It reminds me of the peaceful mountain forests."

"Sugi applied as a suitor, but we became friends instead," Kaori said, immediately regretting his words.

"Ah, so you are not betrothed, then."

Sugi withdrew her hand. "That would appear to be the case."

"I don't mean to interrupt," Taigen said. "Please, do not leave on my account."

"I was about to depart anyway."

"Don't!" Taigen said abruptly, startling even himself. He cleared his throat. "I can have someone bring up another cup for you to join us."

"It's alright," Sugi said, and this time, a self-satisfied smile crossed her lips. "I really do have to leave."

With that, she descended the stairs. At the sound of the door closing, Taigen rounded on Kaori. "Tell me you were lying."

"What do you mean?" Kaori asked.

"I don't believe you've not chosen her," Taigen said. He dropped heavily into one of the armchairs, lifting a cup of tea before instantly setting it back down. Kaori had rarely seen him so flustered, especially when it came to a member of the opposite sex.

"Like I said, we've become friends instead."

"With that gorgeous creature?"

"She's a human being."

Taigen eyed him suspiciously. "So you're not playing some fool's game?"

"No. We met under the pretense of potential marriage. Why would I play a game?" Kaori asked. He sat back down on the sofa and took the second cup. The porcelain was warm in his palms. In retrospect, he should have realized Taigen and Sugi hadn't yet met, given the very fact that Taigen hadn't lusted after her. And now... well, now it was too late. Kaori wasn't especially close to Sugi, but from what he could gather, she didn't respond well to lewd advances. Taigen would have his work cut out for him.

"You are unusual," Taigen said. Uncomfortable with the scrutiny of his gaze, Kaori took a sip of his drink.

The tea scalded his tongue. Kaori tore the cup from his mouth, spilling more of the hot liquid down his front in the process. When he cried out in pain, Taigen only laughed.

"Here is Nokara's great emperor: burnt tongue and wet-crotched!" Taigen wheezed.

"Oh, quit it before I dump the rest of this over your head."

"You know, I only try to bring levity to our meetings." Taigen took his cup again and blew across the surface of the tea. "At least Kento's got a good humor about him. I think Amaya's only capable of vague smiles."

"Maybe she just doesn't find you very witty."

"Ridiculous. I'm the wittiest ox in this damn place." Taigen sipped, managing not to spill any on himself or burn any part of his mouth. Kaori took this as a cue that the tea was safe now.

"Why are you here, if you don't mind me asking?"

"Can't I want to see my friend?"

"Does that mean you've finished sampling all the brothels?" Kaori asked. Taigen showed him his tongue.

"Not at all. Though I can show you around if you'd like."

"I think I'll decline," Kaori said, waving his hand.

Taigen chuckled. "In all seriousness, I was simply thinking that I haven't seen you in a while. As friends, I mean. We used to share a cell, after all. Now, you're always in some lesson or meeting. And you're always acting the emperor, aren't you? You're not just Kaori anymore."

Kaori sat in silence. Taigen meant to say he missed him, though he'd never admit to it in so many words. Kaori might scare away this moment of sincerity if he admitted to feeling the same way. Their friendship was complicated in that regard.

"When I'm not being emperor, you're usually off whoring," Kaori said.

"I knew you would use that excuse," Taigen laughed. He sat forward. "Fucking is great, by the way, especially with girls who know what they're doing."

Kaori rolled his eyes.

"So, we're here then," Taigen said. "And we can continue discussing how everything's changed and we're not ourselves any longer, or we can do something like old times."

"That sounds like getting into trouble," Kaori said. "You know I can't, Taigen. I'm *emperor* now."

"All the more reason! Nobody can punish you, and if they tried, you could have their nose chopped off or something."

"How many noses have I ordered chopped off—"

"What say you and I have an adventure?"

Kaori took another sip of his tea, studying his friend while mulling over the benefits and consequences of Taigen's proposal. Nobody could punish him now, that was true, but he also had the weight of the palace *and* the empire's honor on his back. Any wrong move could disgrace him. That was a much more lasting effect than a reprimand or an evening of punitive labor. Still, it felt good to be discussing mischief with Taigen again, even if he'd never been the one to initiate it. A part of him delighted at the raised stakes.

"What did you have in mind?" Kaori asked.

~

They left the palace through a servants' door, exiting into a near-deserted Tatsu Garden. Kaori wore a simple black robe to keep from being recognized, but though the shadow of the hood obscured his face, he feared it wasn't enough. Each time they passed beneath one of the dim lanterns, Kaori clutched at his hood. The third time he did this, Taigen swatted his hand away.

"You're making it more obvious," he hissed.

"You should've worn something too," Kaori said.

"Two hooded figures are more suspicious than one," Taigen said. "Besides, if they recognize me, they'll just think you're an escort."

Kaori grunted his disapproval. "I knew this was a bad idea."

"Relax," Taigen said. He wrapped an arm around Kaori's shoulders. "This will only work if we're confident."

They approached the gate, Kaori's heart racing. In his rooms, Taigen's plan had seemed so alluring. The thought of leaving the palace without his constant guard tantalized him, but now the whole thing seemed reckless and unnecessary. Amaya and Kento cautioned him constantly about safety, especially after the appearance of the Jade Dagger.

"Keep confident," Taigen muttered under his breath. Kaori didn't know how he could *keep* being something he hadn't been in the first place.

"Good evening, Chamberlain Taigen," a guard said, noticing them. "Leaving?"

"The night is young," Taigen said. He wrapped an arm around Kaori's waist. "Time enough for another round elsewhere."

The guards chuckled. One said, "Some men have all the fun."

"Be wary, Taigen," said the first. "If your friend isn't hygienic, you may develop an itch."

"I don't think the emperor would be too pleased about that!"

Taigen laughed along with them. "Believe me, friends. I pay good money for good company. Only the finest Black Tide has to offer."

Finally, Kaori heard the gates opening. He could only hope the noise drowned out the rap of his heart.

"Even so, be careful in what grass you let loose your snake. I had a cousin who screamed in pain every time he urinated. They eventually had to cut off his manhood."

Everyone groaned at that. Taigen urged Kaori forward and they passed through the gate, leaving the grounds of Kingfisher

Palace. Kaori sensed the change immediately: the air was different out here, wild. The sounds rang clearer, as if within the gates, they were muffled—only you couldn't tell until you'd left. They trod down the road toward the city, and once they were out of sight of the gate, Kaori felt himself breathe again.

"They seemed friendly enough with you," Kaori joked.

"I'm known to come and go."

"And they didn't even question your companion. That was helpful, but I'll have to speak with the guard in the morning. That sort of lapse in security is dangerous." He stopped talking, reminding himself that he wasn't the emperor tonight. "Sorry. I think I'm growing used to my role."

Taigen smiled and nudged him in the ribs. "I think you're beginning to understand."

Kaori lowered his hood and let the cool winter air touch his face. At the Academy, the students had to return from their market trips at sunset. He'd only ever stayed out beyond curfew one time, when Taigen had convinced him to linger. They'd hidden in the forest outside the city, but after the sun had set, they were too afraid to go anywhere. They couldn't very well ask the guard to let them in, lest they be severely punished, so they'd had to wait until the next morning to enter with a group coming to seek counsel with the empress. To their surprise, nobody had confronted them, but he suspected the kumo had known and simply let his obvious sleep deprivation serve as punishment for the one-time offense.

If he was doing this again, Kaori realized, he didn't want to cower in the same way as before. He wanted to enjoy this night.

"Shall we go to the night market?" he asked, raising his hood again.

Taigen grinned. "I was thinking the same thing."

~

Every rumor about the night market was true. All along the main street, spherical lanterns glowed in ebullient colors: reds and greens and blues and goldens. Dancers moved seductively to the plucked shamisen, gold and gems strung across their taut bodies. A woman dressed all in deep burgundy made flower petals dance above her head as she whipped her skirts around. She winked at them when they turned to leave after staring in astonishment, and Kaori pulled his robe more tightly around himself to obscure his face.

Music poured from every alleyway. Intoxicating smells took turns tugging at his nose. Taigen treated them both to several small glasses of strong liquor that burned in Kaori's throat and made his head spin. Then he cheered Taigen on as he played checkers with a man who had more gaps than teeth.

Fighters emerged, and people gathered around them in the avenues to cheer and place bets on the winners. Each fighter had their own band of followers, who screamed for their champion to use their favorite moves. Kaori wasn't much of a fan of these fights, grimacing as blood poured down one man's face from a crushed nose.

Then they passed a building with windows covered by vibrant shades, which cast colorful light out into the street. Thick steam seeped from the propped doors, leaking into the night and rising in a mystifying haze. It smelled like perfume, floral and sweet and heady. Kaori was drawn toward it until he glimpsed a half-naked woman through the fog and recognized the building for what it was, much to Taigen's visible chagrin.

Finally, when his eyes started to ache with exhaustion, Kaori pulled on his friend's sleeve.

"I think it's time we returned home," Kaori said.

Taigen, who was flirting with a female dancer, reluctantly let her leave to perform another routine. "Alright, but just one more stop."

Kaori couldn't believe his ears. "Another stop? Taigen, we've done everything there is to do. We should really make our way back."

"You're such a child," Taigen replied. "And we haven't explored one tenth of the market."

Kaori didn't think he had the stamina to see anything else, let alone the nerve. The pleasant dizziness of the drinks was still in effect, but somehow they'd amplified his concerns about the guards catching him. He rested his hand on Taigen's chest.

"Look, this has been fun. Maybe we can do it again sometime. But I'm really tired."

Taigen stared back at him, a faint smile painted on his lips. Kaori had never been drunk before. He wasn't sure he liked the feeling. His advisor grabbed him by the wrist.

"Alright, but only one more stop."

Kaori sighed and let himself be led away. Rather than continuing through the market, they headed down an alley. The general commotion faded away, replaced instead by a symphony of the night: the wind on the eaves, an infant crying somewhere, and the rustle of leaves.

They entered the forest on the outskirts of the city.

Kaori had to stare intently at the ground, doing his best in his inebriated state not to trip on rocks or tree roots. The cypress swayed above them, black and silver in the moonlight.

"Where are you taking me?" Kaori asked.

"You'll see in a moment."

The steady babble of water emerged from the dark. Consulting his mental map, Kaori reasoned they had reached one of several rivers that emptied into the southern end of the bay—at least a mile from the city proper. What were they doing so far out? Kaori tripped over a stone and clutched at Taigen's arm to keep from falling.

They began to climb. It wasn't a long ascent, but by the time they'd reached the top, Kaori had had enough.

"I really don't think it's safe for me to be—"

"Look."

Kaori raised his eyes and gasped.

A gap in the cypress canopy provided a clear view of the top of Kingfisher Palace. It rose dark against the cloudy sky, pinpricks of light emanating from lanterns strung all across the balconies. The palace hovered amid the stars as if floating in the heavens. He counted the levels down from the peak and found his rooms. They were dark, but he knew they were there, doors flung open to the world. Every night, he looked out from that balcony just beyond the discerning powers of his eyes.

"And down there," Taigen said, pointing to a spot below them on the bank of the dark river, "is where we camped out that night."

He said it casually, as if that hadn't been one of the more terrifying experiences of their childhood. Had they really been this far away from home? Kaori couldn't remember anything but clinging to Taigen in the dark as his friend comforted him.

Then something moved.

Kaori squinted, searching the forest floor. No, that had been a trick of the night. The trees moving in the wind. He waited, staring intently at the place where he'd seen it.

Again. Movement.

He tapped Taigen's shoulder. "I think there's something—"

The creature moved again, and this time, it let out a weak groan. Kaori's body seized. It sounded like a *person*.

They groaned again, louder this time.

"Someone's down there," Taigen said. "We should leave."

"No," Kaori said. "They need our help."

Taigen looked at him, bewildered. But as the person groaned once more, Kaori began to descend from their rocky mound. Over the rocks he slid, shaking away the last dizzying effects of the drinks until he was on the bank of the river. He could make out the figure more clearly now: a man maybe Taigen's size. He lay on his side, his face buried under his arm.

Kaori looked around, but the forest was empty. "Hello?" he said.

Taigen came up beside him, placing a hand on Kaori's shoulder.

"Hello?" he said again.

Dark patches stained the man's shirt and trousers. Kaori had the strong suspicion they were blood. Both the man's feet were bare. He must have been assaulted, but his attackers were gone or hiding now.

"Bandit," Taigen whispered. "We should leave."

Kaori brushed him away. "We can help you," he said to the ailing man

The stranger half raised himself, straightening his arms. His head turned their way, but he didn't look at them. Matted strands of hair hung long enough to shroud his eyes from view. He said nothing, but his breath was labored.

And then a sudden realization overcame Kaori. The man's clothes weren't typical of Nokari. He'd never seen a shirt of that style, and the dark sash tied at his waist looked nothing like those Kaori wore around his own robes. Perhaps he couldn't understand them and that's why he didn't respond. As part of the curriculum at the Academy, they were taught multiple languages—primarily, Wikang of the Kailon Islands—but he had elected to study two more: Luzanti, the language of the ancients, and Luso, the contemporary variant spoken in some eastern lands.

He tried the island tongue first. Crouching low to the ground so that he was level with the man, Kaori asked, "Can you understand me?"

The stranger looked toward him, but rather than being placated, the man tried to crawl away. He barely made it into the underbrush before collapsing again.

"He doesn't want our help," Taigen said.

"Hush." Kaori tried again, this time in the eastern tongue. He wasn't as fluent, but he could remember simple words. "We don't want to harm you."

At this, the wounded man raised his head again. He looked to them, the rising and falling of his chest an effort. Kaori squinted in the dark, trying to better make out the man's face, but the night was too thick.

"Can you understand me?" Kaori asked.

"You speak the common tongue?" the man replied, his voice deep and hoarse.

Kaori crept closer. "We want to help you."

"Please..." And then he muttered something else Kaori couldn't understand before collapsing.

"Let's get him to the palace," Kaori said. He rushed over to the man and picked him up by the ankles. Taigen hesitated, looking around as if they might be able to push the job off on someone else. Or perhaps still worried that the attackers might return. More insistently, Kaori urged, "Taigen, look at the blood. He might not have much time."

"Why can't we take him to a regular healer?"

"Because whoever attacked him will be able to find him there."

"And what if he deserved the beating?"

Kaori looked his friend straight in the eyes, his tone resolute. "Even if he did, we can't just let him die."

Reluctantly, Taigen lifted the man under the arms. "I'll do as you say, but I don't know how we'll get him past the guards."

~

Trekking back through the forest while carrying the man required all the strength Kaori had. They did their best to avoid the main city streets. At this hour, most of the activity had finally died down, but they couldn't take any chances. By the time the palace gates came into view, Kaori's sweat had soaked through his clothes though the night chill crystallized his breath. He was surprised the sun had not yet risen.

"About time you came back," one of the guards joked. Then he noticed the body. "Who's that you carry?"

"He was in a fight," Taigen said. "I found him this way. He's hurt."

"Well, take him to a healer in the city. Don't drag him here."

"I can't. His attackers might still be after him."

"You can't bring some stranger into the palace infirmary."

"And look at his clothes," the second guard chimed in. "Is he even Nokari? His skin is darker."

"Please," Taigen said, shifting the man to get a better hold on him. In response, the stranger flinched with a groan, his eyes still closed. "He needs help."

"You can't bring a foreigner into the palace unannounced."

"Then announce him."

"The palace is asleep."

"He may not make it then."

"That's no reason for me to break command."

Kaori set the man's legs down and stepped forward, his pulse racing. He lowered his hood.

"I am Emperor Kaori," he said, struggling to keep his voice level. "Let us in now, on my orders."

The guards took a moment to recognize him, but when they did, both threw themselves into repeated bows.

"Your Grace, we did not know it was you—"

"Forgive us, we were only protecting the palace—"

"If we had known, we would have complied immediately—"

"Just open the gates," Kaori said.

The guards called down to the other side. When the gates opened, two guards on the ground level came out to take the stranger from Taigen and Kaori. They hoisted the man between them as if he weighed nothing and made for the palace. Kaori wanted to go with them, wanting to see that the man was treated kindly and by someone who could speak his language. As he crossed the gateway, however, he realized his exhaustion. The sun would rise soon, and though he'd been awake all night, his duties would not delay.

What a strange tale he'd have for Amaya and Kento when they awoke.

Emilio

Three days passed before Emilio decided to ignore the dining room all together. He and his mother had taken care to scrub the entire place clean from top to bottom, erasing any evidence that a tragedy had occurred, but stains of memory couldn't be so easily eradicated. Even if it made the path from the entrance to kitchen longer, he walked around the stairs through the common room. His mother did the same, and they took to eating on the hearth rug. When he was a boy, Emilio would've delighted in this privilege. Now, it was a thinly veiled reminder of how things were different.

On the fourth day, he volunteered to go to the market. His mother was busy as of late, shut up in her room at all times. He wondered if this secrecy had to do with Afonso's Light, but she refused to say. Her silence frustrated him. It was bad enough that he'd lost his brother and father. Her absence only accentuated his loneliness. Maybe she had responsibilities to fulfill, but he wanted her comfort when the waves of grief crashed over him at night. To reassure him that she, too, shared his pain. They were in this together. They were all each other had left.

Instead, he was alone.

Before shutting herself away again, Mamãe gave him two knives for protection on his solo journey to town. She hadn't done much in the way of teaching him to *use* the knives, only instructed that his first defense should be to hide. The knives were a last resort.

But none of the Tyrant's men came his way. He trudged along the gravel path, dragging his cart, kicking the rocks underfoot and singing songs to himself with his own morbid versions of the lyrics. He called to the birds perched in the trees, emulated their sounds, and watched, angry and disappointed, when they flew away.

Without much money, and not wanting to draw attention to their murders, Mamãe had built both Papai and Davi crude coffins using leftover wood from their chicken coop. Behind the house, where the sunset peered through the trees every night, they'd buried their kin. As a final touch, Emilio had fastened a woven tetrahedron to each coffin to symbolize the Holy Order, that Deus might take their souls.

The first sounds of Old Mandibula emerged through the trees. Emilio wheeled the cart onto the cobblestone road, threading his way through the town and doing his best not to make eye contact with any of the townsfolk. At the market, he made quick work of his list, not spending too much time finding the fattest or ripest fruits nor haggling with any of the merchants over price. When he was finished, he decided to treat himself to Pão de Deus while he sat on a low wall.

He found that if he kept his head down and a frown in place, people passed him by without noticing. He was happier this way, savoring the sweet, bready treat in solitude. While it had been a struggle to convince himself to leave the house, he found himself more at peace out here. The bloody memories were not as suffocating.

Someone was beside him. He hadn't noticed them there before, but now that he had, they were much too close.

Trying not to be too obvious, but just conspicuous enough that his visitor would understand his meaning, Emilio turned away. He shoved the final bit of the Pão in his mouth and took up the handle of the cart.

"Beautiful day, isn't it?" the visitor asked.

Emilio acted as though he hadn't heard.

"The sun's just warm enough that you can pretend it's spring. Of course, it won't last. The rain will come again."

He looked over at the woman. She wore a headscarf with red, geometric patterns over most of her face—all except her hazel eyes. Her dress was a deep crimson, almost black, and hung loosely on her frame. Emilio turned away again. He should go home. He had spent enough time in town. However, something warned him that if he left now, the woman might follow.

"You are a good son, going to market for your mother."

Emilio didn't answer. He stood. If she wanted to follow him, let her. Maybe he'd have the chance to pull out the knives. That might teach this imposing vagrant a lesson about bothering strangers. He realized he was clenching his fist so tightly the nails were cutting into his palm. He unclenched. *I shouldn't be so angry.*

He made to leave.

"Terrible thing," the woman said next, "what happened to you."

Emilio's heart skipped a beat. She couldn't possibly know. Neither he nor Mamãe had breathed a word to anyone. This had to be a witch woman, someone who went around using lucky guesswork to prey upon people's misfortunes. She probably said that to everyone she hoped to ensnare. The words had little to do with his family's recent tragedy. He'd never met her before in his life.

How can you tell? Her face is covered.

He spun to look at her, to study her eyes again. She didn't flinch, staring straight back at him. No, he didn't know those eyes.

"Have a good day, miss," Emilio said, brusquely. He turned to leave again.

"Losing any loved one is hard, much less a father and a brother at once."

This was too much. Feeling his eyes welling with tears in spite of himself, Emilio snapped, "Fuck off, hag."

Again, the woman did not shift or appear to react to him at all. In fact, if not for the ruffling of the scarf when she spoke, he might not have known she was the one speaking.

"I will," she said, "but I hope that you will hear me first."

"What do you want from me?" Emilio asked, swallowing the lump in his throat.

"To help you, Emilio."

She knew his name. Emilio wanted to ask for hers, but something told him she wouldn't answer. She didn't want him to know who she was or, at least, she didn't want anyone around them to recognize her.

"You can't help me," he mumbled. Nothing good could come from listening to a stranger who hid her own identity. Even if she did claim to want to assist him, that spelled trouble.

"What if I told you we could figure out who killed your family?" she said.

Emilio's heart leapt. Her hazel eyes never wavered. They were the eyes of someone who had seen many things in her lifetime—many terrible things, many *impossible* things.

"I already know who killed them," he said in a flat tone, though it wasn't exactly the truth. Of course, he knew it was the work of Fogosombre. Maybe not the direct result of the king's hand, but even perpetrated by another in the king's name, he was still at fault. Perhaps the nobles they'd passed on the road to Old Town had doubled back to their quiet dwelling to wreak havoc for sport. Emilio had even wondered if a loyalist to the Granite Throne had killed his papai after discovering his ties to Afonso's Light—though this explanation was less likely, given Mamãe was alive. He knew who was to blame even if he didn't know who had plunged the blade into his father and brother's hearts.

But he could find out.

Did she know who had killed Papai and Davi? If so, why was she offering to tell him? Did the reason matter? She might have known and seen a great many things, but that was no reason to trust her.

"You know who murdered them?" Emilio asked, sinking back down onto the wall beside her.

She shook her head. "No, I don't."

Emilio frowned. Of course, she didn't. He was back to believing she was just a witch woman. Someone looking to feed off his vulnerability. He'd eaten right out of her hand. He didn't know how she'd guessed about his father and brother, but it was nothing more than that. A guess. His disappointment turned to irritation. She was wasting his time.

"I don't know," she said again. "But I know how to find out."

And there it was again: the desire to hear her out. Emilio was torn in two. On the one hand, he knew he couldn't possibly trust her. Assuming she told the truth—and that was a very big assumption—her solution likely entailed malign magic. He certainly didn't want to get entangled in any of that. But on the other hand, if he knew the murderer's identity, then he could avenge his father's and brother's deaths. He could hunt the person down and... and drive a blade through their heart.

The images of Papai and Davi emerged again in his mind, twisting Emilio's stomach into a knot. None of the clarity had been lost. He could see them as if they lay before him now on the street, drenched in their own blood. How satisfying vengeance would be. How satisfying for both him and his mother.

"Show me," he said.

The woman nodded. "First, we will need one of their bodies."

Arsenio

Pain woke him from a dreamless sleep, but he kept his eyes closed, listening to his surroundings. Confusion came first. Jocaste and the two other crew members had attacked him in Black Tide Cove; retaliation for his lack of punishment after stowing away aboard the *Flaming Virtue*. Or maybe they believed he'd garnered preferential treatment from the captain. If that was the case, they were sorely mistaken. Perhaps they just didn't like him. Though he'd never spent a day at sea without working until his back ached, few crewmembers had missed a chance to harass him for any perceived ineptitude. Whatever the case, the trio had caught up to him in the forest.

So, assuming they'd left him alive—which he very much hoped was the case—then he should have awoken in the forest, strewn across the ground. Instead, he found himself on a bed softer than any he'd slept in before. Not only that, but he'd been covered in silken sheets.

The more he probed his senses, the more confused he became. Many parts of his body—the places which hurt most—were wrapped in bandages. Both of his arms, his ribcage, and his right leg. Surely Jocaste had not taken the time to carry him back into the city to get his wounds treated. And he definitely was not back on the Flaming Virtue; he sensed no rocking nor heard the creak of the cabin. Could it be that perhaps Elwin found out what had happened to him and sent help?

And then another memory surfaced: crawling through the forest in the dark. A stranger speaking to him in a foreign tongue. No—two strangers, arguing over him. One spoke his language. Then nothing.

Had someone from the city found him?

Arsenio tried to raise a hand to his face. A bolt of pain through his body and he gasped, eyes flying open.

He was certainly no longer aboard the ship.

Around him, an opulent infirmary came into focus. The walls were a brilliant red, trimmed at the top and bottom with colored tiles of black, white, teal, and yellow. High above him, complex patterns of copper filigree divided the ceiling into square segments, from which hung matching hung copper lanterns. Although multiple other beds filled the room, his was the only one occupied.

Where was he? Arsenio tried not to succumb to the terrifying thought that he was lost in a foreign land, but it permeated his skin and sank into his bloodstream. A chill ran through him. Was he still in Black Tide Cove? He thought it unlikely that whoever had found him would transport him somewhere else, but he had no basis for assuming they hadn't. Nor did he know what sort of person they were. If they were privy to such wealth, they might be a slave owner. What if he were being allowed to heal only so he could be sold off? What if—

Footsteps approached.

Arsenio tried to turn his head to view his visitors, but the movement sent a spasm of pain through him and he sucked in a sharp breath.

A tall man in black appeared first, carrying a spear: most likely a guard. Arsenio tensed.

Then there was talking. A younger man's voice, by the sound of it. Someone whose tone had not yet acquired the timbre of age. Arsenio couldn't see him yet, but he was close by. The guard responded monosyllabically.

And then the speaker stepped into view.

The stranger had ink-black hair with a silky luster to the thick strands. His skin was fairer than Arsenio's, the color of sunbaked fields after a long and scalding summer. His eyes were shaped like the tip of a new paintbrush, the irises a brown so dark they reminded him of midnight. He was slender, smooth, elegant, and *beautiful*. Though his command over the guard spoke of power, the man's strength betrayed a sense of delicacy. Like a young tree braving life on a windy mountainside.

Arsenio wished he could turn away. The man's splendor shamed him.

"You are in much pain, but I hope there is ease too," the man said. He spoke the common tongue hesitantly. Arsenio knew at once he was the person who'd found him in the forest.

Thank you, he wanted to say, but the words wouldn't come out.

"I hope it pleases I brought you here," the man continued. "You were injured. Nowhere else I could think to go. I am happy to see you have awaken."

Arsenio's throat was dry. If only they gave him water, he might be able to respond. His heart continued to flutter. His tongue struggled against him, lips refusing to heed his command.

"I will return," the stranger said, and looked away. He made to leave.

"Thank you," Arsenio said, finding control of his voice.

His rescuer turned back, eyes wide and inquisitive.

"How do you feel?" he asked.

With great difficulty, Arsenio responded again. "Pain," he said truthfully, "but better than it could be. I appreciate your help."

The man nodded. "What is your name?"

"Arsenio."

"I'm Kaori."

Kaori. Arsenio mouthed the three syllables, marveling that a word could so perfectly embody its owner. He wanted to repeat the name endlessly, already imagining what it might mean in its native tongue.

Apparently satisfied that his patient would be alright, *Kaori* turned to leave again. Arsenio wondered when he might return. He had many questions to ask Kaori, about where he found himself and who he was. Why he'd seen fit to save him. But Kaori must have important matters to attend to. Someone who kept a guard had to be powerful. Perhaps he served the empress.

The empress!

Arsenio remembered his purpose. He tried to reach out for the stranger, which sent another wave of pain through his body. This time he cried out, a guttural, meaningless sound. Kaori turned back to his guest, brow raised in concern.

"I must see your empress!" Arsenio blurted.

"Empress?" Kaori asked.

"Yes, your leader."

"Oh." Kaori shook his head.

"Please, I must meet with her at once."

The young man smiled. "You have already met him."

The simple expression enraptured Arsenio, whose heart felt like it might burst. But he couldn't let his strange reactions lose him his one contact in this foreign land. "Please, it's urgent!"

Kaori cocked his head, concern deepening. He exchanged a glance with his guard, but it was obvious they spoke no Luso.

Another individual entered the room: an older woman dressed all in black. She didn't acknowledge Arsenio, but kept her eyes trained on Kaori.

"Emperor Kaori," she said, and then continued with words he didn't understand.

Arsenio's mouth hung open. He watched the exchange, the pain retreating to the back of his mind for the moment. *Kaori* was the emperor? The king of this nation's people had rescued him from dying alone in the forest? Somehow, he'd found his way into the care of the exact person for whom he'd set out from home, an ocean away. And here he lay before him, wrapped in bandages, fragile and weak.

When they had finished talking, Emperor Kaori faced him. "I come back to see again, Arsenio," he said. "I hope the pain is ease."

And with that, he was gone.

~

At least an hour had passed before Arsenio's rampant thoughts melded into an obscure fog and he drifted to sleep. Again, his rest was dreamless and black, but he preferred this to nightmares about his sister's fate and his departed family. When he awoke again, he found the pain had subsided enough that basic movements no longer paralyzed him. He could turn his head slowly, though he couldn't raise it off the pillow, and he could move his right arm.

He no longer wore his own clothes. Instead, he was dressed in a plain black tunic, the same silken material as the sheets. Such expensive fabric felt foreign on his skin, but it was a novelty he welcomed.

A medic visited, a sturdy man who never stopped eyeing Arsenio with suspicion. He spoke constantly, but never said anything Arsenio could understand. This language barrier frustrated the medic to no end, and his tone grew more aggravated whenever Arsenio didn't respond correctly to his gestures.

He changed Arsenio's many bandages, cleaning the gashes that had turned purple and black. Arsenio determined that his leg had been broken and so had a few of his ribs. Removing his shirt was the most arduous part of the visit. Arsenio could not lift himself, and when the medic did it, he was forceful and unapologetic, grumbling to himself the entire time.

The medic left after applying several ointments and feeding Arsenio several drops of medicine. Arsenio had no idea what he was taking, but after a few minutes, he found the pain had returned to a comfortably dull state.

As promised, Emperor Kaori returned.

Arsenio was able to turn his head to watch him approach. The same swelling occurred inside his chest at the sight of the emperor. This time, Kaori brought multiple other individuals in addition to his guard. Each was dressed in similarly elegant attire: robes with bold floral or geometric patterns woven into the fabric. Two were men: one with a lined face and whose remaining hair had begun to gray, and one who looked about Kaori's age, though taller and broader. The other two were women. Arsenio recognized the older woman as the one who'd come to fetch Kaori the first time he'd visited. The other had a round face and a uniquely observant gaze. They stood around the bed, looking down upon Arsenio, who immediately felt on display.

"Arsenio." Kaori pronounced his name perfectly, without hesitation. "These are my people who advise: Amaya, Kento, Sugi, and Taigen."

Arsenio stared back as the assembly bowed their heads respectfully. The ones called Amaya and Kento greeted him in his language, but the younger two did not. Perhaps they didn't speak the common tongue. Taigen turned to his emperor and said something with a sly grin on his face. His familiarity told of a long friendship. Taigen laughed, and though Kaori didn't, he wore a small smile. Amaya eyed Taigen with reproach.

"I am thanking Taigen does not speak Luso," Kaori said. "With me he was when found you. I have told them all events. Can you tell me who attacked? Was it Nokari?"

Arsenio shook his head as best he could without straining himself. "They were from my own ship, people who didn't like me."

"Not comprehend."

"They were not friends."

"Why?"

"I didn't fit in well with them."

"Were they not from your homeland?"

"No," Arsenio answered. The emperor took a moment to translate all he had said to Taigen and Sugi, who nodded.

"You are from the east?" Amaya asked. Her voice was soft and kind.

"Faron," Arsenio said, and the one called Kento made a sound as though he had assumed this all along. He said something to Kaori which made both Amaya and Sugi protest. Kaori contemplated Kento's statement while biting his lip.

"Your ship *not* from your country?" Kaori asked. "Which, then?"

Arsenio thought about telling them the truth—admitting that the *Flaming Virtue* hadn't sailed under any flag—but he felt this information wouldn't earn him any trust. Though Kaori felt a sense of goodwill toward him at the moment, that attitude was tentative at best—based upon how much they knew of him.

"I'm not sure. A land south of mine," he said, thinking of Redthumb.

"Why did you do this?" Kaori asked. "Why come here?"

"I've come to plead with you," Arsenio said.

Kaori frowned. Amaya said something to him that must've translated the message in a way he could better understand.

"What do you mean?" the emperor asked.

And so Arsenio explained as best he could. He told them of Fogosombre's rule, his stranglehold on the realm ("I have heard of Fogosombre before, though had not aware of cruelty."). Arsenio described the attacks, the fear Fogosombre spread throughout every city and village. He had usurped the throne a dozen years ago, and though Arsenio had been young, he could still remember the darkness that had descended across the land. Fogosombre burned those who opposed his rule, claimed resources that had once belonged to the people and distributed them only to those he deemed worthy. By the time Arsenio had reached the attack on Corva sum Rio and the death of his family, he found his voice shaking and his vision glossy. Though he spoke to Kaori, Amaya seemed to understand him best. She translated as he went, and her words elicited sympathetic reactions from the younger advisors. Only Kento remained stony-faced and silent the entire time.

"I crossed the Great Ocean," Arsenio said, "to ask your help. My people are suffering. Though some are willing to fight, we can't hope to overthrow Fogosombre alone. He's too strong."

Arsenio reached out to take the cup of water from his bedside table. In the process, he revealed his arm; bruises patterned the skin around his bandage. The sight of his injuries brought the weight of his journey and all that he'd lost crashing down upon him, and he felt the first tear roll down his face. He drank, facing away from the assembly so that they wouldn't see.

They talked among themselves. Amaya and Kento spoke most, though no member of the group stood silent. When he finished his drink, Arsenio wiped his eyes and lay watching the conversation unfold. Without understanding, he could see that most of those gathered looked unsure but concerned. Only Kento appeared aggravated. Each comment garnered a gruff response. The longer the discussion continued, the softer the rest of the group became, until Kento was the last to speak and a long stretch of silence followed.

"What would you decide?" Amaya said in words Arsenio could understand.

Kaori stared unfocused at the bed, lost in an internal struggle. His downcast eyes and solemn expression didn't bode well for Arsenio's chances. His heart sank. What was he supposed to do if they refused him? The one task Galina had given him and his sister was to find help. He had traveled so far. They couldn't possibly turn him away.

"The problem you have is difficult," Kaori said finally. "I feel your pain; I give my heart to the people."

Arsenio felt a glimmer of hope.

"But I have to think on my people. Our countries, no ties. If send help, it will be an attack. Will make for retaliation, my people in danger."

Arsenio felt himself collapsing, sinking into the soft bed. A comfort he didn't deserve. A comfort he couldn't share with the people of Faron. "No!" he shouted, louder than he meant to.

"Please—"

"Don't you understand? My people need help!"

Kento said something in a warning tone.

"You must understand," Amaya said. "For Nokara to take a stance against—"

"But we are dying!" Arsenio tried to sit up, but this was too much for him still. He cried out in pain and fell back against the pillow.

The emperor said something Arsenio couldn't understand, followed by, "But I don't know that I can help you at this time."

The gathering began to disassemble. Kento led the way out of the room, followed by Taigen and Sugi. Amaya went next, her head bowed as if she couldn't bear to look Arsenio in the eye. Last to go were Kaori and his guard. The emperor's eyes lingered on Arsenio, heartbroken and afraid.

The look of someone whose resolve could be shaken.

Arsenio knew he was in no shape to go anywhere, but he figured that he had no need to. If he had access to the emperor, then he would keep it. Perhaps today he couldn't persuade this foreign power to aid his cause, but tomorrow was another chance. He wouldn't waste the opportunity.

Queen Yiscel

On the morning which marked the start of the Flower Festival, Queen Yiscel rose before the sun. This had become an unfortunate and frequent habit she couldn't shake no matter how much she might want to. She blamed grief. After all, she'd only begun her early risings upon the death of Nokara's late Empress Mai. The first time had been the morning of her friend's passing, days before the sparrow would arrive announcing that Mai was gone forever. How had she known then before word had reached Kailon?

The ocean had told her.

The ocean told her many things.

Yiscel went to it now, leaving her bed chambers and her sleeping husband behind. She would be back before he woke, his quiet snores a low drone in the darkness. After slipping sandals onto her feet, Yiscel navigated the halls of the Lily Palace, dodging candlelight where it betrayed the position of those rare souls already awake. The corridors led her out into the moonlight, where the warm breeze brushed her skin.

Yiscel crossed the path to the wooden stairs leading down into the palace's private cove. She left her sandals on the bottom step and walked out onto the moist sand. With the tide out, the waves entering the cove barely made it halfway up the small beach.

But the cool, wet sand they left behind shone smooth in the moonlight. Yiscel left tracks behind her as she walked to the water.

Why, two months later, was she still grieving?

Yes, Mai had been her closest friend, someone with whom she could confide, someone who was her equal in power. Though they only met in person twice a year—once when Yiscel visited Nokara in the rising season and again when Mai would visit Kailon in the waning season—they'd kept a correspondence at all times. An unspoken pact had existed between them, that in these letters they never wrote on matters of state. They were personal, often featuring humorous thoughts, private fears, words of admiration, advice, and thoughtful anecdotes.

Now that correspondence was over.

Yiscel had sent well-wishes to the new emperor: a young boy, she'd heard.

Writing the letter without a trace of skepticism or spite had been a struggle requiring multiple drafts. It wasn't the boy's fault the empress had died, and Yiscel knew that he hadn't chosen to become her successor either. Still, she doubted the young emperor would carry any of the qualities she held most dear in Mai. In the place of a friend, the position was now held by an *other*.

Would the biannual visits continue between the two thrones? That had yet to be decided. Yiscel had of course attended Mai's funeral, but that hadn't taken the place of a formal visit. Neither had Yiscel stuck around for the boy's appointment, much to the opposition of her husband and her head advisor, Locaya. Instead, she'd braved the funeral ceremonies and then hopped aboard her ship again for the nine-day passage home. She hadn't the stomach to face the Elliptic Council without her friend to mediate.

White moonlight danced on the water.

"Harana," Yiscel said, and sang three loud notes.

A moment passed. And then another.

From the depths of the ocean emerged an elongated shadow swimming toward the shore: a snake as long as a ship and as wide around as its mast. The animal lingered below the surface, gliding toward the spot where Yiscel stood in the water. When it reached the shallows, it reared up out of the tide.

The serpent had a narrow head with webbed ears. Pointed scales of dark, glossy indigo covered her back, but along her belly, the scales transformed into a brilliant, shimmering gold. A bakusawa, a great sea snake. One that had bonded with Yiscel.

Watching Harana's head eclipse the moon, Yiscel grinned. She put her hands out, feeling the spray of the ruptured ocean surface as the droplets raced to rejoin the waves.

For the Nokari people, death meant a place in heaven among the gods. For the Kailonese, the afterlife meant joining the Endless Ocean and the riches hidden beneath the water. Now standing in the calm waves, Yiscel felt a greater sense of peace. A comforting connection with her old friend.

If Mai was in the water, Harana could know her then.

The bakusawa lowered her head so that Yiscel could touch her scales.

"The Flower Festival begins today," Yiscel said, and sighed. "Such a happy celebration, and yet, I hope it's over and done with quickly."

The queen confided in her marine friend until the receding tide had nearly stranded Harana. Then she let the creature go, watching her tail disappear beneath the water. She shed no tears—she never did, even when watching the procession carry Mai's coffin away from the palace—and made her way back up the shore.

~

Yiscel entered her bed chambers just as her husband, Ilocoy, awoke. Without saying a word, she crossed to him and kissed him on the mouth. They made love by the rising sun. Love which was, at first, slow and soft, but grew desperate by its finale, heavy with the sounds of passion. When both had finished, Yiscel lay naked on the bed, staring up at the ceiling.

After, she prepared for the festivities. She bathed, then called in a half dozen handmaids to her side. As the girls fussed over her garments and her hair, Locaya read the list of events for the opening day. The queen's head advisor already wore her festival attire, her baro't saya appropriately colorful as it cascaded to the floor in swirling patterns of cream and fuchsia. The pronounced, lacy shoulders had been embroidered with lilies: the symbol of the capital island and the throne. Her thick black hair was pulled back into a bun at the nape of her neck, a hair-tie holding it in place with strings of white pearls dangling beneath. Her preparedness had never been surprising, Yiscel couldn't remember the woman ever being caught off her guard.

The queen's own dress had been crafted of Nokari silk. She'd specifically requested the fabric be dyed the deep blue-green of the Endless Ocean. Though the festival was meant to celebrate the vibrancy of the nation's flowers, the water never strayed far from her mind. Black ornamentation decorated the hem of the skirt, and pleats gave the fabric waves. Over her shoulders, the handmaids wrapped a violet panuelo: an embellished triangular cloth pinned at her sternum.

As usual, the wooden head-piece they used to structure her massive hairstyle was bulky and heavy. It was Yiscel's least-favored aspect of her regal costume, and she wore it with great reluctance despite how ridiculous it made her feel.

The girls finished and followed Yiscel out into the corridor, where her husband awaited in his white and gold robes. Locaya's husband, Mo'one, wore a similar outfit. During the Flower Festival, men donned muted tones to emphasize the florid, traditional costume of the women. Their robes were made of a sheer fabric, under which they wore a plain white shirt. Yiscel envied them the breathability of their clothes. In the hottest part of the day, the large dresses could be stifling.

Together, the queen and her entourage boarded a carriage to the festival grounds, where great tents and competition pens had been temporarily erected. At first sign of the queen, the people took notice. Chatter gave way to applause and cheering. Loud chants of "Gods' favor, Yiscel!" rose into the air. They greeted her with such enthusiasm that Yiscel couldn't deny them a smile and a wave.

"As always, my love, the people are thrilled to see you," Ilocoy said in her ear, an encouraging smile on his face. He knew the festival wasn't one of her favorite events. The vibrant, floral displays celebrating beauty and fertility could be indelicate affronts. Additionally, the villagers could come and go as they saw fit, or as their interest piqued and waned. But as the queen, Yiscel was obliged to attend one event or another from sunup to sundown. At the very end, she also had to congratulate all competition winners. Ilocoy delighted in the chance to do so, but Yiscel couldn't help feeling her time was better spent elsewhere.

"As always," she breathed, and led the way to where the first of many dance competitions would take place.

So, the day began. Allowing herself to be entranced at first, Yiscel soon found her mind wandering. She thought of Harana, somewhere beyond land, free to roam the depths of the sea as she pleased. For all that the bakusawa knew of Yiscel's home, Yiscel had no idea where the great sea serpent went when she wasn't beside her. The ocean was endless.

As the sun rose and fell in the sky, Yiscel played witness to drum circles, fire dancers, galleries of elaborate floral displays, jugglers, and acrobats. She let Locaya guide her around, waving and smiling to villagers everywhere she went. Yiscel had to admit that though she found the festival to be superfluous, it gladdened her to see the happy faces of her subjects. They ran between events, excited bursts of conversation following wherever they went. They gasped in unison as the fire dancers caught flame and laughed when the jugglers stood on their hands instead of their feet. At no other time of the year was Yiscel this close to so many of them.

The sky dimmed, the torches came to life, and everywhere she went, shadows added a layer of kinetic energy to the celebration. Only one event remained for the queen to attend this evening, Ilocoy's favorite: the storytelling tents.

If Yiscel had to choose an activity to obligatorily attend, she would have chosen spear throwing or buno wrestling, but storytelling was a close third. Banguet City's Flower Festival was known to attract the best storytellers in all the islands, people who incorporated magic and music and movement into their tales. Two years ago, a woman had sliced her leg onstage in order to bring authenticity to her performance. Now *that* had been enthralling.

"Venancio Canete came back this year," Ilocoy said to Yiscel, as excited as a young boy about to receive a treat. "I heard he lost *two fingers* preparing for his performance."

"Two fingers?" Yiscel said. "I wonder which ones."

They sat in their thrones at one end of the oblong interior, Yiscel after some maneuvering, given the size of her dress. The tent filled with low chatter as festival-goers wandered in, and continued until the first presenter of the night took their place onstage. The openings in the tent fell closed and he began.

The assembly enjoyed several stories from a handful of entertainers: one, the harrowing journey of a young kaicat—the water cats who lived on the coasts of the islands and swam in the shallow sea—across Kailon, and a few about great battles of the past that featured Kailon's mighty gold-sail fleet. This was typical of first-day storytellers since it was the only night you were guaranteed the queen's attendance. Yiscel applauded them all, particularly one gentleman who made sounds with his mouth that could have been mistaken for actual wind in a sail and the clash of bolo knives.

And then came the last storyteller of the evening.

She was introduced as Agueda Gamboa, a newcomer from the island Sampaguita. Contrary to the elaborate fashions of most women, Agueda wore only a plain tan saya about her waist. Her long black hair hung loose over her shoulders, a strand covering her right nipple, the other bare. She walked to the center of the stage and spun on the spot, looking into the faces of all the people watching her. The firelight cast flickering ripples across her deep brown skin. She seemed to be waiting for some cue before she began, and Yiscel had half a mind to call out to her, to let her know that she had permission to start, but then the woman raised her hands over her head and sang a long, resounding note.

The firelight dimmed.

"The Bringer of Day," Agueda said. Her voice resounded in the tent, unchallenged. "In the beginning, when the Endless Ocean appeared, the Greater Gods saw fit to fill it. They created the volcanoes to warm the waters, the corals and weeds to give it color, and the waves to give it life.

"But they needed creatures to appreciate the beauty they had made. First swam the fish, simple dwellers who never left the deep. But the fish were *too* simple; they could not appreciate the ocean's full majesty. So, the gods created the whales and the kaicats who swam the depths but had to leave for air, reminding them of the ocean's power. These superior beings saw the ocean for what it was and were awed.

"Still, this was not enough. Laluwang claimed ownership of the ocean, as the other Greater Gods moved on to create the land and sky. To keep watch over her kingdom, Laluwang made the first mighty bakusawa. All the ocean feared the bakusawa, for though it was fair and gentle, it was vast and more powerful than any other creature." Agueda's force of presence was so strong that nobody in the tent breathed. She didn't stoop to the effects of the other storytellers whose smoke and mirror accompaniments were reduced to gimmicks by comparison. Instead, her intonations were nails that pinned her audience to their seats, unable to look away.

"The first bakusawa had many children who spread throughout the tides. As the giant island arose, humans were created. Humans who found that they could bond with one of the bakusawa's children if that serpent was so inclined. These were deep connections that lasted a lifetime. Indeed, the bakusawa, who live much longer than humans, could sense everything about their imprinted companion and even mourn their death from afar. But no human bonded with the first bakusawa. While her children fled to the surface in droves, she kept to the depths, maintaining the balance of the ocean as she was created to do.

"Peace above did not last long. The Lesser Gods of the land waged wars against each other: wars of boastfulness, of territory, and of pride. They set their humans against one another to aid in their great battles. They tore the land to pieces, separated by water, and tainted the ocean with blood. Finally, they threatened to tear apart the world.

"Daliya, the Greater Goddess of the moon, became angry with the people and the gods of the land. She decided that humans were a mistake, and because of this grave mistake, the world would have to be recreated all over again. Enacting her secret plan, she lifted the moon into the sky after the sun went down and left it there permanently.

"At first, the people and the Lesser Gods of the islands did not notice. They continued to wage their wars, tearing the land and staining the ocean with blood. They fought and hated and murdered and appreciated none of the beauty the Greater Gods had created for them. But as the endless hours of night dragged on, the world grew cold. Without the sun, the plants began to die. The people could not grow food, they could not see, and they shivered. The fighting stopped as they turned together as one to beg the Greater Gods for forgiveness.

"'We know what we have done,' they said. 'Our fighting has caused you to punish us. Please, return the sun to the sky so that we may grow food and feel warmth, and appreciate the beauty of the world you have given us.'

"But though Daliya heard their pleas, she did not believe them. If she did as they asked, she knew they would only go back to their ceaseless fighting. She was determined to start creation anew. The other Greater Gods heard the pleas of the people and asked Daliya to lower the moon again so that Yarin could lift sun, but she refused. Conditions worsened.

"On the island Banguet, a famous warrior lived. Known for her many achievements in battle, she'd sought isolation once the humans and the land gods had realized their folly. She meditated endlessly on the damage she had helped cause to the world and wondered that there was no way to appease the moon goddess.

"Searching for answers, she swam farther out into the Endless Ocean than she'd ever gone before. A great shadow overcame her. Afraid, the warrior tried to swim back to land, but she couldn't. In darkness, she could no longer tell which way was home. Then a gigantic face appeared in the depths beside her: the face of the first bakusawa. The giant serpent explained to the warrior that Laluwang sought to help the people, but could not do so without angering her sister, Daliya. The first bakusawa had decided to take her own stance.

"She made a promise to bond with the warrior if the warrior would help her. Agreeing, the warrior said she knew what they must do. She mounted the first bakusawa and together they dived deep beneath the waves. Once they had dived deep enough that the world was blacker than night, the warrior pulled on the bakusawa's scales and they headed for the surface. Faster and faster they swam until it was all the warrior could do not to let go and be flung into the Endless Ocean. Still faster they went, and some of the bakusawa's scales came flying off. Then they soared out of the ocean and into the sky, climbing up into the air like a bird.

"'Open,' the warrior commanded, and the first bakusawa unhinged her jaw. She swallowed the moon in one gulp and fell back to the Endless Ocean. Now that the moon was gone, Yarin could raise the sun back into the sky. The people and the land gods were so grateful, that they vowed to worship the names of the Greater Gods every day. Betrayed, Daliya searched for the human warrior and the serpent, but they were gone: the human into the islands' many jungles, and the first bakusawa into the unfathomable depths. Still, when the sun set, the moon rose again, restoring balance to the world. Appeased by the respect the first bakusawa showed her by releasing the moon, Daliya took back her wish to destroy creation and start anew.

"From that day, the people named the first bakusawa Asanisol, 'the snake as large as an island,' and the warrior, The Bringer of Day."

~

The audience applauded: not the rapturous cheers that followed performances of fire and magic, but the admiring applause of those entranced by words. Queen Yiscel thought she knew why. Many had heard Agueda's tale before in some form or another—it was one of the creation stories you were told as children. Few had heard it in such detail or layered with such grave warnings against war and violence.

Still, Agueda's effortless command of every eye and ear left an impression.

Islanders began filing out of the tent. The muffled sounds of music wafted through the exits. Dancing would continue for many more hours, but Yiscel's obligations had been fulfilled for the day. She would return to the Lily Palace, perhaps lie with Ilocoy once more, and then retire for the evening. Tomorrow's schedule, though not as full, would be similarly demanding.

Several handmaids became occupied suddenly to Yiscel's left. She looked their way and saw three women attempting to approach her. The trio argued with her handmaids now, drawing some attention not because of their conversation—which they wisely kept to a low level—but because they obviously didn't belong. They wore no elaborate baro't saya, or even plain saya as Agueda had worn. In fact, their clothing didn't appear to be Kailonese at all, which was not so surprising when she considered that none of them looked to be from the islands.

"It appears you have company," Ilocoy said, standing beside her. When Yiscel said nothing, he continued. "Are you going to intercede?"

"I've yet to decide."

"Nobody has sent for help removing them," Locaya observed. "Shall I call for a guard?"

"No," Yiscel said. By rights, she probably should have—foreigners were rarely a sign of good news—but something told the queen such force wasn't necessary.

"At your command, my love," Ilocoy said.

"You may all leave," Yiscel said. "I want to know what the fuss is about."

"Shouldn't we stay with you?" Locaya asked. "What if—"

"No, this won't take long," Yiscel said, raising her hand with finality.

Locaya bowed her head and took Mo'one's hand. Then she and her husband left. They were young still. Now that the advisor's duties were fulfilled, they could wander the festival as they pleased, dance if they wanted to.

"My blossom?" Ilocoy asked.

Yiscel shook her head. "It's alright. I'll ask what they're doing on our lands, then I'll be on my way." Not wanting to sound harsh, she added, "my king."

"I will wait for you in the palace," Ilocoy said. He too left.

Yiscel approached her handmaids, who still formed a barricade between herself and the trio of women. The one in the middle looked to be the leader. She had skin several shades darker than the islanders even, her hair twisted in thick plaits. To her left was her opposite, a thin woman with crimson hair whose skin was so pale Yiscel thought she might be sick. Perhaps that was why they'd come to her. The last of the women was shorter with dark brown eyes. With her skin tone, she could have passed for Kailonese, but her facial features were too sharp, her hair auburn instead of black.

"What seems to be the problem?" Yiscel asked.

One of the handmaids turned to face her. "They want audience with you. We told them that's not possible."

The two women to either side began speaking at once, and Yiscel realized that neither spoke Wikang. She only understood phrases here and there, a language from the east. This worried Yiscel, who'd had few good experiences with easterners. Mostly, their hearts were set on conquest and riches, things that didn't bode well for her country. Then the one in the middle spoke up.

"Your Majesty," she said, in formal Wikang, though with a heavy accent. Had she learned from a linguist? "If we could hold council with you, our matters are urgent. We come from eastern lands seeking help from you and your people. If you would—"

But Yiscel had heard enough. Just as she'd feared, these easterners dared to barge in during her festival demanding aid. The arrogance of it all was quite stunning. She should have listened to her advisors and left without question.

Yiscel waved a hand to silence the woman. "No, I will not hear you. Kailon doesn't concern itself with the matters of eastern lands. This is a celebration of life, of fertility, of beauty—if you haven't noticed. Please, take your matters elsewhere."

The two who couldn't speak the language of the land waited for their companion to translate for them, but the woman in the center only stared with a hard gaze. Before she could protest, Yiscel swept away, her long dress billowing out behind her as she ducked out into the humid night air. Above her, the moon shone silver in the black sky.

CHAPTER FIVE
BLACK WATERS

Helena

Night had fallen and Helena had retired to her bedchamber by the time Jacinta came to find her. The Magistrata knocked on her open door to let the girl know she was there, then entered the room and closed it behind her. Helena rose from her cot, tense with anticipation. It had been weeks since her friend had promised to answer her questions about the north wing. Weeks of nothing but cleaning and keeping her head down. At least she'd healed in the interim. Her bruises had vanished, and the cuts were fading into memories.

"You will follow me tonight," Jacinta said. She wore a heavy cloak over her usual blue dress. From within, she drew folded garments, which she handed over. Helena let the clothes fall open, revealing a long blue linen dress and a black cloak similar to

Jacinta's, though the fabric was not as fine. Without hesitating, Helena began to undress.

"You won't say a word; try not to make any sounds at all. You will keep your head down and your hood raised. Follow close to me and no one will question you. Once we are finished—" Jacinta gave her a stern look,"—then you may ask questions. And you *will* have questions."

Her tone turned Helena's blood to ice. She paused only a moment, then resumed changing her garments by slipping the linen dress over her head. It was slightly too long and dragged on the floor, but it would do for one night. Then Jacinta wrapped the cloak around her shoulders and tied it beneath her chin.

Helena raised the hood, which was also too big. Every time she moved, she found that it slipped over her eyes, requiring her to adjust it again. Seeing this, Jacinta *tsk*ed, but they didn't have time to find a replacement.

"Did you hear what I said?" Jacinta asked.

"Yes."

"Good. Then let us depart."

The Magistrata opened the door and they left the bedroom, moving down the corridor at a brisk pace. Helena found it easier to hold the hood in the right place with one hand at her cheek, rather than to keep adjusting it. The backs of her fingers were cool and clammy, betraying her anxiety. A plethora of possibilities tried to force their way into her mind, but she held them all at bay. She didn't want to guess what might be waiting in the north wing. Better to let it present itself.

They met few people. The odd person that poked their head out of a doorway glanced at the women in blue and retreated back to their own business as if knowing whatever purpose the pair served didn't concern them. Helena kept close, mindful that she didn't tread on Jacinta's heels.

When the doors to the north wing appeared before them, Helena held her breath. Two sentries stood at attention, one to either side. They did not stop the women from entering.

As Helena crossed the threshold, the air became clearer and colder. A breeze permeated the corridor, billowing her cloak. She looked around at the doors lining either side of the passage, each marked with symbols she couldn't understand.

"Where—" she began, but Jacinta threw her a dark look and she shut her mouth.

The fires, which lined the wing and did nothing to fight the cold, cast spheres of orange light. As they navigated the corridor, several other people joined them. Helena blinked, wondering where they'd come from. If they'd approached from behind, she hadn't heard. If they'd come from any of the closed doors, she hadn't seen them open. The company all wore the same cloaks as Helena and Jacinta, and each kept their gaze straight ahead, unwavering.

A woman appeared at the front of the group with a lit torch in her hand. At the end of the corridor, they passed through another set of double doors which opened unto a stairwell that descended into darkness. Helena found she had to dart between a few cloaked figures in order to stay by Jacinta's side. Nobody said a word or tried to stop her.

They followed the woman down the spiraling steps, heels echoing softly on the dusty stone. Down and down they went, descending until the air grew stale and moist. The walls turned from masonry to rough stone, black mold painting abstract patterns across the surface. Helena felt slightly dizzy at the constant turning, wondering how far they'd burrowed beneath the basilica. She would have never imagined such a passage existed, never considered that while she toiled at her cleaning above, members of the Holy Order might be a hundred meters or more beneath her.

Finally, the spiraling passage ended and they emerged onto uneven ground, which sloped forward at a shallow decline. The woman holding the torch raised it above her head and stepped out into a black cavern, leading the congregation away from the stairwell. Helena watched her go, wary of where they were being led. She had to shake herself, blinking hard to make sure that what she saw was real.

Water. The sloped ground was a stone shore.

As the woman proceeded, her fire reflected off the surface of a pool that stretched out into the darkness. The water was calm, placid, as still as ice. And maybe it *was* ice; Helena couldn't know without touching it. But how could that be?

She didn't have long to ponder.

The congregation began to line up in two rows, creating a path to the water's edge. Helena jogged to keep up with Jacinta, taking her place by the woman's side, right where the shore ended and the icy surface began. Once they'd lined up, they stood in silence, the entire assembly waiting patiently. Every head had turned to face the stairwell, hands tucked inside their cloaks, the firelight barely gracing the mouth of the passage.

A low and constant hum filled the cavern, seeming to come from all around her at once. It grew, ringing throughout her body, bouncing off the rocks, sliding from beneath the glassy water. And as it became louder, Helena recognized it as chanting. At least half a dozen voices spoke words she couldn't understand. Asynchronous, the words folded over one another, but instead of creating a cacophony, their monotony produced a drone.

She didn't like the way they sounded. Not one bit. In fact, the eerie tone made the back of her neck prickle. For weeks, she'd wanted to know what happened in the north wing, but standing there in the depths of the basilica beside a black grotto with the chanting reverberating around and through her, Helena cursed her curiosity. She wished she was back in her bedchambers, stoking her self-pity. Still imagining what went on beyond the guarded doors.

Light grew in the stairwell. A septet of individuals all draped in the same black cloaks emerged. Six men led the way, carrying a wooden casket between them. The two in front also carried torches in their free hands. They chanted in low but powerful voices. Several steps behind the procession, a woman followed. Beneath her black cloak, she wore a linen dress similar in its simplicity to Helena's, but pure white.

Helena's skin prickled, her breath coming in short gasps. She fixed her eyes on the casket as the procession halted and bent as one to rest it on the rocky ground. In unison, they lifted the lid of the wooden coffin, revealing the blanketed body within. Helena's eyes widened. She remembered the horror stories children told each other about corpses reanimated by malign magic and she hoped dearly that the body wouldn't move.

The men lifted the corpse out of the casket, blanket and all, and carried it toward the water. They passed between the assembled viewers, their chants escalating into terrifying exclamations. Though Helena still couldn't understand the words, she heard wicked jibes, sinister threats, and pleas for mercy within their wildly divergent tones as if each man were possessed by a desperate soul crying out. Her breath came in gasps. She wanted to break the line, to flee up the stairs back to the ignorance of the basilica. And yet, she held her ground, knowing it was too late to run.

The men carried the body out into the water, their slow steps barely disturbing the lake. They walked until they were submerged up to their waists and the corpse they carried had just touched upon the surface. Then they stopped, and so too did their demonic intonations.

Silence hung thick in the cavern.

The woman who'd worn the white dress stood beside Helena at the water's edge, all of her clothing removed. Her hair fell straight down her back. Though she wore a somber expression, Helena thought she saw a flicker of apprehension there as well. Maybe fear.

The woman waded out into the lake. Water curled around her calves, the only sound in the cavern.

She hadn't made it more than a few steps before the men suddenly dunked the covered body beneath the surface. A wave rippled out from the disturbance, spreading into the darkness beyond the torchlight. For a second, Helena thought the water might wet the hem of her cloak, but the wave stopped short. Nobody moved.

They listened to the dying disturbances.

The woman in the water cried out, clutching at herself as she doubled over, as if in pain. Helena gasped, unable to control her surprise. The woman stumbled around, the muscles in her jaw and neck bulging as she gritted her teeth. She flailed, splashing water with every jilted step. The assembly watched, not a single soul moving to help her. Droplets of water clung to her legs, the dancing light exaggerating every movement. With a loud cry, she flung herself around, facing the shore.

Helena had to clench her mouth shut. The woman's body had deformed, her womb swelling as if she were with child. She collapsed, splashing down into the water as the protruding stomach continued to grow. Scrabbling onto her elbows, she flung her head back. Her hair draped into the subterranean pond.

Red leeched into the water from between the woman's legs. All the while she screamed, her body morphing at a grotesque pace. Helena could barely mask her terror, tears spilling from her eyes as the woman shuddered. She gave one loud, final shriek that curdled Helena's stomach, and she averted her gaze.

And then a white light washed over them all.

Helena had to will herself to look. What she saw only deepened the confusion brought on by the bizarre events. Hovering in the air before the prone figure was a tuft of hanging smoke, white and luminescent. For a moment, all eyes were fixed on this new *presence*. What it was, Helena couldn't identify. All she knew was that she could not, and did not, want to look away.

The brilliant wisp of smoke began to drift toward the six men who still stood out in the black lake, holding the corpse below the surface. It morphed constantly like mist in a wind, but all the while, it advanced on them with purpose, a magnetic draw.

Before it could get to them, however, the torch bearer who had led Helena and Jacinta down the spiral steps lunged into the water. She drew from her cloak a small box and, with a sharp snap, she trapped the wisp inside.

It was all over. The men waded toward the shore, their corpse floating away into the darkness behind them. Several onlookers went to help the woman who'd given birth to the smoke out of the water. She shivered, naked and wet from head to toe. But she didn't cry any longer or even whimper.

Helena tried to catch Jacinta's eye, but the Magistrata wouldn't look at her. Instead, they followed the congregation to the steps and, in silence, began their climb back up into the north wing.

~

The moment the bedchamber door closed, Helena hissed, "What in Deus' name was that?" as she rounded on the Magistrata.

Jacinta removed her cloak though the room was cold with winter. Her midnight-blue dress was dimmed to black by the candlelight. "What you observed is called a Graylife."

"I have no *idea* what I just observed."

"The dead man was believed to have witnessed something of importance—either that or he'd been murdered."

"How do you know that?"

"It's why a Graylife is made."

Helena sat on her cot. Several times, she thought she was ready to speak, but every time she opened her mouth, so many things rushed forth that she couldn't choose just one to voice.

Jacinta sighed. "Many hundreds of years ago, miners high up in these mountains stumbled upon the Pool of Iniquities. When they bored into that cavern, they released shadows and demons into the world. Naturally, they summoned the Holy Order to reconcile their mistakes.

"In driving out the malign forces, the Holy Order discovered that the pool changed nature, almost as if in gratitude for their services. Instead of birthing demons, they found the waters would produce Graylives."

"But what *is* a Graylife?" Helena insisted.

"You saw what happened to that man," Jacinta said. "When the body dies, a piece of the soul clings to it."

"I thought our souls went to Paradise? Isn't that what the Holy Order teaches?"

"Yes, most of the soul does, but a part of it—a significant part—clings to the body. It's like flesh. The remaining soul decays as all dead things naturally do, but so long as there is flesh, you can assume there is a piece of the soul."

The only notion this conjured for Helena was that her soul was embedded in her flesh, but she knew that couldn't be what the Magistrata meant. She looked down at her palms, imagining white vapor churning beneath her skin.

"When a body is brought to the pool," Jacinta continued, "the waters use the remains to summon the rest of the soul and reassemble it into its purest form: a Graylife. But life cannot enter our world without passing through the womb—"

"The woman who birthed it."

"Yes."

"And the carriers were all male because—"

"Because the Graylife reassembles inside the first inhabitable womb that touches the Pool of Iniquities alongside the corpse it once embodied."

Helena pondered this alarming fact for a moment, considering how close she'd stood to the water, how she'd considered touching it to see whether or not it was frozen. She shivered to think that what had happened to the woman in the water might have happened to her instead.

"Why?" she asked.

"That is harder to answer." Jacinta sat down beside her. "Magistrata can contain the Graylife in specially blessed boxes made of marsh wood or quartz stone. When a Graylife is viewed through crystal, we can enter a state of immersion. It's difficult to describe. You are transported, but only spiritually.

"The Magistrata who discovered this ability also discovered that Graylives experience a reality of their own: a rebuilding, if you will, of the circumstances their human form faced in life. The people they encountered, the events they experienced, places they visited.

"They took this as a sign from Deus that it was their responsibility then to enact judgment. Who could deny them, after all, if they could view a murder from beside the victim? There could be no doubt when it came to blame. By observing Graylives, the Holy Order could catch killers, they could find stolen objects, complete unfulfilled wishes to surviving loved ones."

"You mean, you can view their memories?" Helena clarified.

"No. That's the tricky part," Jacinta said. " That's what they initially thought, for most often, the Graylife will make the same choices and have the same responses to these circumstances as their living form did. But this isn't always so."

"What do you mean?"

"The Graylife is not a memory. It's a spiritual reconstruction of the being. After several decades of wielding this power, the Holy Order discovered that even in its purest form, human souls are inconsistent. A particularly imposing viewer could influence the subject, bend them to a strong will, appear to them in corporeal form. Even without such stimuli, sometimes the subject would decide upon a new course of action. While being viewed, they might place an object where it very obviously wasn't in our world."

"You mean, they're living a new life?" Helena asked.

"No," Jacinta said. She took a deep breath, eyes raised to the heavens as if pondering how best to explain what she was trying to convey. "Their soul uses the same experiences, the same knowledge, as the person when they were living, but it extrapolates. Souls absorb everything around us, whether we're aware of these things or not."

The idea was ridiculous to Helena, who couldn't help but lean away from her friend, wondering if maybe the Magistrata was testing her imagination. Helena hadn't forgotten the events she'd witnessed only an hour ago, which had certainly appeared paranormal, but what Jacinta said now couldn't be true. Could it? Souls living lives beyond the body—living new lives under the observation of the Holy Order. The implications were too grand. Unfathomable.

"I don't understand. So, after being captured, a Graylife starts over and reconstructs the person's life again?"

"Time for them doesn't move in a linear fashion the same way it does for us. Think of your mind recounting events several times in quick succession, considering many possibilities at once. When a Magistrata observes, we choose to view the particular thread of a Graylife linearly.

"All of this certainly poses some questions about fate and free will," Jacinta continued. "If some decisions are embedded in our soul and others aren't, what does that mean for us as humans?"

"I don't know," Helena said. She'd never been one to show an interest in philosophy. The sit-and-thinkers wasted their time, in her eyes. She preferred to explore the woods, to discover the cracks and crevices. Considering what choices she made and what choices were made for her was something she'd never paid much mind. "Why do they do it still, then?"

"What do you mean?"

"If they can't rely on Graylives to get answers because the soul or whatever might be making different choices than their former life, why does the Holy Order still create them? I thought our souls were meant to enter Paradise after the death of our bodies. Isn't summoning the soul back to our world keeping them from their final resting place?"

Jacinta smiled sadly. "I knew you had the right mind for this," she said. "For almost as long as we've known about Graylives, the courts have looked to the Holy Order for truth. How could they deny us, after all, when we could show them visions of the events? The Holy Order doesn't, however, disclose knowledge of the disparities. As far as the judges know, our findings are indisputable. In this way, the Holy Order can keep using the Graylives as they see fit to serve their own ends."

Helena sat in silence, processing what Jacinta had said. The more time passed, the heavier the weight of her words became, until Helena feared its magnitude. She frowned. There were so many pieces to fit together. "But you are a Magistrata."

"I am. I sought the Holy Order at a time when I believed them to be a source of good in the world—and to the credit of some members, they are a source of good. Some enact the teachings and ideals of the Scriptures selflessly. So long as they haven't lived in the Quartz Basilica, they might never know the deeper levels of malintent that underlie the foundation. But membership to the Holy Order is for life, and even though *I've* discovered the questionable side of things, I cannot leave."

"Would they kill you?" Helena asked. She couldn't imagine, from all the things she'd been taught about the Holy Order, that they would sanction the taking of anyone's life. But then again, she was coming to understand the complexities of a world she'd never been aware existed.

"Death isn't always a good form of punishment. They can find other ways to keep me chained to my life of service."

Helena continued mulling over everything she'd seen and heard since the night began. She was a long way from the life she'd once lived as a girl in Corva sum Rio. She felt as if she'd aged immensely since fleeing her village. Exhaustion came crashing down upon her, but how could she possibly rest knowing what went on in the bowels of the mountain? The horrific chanting rose in her mind, the gravelly monotone sending chills up her spine. That was a sound she hoped to never hear again.

"Have you done it before?" Helena asked.

Jacinta tilted her head quizzically.

"The woman who gave birth to the mist. Have you ever had to do that?"

The Magistrata's eyes unfocused as she recalled a history Helena couldn't see. "I have, yes. I was selected to be surrogate several times, in fact. But then I did something I wasn't supposed to; I gave a mother and father a second chance. I rebirthed their child's soul for them and let it reunite with the body, which is strictly forbidden."

"What? How is that possible?" Helena asked.

"Didn't you see? When the Graylife was created, its first instinct was to rejoin its physical form. The Magistrata trapped it before it could get there, otherwise we'd lose the ability to observe it." Jacinta said this with a hard line in her jaw. "If you don't contain it, the soul is reclaimed. The person continues living. I did this for a couple who came to me in need. I pitied them and it cost me."

"What happened?"

"You mean, what was my punishment?" Jacinta asked. Her eyes shined in the candlelight, glistening like mourning stars. "They mutilated me. Made me infertile so I could never do it again."

"That's horrible," Helena whispered.

"Even after I was forced to fast for weeks on end, even after I was flogged, even after I'd pleaded that I'd learned my lesson and I'd never repeat my crime, they still mutilated me. The greater the offense, the less mercy they show. Do you see now? Death is not always a punishment, Helena." The stars fell from her eyes. "Death is sometimes an escape."

Mariana

"I am sorry your meeting with the queen did not go as planned," Nohea said.

"I thought it went rather well," Mariana said dryly.

Ramil's brother, Nohea, displayed almost no resemblance to the innkeeper. Whereas Ramil was chinless and short, Nohea stood tall and muscular, with even features that formed the most disarming smile on command. He kept his hair cut close, though his beard was long enough that he kept it in two beaded braids. From beneath his sleeves, tribal tattoos detailed a story of his travels that Mariana was curious to know.

His ability to speak Luso was also far better than his brother's, probably a result of his experiences.

"You'll have to find another way," Lenora said.

"Yes, I suppose simply walking up to her was an idiot's strategy," Mariana said. "Are you still planning on leaving me then?"

"Me came for the festivities and a ship off this land," Redthumb said. "Nothing against you, Mari, but this not me fight."

"Nor mine."

"Maybe not," Mariana said, "but it's a fight for the good of many, many people. An entire kingdom. That has to mean something to you."

"What does I owe them?" Redthumb asked. "I have me life risked plenty on me own, thanks."

Lenora nodded in agreement.

Mariana looked back and forth between the two of them, disbelieving. Even though they'd said they were only joining her on the way to the capital, she'd expected them to realize the importance of her mission once they were there. An entire kingdom of people needed help, after all. They couldn't be so heartless, could they?

It would appear she'd been wrong.

Frustrated, she crossed her arms, aware of how childish she looked. "What am I supposed to do then?"

"Does the queen hold counsel?" Lenora asked. "You could wait until after the festival is finished and go to her then."

"But not all who seek counsel are given audience with the queen," Nohea said. Mariana had almost forgotten he was there.

"No?" she asked.

"Smaller matters are handled by less important officials, and those who have already been turned away once are likely to be turned away again without second opportunity."

"She not take kind to our faces," Redthumb said.

Mariana grunted in frustration. "I can't leave without having a fair chance to convince her."

"What? You try thiefin' then?"

"If she won't listen to a band of foreigners, she certainly won't listen to a foreign *thief*," Lenora said.

"Have you a better idea?"

"No—"

"Then you do well not to shave me words."

"A bad idea doesn't take the place of no ideas."

"Stop arguing!" Mariana said, massaging her temples. "It doesn't help to be at each other's throats."

Lenora and Redthumb exchanged angry looks but refrained from saying more. Mariana was thankful for their silence. The bickering only aggravated the hopelessness and frustration that gripped her. If only she had another way to attract the queen's attention. If only they could have made it to the queen first and not her handmaids. If only she wasn't stranded on this island with her brother across the sea. If only her parents and her sister hadn't been killed in Corva sum Rio. If only Fogosombre hadn't taken the throne in Faron.

It seemed there was always another layer of *if only* to peel back.

"Does the queen meet the competitors in the festival?" Mariana asked.

"Not all of them," Nohea said. Then his eyes lit up. "But in addition to their prize, she does meet with the winners."

All three women turned to him.

"So I need to win a competition," Mariana said.

"What kind of prize?" Lenora said.

"Gold usually," Nohea said. "Piloncitos. A tidy sum, I've heard. But I've never competed. I've not the truest aim—"

"Mari, you need to win something!" Lenora said.

"A sad trio of stranded travelers, we are," Redthumb commented. "Don't have nothin' but the clothes on us. What competition you think she win? She going to strip for her then?"

Mariana began counting off her fingers. "We don't know any of the dances, we haven't got flowers with us to arrange, nor an oven or ingredients to cook with—"

"I've got my bow and arrows," Nohea said, gripping the handle of the recurve bow slung across his chest.

The women looked at him.

"Them have a shooting competition?" Redthumb asked. "I thought this a damn festival of flowers. *Quat je duvelne.* Why them shooting?"

"Well, they're not shooting each other," Nohea said. "It's about aim and strength. Nobody's bringing blades to the festival."

"Three knives I have strapped to me waist beneath this skirt," Redthumb said.

"Maybe that's why the queen wouldn't talk to us," Mariana mused.

"When is the next archery competition?" Lenora asked.

"The last day," Nohea said.

"Great. That gives us time to prepare." Mariana rubbed her hands together, sitting back against a rock. Nohea had brought money, but he hadn't enough to buy them lodging as well as food. They'd decided the latter was more crucial. As such, they were sleeping beneath the stars every night, though Mariana didn't mind too much since the nightly breezes countered some of the worst effects of the unrelenting humidity. "Which of us is competing, then? I've only ever used a sword."

Mariana looked to their guide.

"I've admitted already I'm no great shot," Nohea confessed. "I can use it decent enough if I have to."

"Me specialty swords and knives only," Redthumb muttered.

Mariana looked to the last member of the group and felt the others do the same. The red-haired woman sat impassive for a long moment, staring straight at the ground by her feet. Of them all, Lenora had perhaps been the most vocal about not sticking around once they'd arrived in Banguet. But the allure of a monetary prize was tempting her.

"You can keep all the winnings," Mariana said.

"All of it?"

"Hey!" Redthumb interjected. "If it weren't for me, the both of you'd be miming your way 'round Medinilla still."

"But *I'm* the one competing."

Mariana rolled her eyes. "Alright, if you stick around and win the archery competition, I'll hand the prize off to both of you. You can split it how you wish at that point. I don't care."

Lenora let out an exasperated grunt and crossed her arms. "Fine, I'll do it. But I'm only staying until I've collected my winnings."

"*Our* winnings."

She nodded. "Then we'll be off."

"Thank you," Mariana said, leaning forward with a smile.

"And then we'll be off," Lenora repeated.

"Of course," Mariana said.

Redthumb sighed. "Me pale friend, you better win." She put a hand on Lenora's shoulder. "I'll be having me share of the prize either way."

"Alright," Mariana said, her spirits raised. "Then we should begin."

~

Keeping to the outskirts of Banguet City, the trio hid among the foliage to help Lenora prepare for the competition. Nohea went into the city to sign her up, and returned several times throughout the day to bring them food and news about the queen's temperament and whereabouts.

Lenora trained. Her family had been hunters, and she'd learned the bow and arrow as a very young girl. But she expressed a nervousness that in the intervening decades since the bow was her primary weapon, her skills had diminished. Not since she'd taken to life on the Great Ocean had she hunted for her meals by way of archery. As such, she took a few hours to refamiliarize herself, but once she had the hang of things, Mari could see she was a natural. By the next day, she was hitting close-range moving targets with relative ease and, more often than not, could hit a bamboo stalk from forty paces.

But this wouldn't be enough.

Nohea informed them that the competition consisted of a series of eliminations. In the first round, contestants moved down a line of targets at twenty paces. A third of the contestants would be eliminated depending on how their marks lined up to the others. For the second round, they would each face a pole at half a field whose height was divided into segments. Competitors had to land one arrow in each section starting from the bottom. This was done until another third of the original number had been eliminated. Finally, entrants would face a challenge course with a multitude of targets spread throughout. They had one minute to hit as many targets as they could. Whoever hit the most won.

By the last evening, Mariana felt their chances of winning were good. Lenora was quick and comfortable with the recurve bow. She could hit the vast majority of what they threw at her and didn't seem bothered by nerves or the pressure to succeed. Even Redthumb paid her a compliment as they ceased training for the night. A look of understanding passed between the two women that Mariana couldn't help but appreciate. Her struggle was not their struggle, the treatment of her people did not affect them in any way, and yet they'd come together to fight for her cause—albeit, with some monetary incentive, but she allowed herself to think this wasn't the *only* reason they'd stayed.

"Do you believe the queen will listen to you if we get her attention? If I win, I mean?" Lenora asked, sitting beside the fire Redthumb had built. Nohea handed her a bowl of rice, which she took gratefully.

Mariana nodded. "I hope so. We're out of options if she doesn't."

"She has to," Lenora reasoned.

"Queen Yiscel is tough but fair," Nohea said. He spooned a piece of chicken into his bowl before popping it into his mouth. "She is a hard woman, but those who have interacted with her swear upon her kind heart."

"She looked like she'd kindly raise a hand to the back of our heads in that tent," Mariana said, and they all laughed.

"She's not a woman I'd want to cross," Lenora agreed. She leaned over and put a hand on Redthumb's shoulder. "But then again, we've got one of those right here. Eh? Maybe if it doesn't work out, Redthumb could have a go at impressing her."

They laughed again, all except Redthumb, who put her bowl gently on the ground, her eyes averted.

"Sunev," she said.

Lenora's chuckles died out. "What was that?"

"Me name Sunev," Redthumb said again. Her voice had never come so soft. "Please, me prefer me name."

In the center of their circle, the fire crackled, sending sparks floating up between the dense canopy of wide green foliage. Despite the marks across her features and the weight of experience that tugged at her brow, the light across her face showed that Redthumb—or rather, Sunev—was much younger than Mariana had originally assumed. In fact, the woman couldn't be much older than herself. Only, she'd seen more of the world's cruelty than even Mariana had.

Lenora broke the silence, smiling and letting out a nervous laugh that might have only been another breath.

"Alright then, Sunev," she said, and gave her shoulder another squeeze.

~

The next morning, Mariana rose with the sun. Her companions awoke soon after and Nohea went into the city for food so they might break their fast. Lenora seemed unbothered by her looming competition. She laughed and joked as she usually did, unencumbered by the fact that the coming hours would decide whether or not they earned a place before the queen, and if Mariana would have the chance to plead her people's case.

Deciding that further training would be of no use, the four spent their morning at the Flower Festival. As it was the last day, there were clear signs that the event neared completion. Several merchants had disappeared, likely packed up and gone home, their wares sold. By no means were the streets empty, but their departure could be felt.

Around the time the sun reached its zenith, Lenora grew quiet. She seemed deep in concentration, with her gaze either intent upon the ground or far over the heads of everyone around her. Mariana gave her what she hoped were encouraging words, but Lenora didn't respond.

Finally, it was time. They made their way to an oblong field surrounded by a waist high fence. Lenora left them, gathering alongside her competitors inside the enclosure. The trio stood on the outside, as close as the canvas fence would let them.

"Sport like this bring me back to Lord Fausten," Sunev said. "Him would watch fighting men in rings like animals. But them weren't free none to choose competition. Didn't win no prizes neither. Them was forced, and fought to death."

"Let's hope the same fate doesn't befall our friend," Mariana said.

Around the other side of the oval, Queen Yiscel sat on an elevated platform. Mariana pointed her out to Sunev and Nohea. They were so close, and yet so many things could go wrong. She would have to put her faith in Lenora, who stood immobile in the group of competitors, Nohea's recurve bow strung over her back. Other competitors were stretching, surveying the onlookers, or playing to the crowd. She wished Lenora would do the same, anything to show that she had fight in her, but the woman only stared at the ground.

At the start, there were thirty-four competitors.

Within the first few minutes, it was obvious that some folks had entered with far more confidence than they deserved. They went down the line, firing at the hay disks, but accidentally launching their arrows over the side of the pen into the jungle beyond. A few did decently, and about a dozen did fairly well, Lenora included. One man with a kaicat tattooed across his entire back went down the line and hit every target dead center with the exception of one, which landed in the first ring. The crowd cheered for him, but Mariana gritted her teeth.

Twelve competitors were asked to leave.

As Nohea had described, the next challenge was the poles. At either end of the field stood stripped trunks of the tall, thick palm trees Mariana had seen across the islands. On each were painted several white lines, which divided the trunks into segments about half her height all the way up. Lenora hit each of these and smiled with satisfaction. The way her movements had loosened, it seemed she was beginning to relax. Three competitors away from her, the kaicat man did the same. His disgusted frown never changed, no matter how well he did.

Another twelve were asked to leave.

A woman walked out onto the field to escort the remaining competitors to a tent while dozens of field hands emerged, arranging props in specified locations around the oval—hay bales, painted masks, and carved bamboo figures among other things. Someone also brought out a bell which would ring each time a contestant successfully hit a target. Placed on a table beside the queen was an hourglass with brilliant white sand inside, easily visible to everyone gathered.

The first contestant hit six targets. The second hit eight. It wasn't until the sixth competitor was summoned that the kaicat man emerged, his scowl firmly in place. The crowd held its breath as he ran, spun, and fired. Even the queen was visibly more attentive to his performance, her hands gripping the armrests of her seat. In fifty-one seconds, he hit all twenty targets and then stood in the center of the course until the time ran out. Mariana's heart sank. If he had achieved a perfect score, then there was no way to beat him. Lenora could only tie. Would they be allowed to share a visit with the queen?

Lenora held the penultimate spot and came charging out of the tent with determination. The crowd went silent. As the hourglass flipped, she launched herself onto the field. Hands flying, she knocked out four targets in the first eight seconds.

Every part of Mariana seized with anxiety. Beside her, she felt Nohea and Sunev tensing as well. Lenora hit her fifth target…her eighth…her twelfth—her grunts of exertion the only sounds that proliferated in the enclosure. All the while, Mariana's eyes darted back and forth between her flying crimson hair and the trickle of white sand.

She was doing better than every other contestant beside the kaicat man. *Thirteen. Fifteen. Nineteen.*

The last target was at the very end of the field, but there was so little time left. Lenora wouldn't make it. She couldn't possibly. She leapt up into the air as she pulled back the bow. Just as the last grain fell, Lenora released the arrow and tumbled to the ground, rolling to a stop.

The crowd gasped.

And then cheered.

The arrowhead had sunk straight through the hay target.

Mariana felt like she might explode, the pressure in her chest slow to release. She wiped sweat from her brow, then turned to Nohea, who grabbed her in an embrace, his arms tight about her shoulders. Sunev looked relieved, turning away from the competition as if she couldn't watch any longer.

The last competitor didn't do nearly as well, and now there remained only Lenora and the kaicat man, who had *tied*.

The woman who guided the competitors away, stood before the crowd. Her vibrant yellow dress swung around her like the petals of a sunflower as she walked. She smiled and bowed politely to the queen and her company. Mariana noticed now that the queen was staring at the two remaining competitors with a look of shock and mild outrage. She'd recognized Lenora.

The sunflower woman spoke while Nohea translated in a whisper. "In the event of a tie, a final round of sudden death is necessary. The competitors will stand at one end of the field with a simple target before each of them. They will take turns requesting the distance at which they'll shoot until one of them fails to make their mark."

Lenora and the kaicat man were led to the far side of the oval. As she didn't speak Wikang, Lenora looked more than a bit confused. But once a hay disk target on an easel was set twenty paces from each of them, she understood. The man went first. He sank his arrow easily through the center. Lenora did the same, her poise and calm returned to her.

The kaicat man called out.

"Him say forty paces," Sunev translated.

The targets were moved back twenty steps.

Again, they loosed their arrows. Again two marks, though Lenora's was somewhat off center. It was her turn to call.

"Fifty paces!" she announced. There was a bustle of confusion as the crowd waited for someone to translate. Another person was brought out, a translator for the field workers. He relayed Lenora's request and the easels were moved an additional ten steps. Now at fifty paces, the targets were half a field away from Lenora.

The kaicat man raised his weapon. He took aim, his body rigid and precise, and let his arrow fly. The tip pierced the hay right on the line separating the center from the first ring. Lenora took her time, breathing calmly in through her nose and out through her mouth. Mariana watched her tense before letting the arrow slice through the air.

It sank with a thud into the second ring. She was safe. The crowd cheered again.

This time, the man looked at his challenger with a mischievous grin. He gave a loud command that sent the audience into a flurry of discussion.

"He says one hundred paces," Nohea explained.

"What?" Mariana stared in disbelief as the field workers jogged out to the easels. Sure enough, they doubled the distance between the targets and the competitors. Though she was far away, Mariana could see Lenora's expression turn visibly shaken. One hundred paces? They'd practiced that distance maybe a few times, but her ability to hit a target from that far away was questionable. She was first.

Lenora nocked her arrow. She closed her eyes, breathing for a moment as a breeze swept across the field and brushed the loose strands of hair out of her face. When Lenora opened her eyes again, Mariana saw determination. The arrow flew.

It stuck at the very edge of the hay disk. Any farther off center and it would have missed the mark. Mariana felt like her knees might give at any moment. Her palms were sweating, but she didn't dare unclasp them. She could only watch.

Although he didn't look scared, the kaicat man had obviously expected Lenora to miss. He glowered at her as he nocked his own arrow. When he fired, his arrow found the mark, but it landed in the third ring, one away from the outer edge.

Now it was Lenora's turn. She didn't speak for a long time, judging the distance between herself and the easels. Mari hoped she would be confident enough to suggest another large bump, anything to intimidate the kaicat, but how much further could they go until they were beyond the range of the recurve bows? As it was, they'd reached the end of the oval and were threatening to move into the space beyond the opening in the canvas barrier.

"Ninety-five paces," Lenora said.

As her request was translated, her challenger scoffed. He took aim even before the workers had finished moving the targets. With a smug smile, he let his arrow fly and it sailed away from him at lightning speed. All heads turned to follow its swift progress, searching for the place where it would land, watching the target for its point of entry, for the slick thud that would signal his success.

Instead, the arrow sailed just over the top of the hay and implanted itself in the back of the head of a retreating field worker.

The man gave a short cry, his dark blood spurting out where the arrow tip protruded from his forehead. After a brief stumble, he tumbled forward. Dead before he'd hit the ground.

The crowd groaned, all eyes quickly turning back to the kaicat man, who stood frozen at his release. As his failure dawned on him, his expression of cocky confidence fell. He rounded on Lenora with veins bulging on his neck and forehead, but didn't move.

The other field hands scrambled from the field.

Lenora wordlessly lifted her bow, took aim, and released.

Her arrow landed in the first ring.

The audience erupted into cheers, jumping up and down to celebrate her victory—the unfortunate death forgotten for the time being. It didn't seem to matter that Lenora was a foreigner who didn't speak their language. The adrenaline of the match flowed through them. Mariana watched the queen applaud calmly, though her face was a mask of distaste. Her husband muttered something in her ear which the queen didn't appear to appreciate, but she continued to applaud reluctantly.

Prepare for our meeting, Your Highness, Mariana thought. *You cannot avoid us again.*

~

After reuniting, they lingered in the field until a representative with a paper invitation approached them. On it were instructions to meet in the Lily Palace at sunset, though the four went straight there, not wanting to attend any other events.

When it came into view, Mariana couldn't help but stare. The Lily Palace was unlike any other place she'd encountered. All the grand buildings in Faron were made of stone with tall, painted glass windows, steeped roofs, and balustrades. In contrast, the Lily Palace was sprawling—a wide cluster of round buildings constructed of bamboo. Each of these buildings was topped by a domed roof made to look, Mariana realized, like the bud of a flower. The largest stood at the forefront, noticeably bigger and more decorated than the rest. Sheltered walkways connected the round segments, winding this way and that between trees, rocks, and foliage. As far as she could tell, the Lily Palace was built to celebrate artistry, and the only word that came to mind to describe it was *entrancing*.

As the sky darkened, a couple dozen other individuals gathered in the largest bud. Mariana assumed these were the day's contest winners. She waited as each in turn was invited into the counsel room to meet with the monarchy. The winners and their guests were invited in chronological order, which didn't bode well for Mariana's patience.

"We're going to be here all night," she said, taking a seat on an oversized violet cushion.

"Perhaps longer," Nohea agreed, though he smiled as he said it.

Lenora took a seat as well, her face still glowing from her victory. "It might not take too long. I imagine most people just want a congratulations."

"So long as them don't upset her none," Sunev said. She remained standing.

"That'd be preferred," Mariana mumbled.

"Do you think the Queen herself hands out the prize money?" Lenora asked.

Mariana watched each group take their turn, the crowd in the antechamber thinning slowly as the minutes ticked by. Each time the attendant returned, he softly beckoned to the next group and they disappeared through the double doors at the other end of the room. Mariana sighed. Spotting a table against the wall with a pitcher of drink and glassware, she grabbed a cup and poured herself some of the orange liquid. Her first gulp was much too large, and she coughed as the liquor burned her throat.

"Pogtat," Nohea said, grinning.

Their last challenge was to figure out how to approach Queen Yiscel about their request. Sunev and Nohea had to do the talking, unless the queen spoke Luso, which wasn't entirely impossible. As a member of royalty, Mariana guessed that she'd learned at least some of the major languages. The common tongue was the most spoken dialect in the kingdom of Faron. Mariana would be hard pressed to imagine that the ruler of the island nation had never interacted with the granite throne before.

She supposed the best strategy would be to act with humility and respect. They'd have to control their tone of voice—even if the conversation was not going their way—and always remember to flatter the queen as necessary. She imagined the even-tempered Nohea would have no problems with this, but Sunev and the queen might clash. Once they'd described the situation, however, Mariana didn't see how anyone could deny her. The fates of hundreds of thousands of innocent people were at stake.

Outside, the vermillion sky darkened to inky black. When there were only two other groups left waiting in the hall, the attendant summoned them. He led them next door to the throne room, where sat Queen Yiscel, her husband, an advisor, and a selection of guards and handmaids. Mariana reasoned they must be beneath the center of the flower bud, for the ceiling stood high above them and came to a point above the monarchs. The queen and the king sat in bamboo thrones wearing headpieces made of light wood and inlaid with gold and colorful gems. High on the wall behind the thrones, an arched window foretold of the night beyond. As she drew closer though, Mariana realized it was not an ordinary window. A vibrant array of stained glass formed the shape of a flower: a blossoming jasmine.

The queen's advisor spoke first. She chose to communicate in Luso, not bothering to wait for them to request a change of language. "Queen Yiscel Baquiran congratulates you on your victory in the archery competition. As a reward, you are presented with two hundred Piloncito to commemorate your triumph."

One of the handmaids came forward with a violet pouch that they presented to Lenora. She took it, staring down at the money with hunger and pride.

"She also hopes you've enjoyed your stay during the festival. Not many outsiders experience this vibrant display of Kailonese culture."

"Please, thank Her Majesty for us," Lenora said. "The Flower Festival has been a tremendous experience—there's been an overwhelming array of things to see and do."

The advisor smiled and nodded. She looked ready to dismiss them. Now was Mariana's chance.

"If it pleases Her Majesty," Mariana began. "We were hoping to have a word with the queen."

At this, Yiscel erupted into a fast stream of Wikang, turning in her seat to face her advisor.

"The queen is disappointed that you would soil your companion's moment of victory. She remembers you from the storytellers' tent, where you and your friends ambushed her. She was hoping you would not attempt to do the same here."

"Please," Mariana said, stepping forward. The reaction was immediate. The guards assumed attack positions, converging on her. The handmaids drew knives from their skirts, ready to defend their beloved ruler. Mariana only clasped her hands together. "I need help! My people are under the leadership of a tyrant. His hold over them has resulted in rampant poverty and danger for everyone. Only months ago, my home was destroyed. I lost almost my entire family. I was sent here to ask you—no, to beg for your help. Please." Mariana sank to her knees on the throne room floor. "Your people are kind and generous, but also strong. If you supported our rebellion, I know you could help us overthrow Fogosombre."

Sensing she was no longer a threat, the queen's defenses relaxed. The handmaids sheathed their knives and the guards resumed their watch from either side of the dais. Mariana had seen the queen's advisor place a hand to her chest upon hearing that Fogosombre had killed her family. The gesture had not gone unnoticed by the queen. Mariana felt a twinge of hope. If she could convince the advisor, that was a step in the right direction. She didn't want to break the eye contact she held with Yiscel, so she hoped that Lenora, Sunev, and Nohea had struck similarly humble stances.

Around Yiscel, her own people looked to their leader, unsure of her judgment. Mariana had expected the advisor to translate, but she said nothing. Instead Yiscel spoke.

"You say you need my help," the queen said. "Why do you not go to the other realms on your own continent?"

"I volunteered to come here and ask you," Mariana said.

"A foolish endeavor."

"Fogosombre's reach is wide—he has spies and supporters in all the realms surrounding Faron. Please, I've seen your ships in the harbor. I've seen how formidable you can be."

"Quiet," Yiscel said. "Why should we help you? Faron has never been kind to the Kailon Islands. Because our lands are small, they think we are small."

Mariana bowed her head. This wasn't going the way she'd hoped. "I cannot speak for our leaders, but I wish to speak for my people. We would never look down upon you. To tell you the truth, I did not know of your existence—"

"Typical eastern ignorance."

"But now that I know, I see how beautiful your lives are. How inspiring! We only want relief. We would be eternally grateful."

The queen played with one of the rings on her fingers, a garnet jewel whose hue made Mariana think of blood.

"A queen cannot simply involve herself in the struggles of another country. "That would be an act of war."

Mariana wanted to scream. She'd lost her home, her family, her twin. She hadn't come all this way to be refused.

"I feel great sorrow for your people," Yiscel continued, though her stoicism did little to convince Mariana, "but I have heard tales of this Fogosombre. I know how he usurped the throne twelve years ago. I know of his cruelty, his reputation. For these reasons, I cannot involve my queendom."

"You're afraid of him."

"I understand where my priorities must lie."

"Then you condemn us!"

"I will not trade the deaths of my people for the lives of yours."

Mariana opened her mouth to rebuke the queen, but as she did so, the king stood. All eyes turned to him in surprise, including his wife's. His gaze swept over the pleading visitors before settling on Yiscel.

"Do you remember, my love, when I had you install that window?" He pointed to the stained glass overhead. Then faced Mariana, a smile on his kind lips. He seemed to be the opposite of the queen; soft-hearted and warm. "You cannot tell now, but in the light of day it is vibrant. I cannot begin to describe how it paints the floor there."

"What about it, Ilocoy?" Yiscel asked, her lips pursed.

"I had you install it because I saw it first as a boy."

The queen rolled her eyes. "Not this again. Please, spare me."

"Perhaps you will grant just one more retelling?" Ilocoy asked. He continued without waiting for a response. "When I was a young boy living in my family home on Sampaguita, I loved to explore. Impetuous to a fault, I roamed the hills of my home and swam out into the Nieves Sea, separating Kailon's beauteous islands. The older I grew, the more I pushed my boundaries, swimming farther and farther out into the waves.

"I was bitten by a water snake one day, off the coast somewhere I'd never been before. A poisonous snake that caught me off guard. I was terrified, but there was nothing I could do. I could barely make it up to land, the pain was so great. Knowing I was going to die, I collapsed on the shore and woke up in a house.

"Of course, this was almost more terrifying: awakening in a strange house after passing out from a snake bite. I didn't know where I was, who was with me. But the window in my room was made of stained glass with that exact picture. It calmed me, made me feel at peace. I thought I might be okay, because what evil person could own something so beautiful?

"I was right. The one who'd found me was a boy by the name of Rizaldo Florenzia, who took me to his mother, Rosalind. She was a healer, he said. She remains the kindest person I've ever met. The woman nursed me back to health. Day by day, she took care of my every need, cooking for me, washing me. By the time I was strong enough to walk again, her son had found my parents and returned me to them." The king stared at the dark window for several long seconds. "I asked that the window be installed here, because I hoped that whoever came to the throne seeking help would always find that same kindness. A reminder that, were it not for Rosalind's mercy, I would not be here today."

He finished and nodded at Mariana before sitting down, a small smile firmly in place.

All eyes turned back to the queen who seemed physically distraught by his anecdote. Grunting in frustration, she threw up her hands. "Dammit. This business of soft-heartedness will be the end of you."

"Does this mean you've changed your mind?" Mariana asked cautiously. She knew she shouldn't have lost her temper with the queen and kept her voice at a softer tone as best she could.

"No," Yiscel said plainly. "Setting foot on Faron with warriors would set Fogosombre's forces against us."

Mariana sighed, angry and defeated.

The queen pointed at Mariana, who still knelt on the ground before the dais. "But my heart goes out to your people. Perhaps I am growing sentimental with age. I will allow you *two* ships, and the necessary crew to sail them. I will grant your refugees sanctuary, but only if you bring them under the utmost secrecy. If you return with Fogosombre on your heel, I will turn you away and claim the ships were stolen. Better to lose a pair of ships than thousands of Kailonese lives."

Mariana searched for a response. This was not the help she had hoped for, but it was better than nothing.

"Your words have moved me," Yiscel said. "Do not make me regret my decision."

~

Mariana stared out over the harbor at Banguet City, darkened ships bobbing in the water by the light of the moon. Though the sun was long gone, she'd never felt such light in the darkness. A part of her mind—the part often so quiet it could only be heard when she was most still—marveled at where she stood. A world away. In a different land she could only dream of before. If her parents, if Helena, were sitting together in Paradise watching her now, she hoped they were proud. No, she was not bringing an army to fight Fogosombre, but she was bringing refuge. She would make sure to save as many as she could.

Her hand went to the chain about her neck, the pendant that hung by her heart. Maybe her mother and her brother had been right in some sense. The necklace wouldn't protect her—it couldn't fight off any enemies—but it reminded her of her family. That was comfort enough for now.

Mariana had been promised two ships with crew, and that was what she would receive. Until then, she could stay at the Lily Palace. Nohea had been all smiles after the conversation with the queen. She'd asked him if he wanted to accompany her on the voyage home, her mind full of hope. But much to her disappointment, he refused, saying he'd been away from his brother for too long, and Ramil would fire him if he didn't go back to Pauwe. Mariana's companions from the *Flaming Virtue* were nowhere to be seen, but that was to be expected. Though she had hoped they would stay, she recognized there was nothing in it for them but danger.

Part of her was happy just to be headed home, a part that filled her with guilt whenever she acknowledged it. She was meant to be part of a group—several folk traveling from Corva sum Rio, not just her family. Now, it seemed very likely she was the only one to have survived. Why her? What factor had singled her out?

Mariana knew the visit would be brief; perhaps less than a day on land even, but stepping on her own soil would bring comfort. Breathing the air she'd breathed all her life might clear some of the anxiety that had permeated her mind since they'd fled the ruins of Corva sum Rio. It would be an invaluable luxury. One that she should be sharing with Arsenio.

Footsteps approached.

"Them the ships, yeah?" Sunev asked.

She nodded at the two vessels in the harbor.

"That's them." Mariana

"Certainly not the *Flaming Virtue*," Sunev scoffed.

Mariana smiled. That was true enough, though she didn't think it was necessarily a bad thing. Below the gold sails which fanned out like fish fins, each ship had two exposed decks for passengers or rowers. Outriggers extended over the water from either side, and as far as Mariana could tell, these too could be loaded with either supplies or people. Unlike the ship she'd ridden to Kailon, there was no exclusive cabin for the captain or privacy for that matter, but perhaps the streamlined dedication of space would be better for transporting larger numbers of people.

"The captain would shit him pants to see a Gold Sail so close. How many of you are there?" Sunev asked.

"Too many for one trip," Mariana answered, "but we will take as many as we can."

"Aye." Sunev put a hand on her shoulder. "That's the truth of it."

More footsteps. This time Lenora appeared.

"Both of you?" Mariana asked, the heaviness inside her lifting. "What about all that talk of taking your winnings and leaving?"

Lenora nodded. "Aye, that was the plan. But after hearing you argue with that Yiscel woman—Sunev changed her mind. She said the right thing to do would be to help you."

"You said as much yourself. Don't make lies none!"

Mariana laughed. "I got to you, did I?"

Lenora crossed her arms. "Don't think too much about it. Besides, there'll be plenty of time to spend my two hundred Piloncito—"

"One hundred!"

"My *one hundred* Piloncito once we've shuttled all your refugees back over here."

"I'll make sure of it," Mariana said, grateful beyond words that her companions had changed their minds. There had been such a flurry of new people entering and leaving her life lately, that having a couple familiar faces as allies was enough to reassure her. At last, some things were going right. At last, her efforts felt meaningful.

Kaori

The emperor was feeding Piko chunks of squash when Amaya entered the garden, walked over, and stood beside him. Kaori ran a hand along the sloth's back before the languid animal began its return into the foliage..

"Your Grace," she said. "You summoned me?"

"Yes." Kaori willed himself to remain calm despite the tightness in his chest. "I find myself in need of advice—or rather, I have a question that needs answering."

"In that case, my title might make me of use to you," she said, winking at him. They moved to a garden table in the shade of a maple tree. The star-shaped leaves were just beginning to appear again, shyly emerging now that the worst of the waning season was over.

"The question, Your Grace?" Amaya prompted.

Kaori sighed. "My thoughts are a bit scattered today. It's difficult."

"Of course, this happens to the best of us. Only yesterday I was headed for the baths when I became completely turned around. I found myself in the dungeons instead. That took a bit of course correction." She smiled and shrugged at her folly.

Kaori appreciated the gesture, but it did little to ease his tensions. "I suppose it's best to cut straight to the issue."

Amaya nodded.

"I—how is the search for the one who hired the Jade Dagger progressing?" Kaori asked, changing course in a rush. His stomach churned. *Coward.*

Amaya frowned, no doubt aware of his last second redirection. "Why, the situation hasn't changed since the update three days ago. Nothing has been discovered for certain, but the search continues."

"Oh, that's—that's good," Kaori said absentmindedly, too busy goading his lips to obey his mind.

As expected, his Head Advisor surveyed him with suspicion, her eyes narrowing. "Surely, you remembered that. Is there another, more delicate matter the emperor is hesitant to discuss?"

Kaori cleared his throat. It was now or never. *Do not be a coward.*

"Actually, yes. I've done a bit of digging in the Halls of Heritage. My search yielded nothing, but perhaps you'll know better. To your knowledge, has an empress or emperor ever taken a spouse of the same sex?" His heart was racing now. Kaori hoped she couldn't see his hands shaking. He lowered them under the table anyway.

His former kumo's smile disappeared. She eyed him warily, her mouth flattening into a thin line.

"This is an unusual question, Kaori," she said. "One the emperor needn't ponder."

Kaori forced out a laugh. It rang false even in his own ears. Inside, the pressure continued building. He could feel perspiration beading on his brow. "Yes, but for the sake of knowledge."

Amaya clasped her hands in her lap, looking down at her thumbs. Her mouth remained thin and straight. Hurt welled up inside Kaori. He'd never seen her cross before, especially not with him, but there was no mistaking her expression.

"It has not been done," she said.

Kaori's disappointment was palpable. He hadn't realized how hopeful he'd been for his advisor to tell him the opposite. But now that she'd given her response, a hollowness opened within him. He wished he could take the question back. He'd known, prior to his inquiry, that romantic involvement between two men or two women was unlawful in Nokara. The gods frowned upon such entanglements. But he also knew that these things happened in secret, whether they were allowed or not—fleeting trysts in dark alleys or the hazy rooms of certain brothels—and some people would turn a blind eye to them. He'd never considered such circumstances might apply to himself, but in recent days, he'd caught his own mind wandering into dangerous territory, and couldn't deny the desires of his heart. This was only exacerbated by the push to find him a wife, which continued to yield poor results.

Amaya sighed. "You shouldn't bother yourself with such thoughts. The issue is simply that we haven't found you the right woman."

"I'm the emperor," Kaori said, as more of a musing than a proclamation. "Can I not deem it appropriate?"

His advisor and friend pursed her lips again, but now she seemed almost fearful. She chose her words carefully. "We haven't had a male emperor in five successions," she said. "And that string of five female leaders introduced an era of prosperity and peace previously unknown to our realm. Not only that, but each of them had already lived for twenty name days by the time they were elected.

"I don't mean to doubt your capabilities, I merely report the opinions of the people," Amaya said, and she looked at him with concern. "And the people are wary. They question whether or not you will be good for the empire, whether you can live up to the legacies of those who came before you, not in the least your direct predecessor.

"You ask me my advice, Kaori, and I give it to you freely as someone who wants not only what's best for your people, but what's best for you. I would advise against breaking traditions at this time. No matter what your mind is telling you. Ignore it, and the thoughts will pass."

Ajira appeared, striding toward them at a steady pace. *Elegance and power.* Kaori held out a hand to her, and she rested her chin upon it. Purred when he scratched at her fur. He wished he could erase the entire conversation. Start over at the place when Amaya first entered the garden. His heart was heavy, and a sickening feeling was building in his stomach that made him wish he was alone. The implications of what he'd just admitted to both his advisor and himself weighed heavily upon him. What hurt more was that at the very least, he'd hoped Amaya might comfort him about his desires. She hadn't. Far from it.

"I hear you have taken to playing the flute again," Amaya said, attempting to refocus the conversation elsewhere. "The shinobue is a magnificent instrument."

"Thank you for your advice, *Akedi* Amaya," Kaori said. It was ridiculous to keep calling her "kumo." She was no longer a teacher at the Academy. He used the formal title instead, and watched her expression twitch. "I think I would wish to ponder my thoughts alone now. I desire some meditation."

"Of course." Amaya stood and bowed to him, then left the garden without another word.

Kaori had half a mind to do exactly as he'd suggested he would. After all, he knew the root of his inner turmoil now. He should confront it through mindfulness and hopefully find the strength to move past his errant desires, come to terms with what was right and proper. But another part of him had other ideas. Ones that elicited sparks of excitement within him. He knew the excitement was fleeting, and that soon, it would be replaced with even greater guilt and perhaps despair, as it did most nights, but the idea was too alluring.

He wished to visit the man he'd rescued. *Arsenio.*

Kaori stood and darted back into the palace, careful not to take any well-traveled corridors.

~

Inside the infirmary, all was quiet. Because the weather had improved, someone had opened the windows, allowing cool air into the room, along with the sweet smell of the Rising Season—when the coldest days of the year had passed and the dormant foliage came alive again. Arsenio's bed was the third down, a curtain drawn on one side to shield him from sight. Kaori knew the man had asked for it to instill some sense of privacy, but the emperor wished it wasn't there. He didn't want to wake him if he was sleeping.

He drew level with the curtain and tried listening for any sounds of movement: rustling, an irregularly timed breath. But he heard nothing.

"I am awake," came the foreigner's lilting voice.

Kaori stepped back, feeling guilty.

He stuttered, switching between Nokaran and Luso. "I'm sorry, I don't mean to bother you."

"Your presence is not bothersome, you may come in," Arsenio said, as if he were in a room Kaori could enter. Kaori stepped around the curtain. The man was sitting up in his bed, propped on pillows. His robe hung open in the front, so that Kaori could see the bandages wrapped around his torso. There were considerably fewer than before. Underneath, the skin peeking through appeared smooth.

"I came to check on your well-being," Kaori said, averting his gaze. Guilt flared in him again.

"Where is your cohort?" Arsenio asked.

"I asked my guard to wait at the door."

"Ah, then you are not alone." Arsenio smiled.

"I'm never alone," Kaori replied. He tried to gauge Arsenio's view out the window from the bed. He could see treetops and not much else. That was a shame. Looking out from the infirmary would have given him a view of Moeru Garden, brimming with plants of warm colors like the flaming silver pieris and the camellia.

"Has the pain subsided?" Kaori asked.

"Some," Arsenio said. "I still cannot walk, but I can breathe and laugh now without cringing."

"I am glad to hear of it."

The man seemed to realize himself, cleared his throat, and donned a more formal demeanor. Kaori didn't understand half of what he said next, but he caught the last few words: "gracious host, Your Highness."

"Please, just Kaori."

"Do any of your advisors refer to you as such? They are much more noble than I."

"They don't always listen to me," Kaori said with a crooked smile. He wished Arsenio could speak Nokaran. Translating in his head made him slow to answer, and he never knew whether he expressed himself adequately, but Arsenio didn't seem put off by anything he said. Taking a chance, Kaori sat on the edge of the bed, though this was highly improper. The gamble paid off. Unacquainted with their customs, the foreigner didn't register scandal. "But you are correct in thinking their nobility exceeds yours. Therefore, you *must* listen to me."

"Oh?"

"And I demand that you refer to me as Kaori."

Kaori let his gaze fall briefly to the chest still peeking between the fabric. In the shallow valley of his sternum, Arsenio's skin was amber brown and unblemished. Inviting. Kaori snapped himself away again, inwardly admonishing his eyes for betraying him.

"As you wish, Kaori," Arsenio said. "You are unlike any ruler I have known."

"You have met many rulers?"

"No," Arsenio admitted. "I've lived through a couple, though I'm only old enough to remember one. I know others through their actions."

"In what way am I different?"

"For one, you're quite approachable." Kaori's chest swelled with warmth at this analysis. "I've only known kings who stand upright and never deign to look you in the face. They're surrounded at all times and dictate from a throne and—"

"I'm surrounded at all times and have a throne," Kaori interjected.

"And yet you sit on the end of my bed," Arsenio said.

Did the man jape with him? This foreigner was either arrogant or bold. Kaori couldn't decide which it was. Either way, he found he didn't mind.

"How else would you compare me?"

"You're also much younger. Though, I wouldn't guess your age."

Kaori nodded. "Here in Nokara, our emperors are elected by council from a pool of candidates. Even by our standards, I'm young. I was elected in my eighteenth year."

"And how old are you now?" Apparently, he *would* hazard to ask.

"Eighteen, still," Kaori said.

"Then your appointment was fairly recent?"

Kaori nodded. He wondered how old Arsenio was, and if the difference in their years changed something about the way the young man saw him. *How long will my youth be of concern to those around me?* Kaori wondered. Would it be until he was twenty? Thirty? Or, perhaps people wouldn't stop eyeing him skeptically until he was Empress Mai's age when she died.

"I'm sorry," Arsenio said, blushing suddenly. "I tend to say too much when I'm nervous."

So he was nervous?

"You have a beautiful palace," Arsenio said. "And a beautiful country, though I haven't seen much of it."

"Neither have I," Kaori replied before he could stop himself.

"You haven't?" The foreigner raised an eyebrow. "If it's not too forward to ask, how can that be, if you were made emperor?"

"To become emperor, you needn't be well-traveled as much as—what is the word—*knowledgeable* in the empire's heritage, and the way it operates," Kaori said, feeling a little defensive.

"It probably wouldn't hurt, though," Arsenio said, struggling to mask a grin.

"You're quite impertinent today," Kaori said. "Perhaps I've granted you too much familiarity."

"My apologies again, Kaori." Arsenio raised his palms in a gesture of peace. "I've been fed many medicines as of late."

"More excuses." Kaori smirked. He liked that the man was willing to press his boundaries. It was refreshing to have someone doing so besides Taigen. Everyone else fell at his feet the moment they saw him. Even if they were more relaxed, such as with Sugi or Amaya, he could still feel them measuring their words before speaking.

"I was raised here on the palace grounds. In the Academy. We're selected to attend at a young age and taught how to be leaders," Kaori explained.

"You lived here?" Arsenio asked, looking at his opulent surroundings. "Your whole family moved?"

"No."

"You came on your own?"

Kaori nodded.

"And how often do they visit?"

"We are made to let go of our kinships. Our parents aren't allowed to visit us after we're honored with selection. That's why we don't carry family names," Kaori said, reciting the lessons that had been repeated to him since he was young. "Familial ties inspire problematic loyalties that can usurp the motivation to serve the people."

"None at all?"

Kaori shook his head.

"Do you remember them?"

"My family?" Kaori considered the question. He'd never given it much thought, as he generally agreed with the doctrines regarding kinship. The problems that followed familial loyalties were all over the historical texts. Still, there came times when he had flashes of his life before. Faces that jumped out of the fog. He'd been so young then. The memories were little more than ruins. "I don't remember much."

"And that doesn't bother you?"

"No, I have made friends here."

"I can't imagine life without my family."

They were silent for a time, enough that Kaori could make out the wind whispering through the barren trees, looking for the leaves to regrow. While the world outside was still cool, the change of seasons had made themselves known.

"Where would you go?" Arsenio asked.

Kaori looked to him, confused.

"You're the Emperor—you can be well traveled too now. Where would you most like to go?"

Kaori needed only a brief moment to decide. "There's a famous flower in Nokara known as the, uh, how can I translate... the 'snowdrift vines,' because they grow in intertwining pairs, and their blossoms hang like falling snow, pure and white. We often compare things to these flowers when we want to emphasize splendor.

"Snowdrifts are very rare in Nokara—most actually grow outside the empire, in the Taischon Mountains to the north. That's where I would go. I want to see them on the mountainsides, growing together. The sight is said to be breathtaking."

"That sounds like a very worthy choice," Arsenio said. He smiled, and Kaori knew whom his heart wanted.

Ira

She could hear the bells in the church tower ringing, even though the church was nearly half the city away. The tolls added their anxious melody to her percussive footsteps on the stone floor.

Ira Marchosias wore a long green dress, which she held up in the front to keep the hem from catching underfoot. Each of her fingers were decorated by rings: some gold, some copper, some adorned with precious stones. Her face was constructed of sharp lines that met at angles and emphasized her stern expressions. She kept her pitch-dark hair half up, so that it fell straight down her back, but never over her shoulders.

This afternoon, Ira had little patience for anything. She'd left her husband standing in the courtyard of Desiderio the Dreadful, raging beneath the fountain where the conqueror's massive stallions wept into a pool. Things were not progressing as Fogosombre had hoped, and when Fogosombre was unhappy, she was the first to know. She could only stomach his irascibility for so long before she no longer trusted herself to be in his presence.

Instead, she went to the Tower Archives.

She mounted the steps to the entrance just as the bells ceased their chiming. As the sound died, Ira was surprised to hear voices conversing inside. Her frown grew, and her hollow cheeks deepened. Without having to say a word, the guards at either side of the entrance pushed the doors open for her and she swept inside.

The curved walls of the tower were stacked endlessly, with bookshelves reaching up toward the ceiling some hundred feet above her. Spindle ladders on wheels climbed the shelves. They were thin enough that by the top they were indiscernible from the wooden bookcases. In the center, beneath the point of the conical roof, a wooden banister cordoned off a raised platform covered by plush red carpet. Atop this were arranged several desks piled high with open books and shuffled papers.

A man sat at the desk in the middle, a thick tome open before him, though Ira could clearly see he paid it no attention. Instead, he was focused on a young boy, her son Fernão, who sat across from him with one leg on the tabletop.

"…and I thought they were only armor, but Ma Eliana says there are skeletons inside," her son was saying, talking animatedly with full use of his hands. "Imagine that: dying inside your suit, and nobody takes the time to pull you out and bury you. How will you reach Paradise then?"

"Have you looked inside one yourself?" the man asked casually, as if it were his place to suggest anything to the boy.

Fernão considered his question for a moment, raising a hand to his chin. His sleeve slid away from his wrist, revealing a bronze cuff embossed with western characters Ira couldn't read. She bristled at the sight of it, appalled that her son, inheritor of the Granite Throne, was adorned in the prisoner's foreign language.

"No," Fernão said, "but I don't want to see a skeleton."

"Then how will you know if Ma Eliana speaks true?"

She'd heard enough. Ira's anger flared, though she mounted the dais steadily.

"Fernão, my love, what are you doing here?" she asked, a thin smile curling her lips.

The boy twisted around to look at her, his face full of fright. The man, realizing his predicament, straightened in his chair and looked down at the book before him as if he were deep in study.

Satisfied, Ira strode to her son and ran the back of her thumb across his youthful cheek. The boy had signs of both her and her husband in him. He was thin in body like her, but his face was broad and square, like his father's.

He seemed reluctant to answer. "I was only talking to Otohiko."

"Hmm," Ira breathed, eyes flicking to the man across the table. "I was unaware you visited Otohiko."

"The guards outside never told me I couldn't," Fernão said, though he wouldn't make eye contact. They both knew the guards would not refuse Fogosombre's only son—not unless they had been threatened by Fogosombre himself to do so. She held Fernão's chin between her thumb and forefinger, turning his face toward her.

"You know Otohiko is *very* busy doing work for your father, don't you, darling?" she asked. She held him there until the boy's gaze flickered to meet hers. He had his father's eyes. How unfortunate. Irritation bubbled in her chest.

"Yes, I know," he muttered.

"Then maybe you shouldn't be bothering him." She grabbed Fernão's wrist and held it up. He tried to yank it from her grasp, but it was too late. "What's *this*?" she asked, lacing her calm tone with a threatening air. She twisted his arm to view all sides of the cuff. The dull metal was warm from the boy's skin.

"It's nothing."

"Where did you get it?"

"Otohiko gave it to me."

She released his arm—nearly threw it down onto the table—and her son slid to his feet, backing away so that he was out of reach. Ira rounded on the seated man. Every time she had to look at him, she was reminded that he wasn't from their land. He was a foreigner with almond eyes and peach skin. Even his hair was different. Though it was black as ink like many Faroni, it was silken and fine instead of thick and wavy.

"Did you give that to him?"

"He was interested. It was just a trinket—"

"That is not what I asked."

The man froze, his head bowed. She could see that he wore several bands on his right arm, but his left was bare. After a few moments of silence, he turned his face up to look at her. Ira delighted at the hatred in his eyes, the loathing he kept for her. "Yes, I gave your son the cuff."

Ira smiled. "We have been very gracious and patient with you, Otohiko. We could have locked you in a cell while you worked, but instead we have allowed you to roam this tower freely."

The man nodded. "I am grateful for your generosity."

"I had hoped, however," Ira continued, "that you could keep from being distracted by a child."

Otohiko's eyes flicked to Fernão, who stood behind her. His gaze was one of apology and regret. "The fault is mine," Otohiko said quietly.

So he thought she would punish the boy and wanted to take the blame instead? Ira didn't know what to make of this. The man's misplaced loyalty was laughable, but it meant he and her son had spent far more time together than she was aware.

Regardless of the anger the man meant to suffuse, Ira would talk with Fernão later.

Otohiko finished his apology, "I will not let it happen again."

"Good." She had half a mind to hit the prisoner, but she didn't want to mar his face. He was, after all, a handsome man—made more beautiful when he looked at her fearfully. She wore a joyless smile. "Come with me," she said to her son, beckoning him to follow her out of the room.

But then the door of the tower burst open again.

The room seemed to darken. Ira's hand fell to her side as her back straightened. She faced the doorway. Only one other person could enter the archives unannounced.

His heavy boots echoing across the floor, Fogosombre Marchosias swept into the tower. A black cape draped his shoulders like the leathery wings of a bat, just barely trailing the ground. On any other man, the cloth might have dwarfed him, but Fogosombre Marchosias was no other man. He stood a head taller than anyone else, no matter who was in the room. His black hair hung, slick and oily, down the sides of his face. His round eyes were ringed with gold, and all along his jaw and throat were black scars, as if someone had slit his throat many times and still failed to kill him—as if the flesh had been mended by shadow. If you stared too long, you might imagine the scars moving like snakes, writhing across his broad neck. He looked down upon his wife and son, disdain as apparent on his face as his pointed nose.

In his wake, as always, trailed the sinister mavens, Vida and Morta. His Fates. The malevolent grins never left their faces, as though the two always knew some terrible misfortune would soon befall you. Before the door could shut, a last straggler came stumbling in, this one flustered and anxious: Ximeno, the advisor to the throne. He sputtered in Fogosombre's wake, trying to get the king's attention.

"You can't possibly mean to use it, my king," Ximeno said, running around in front of him.

"Be silent," The King commanded, not bothering to look at him.

"But, Your Majesty, the amount of damage—"

"You should know I don't like being told what I can and cannot do," Fogosombre said, fire simmering beneath his even tone.

"It is too far," Ximeno pleaded. Ira kept quiet, though she wanted to urge the advisor to step down. He should know better.

"Hold your tongue!"

"My king—"

"Ximeno!"

"Think of your—"

Fogosombre reached out with one massive arm, grabbing Ximeno around the throat. It was then Ira casually stepped in front of her son, knowing all too well what was to follow. His gold eyes alight, Fogosombre tightened his grip.

He lifted his other hand to Ximeno's mouth. The advisor clenched his jaw, shaking his head to keep Fogosombre at bay. But the king was too strong. He held Ximeno still and pried his teeth apart with his fingers. Ximeno's eyes bulged, sweat running down his flushed face. His jaw wasn't wide enough to admit Fogosombre's hand, muscle and bone straining against the intrusion. With an audible crack that resounded through the tower, his jaw dislocated.

Fogosombre's pleasure shone on his face. He leaned in close to Ximeno, who was crying muffled sobs, trying desperately to loosen the grip around his neck. The last thing Ira saw was the king's hand closing around the advisor's tongue. Then she looked away, not caring to see anymore.

What followed was a loud, anguished cry, the dull, wet tear of ripping flesh, and then Ximeno's silence. Perhaps he had passed out from the pain. Ira kept her gaze trained on Otohiko, listening as guards came to drag Ximeno away. Only when the tower doors fell shut again did she move.

Ira looked her husband in the eye, wary of his approach.

"My phoenix," he said, his deep, growling voice vibrating in her chest. He acted as though nothing had happened. "You left so swiftly. I hope I didn't scare you."

Ira didn't let her expression waver. "Why would you have scared me?" she said. Her jaw pained from clenching.

"My frustrations get the best of me sometimes. I know this"—he stepped up to her, close enough that she could feel the leathery cape against the back of her hand—"and you know this." She had to tilt her head as far back as it would go in order to continue looking into those eyes. They held this gaze until Fogosombre let out a hoarse laugh and swept away, going instead to their son. He ran a hand through the boy's hair, with the same fingers that had ripped Ximeno's tongue from his mouth, while he continued to address her,

"You left so quickly that you missed the good news."

So something had happened to brighten his mood? She should've known that was the case, his bouts of anger were usually much lengthier. Ira looked to Vida and Morta, but the two women were whispering between themselves, eyes glinting maliciously. If they'd been the ones to give the good news, she was sure they'd be gloating, which meant it came from elsewhere.

"What's happened?" she asked.

"Belinha says she has had a breakthrough. A glorious discovery which further proves Deus's favor shines upon me."

Belinha was Fogosombre's Chief of Sciences. For years, she had been laboring away to develop a mysterious weapon for Fogosombre, something very powerful indeed. Ira didn't know many of the details, though her husband bragged that it was beyond anything the known world had seen before. If Belinha had had a breakthrough, it could only mean that Fogosombre was closer to his weapon.

"That is good news indeed," Ira said, indifferent. She didn't want to grant him the satisfaction of emotion. Not when she was still irritated with him. Not when he'd bellowed in her face less than an hour ago.

"Fortune favors the Benevolent Leader," Vida croaked, her eyes full of admiration.

"His will is word," Morta hissed. They cackled in unison, as if knowing how much this annoyed Ira.

Fogosombre's brow darkened. In spite of herself, Ira shied away, half raising an arm to shield herself from him. Flames danced in his eyes. The thirst for power, for conquest, ran as deep in him as blood. She could see cities falling before him, crumbling to the ground under his great weapon. This made her pulse quicken. He couldn't be denied. That had always been true.

"Come with me, my wife," Fogosombre said. He placed a firm hand across Ira's back, driving her away from the dais. She glanced behind her to where Fernão looked on and the prisoner kept his head down, scribbling furiously on a sheet of paper. If only she'd been faster to leave, she might've made it out of the tower with her son before Fogosombre arrived. As if sensing her thoughts, her husband called out, "My son."

Fernão hurried after them, drawing level with his parents just as they reached the doors.

"Yes, Papai?" he asked.

"You should not be with the prisoner. If he slits your throat, then I will have to do the same to him, and I'd rather not have to find someone else for his task."

"Yes, Papai," the boy said, looking ashamed.

Their son was dismissed by way of Fogosombre's disinterest. He disappeared into the stony corridors with a new purpose in his pre-adolescent mind.

Fogosombre led Ira through Braecliff Citadel, down the lengthy hallways, into the depths of the structure. The stronghold had long been Faron's capital, nestled safely in its infamous alcove, surrounded by cliffs of solid, impenetrable granite. The only way in and out of the citadel was through the city. Legend told of tunnels carved into the cliffs as a means of quick escape, but knowledge of their entrances had long since been forgotten, probably caved in by centuries of shifting earth.

They emerged onto a sheltered walkway, a stone wall to one side and open arches onto an interior courtyard on the other. Above the turrets and pitched rooftops, Ira could make out the surrounding cliffs looming over them.

"I'm inclined to believe there's more you wish to say." Ira's heart sank when she noticed the Chief of Sciences waiting for them in the courtyard, a torch in her hand. She thought the fire a bit unnecessary. Though the afternoon waned, daylight was far from gone.

Belinha Gaioso had pure white hair she kept just long enough to tuck behind her ears. Although she could only be five or six years older than Fogosombre, her face had begun to show signs of age. The corners of her mouth sagged into a permanent frown and crow's feet had etched themselves into the corners of her eyes.

Fogosombre stepped down into the courtyard. "Vida and Morta have divined the location of yet another resistance outpost."

"Yes, indeed," Vida said, pressing against Ira's left side.

"A sizable one," said Morta, appearing on her right.

Ira grimaced and extricated herself from their grasp. She longed to swat them away like flies, but like most, held the superstition that should she upset the Fates, they would foresee her downfall.

"Really?" Ira said, descending into the courtyard. "And where is this one?"

"Red Cliff," Fogo said. He swept to his Chief of Sciences, holding out the palm of his right hand. Belinha looked wary, but she knew it was better to give the king what he wanted, even reluctantly. Ira had assumed she would hand him the torch, but instead she brought a small black rock out of her pocket.

Fogosombre held the rock up to the light, eyeing it with great excitement, a hunger Ira knew from only his worst achievements. The same look as when he'd wiped Corva sum Rio from the map. He spun on the spot and tossed the rock into the dry fountain at the courtyard's center. Then he snatched the torch away from Belinha, who protested.

"You can't, sire! It'll burn—"

"Out of my way," Fogosombre roared. He lifted the torch high above his head and in one swift movement threw it down atop the black rock.

There was a flash of white light and a loud, sharp roar. Ira shielded her eyes with her arms and had to turn away, gasping in surprise. The courtyard was igniting! Something had gone wrong.

Around her, she could hear dirt and pebbles raining from the sky. A few hit her arm, though no piece was large enough to do more than sting.

When the rain stopped, Ira opened her eyes. She peered out, heart pounding in her ribcage. *What was that?* It was as if the whole courtyard had spontaneously caught fire. She could still feel the heat on her skin, and her ears rang from the sound.

Belinha lay on the ground, shielding the back of her head. She shook with fear, whimpering softly at Fogo's feet. The king stared at the spot where the fountain had been but moments ago.

The fountain! In place of the sculpture only a shallow crater filled with chunks of rubble remained. One large piece of the basin lay several meters to the left, and another several meters to the right, but the rest of the fountain had disintegrated into shards of debris no bigger than the tip of Ira's little finger. How could that be? That fountain had been made of solid granite. It had stood unblemished in the courtyard for a hundred years. Yet somehow, the rock Fogosombre had thrown had reduced the fountain to pebbles.

"Behold," Fogosombre said, enjoying his own presentation.

"But you just…How did you…" Ira couldn't get the words out.

"It's made from black chalk mined in the Urse Mountains," Belinha explained, rising slowly to her knees. "Mixed with extract from an olive tree."

"I call it Shadow Fire," Fogosombre proclaimed.

I call it death.

The rock he'd thrown had been so small and yet it had caused enough damage to destroy a fountain large enough that she could've lain comfortably inside. Imagine what he could do with more. She kept repeating to herself, *The rock had been so small. The rock had been so small.*

"The Red Cliffs," Fogosombre said, "may not stand for much longer."

The rock had been so small.

Suddenly, she understood why Ximeno had protested so.

"How much have you made?" Ira asked, looking from her husband to Belinha, who was only now getting to her feet. Blood trickled down the side of her head where she'd been struck by flying debris. "Is it hard to get?"

"The black chalk takes time to mine," the Chief of Sciences said. "Veins are easy to miss and even easier to lose, and they must be extracted carefully, but we should have enough for a healthy display of power."

Ira looked to her husband. She'd willed herself to calm, but the vision of the sudden explosion kept replaying in her mind. Such instantaneous destruction had never been heard of before, not from a human at any rate. The savage races who kept polytheistic religions spoke of gods with violent, destructive powers, but very little evidence suggested that those stories were anything but the myths of heathen minds. This…this was something different. Fogosombre was no god, of that she was certain, but he held in his hands a power which separated him from mortals.

While he sketched his plans, Ira lingered against the arches of the portico, wondering what this meant for herself and for her son.

Queen Yiscel

The doors creaked as they swung open, making Yiscel grit her teeth. She'd hoped not to be noticed. She'd gone down to the inlet again to visit Harana, and the cool sand still clung to her feet and her sandals. Yiscel had sung to the serpent, one of the folk songs that every child heard growing up in Kailon. An ode to the homeland: the provider for the people.

From the sands of Medinilla, to the reefs off Aster's coast
The sun will shine upon you and blue waters will you boast
From the rains of Sampaguita, to the trees of Mauhele
May your neighbors never leave you and in glory may you stay
My love for you, my love for you
Is what I'll hold inside
Until I say farewell and join
The waters of your tides

The great beast had lingered long enough to listen to her whole song, and when she finished, dipped back into the Endless Ocean. Though her friend had gone, the song remained with Yiscel, its melancholy stirring her spirit. Even now, she hummed softly to herself as she came to stand in the center of the throne room.

This was where her subjects stood, looking up to the thrones on the dais. Her eyes gravitated overhead to the stained-glass window. When they lit the torches in the throne room, the window was dark and dim, but now that the only light came from the moon, she could make out the image. The colors washed out in the pale glow so that the picture appeared only white and gray, the blossom and that which surrounded it.

The door behind her opened.

In walked Ilocoy, Locaya, and Mo'one, an abrupt end to her solitude. But their presence was not unwelcome. After allowing herself one last moment to consider the stained glass, Yiscel turned to face her company.

"We were hoping we might find you," Ilocoy said, hands clasped behind his back. His smile was bright and cheerful.

"And here I am," Yiscel said. "Why have you sought me out?"

Ilocoy chuckled. "Not for anything so formal."

"We merely wanted to see how you fared," Mo'one said. He shut the door and joined the others in the center of the room.

Yiscel allowed herself a smirk. "You should all know there's no need for that."

"The past few days have been eventful," Locaya said. That was putting it lightly. The confrontation with the trio of Eastern women, summoning two ships from the royal fleet, and gathering the supplies and personnel to crew those ships mere days after the Flower Festival had been feat of sheer determination.

"Nothing your queen cannot navigate." Did they think her so soft? She had handled strenuous situations before and never had her company come to sidle up beside her. Surely they would think this situation no different.

"Yes, but these are uncharted waters, Your Majesty," Locaya continued. "Kailon doesn't have many dealings with the east, let alone ones that might stir conflict."

"And yet you were all practically begging me to take in the refugees," Yiscel said, "if I remember correctly."

"We mean no insult, my blossom," Ilocoy assured her, palms raised to offer peace.

"Not all of us were campaigning for that particular brand of generosity," Locaya said, her tone even.

Yiscel faced her advisor, an eyebrow raised. "Are you suggesting that you would've had me take some other course of action? I don't remember you saying as much at the time."

"Her Majesty's decision is the law of the land, but no, I wouldn't have advised that you engage in any manner with Faron," Locaya said.

Pity she didn't say anything, Yiscel mused. Maybe she'd made the decision rashly, but at the end of the last day of the Flower Festival—having seen and greeted every champion—she'd been a bit blindsided by the request. Rather than putting it off for another time, she'd made her promises then. Perhaps her judgment had been affected by exhaustion, perhaps her mind had been softened by her husband's pleas for kindness. Whatever the case, while she didn't regret her decision to help the women, the possible consequences gave her pause.

"Well," Yiscel said, "perhaps you should have *advised* me then. My mind had been wrung of fortitude, of obstination, and of patience. All I had left was pity."

"I am sure the people of Faron will feel indebted with gratitude."

"I don't want their gratitude. I want peace," Yiscel said.

"Which brings us to another matter," Ilocoy said, stepping forward. "Where do you mean to put them?"

The queen had not yet come to a decision in this regard. In fact, while the ships were prepared for the journey, she'd belabored their return many times. Ideally, the refugees should be brought to Banguet. She was, after all, the one graciously hosting them. The problem was that Banguet was the most populated of all the islands, and wedging thousands of people into the city was bound to create overcrowding. Her people might not take kindly to the sudden, permanent appearance of outsiders in their home.

Medinilla was the obvious second choice. It was the largest island. In addition to its dense jungle—portions of which would require clear-cutting to be made habitable—Medinilla boasted sprawling fields sheltered by the inland mountains.

The only trouble was that Medinilla was the farthest major island from Banguet City. Yiscel hesitated to place the refugees somewhere she couldn't reach quickly. Sampaguita and Aster were too small. Ignoring the other interspersed dots of land, that left Mauhele.

Singobet was the largest city on Mauhele, with room on all sides for expansion. She'd put them there.

"Singobet," Yiscel said, looking each of them in the eye and searching for protest. She found none. Ilocoy smiled, Locaya nodded in reluctant agreement, and Mo'one stared back at her, impassive.

"The ships will be ready to sail tomorrow, I'm told," Locaya said. "Shall I inform them of their return port?"

"You may wait until morning," Yiscel said.

"As your Chief Architect," Mo'one said, "I will bring builders to Mauhele and oversee the construction of shelters for the refugees."

"Good," Yiscel said. "You may leave in the morning. We don't have time to waste."

Locaya looked at her husband and took his hand. Yiscel knew she didn't wish to see him leave, but his absence couldn't be helped. He was needed in Singobet. Their separation wouldn't be for long, and he was only an island away.

"Now if that's all the business we need to discuss tonight," Yiscel let the sentence hang. Locaya and Mo'one bowed their heads respectfully and departed the way they'd entered, while the queen and king headed for their bed chamber.

~

Yiscel lay on her back, staring up at the ceiling and imagining the night sky beyond. The world was quiet, and the feather bed was soothing as ever, and yet, sleep would not find her. She reached over to where her husband lay and stroked Ilocoy's shoulder.

At first, she thought the gesture too soft, but then the man opened his eyes. A smile spread across his lips. Everything about him was so peaceful—his demeanor, his rationale. Even when his slumber was interrupted, he awoke without irritation. What must that be like? Was that why she'd chosen to marry him?

He rolled onto his side to face her. "My queen," he said softly.

"I cannot sleep," she whispered.

He ran a hand through her hair. She closed her eyes as the pleasant sensation spread across her scalp.

"Do your decisions haunt you?" he asked.

In the dark, his normally honey-colored eyes shone like black silk. She wanted to touch the peace they held, to reach out and pull from his gaze the understanding that allowed him to rest. *No*, she wanted to say; it wasn't this business with the refugees that kept her up. Somehow, she was still grieving the loss of her friend, the woman she only ever saw in person but twice a year. She wanted to express how ridiculous that made her feel, that the stranglehold this grief had over her was absurd and aggravating and made her want to scream in frustration.

At least, these were the things that she believed kept her up at night.

"You're doing the right thing," the king whispered, taking her silence for confirmation. He let his hand move down to cup the back of her head. "If you fought, you would bring your people to danger. But in this way, you are still helping."

"I know," she said. "I worry though. What if I've condemned them to danger anyway?"

"You love this land and its people more than anyone," he said. "I think your subjects know that. They'll recognize the generosity you're granting the foreigners."

She nodded, and suddenly she wanted more. Not for him to speak, not for him to guess at what troubled her. She wanted the physical. To be wrapped in his arms and to absorb him inside of her.

"Make love to me," she said.

He smiled and began to laugh until he saw how serious she was. "My blossom, the Flower Festival is over."

They had made love every evening of the festival—to celebrate its symbolism, she told herself. But that didn't mean they had to stop simply because the week was over. She slid until she lay on top of him, staring down into his eyes.

"Please," she said. "Make love to me."

"Of course," he said. "Anything."

And so they did, writhing on the bed until beads of sweat dripped down their skin and they gasped their quiet pleasure into climax. At the end of it, Yiscel rolled onto her back again, listening to her own breaths slow until she fell asleep at last.

CHAPTER SIX
AT THE RED CLIFFS

Kaori

Like gravity, the pull was undeniable. Every day, during any moment of free time he could squeeze from his duties, Kaori disappeared to the infirmary to visit Arsenio, lingering for as long as he possibly could without getting into serious trouble. When it was time for the foreigner to walk again, the emperor was there helping him to his feet. They strode up and down the length of the room together, Arsenio holding tightly to his hand as if afraid of falling. Even when his strides were steady and strong enough not to feel precarious, he clung to Kaori, who didn't mind at all.

On a handful of nights, when Kaori couldn't control the giddiness in his mind, he stole away to Arsenio's bedside. By candlelight, they'd chat into the early hours of morning. Kaori did his best to teach Arsenio Nokaran, while his friend helped improve Kaori's mastery of Luso. Arsenio had the worse end of the bargain. Having only learned one language his entire life, he struggled to adapt to the changes in sentence structure and to memorize the entirely new vocabulary. Yet, after a few weeks he showed impressive progress and could understand simple phrases.

Arsenio wanted to see the city of Black Tide Cove. He felt his rough introduction had been unfortunate, and maybe by Kaori's side, that impression could be changed. Kaori was struck nervous by the idea at first, wary of how that might look to his advisors and to his people—what was the emperor doing spending so much time with an undistinguished foreigner?—but he agreed, eager to expand their world beyond the infirmary.

So when the medic deemed Arsenio well enough to venture outside, Kaori arranged a trip into the city. Taigen and Sugi accompanied them in addition to the customary guard, though Taigen gave him a questioning look when Kaori first asked. Kaori explained that Arsenio had simply never been anywhere beyond his home village, let alone the capital of another empire. Though unconvinced, Taigen complied anyway, glad perhaps for the opportunity to spend time with Sugi.

The group left in the early morning, when the sun had just breached the horizon over the sea. They had to move slower than normal, not wanting Arsenio overexert himself.

The daily market was bustling when they arrived, the streets crowded with the usual throngs of vendors and shoppers. Kaori was familiar enough with it that he found more enjoyment watching Arsenio's reactions to the sensory overload than the market itself. At each stall, Arsenio would enthusiastically examine every object and inquire as to its purpose. Kaori gladly explained, though this became a troubling practice as lingering in one place for too long encouraged the vendors to harass them. Several times, the guards had to stand in between Kaori and a vendor who was too eager to sell crystal goblets to the emperor.

By mid-morning, Kaori had purchased for Arsenio a kikukarakusa robe, several steaming buns, a handkerchief with snowdrift vines embroidered in one corner, and a wooden shinobue from an old blind man who sold his wares in a courtyard off the beaten path. Taigen and Sugi joked that Kaori was doting on Arsenio like a grandfather on his grandson. Kaori also caught the cautious glances they exchanged when they thought he wasn't looking, but, though he knew he was displaying his affections too obviously, he was powerless to calm his impulses.

The worst came when they rounded a corner and met a squat, dirty woman selling liquids in glass bottles. Each liquid was of a different color, some bright and alive with energy, and some cloudy and swirling like fog.

"What is this one?" Arsenio asked, pointing to a vial with a deep scarlet liquid inside.

The woman drifted over to them, eyes alight at the prospect of selling to a friend of the emperor. "If you wish to pleasure your woman as she has never been pleasured before, then this is just what you need, my friend," the woman said, not realizing that Arsenio couldn't understand her.

"What did she say?" Arsenio asked. He couldn't possibly get any closer to the crystal bottle without pressing his face against it.

The woman chuckled; she couldn't understand Arsenio either. She turned to Kaori. "Your friend must have a strong lust. This is oil to sweeten the acts of love. No more painful, dry penetration. Midako has added her own kick as well, to spice things up." The woman winked at him, and Kaori felt his face burn. He wished nothing more than to drag Arsenio—who was still oblivious to the conversation—away from the stall. But it was too late. Taigen's barking laugh preceded his arrival.

"Interested in sexual lubrication, are we?" he asked, nudging Kaori's arm. "Have you found a woman after all? Taking my advice and bedding her first?"

"Taigen!" Kaori hissed. He didn't think his face could get any hotter. In fact, he could feel himself beginning to perspire.

"Don't worry," Taigen whispered, though it was loud enough that Kaori was sure Midako, the vendor, could still hear them. "We have much better oils in the palace. Ones that won't give you a rash."

The vendor exclaimed indignantly at his implication.

"Do you have to be so crass?" Sugi asked, rolling her eyes.

Taigen backed away from the emperor, looking somewhat ashamed. "Not that I would know, of course. My partners have always been able to produce ample lubrication all on their own."

Unable to take any more of this topic, Kaori grabbed Arsenio by the arm and led him away from the stall. Taigen and Sugi made to follow, bickering over the moisture quantity of Taigen's previous exploits, when Kaori called over his shoulder, "We'll reconvene later. I wish to show Arsenio the Temple of the Four Winds."

"Alone?" Taigen asked.

"We'll have half the guard," Kaori said.

"Are you sure?" Sugi asked.

"Completely," Kaori mumbled as they fled the alley, Arsenio at his side looking highly confused.

~

They walked through the city until the crowds began to thin and even the temple, with its tower piercing the clouded sky, stood behind them. Kaori had been looking for an opportunity to split off from his advisors, and seized the chance when it presented itself, but he realized he was moving too fast for Arsenio to keep pace. Though he tried not to let his distress show, the man was panting and listing to one side.

Kaori slowed.

"Where are we going?" Arsenio asked, fighting to breathe normally.

"I thought we might like a change in scenery," Kaori said.

"Are we going outside the city?"

"No," Kaori said, spinning on the spot. He hadn't given much thought to where they were headed, only that they should do so with minimal accompaniment. Arsenio seemed to realize this, for he snorted at Kaori's dance of indecision.

"You're making this up as you go along, aren't you?" he asked.

"No, it's just…I'm—well, yes. Alright, maybe I am, but to be fair you only expressed an interest in seeing 'the city.' And that's not very specific, is it?"

"So now you're shifting the blame to me?" Arsenio shook his head. "Typical. Any man with power sees himself as blameless."

Kaori took a chance and hit him playfully on the arm. Arsenio's mouth opened in shock. "And now I'm being assaulted by the emperor himself. I don't know whether to feel ashamed or honored."

"Well, then," Kaori said, unable to mask a grin. "Where would you have me take you?"

Arsenio raised his head, accentuating his slim neck and prominent chin. He peered between the buildings that surrounded them, checking the roof-lines visible through the many alleyways.

"That one," he said, pointing. "The large one sticking up over those trees."

It took a second for Kaori to figure out which building he meant. He cocked an eyebrow. "That one with the square roof? That's the Halls of Heritage. I don't think you want to go there."

"Why not?"

"It's nothing but a collection of wealthy families' heirlooms and corpses."

"Corpses?" Arsenio looked surprised, but not discouraged.

"Yes."

"Well, that doesn't seem so bad. It's like a graveyard," Arsenio said.

Unable to find a good reason to refuse—and wanting to give Arsenio whatever he asked for—Kaori complied, leading the way through the city streets until they stood beneath the grand arches of the Halls of Heritage. They stared up at the monumental structure. In Black Tide Cove, it was second in size only to Kingfisher Palace, and second in age as well. Guards stood watch at all hours of day and night, protecting the treasures within from thieves and vandals. When they saw the emperor, his guest, and his protection, however, the guards stepped aside to allow them through.

Inside was a maze of grand chambers, each dedicated to a particular subject or an influential family, Kaori explained.

"When the capital was moved from Shondai to Black Tide Cove, Empress Kuriku considered moving the Halls of Histories as well. That was a sanctum for Nokara's past, an archive of the stories and dealings of the empire. However, Empress Kuriku ultimately decided not to move the sanctum and opted instead to build the Halls of Heritage.

"It's meant to be a living preservation of our culture. Scholars submit everyday items or record important happenings. Likewise, the bodies of every ruler of the empire are kept here along with accounts of their achievements."

Arsenio stared up at the granite walls and ceiling. Porcelain urns dotted the corridor, each hand-painted to recall historical events. After a minute of transfixed silence, he turned to Kaori. "Do you mean to say you'll be kept here someday?"

"Someday, yes," Kaori said. "And hopefully with a long list of accomplishments to my name."

"I don't doubt."

Kaori grinned, then continued his explanation. "But scholars and historians aren't the only ones to decide what's kept in here. Influential families may also lay claim to a chamber if they can argue the significant impact their line has provided the empire."

They entered a room labeled Gaya.

Kaori watched Arsenio marvel at the mounds of artifacts inside. When it came to the family-owned chambers, their organization was hit or miss. Some families took great pride in their displays—even though few people could enter the halls—and stacked everything inside neatly on shelves or in cases. They brought few items: only those which they felt were most important in portraying their legacy. Other families threw everything into the room that had the slightest chance of being useful. They treated the chamber like a storage facility, housing everything from a mother's broken chair to the ring a great-great-grandfather forged for his wife to earn her favor. The Gaya was a family of the latter kind.

"They have everything in here," Arsenio said, peering at a messy stack of papers piled high on a desk. He couldn't read the text, though he glanced at the top page with interest as if he might understand. He moved on to a black jewelry box with green mountains and cherry trees painted on its faces. Arsenio tried to open it, but it'd been locked.

At the next stack of refuse, Arsenio gasped, recoiling in surprise.

"Is that...?" he asked.

"Yes, a deceased family member," Kaori replied.

In the place of another table stood a casket. Wood framed the edges, though each face was mostly glass, allowing a clear view of the body inside. She'd been a middle-aged woman, long black hair beginning to show signs of intruding white. Clusters of silky white flowers lay across her black dress. She could've been sleeping, her face delicately arranged to resemble a peaceful rest.

"She must've just died," Arsenio said. "It can't have been more than a few days."

"The Halls of Heritage are infused with a subtle magic," Kaori answered, eyes still transfixed on the woman before them. "The wood of the casket comes from Tamashi trees—I believe they grow in the east too, though they're known as marshwood there. They have special properties of preservation."

Arsenio looked up at Kaori, somewhat horrified by the news. "You mean all the bodies in here look...*fresh*? Forever?"

"Yes."

"Even the emperors?"

"Yes."

"Forever?"

"So long as the magic remains intact."

Arsenio went silent, turning back to the woman's still form. He contemplated her for a minute longer before taking Kaori by the hand and leading him out of the room. Shocked by the gesture—in sight of his guards no less—Kaori allowed himself to be led without resistance. His heart fluttered. They navigated back through the corridors, passing the painted urns one at a time until they crossed the threshold into the light of day.

Once outside, they slowed, Arsenio breathing hard again from the exertion. He led them away from the entrance, to a copse of trees encircling a bench off the path.

"*Anaguro, mitsuane.* I'm sorry," Kaori said as Arsenio released his hand to sit on the bench. "Should I not have taken you in there?"

"No, I was the one who asked," Arsenio said.

"I knew what was kept inside. I—I could've refused." Kaori sat beside Arsenio. The guards didn't enter the circlet, standing outside the ring of cypress trees to keep watch. "I apologize for disturbing you."

"I'm not disturbed."

"What troubles you then?"

"I..." But Arsenio couldn't seem to find the right words. He squinted against the sunlight, staring up at the swaying tips of the cypress pointing toward the heavens as so many things seemed to do—the arrowhead mountains, the pitched roofs of the buildings, the tower of the temple. "I'm simply amazed by what is afforded different people, different cultures.

"I lost all my family and will never see them again. Not until I die and enter Paradise, at least. If there is a Paradise. I'm not so sure of that anymore. Meanwhile, someone here who is wealthy can keep their loved ones perfectly preserved, can visit them and remember every line on their face any time they choose to. Yet they pile books on their casket and tuck them behind stacks of refuse instead."

Kaori didn't know how to respond. He wanted to apologize to Arsenio though he wasn't the offender, wishing he knew how to wipe the look of distress off his face. He was strikingly beautiful, even in agony. His pain was Kaori's sadness.

"Thank you for showing me the city," Arsenio said.

"I could've chosen better activities."

"No, really. I appreciate it all. We've covered more ground today than I ever did back home."

"Any time you wish."

"At the very least, my impression of Black Tide Cove has successfully been changed, though that wasn't too hard a feat." Arsenio smiled, though Kaori could tell his thoughts still tugged at him.

"I'm glad of it." Their eyes met. Kaori had never sat so close to Arsenio before. Their legs touched. His thumb briefly brushed the back of Arsenio's hand. "I suppose we should head back to the palace."

Arsenio was no longer looking at his eyes, but at his lips. "Not yet," he whispered. This man was so gentle, so polite, and yet so bold at the same time. The privacy afforded by the trees was not complete enough that they should feel comfortable this close, but Kaori couldn't remember any words to call off Arsenio's advances.

And so they kissed.

Kaori could've wept if he allowed himself. A hundred scattered pieces fell into place within him, assembling a portrait of what his life was meant to look like. Giving answer to the questions he'd kept buried inside. This felt right. This felt like the answer. And then a great sadness overcame him, because he knew it couldn't be.

A tear slipped out of the corner of his eye. He hoped Arsenio didn't see it.

When they finally pulled away, too late and too soon, they were both smiling.

"Now we may return to the palace," Arsenio said.

~

They reconvened along the main road with Taigen and Sugi, who were oddly quiet. Kaori wondered whether he was being paranoid or if his advisors had been discussing his and Arsenio's disappearance. Oddly enough, he found he didn't mind much. An airiness had permeated his entire being. He couldn't stop looking over at Arsenio, who more often than not looked back at him, and they'd both smile sheepishly and turn away. So what if two of his advisors suspected something? They were both his friends; he'd confided much in them before and they'd yet to betray his trust. Why should this be any different?

Well, I have never done anything unacceptable before.

He squashed the thought, finding himself staring at the man beside him once again with a halfwit's grin across his face. When could they kiss again? Tonight, Arsenio would be moved to a different room in the palace since he no longer needed the infirmary. Kaori couldn't wait to steal away to him by night. To kiss him again and maybe hold him this time, the way he imagined in his mind.

They entered through the gates, the great teal Kingfisher Palace looming over them against the sky. As they mounted the steps, a rush of bravery overcame Kaori. He wanted to hold Arsenio's hand. Before he could act upon his impulse, however, a voice called from behind them.

"Emperor Kaori." It was Kento, his arms folded into the sleeves of his long violet robe. A look of utmost solemnity straightened his mouth into a thin line. "I might have a word with you, please."

Kaori looked between his advisor and Arsenio, who'd understood enough to know that something serious was amiss.

"I must show Arsenio to his new chambers," Kaori said.

"I'm sure," Kento said, bowing his head, "that someone else might manage to do the same. Surely, there are more important things on the emperor's agenda than showing a foreign civilian to his bed."

Kaori's face fell. He had no argument to make. At least, not one that would satisfy Kento. The man stood at the foot of the steps, one eyebrow cocked so high that it might've been a part of his hair were he not balding. His heart sinking, Kaori nodded.

"I will take him, Your Highness," Sugi said. She continued up the steps, gesturing for Arsenio to follow her. The Faroni man looked back at Kaori before complying.

Kento didn't move until they were out of sight, then he mounted the steps. "Your Grace, it has come to my attention that you may be entertaining certain ideas that are—how may I phrase this delicately—*uncouth* for an emperor to consider. No. Maybe uncouth is incorrect. Shall I say *immoral?*"

Kaori felt his face reddening. He looked over at Taigen, but his friend would not return his gaze.

He stammered, "I don't know what you mean, Kento."

"I think you do."

"I don't know who you—"

"I had a talk with Amaya. She seemed rather disturbed by your implications and wasn't quite sure how to proceed. Of course, I've noticed myself. We all have. You aren't exactly discreet. I told her I would speak to you."

"Kento, I don't think—"

"Please, don't make me say it, Your Majesty."

"I'm not—"

"You cannot *fuck* men," Kento said, his tone sharp and gravelly. For the first time, Kaori wanted to reprimand someone for the lack of respect in their tone—he was the emperor after all—but his shock at the blunt utterance rendered him speechless.

"Kento," Taigen said, a warning that carried no weight.

"My apologies," Kento said dismissively. He cleared his throat and straightened his robe, then gestured for them to continue up the steps toward the palace. "I find that cutting to the heart of matters best intercepts them before they become problems—and certainly before they become disgraces."

"He is my friend," Kaori said, though he knew his continued denials to them and himself were useless.

"You are fooling no one. Your Grace." Kento added the title as an afterthought. "And I think the sooner you come to realize that, the easier this all will be. For the sake of the gods, he's not even one of us. He's a *foreigner.* Think of what that alone would mean to your people."

Kaori kept his eyes trained on his feet as he climbed from step to step, Kento's harsh words echoing in his head. He couldn't fuck men. Of course he knew that—he'd heard Amaya allude to as much. He knew it was frowned upon, even illegal—though there were always whispers of those who participated in such deviant entanglements. But he was the emperor. If he was held to such high esteem, and the throne carried as much power as everyone seemed to think it did, then why was he being browbeaten for his own desires? Would he really be removed if he declared a change? He wanted only to hold Arsenio, to kiss him again, be with him as lovers were. That wasn't such a bad thing.

His throat ached, holding back tears.

"I cannot help what I feel," he said. He looked at his advisors. Maybe part of him was pleading.

At his admission of guilt, Kento's features were stern, reproachful. But while his disappointment carved guilt into Kaori's conscience, it was nothing to how Taigen's expression affected him. Kaori saw confusion, hurt, and even a flicker of disgust. That he couldn't beg then and there for the chance to defend himself to his closest friend suffocated him. His lungs felt too small, his chest constricted.

"Maybe not," Kento said, "but you *can* help how you act. Perhaps you should spend some time with Taigen."

"Me?" Taigen asked, surprised to suddenly find himself the subject of conversation.

"He knows enough whores. Perhaps he can find a cunt skilled enough to sway your unnatural interests."

Kaori had come to a halt, but Kento continued moving up the stairs until he was passing beneath the black doorway and disappeared into the palace. Kaori teetered on the edge of emotion, unsure whether he wanted to stay frozen there on the steps until the night covered him or if he wanted to escape to his own secluded area of the palace. Either way, he couldn't remember a time when he'd ever felt so ashamed of himself, so completely embarrassed that he contemplated whether he shouldn't simply throw himself over the banister. Taigen stood beside him, but Kaori was too afraid to look at his friend. The disgust Taigen had shown was haunting.

"Kaori," Taigen whispered.

Not prepared to hear another lecture, Kaori turned and walked swiftly into the palace, both relieved and distraught that Taigen did not decide to chase after him.

Emilio

The white blanket seemed too thin a barrier to protect Davi's body from the elements. Although Emilio sat behind the witch woman, holding to her waist as the horse trundled along, he'd spent most of the journey looking back over his shoulder. Every bump in the road made him cringe, made him want to hop down to check that his brother's body hadn't been damaged. Even just to make sure that it *was* still Davi's body beneath the blanket. But the witch woman had said he couldn't lift the cover or the preserving magic in the marshwood blanket would be broken.

They'd traveled for many days, a journey of firsts for Emilio. For one, he'd never been on a watercraft much larger than the fishing boats he and his father took offshore. Yet, he found himself spending multiple days aboard a ferry crossing the mouth of the Moor sum Portes. He'd never left the arid Iron Peninsula, and yet, there he was stepping foot on the lush green shores of Port Esperancia—only miles from the capital. The witch woman had secured them a horse for travel then, and a cart for his brother's corpse. They'd continued from there, riding through the endless forest beside the Urse River.

Needless to say, he was now farther from home than ever before.

The other matter which weighed heavy on his heart was the guilt he felt at having left his mother. She didn't know that he'd defiled his brother's grave—such an act may have been too much for her to take—but he knew he couldn't leave without saying goodbye. So he'd crept into the house, after returning from the market, his mind still rife with doubt, and found her sitting in her bed chamber hunched over a map.

"Mamãe," he'd said. She spun to face him, eyes bloodshot with heavy bags hanging from the lower lids. She'd looked almost surprised that he was there, too consumed by whatever project occupied her mind. Sadness nearly wore him down then, but he'd already given the witch woman permission to uncover his brother's casket.

"What is it?" she asked. She wasn't angry. No, she seemed frantic. This didn't scare him. He approached her, reaching out to touch her shoulder.

"Nothing," he said. "I only wanted to let you know I'd returned from the market."

"Did you find everything I asked for?"

"I did. The items are in the kitchen."

"Thank you." Her features had broken then, eyes squeezed tight to dam the tears. Grief had reduced her to a shadow of herself, a shell of the woman she'd been before. Seeing her weep for her lost husband and son, Emilio felt a stiffening resolve within him. He *had* to go with the witch woman. He had to know who'd done this to his family—who'd brought his mother so much pain. He wouldn't be able to sleep soundly until he did.

Mamãe had leaned forward then and wrapped her arms around his neck, pulling him close. In his ear, she'd whispered, "I love you so much, Emilio."

He'd held her back, squeezing as tightly as he dared, staring past her at the window. Determination filled him.

"I love you too, Mamãe," he'd said. "I'll be back."

She'd held him at arm's length, her brow furrowed. "Where are you going?"

"Just to the field." And suddenly, there'd been tears on his face. "I want to watch the sun set. It reminds me of Davi."

"Of course." She'd let him go.

His heart had broken as he'd left the house, hoping he hadn't said goodbye to Mamãe for the last time. With each sunset that followed, Emilio wondered if maybe he should've told his mother where he was going after all. She would've done her best to stop him, he knew, but she might've relented in the end. He may have even been able to convince the witch woman to let her come along, but it was too late for that now.

Instead, weeks had passed with only the witch woman as company. He didn't dislike her, but he found her very strange. With another companion, he might have grown friendly over the course of a fortnight, but, while the witch woman was never unkind to him, she didn't speak much unless to give necessary direction. She never gave him her name, though he'd asked several times. Besides her initial explanation of their quest—a bewildering description of disturbing mysticism he didn't fully comprehend—she'd remained uncommunicative of further details.

He knew they were headed for the Quartz Basilica, that she was a member of the Holy Order, a Magistrata. Though the Magistrata didn't typically cover their faces, she refused to remove her scarf. What they were going to attempt had something to do with a Graylife. She gave him some explanation, but the particulars eluded him.

Beyond that, he had to rely completely on faith.

Faith that he wasn't headed into danger. Faith that he hadn't defiled his brother's grave for no reason. Faith that the witch woman could deliver on her promise.

He'd never relied much on faith before.

~

When he opened his eyes in the morning, she was already awake.

The witch woman handed him a torn chunk of bread. "Eat. We will reach the Quartz Basilica before the sun sets again."

"We will? We're close?"

"As close as a day's ride," she said.

His eyes went to Davi, to the white blanket.

And then I will see my brother alive again. Or at least, as close to living as he'd ever be. The witch woman sighed as if understanding the thoughts running through his mind. He knew she'd discourage him from this view of the preternatural ritual, but he couldn't see the difference.

"Just remember," she said, "you mustn't force an interaction with him."

"But I *can* interact with him?" Emilio asked, hopeful.

"It's possible." The witch woman chewed a mouthful of the bread and swallowed, avoiding eye contact with him.

"The soul will be reluctant to talk to you because it senses you are not of its realm, but with focus you can convince it to interact." She slid another piece of the bread under her scarf, and Emilio waited for her to swallow, his mind wrapped around the idea of conversing with his brother once more. "But we are here to observe the course of things as they happened. The moment you influence the Graylife is the moment it deviates from the path."

"Which means—"

"It'll make decisions it didn't have the chance to make in life." She contemplated the bread, but decided not to have any more, slipping it back into the pouch from whence it came. Emilio continued to nibble on the piece she'd given him. "If you talk to your brother before the murderer comes along, he might not be in the right place at the right time. The murderer may decide to stay away when they see he's missing, and you won't have the opportunity to discover their identity."

"The moment he deviates is the moment that what we view in his Graylife loses credibility and no longer reflects what truly happened."

"But I thought you said sometimes they deviate all on their own?"

"Sometimes, but it's much less likely without influence."

Did he want the murderer's identity more than a last conversation with Davi? Emilio considered this, wondering if the witch woman would feel he'd wasted her time if he simply altered the Graylife in order to tell his brother he loved him. But then another thought occurred to Emilio. If he talked to his brother, if he *influenced* his Graylife and Davi wasn't killed, could Emilio simply stay in the observing state, living alongside his brother in that mystical consciousness? If Davi survived his murder, there'd be no reason to leave.

Mamãe's face drifted into his mind. Though it would feel like Davi was alive, he wouldn't *truly* be alive. Their mother was. And she would be alone and grieving until Emilio returned. He had to go back, he had to tell her who'd killed their family so the both of them could seek justice and know peace.

"Alright," he said, nodding. "I understand that I can't interact with my brother."

"Good, then let us continue."

They arrived at the Quartz Basilica just as the sky pinked over the endless hectares of forest. The grand structure loomed ominously over them, stark pale against the black rock that surrounded it. Emilio expected them to enter through the front, but the witch woman led him around the side, where she tethered the horse. Then, she and Emilio lifted Davi off the cart, careful not to touch any part of him but through the blanket. The witch woman placed the boy's small frame in Emilio's arms. He paused, feeling his brother laid against him and wondering for the countless time whether he had the strength to follow through with their plan.

He carried the corpse through a side entrance into the basilica, his and the witch woman's footsteps echoing around the dark halls. Every time they passed another Magistrata, he averted his gaze, trying not to give the impression that he didn't belong.

Though his brother was small and light, Emilio was uncertain how long he could continue to carry his body. Emilio's arms and legs were already sore and stiff from the many days of travel, and their quick pace through the halls did nothing to ease his burden. The longer they went, the heavier the body felt, until he worried he might collapse under what had begun as a perfectly manageable load.

Finally, they came to a pair of doors that were guarded by two intimidating sentries. They came to a halt, Emilio shifting his weight in order to cling to his brother's body. Perspiration beaded at his lip and rivers ran down his spine. His muscles screamed at him to let go, but he fought against them. He could not drop Davi.

The witch woman muttered to the sentries something Emilio couldn't hear. They considered her words, exchanging a glance with each other, before nodding and allowing her to pass between them. Emilio ran after her.

"How much farther have we to go?" he grunted as they entered yet another long corridor.

"Not much," the witch woman said. She took a torch from the wall, her hands as steady as her gaze. Suddenly, they weren't alone. They were surrounded by a handful of other Magistrata, their hands pressed together at their chests, some chanting in a language that Emilio didn't understand, nor did he want to.

As a group they proceeded down the corridor to the doors at the far end. Fear and apprehension ate at Emilio. He was beginning to regret his decision to follow the witch woman here. Though he was eager to learn the identity of the murderer, the chanting made his blood run cold, and he was further unsettled by the inhumanly precise way in which those around him marched onward. He'd forgotten the weight of his brother's corpse, adrenaline compensating for the toll on his body. The Magistrata surrounded him, but surely if he ran, he could break away. If he caught them by surprise—

I'm sorry, Mamãe, he thought. He could only hope this wouldn't cost her anything.

They reached the doors at the end of the corridor. The witch woman reached out with her free hand and pushed them open. A wave of cold air wafted out of the opening. Emilio peered over the shoulders of those in front of him, trying to get a glimpse into the stairwell leading down into complete and utter darkness.

Mariana

The tile clattered to the table. Mariana eyed the quartet of bamboo symbols painted delicately in black. She tried not to let her expression falter. For a moment, she'd thought the tile had three symbols, which would have completed her triplet.

Bahala was next. She drew, a sneer plastered over her face.

"Nolie always plays *dirty*. You know? That's why I don't like to play with her," she said.

Although Mariana had begun learning Wikang from Sunev and some of the other shipmates who spoke the common tongue—which wasn't so common in these parts—she didn't understand enough to carry on full conversations. Thus, she spent much of her time with a group of older women sailors who obliged her by speaking Luso. They delighted in teaching her Mahjong, which they played after each day was done. Mariana had grown quite fond of the game, in which four players drew and discarded tiles to form sets or sequences. But it was really watching the three women banter that entertained her. Bahala continued her rant. "She is always trying tricky things, you know."

Nolie clicked her tongue. "Everything that comes from Bahala's mouth is lies—why you are always asking me to play then, huh? *Ng homali ke!* She's full of shit, that's why she smells."

"Ah! You both drive me nuts," Monina said, throwing up her hands. She turned to Mariana. "You'd better get far away from these two, *siban*. You are going to catch their stupid. Look—Nolie doesn't even realize it's her turn."

"Ha!" Nolie exclaimed. "How am I supposed to go with *this one* always shouting in my ear."

"Maybe I wouldn't have to shout if you could hear properly," Bahala said. She crossed her arms.

"I may be hard of hearing, but don't forget I've saved your ass more times than you can count."

Monina scoffed. "As if we all haven't done the same, Nolie. You are not so special."

"She's going to hang that over my head always. Even when she dies, they're going to say at her funeral, '*She saved your ass, don't forget.*'"

Mariana couldn't help laughing. This only encouraged the women, who she suspected, exaggerated their strife just a bit when she was around.

"Are you going to go or not?" Monina asked.

"Ha! I thought I was a liar. Bahala doesn't want to play with me, right?"

"*Bahala ke mikaha lo.* Do what you want. If you leave, we have to find another player."

Monina drew and discarded. Three bamboo! Mariana moved to take the tile.

Sunev came darting into the room, causing all four women to turn and face her.

"Mari," she said. "Land."

Mariana's heart leapt. She stood immediately, leaving the table without another word.

"*Siban,* but it's your turn!" Bahala called after her.

Following Sunev, Mariana hastened out of the room and into the waning sunlight. The cool wind whipped off the water, immediately misting her with the sea. Her hair flew about her face, lifted by the speed of the ship.

Outside, Sunev led her to the railing, where Lenora waited. The crimson-haired woman pointed ahead of the boat. Her solemn expression worried Mariana, who would've expected relief. She followed Lenora's finger with her gaze.

Ahead of the boat, the forested lands and towering mountains of Faron greeted their arrival, and Mariana felt a swell of homesickness. Even if her village was gone, this was the land she'd grown up in. Several months away had strained her sense of belonging, but it remained—thin, yet strong. Here, she knew the language, the culture, the buildings, the trees. She was no longer foreign on this soil.

For a moment, Mariana wondered why her friends seemed so solemn about their arrival. The answer came in the form of smoke billowing into the sky. The column rose, dark and ominous in the distance.

"The Red Cliffs, Mari," Sunev said. "Them that's burning."

"That can't be," Mariana said, eyes wide.

"It is," Lenora sighed.

Had Fogosombre found Afonso's Light yet again? That didn't seem possible. He couldn't have known.

Galina had said she'd be there. Mariana had brought help for the refugees.

Though they didn't alter course, the trio watched the approaching obelisk of black smoke with apprehension. Mariana said a silent prayer to Deus, hoping that they weren't too late but wary of what they'd find once they arrived.

~

Galina stood waiting for them at the docks, a grim expression on her face as she helped tether off the ships. Mariana made sure to be the first to disembark, jogging up to the stern woman with a heart full of apprehension.

"You came," Galina said, squinting against the sun.

"Did you get my sparrow?" Mariana asked.

"I did, but given the smoke, I was no longer sure."

"What happened here?" Mariana eyed the column of smoke rising before her as Sunev and Lenora appeared at her side.

"All in good time. Let me take you to the people first. We must start organizing them to board." She eyed the two ships, sizing them up.

"We can fit maybe three hundred," Mariana said. "We'll return for more."

"In three weeks?" Galina said. "Hopefully, they'll still be here when you return."

"It's the best I could do."

"I haven't seen ships like these before. Where are you coming from?"

"The Kailon Islands. These are a loan from Queen Yiscel." Mariana turned to her two companions. "I met these women on my journey. This is Sunev and Lenora."

Lenora held out her hand to shake, but Galina only nodded at the two of them, her lips pursed. "Thank you for your help. Now, we really must start loading survivors. The sooner they are out of the king's reach, the better."

She led the way up the ramps onto the shore. Surprisingly, no part of the docks seemed to be damaged, which meant the attack had probably come from land. To their right, the famous Red Cliffs rose over the inlet to the sea of Moor sum Portes. An older city which served as the main trading port with Faron's southern

Iron Peninsula, the brilliant cliffs were known to help sailors locate the harbor. The city itself once had a name Mariana could not recall, but over time, it'd been replaced by its landmark.

The farther they got from the harbor, the more damaged the buildings became. Streaks of black covered walls over shattered windows. Charred remains where structures had once stood lay in heaps upon the ground. The smoke in the sky emanated from the north end of the city, where flames continued to burn. Large chunks of the houses had been blown away. The damage was like nothing Mariana had seen before. She'd seen fire, but what could possibly do *that* to an entire row of buildings?

While they walked these parts of the city, Galina called out in the streets. People emerged from the rubble, from places Mariana couldn't imagine anyone hiding. Ash and dirt smeared gray across their skin, interrupted only by red streaks of blood. Some had burn wounds, their faces melted by the searing heat of the flames. Their clothes, once colorful with the vibrant patterns of Faroni textiles, were now tattered and soiled. Mariana saw villagers with missing limbs, children clinging to their fathers and mothers, devastated elderly. They flocked after Galina, Mariana, and the Kailonese sailors. Though Mariana heard the people talking to each other in low whispers, nobody spoke up to question Galina or the foreigners who had come to take some of them to safety. They only heard a message of hope. The chance to escape the ashes and smoke and shadow.

Mariana didn't know when she'd begun weeping, but her face was warm and wet, and she tasted salt on her tongue. The procession grew and grew until they were marching down the streets in a seamless crowd. Galina led them on a circuitous route back toward the harbor, along a short road where few others hid, and Mariana realized she did this so that the number of followers did not grow to more than they could accommodate. Yet Mariana wished they would continue combing the city, calling every villager out from their hiding places no matter how many or how wounded. She wished she'd been able to secure more transportation, perhaps fought harder with Queen Yiscel, so that she might take every last one of them with her here and now.

When they came around to the water's edge, walking along the quay with the docks in sight, the two Kailonese ships came into view, and Mariana felt a rush of excitement emanate from the congregation. She herself felt energized by their presence, tangible evidence of her contribution. She was helping them. She was helping her people.

In the harbor square, Galina turned to face the followers.

"The queen of the island nation Kailon has promised shelter," Galina said. "Should you choose to leave aboard these ships, you will have a place to live, safe from the horrors Fogosombre has inflicted upon you. But take a look around. Take a look at what he's done to you, to your families."

She paused, waiting as the crowd of refugees murmured among themselves. "Leaving does not rebuild what's been torn down. Leaving doesn't bring justice to those who brought you pain. And leaving does not vanquish the shadows cast over our homeland! I cannot make you stay, but I urge those of you who can, to remain here and fight with me. Join Afonso's Light and together we can overthrow Fogosombre. Together we can take back our lives."

Galina finished speaking and stared out at the crowd, her jaw rigid. Mariana watched as the vast majority of the people trudged toward the ships. The Kailonese who had come with her— including Bahala, Nolie, and Monina, who she could see at the end of the dock—organized them into lines for boarding. A few dozen remained, many fearful but stirred by Galina's call to arms.

When it was clear who meant to stay and who to go, Galina nodded. "There are tents at the base of the cliffs. Go there and you will receive instruction."

Mariana watched this group depart, wandering away from the port with a mixture of determination and uncertainty. She noticed others heading back into the city, most of them elders.

"Where are they going?" she asked.

"I suspected as much," Galina replied. "They've spent their whole lives in Faron. Leaving does not mean much to them, for they expect that they've already done the vast majority of their living. What has happened is terrible, but they'd rather remain than abandon the only place they've ever known."

"And what *has* happened here?" Mariana asked. She watched as Lenora and Sunev spoke to a father and his young daughter, most likely convincing them that the ships were safe.

"I'm still not quite sure." Galina turned away from the crowd. "This morning, I traveled up into the hills to send a sparrow. Even from afar, I heard the approach of soldiers marching toward the city, at least a hundred. They'd brought with them a catapult. I could see its hinge peeking out among the trees.

"I ran as fast as I could, *knowing* the troops would ravage the city, killing everyone they could find. Many of the survivors from Corva sum Rio followed me here—members of the resistance, yes, but also innocent people who had nowhere else to go—and it pained me to know that they'd survived one tragedy only to be attacked again. Although I wanted to believe that Fogosombre couldn't have known the rebellion moved to Red Cliff. I couldn't rule out the possibility. It's very difficult to hide light from the shadows.

"When I came out over the Red Cliffs, I expected to see a slaughter. Instead, I saw the soldiers standing at the edge of the city. They didn't break formation, they only made sure nobody left. The silence was terrifying. The stillness worse. Then they launched the catapult." She paused, watching several families pass them by. Mariana was amazed by Galina's ability to estimate the crowd. It seemed everyone who had decided to board the ships would fit. Despite those who had gone to join the rebellion and those who went back into the city, there would be very little empty space left.

"I have seen catapults launch boulders at city walls before," Galina said. "I have even seen them launch ammunition that's been set aflame. This was neither. What they hurled at us exploded. It tore through entire buildings. It ignited everything in reach with violet flame that burned hotter than normal fire. You saw the damage it caused. They hit us with one projectile, and then they left."

"One projectile?" Mariana's mouth fell open. "This was the result of one projectile?"

Galina nodded solemnly. "The fire spread, consuming half the village. I don't know how many are dead, but this was not a strike to kill. This was a display of power. And if that's what Fogosombre is capable of now, then we have a much harder war ahead of us."

Mariana saw Galina's fierce expression slip for a moment. The change was short-lived, but it was enough for her to glimpse how weary the leader felt inside.

The crowd in the square had thinned significantly.

"We can board now," Mariana said. Lenora and Sunev were looking at her, waiting for her to join them.

"I'm not going," Galina said.

"You're not?" Mariana realized that, on some level, she'd been hoping the leader would return to Kailon with her. Perhaps then Galina could speak with Queen Yiscel in her place and present a more compelling argument for stronger aid.

"You heard what I said. Together we overthrow the Tyrant. My place is here." She crossed her arms, staring off at the buildings and the smoke, which was beginning to thin as the fires died. She said, "I sent a sparrow to Black Tide Cove. It isn't as good a plea as having someone there in person, but I hope this attack will galvanize their support."

"My brother may still have made it," Mariana said. "I haven't heard from him since we were separated."

Galina nodded. "Time will tell. Inform the Kailonese queen of what has happened here. Plead our case. Show her the faces of the young who barely survived."

Mariana didn't have to answer. She began to move away, heading for the ships where the sailors followed the last of the refugees onboard.

"I will look for the returning sails," Galina said.

Then she walked toward the city, her stride deliberate.

"Let the winds be in our favor and the arms of the rowers strong," Sunev said as they climbed the ramp onto the ship. "Elsewise, arduous the journey back will be. I don't pity none the crew what has to tend the passengers."

"*We're* the crew that has to tend the passengers," Lenora said.

"Aye, and I don't pity us none."

With the docks cleared, the tethers were withdrawn and the ships drifted out into the harbor. Mariana took the time to scan the faces of the Faroni people around her: the devastation, the suffering, and the underlying thread of hope. She could do nothing but plead to Deus that she wouldn't disappoint them.

Kaori

He left his quarters by moonlight.

Kaori cautiously navigated the palace corridors, his slippers soundless on the floorboards. If he stopped to think, he would've found his own behavior ridiculous—after all, why was he bothering to sneak about when he had an armed escort following him the entire way—but he was not hiding from attackers. He was hiding from his own entourage, and that required its own form of discretion.

A quiet knock at the door.

For a few gut-wrenching moments, he stood in silence, not wanting to look at the two guards waiting patiently behind him for fear of mind-changing embarrassment. Then Arsenio answered, and all else was forgotten.

The foreign man blinked at him, unsure whether to be relieved or cross.

"Your Majesty," he said simply.

Kaori swallowed, his heart racing. "Arsenio," he breathed. The name still tasted as sweet as it had the first time he'd uttered the four syllables. "I came to apologize."

They'd argued earlier in the day, the same argument they'd had three times now about his inability to help Arsenio's people, but unlike the previous disagreements, they hadn't made up before parting ways. Kaori had been called to another lesson on swordplay before they could resolve the tension, and he'd spent the rest of the afternoon and evening mulling over the poor state in which they'd left things.

"An apology with wine?" Arsenio asked, one eyebrow raised. He didn't turn Kaori away though, and that was not a positive to be overlooked.

"I've found that wine tends to help smooth things over," Kaori said with a hopeful smile.

"Come in." Arsenio stepped aside and Kaori entered his room, eager to get away from the prying eyes of his guard. They knew by now that it was fine to let the emperor into the foreign man's room—he'd done it many times without harm. As the door shut behind Kaori, he felt a slight release. Arsenio grabbed the glasses from Kaori's left hand and set them down on a table, the yellow glow of his lantern reflecting off their surfaces. Kaori set the wine bottle down beside them and removed the stopper.

"The words must feel empty by now," he said, filling the glasses nearly to the brim, "but I am sorry."

Arsenio took his and drank deeply. "I know," he said, brow furrowed as he went to sit on the edge of his bed. "That's the worst part; I understand your hesitance, even if I don't like it." The mattress sank beneath his weight. "And it pains me to consider you might think ill of me, that my affections are contingent upon your ability to help me."

The thought had crossed Kaori's mind, but each kiss they'd shared ate away at its validity. He took his glass and tread gingerly over to Arsenio, stopping only when their knees were all but touching. He took a sip of the pale liquid, unable to tear his gaze away from the young man's features. "I couldn't think ill of you if the gods cursed your name," he said, and felt his face flush.

Arsenio smiled sadly, taking another sip of the wine. "What was it like growing up here?" he asked, looking around at the opulence abundant in every corner of Kingfisher Palace. The painted window screens, the gold plating in the wooden joints, the embroidered blankets on his bed. Kaori appreciate the change in topic though it further highlighted the juxtaposition between his relative comfort and the suffering of Arsenio's people.

"I wasn't raised *here*, per se," Kaori answered, drinking more. "Kingfisher Palace is a great deal more luxurious than the Palace Academy. Don't get me wrong—I wanted for very little, but I don't want you thinking I slept on a feather bed all my life and had servants drawing baths each night."

Arsenio chuckled. "Of course," he said. "If that were not the case, you'd probably be an insufferable narcissist."

"Taigen would've never let me think so highly of myself."

"The two of you shared a room then?"

"Oh yes, since the day we were both selected."

"I could tell you were longtime friends," Arsenio said with a smile.

"Was it the utter disrespect with which he talks to me?"

That enchanting laugh. "Perhaps." He stood to pour himself another glass. Kaori did the same, though he could already feel a lightness to his step. When they'd both topped off, Arsenio clinked their glasses together. "You're like siblings, the two of you."

"Are we?" Kaori asked.

"Oh yes, bickering, japing, but with an underlying bond forged by proximity. I suppose not all siblings carry such affinity for one another, but I'm basing my comparison off my relationship with my own sisters." A flicker of somberness crossed Arsenio's face, but he took another sip and it was gone. "How did he react to your appointment?"

Kaori considered the question. "I'd be surprised if there wasn't some jealousy—Taigen wanted the position far more than I did, but he hid it well. He was supportive. Excited. And I think, in the end, he realized he liked being an advisor more than he would've enjoyed being emperor. He boasts considerably more leeway, at least."

"And you? How do you feel about being emperor?"

Kaori blinked and took his largest gulp of wine yet. As the liquid effects rushed to his mind, he pondered the past months since the Crown of Mai had been placed on his head; the many ways in which his life had changed; the power granted to him, and the powers taken away. He sank onto the bed beside Arsenio.

"It doesn't matter how I feel," he whispered.

"Of course it matters how you feel," Arsenio said.

"I can't do anything about it. I can't give it back."

"Is that what you want? You wish you hadn't been chosen?"

"I'm not strong enough to be Nokara's leader. I'm not brave enough, or confident enough, or—or decisive—"

"You can learn all these traits."

"Can I?" He leaned away from the foreigner, as if Arsenio might need some distance to see him clearly. With his narrow shoulders, his delicate features, everything about him was a hesitation. After an empty moment of staring at one another, Kaori sighed and took another sip of wine. His glass was nearly empty again. He stole a furtive glance at Arsenio's, not wanting to go for more if the other boy stopped now.

"We can only do our best with what we're given," Arsenio said in a low voice.

"Too often our best isn't nearly enough," Kaori replied, then shook his head as if that would rid him of his demoralizing thoughts. "I beg a change of subject. I spend far too much of my days dwelling on my shortcomings. Tell me of Corva sum Rio. What was it like having a family?"

To his relief, Arsenio stood long enough to grab the wine from the table. Sitting back down on the bed, he filled his cup before offering more to Kaori. He nodded, holding out his hand, and watched the pale liquid pour in. Apparently, he hadn't brought enough. They were nearly out.

"I always liked my family," Arsenio said somberly. "We were honest with one another, supportive. I bickered with my sisters, of course—all siblings do, I think. But it wasn't from disliking one another. It was more because we shared everything. Me and my twin especially; Mariana. She—well, she's a fighter, that one. The only family I've got left."

He'd told Kaori about the deaths; how he'd gone from a full family of five to just himself in a matter of weeks. Although Kaori didn't know his parents, he thought of Taigen or Amaya dying, and knew Arsenio's pain had to outweigh his own.

The foreign boy stared into his cup with a frown.

"Is something wrong?" Kaori asked.

"Just wondering what's in this Nokari wine that makes the drinker so morose." Arsenio chuckled, then took another swig. "Much more of this and we'll be reduced to sobbing."

"Hmm," Kaori said by way of agreement. "You might be right. I didn't come here to wallow in self-pity."

Arsenio met his gaze. "Why did you come?"

"I—to apologize, of course," he breathed.

"You have," the other boy seemed to be searching, asking Kaori to say something, though he didn't understand. "You could've apologized by daylight."

"I could have."

"I'm afraid I'm falling for you."

The admission shook Kaori to his core. Stated so plainly in language uncloaked by timidity or fear. Arsenio said the words with the soberest of expressions, his dark eyes boring into Kaori like the roots of a tree burrowing into the ground. He was powerless against that gaze, defenseless.

"The wine is giving you silly thoughts," Kaori said, his heart tearing at the seams.

"It's not," Arsenio said, setting his glass down. He tried a phrase in Nokaran, which came out clumsy and incoherent.

Kaori giggled. "I don't believe I understood that."

"I was trying to say 'I love you.'"

That's not possible, Kaori wanted to say. Men couldn't love men. How strange, how torturous that those three words should feel at home in his ears, coming from Arsenio's lips. Though Kaori had thought the same weeks ago when they'd kissed outside the Halls of Heritage, he knew they couldn't be true. Not when everyone else stood so adamantly against them. He wanted to return the sentiment, the correct Nokaran expression on his tongue, but every time he made to say the words, he felt the sting of approaching tears in his eyes.

"Does such a thing exist, where you're from?" Kaori asked instead. He didn't need to specify to what he referred.

"It's rare, but not unheard of," Arsenio said. Then he slid closer on the bed and leaned over Kaori to kiss him full on the mouth. Every muscle urged Kaori to move away. Yet he fought to remain. He fought until Kento's harsh words weeks ago faded from his mind, until Amaya's urgings were nothing but echoes, until even Taigen's flare of disgust was no longer visible. They kissed until his repressed desires overtook him and he stood, sliding his hands behind Arsenio's head to bring him closer. He wanted more, as much as the young man would grant him. Arsenio pressed Kaori's back against the wall, sliding his hands inside Kaori's robe to touch his skin; his stomach—his chest, his back.

Arsenio's hand slid further south to caress his hardened sex through the silk fabric. Euphoria blazed through Kaori's body, bright like lightning in the night, for the briefest of instants. Then he pulled away, his lips sore from contact. This was too much to handle for one night. Too much for him to comprehend. Every fear came crashing back into place.

"I can't," he said, choking back a cry of anguish. He'd never felt so disgusted by his own needs, his own lack of propriety. Catching his breath, Kaori was reluctant to look up at Arsenio, afraid to find that the other boy was hurt or insulted by the sudden change of heart.

Not a change of heart but a betrayal of my mind.

Arsenio placed two fingers beneath his chin and tilted his head upward so that they locked eyes. He was blushing.

"Perhaps that was a bit too forward," he said shyly. His impish grin calmed Kaori's internal tempest.

"That was definitely the wine," Kaori said, and Arsenio nodded.

The rush of the moment gone, Kaori was suddenly aware of his dizziness. He'd drank a half bottle of wine, and now the effects were catching up to him, making him do silly things like entertain the idea of a lifetime sharing a bed with Arsenio Avilla, wondering what it would be like to hold him and not feel an ounce of shame, to love him as they sat together upon the Golden Throne. He could be the bravery Kaori needed to lead. The certainty he lacked.

"I should go," he said.

"Must you?" Arsenio asked. "You could stay. I promise I won't touch you again."

"My will is weak," Kaori whispered. "And my guard—"

"What will they think that they haven't already?"

He had a point. Kaori searched for words. He had a thousand reasons why he should leave now and return to his rooms, but he couldn't get his feet to move. He still stood with his back against the wall, and he wondered if he had the strength to walk out of this room without it holding him up.

I can't stay.

But how could he leave?

~

The light of the sun woke him.

Kaori breathed in, listening to the silence of his surroundings. There had been so few days when his rest wasn't interrupted by one servant or another announcing that the day had begun and he needed to dress. In fact, he couldn't remember the last time he'd awoken of his own accord.

He rolled onto his back, his hand sliding up to the pillow beneath his head. With a last sigh of satisfaction, Kaori opened his eyes.

He wasn't in his bed chambers.

The thought dropped into his head and spread to the corners of his mind. Strangely, it didn't frighten him even as his memories returned: the wine, his confessions, Arsenio's wandering hands. It all felt like a dream now, the conjured images of drunken sleep, but there he lay atop the sheets of a bed that was not his own in a room that certainly did not belong to the emperor.

I love you, Arsenio had said. He'd wanted so much—more than Kaori could give him, though he wanted it just as badly.

Kaori sighed. Now the night was over, and in the light of day, he could no longer hide. Though he regretted nothing from the night before, it'd represented a precipice at which he could either turn back or let himself fall. He had chosen to fall, and now he would have to discover what awaited him at the bottom of the cliff.

Could he do that? The consequences were so ineffable that he hadn't any idea what came next. Did he act upon his desires? Or did he live the rest of his life as he was supposed to, knowing what he knew about himself but repressing that part of his whole. He could see either scenario playing out, and in only one of them was he happy.

Did he deserve happiness? That might be another man's privilege.

He could lie to the rest of the world, but he couldn't lie to himself. He had fallen in love the way water finds the ocean: no matter the obstacles, the twists and turns, the destination was inevitable.

He stood, not allowing himself to glance back at the young man breathing with the softness of sleep, and left the room. His guard waited beyond the door. Kaori could not look the men in the eyes, he felt too much shame. Instead, he lead them away with his head bowed. The corridors felt unnaturally deserted as he ascended to the upper levels of the palace. He at least expected to pass a steady stream of officials and servants along his way, but perhaps the gods were on his side this morning, for he encountered only two other souls.

By the time he was walking along the latticed corridor toward the stairs up to his chambers, he'd convinced himself that word of his nighttime escapade might not reach his advisors.

He was wrong.

Taigen was waiting at the top of the stairs.

"I thought you'd never make an appearance," he said, his hands clasped behind his back, all the playfulness drained from his voice. "You're needed in the throne room."

~

Kaori burst through the double doors feeling rushed and disheveled. Echoes of conversation died in the rafters. Taigen followed Kaori to the dais where the throne awaited, taking his place among the other advisors. Amaya and Kento watched Kaori, their faces expressionless. Only Sugi appeared relieved that he'd been found at last.

A crowd had formed around the perimeter of the room, members of the Elliptic Council and the courts, as well as officials and nobles from the city. They too watched him settle into his place, though some kept their eyes trained on the space before the dais. There, a man knelt on the floor, flanked by several guards who had their spears trained on him. Kaori thought the show of force a bit excessive. The man was easily in his waning years, with graying hair and aging skin, but though he looked healthy he did not appear threatening or in any shape to fight them.

Kaori straightened his crown as he fought to catch his breath, wishing he'd thought to ask Taigen more details before rushing off.

"What's happening?" Kaori asked, turning to Amaya.

"Your Majesty," she said. Though her usual graceful smile was present on her face, her voice sounded strained. "For this man's crimes, Kento has been eager to deliver justice upon him."

"Justice well deserved," Kento interjected.

"But he must know that a death sentence can only be delivered by *the emperor* so long as the emperor is present in Black Tide Cove." She snapped her head around to glare at Kento, who was unperturbed by her reproach.

"In some cases, this law should be overlooked," Kento argued.

"That isn't for you to decide," Sugi said. Kaori was surprised to hear his friend so aggravated. She was typically even-natured. "The emperor *is* present."

"And I think he would be on my side."

"If I may," the man on his knees began.

"Silence, traitor!" Kento bellowed. A murmur went through the audience.

"You think this man deserves death?" Kaori asked.

"He does! There's no question about it."

"What has he done to warrant such punishment?"

Amaya answered. "He's the one who hired the Jade Dagger to assassinate Hinata."

Adrenaline spiked in Kaori's blood. He had forgotten about the pursuit to catch Hinata's killer. Another murmur ran through the crowd. Kaori suspected that this information had already been revealed before his arrival.

"Is this so?" he asked.

"He was apprehended in his hometown, going about daily life as if he hadn't committed a heinous act of treason," Kento spat.

"I have nothing to hide!" the man called loudly. "I know what I've done."

"So you admit to your actions?" Kaori asked.

"Like I said, Your Majesty, I don't deny anything. Hinata deserved his fate!"

At this, the crowd gasped and the talking grew louder.

"How dare you?" Kento hissed.

"Hinata was a well-respected man of the people," Amaya said. The prisoner only laughed.

"Man of the people, you say? What a ridiculous farce!"

"What's your name?" Kaori asked.

The man drew himself up straight, though he remained on his knees. Pride was evident in every muscle on his face. "Takahiro Kodemi," he said. Beside Kaori, Taigen shifted in his seat. "I wouldn't expect you to recognize the name. You all have lost reverence for the old nobility in our nation! We families who built the lands you live on! We, who are granted no respect ever since the line of the throne was given over to *elections*. I have royal blood in me!"

The talking continued until Kaori raised his hands to quiet them.

"Royal blood," Kento spat. "The dynasties of old have been gone for centuries. You have no more royal blood than anyone else in this city!"

"Please," Kaori said to his advisor. Kento's aggravated tone only incited fervor in those gathered around the room. Their murmurs had grown to rumbling. He turned back to Takahiro. "You say the palace insulted you. How?"

The man seized upon the opportunity to explain himself. "I have had everything taken from me!" he pleaded. "I have only known a simple life, farming in my modest village. The surplus of my crops helps feed the capital, and my family has always been faithful to the throne."

"And yet you go on claiming 'royal blood,'" Kento said. "How does that factor into your faithfulness?"

"Kento, please," Kaori said more firmly. "Takahiro, continue."

Kento growled, but held his tongue.

"Thank you, Your Majesty," Takahiro said, bowing his head. "We have always done what we could to aid the throne, but I lost everything! Everything! My family has been shamed. Of my three children, the two youngest were selected to join the Academy. This was meant to be an honor, though I was never to see them again. And yet, they've been chosen for nothing! I thought maybe they would become members of the Elliptic Council, or lords of their own cities. But I hear nothing of their appointments. The older of the two approaches her twenty-first year. When that happens, she will be relegated to the military. A fate anyone could have chosen! And the younger is not far behind. They were stolen from me for no reason!

"And then my eldest child, the only one I had left, was taken from me as well. Nobody knows where he has gone. Vanished. So I did the only thing I could do to avenge my family's loss of legacy. I sent someone to kill the man responsible! The one who selected both my younger children for their worthless fates: Hinata!"

The crowd erupted into shouts protesting Takahiro's statements, defending the Academy system. Kaori held out his hands, but this time they paid him no mind, voicing their outrage without heeding him.

"Silence!" Akedi Amaya said in a loud voice. The tone she had no doubt learned from decades of teaching was powerful enough to quiet the uproar. "You speak of the worthlessness of your children's future, and yet students who aren't chosen for other roles enter the military as leaders or as teachers in the Academy. There is honor in this."

Takahiro scoffed, his disgust apparent.

"And did you not know the treatises when you brought both your children to selection day? No parent is forced to bring their child. It is only said that the child may be presented at five years of age. You come knowing that if they are selected, you are offering them to a greater purpose: the chance to serve the empire."

"A greater purpose!" Takahiro said scornfully. "A chance at honor! But not if they're ignored."

"Again, you knew this to be a possibility." Kaori had never seen Amaya so livid. "No child is guaranteed a particular position. They're equal in the eyes of the gods."

"But not in the eyes of man. One child taken and relegated to insignificance is an insult, two is murderous. So, I delivered murder." Takahiro rose to his feet. At this, the guards flanking him aimed their spears once again. One came forward and shoved him back onto the mats. The shouts began, members of the crowd calling for Takahiro's death then and there. They chanted, raising their fists as if they wished to assault him themselves though they remained behind the banisters.

Kaori could feel his influence over the room shrinking. On Amaya's other side, Kento encouraged the audience, his fist bared in anger. Amaya looked disdainful, though she remained silent and poised. To Kaori's left, Taigen seemed stricken, his eyes wide and his face pale. And beyond him, Sugi stared in horror at the bloodlust of the nobility, her knuckles white on the arms of her seat.

Kaori was at a loss. In times where the right choice was mired by shades of gray, he looked to his advisors for their opinions, but now they were all preoccupied by the events, their attention drawn away from him. He'd yet to sentence anyone to death, and though the man's crimes were treasonous, Kaori was reluctant to have blood on his hands. Yet, he feared the crowd's anger turning his way should he not order Takahiro's death. The warnings both Sugi and Amaya had voiced about the public's opinion of his rule lingered on his mind. Their respect for him felt tenuous.

But he needed the chaos to end.

He raised his hands. Again, the crowd ignored him. Amaya didn't intercede this time, her focus elsewhere. He tried calling out to the people—"Quiet!"—but his voice didn't carry.

Finally, his frustration peaking, Kaori lunged off the Golden Throne, robes trailing behind him. His hands still raised, he screamed at the top of his lungs, "I WILL HAVE ORDER!"

Silence fell heavy like a curtain. Kaori was out of breath, trembling from head to toe beneath the silks. He stood a meter from Takahiro, all eyes focused intently on him. The faces shone a mixture of anger, surprise, bloodlust, and intrigue.

"You have committed a treasonous act," Kaori said to the prisoner, his eyes downcast on Takahiro's fearful expression. "You don't deny this. You've confessed. For this, I will not sentence you to death *at this time*." The audience threatened to devolve into commotion again. "*But!* You will be detained in the palace dungeons until enough of this emotion"—he gestured widely to the crowd— "has passed that a clear course of justice may be determined."

Takahiro was hoisted off the floor, shouting at the guards, who made no allowances for delicacy. They dragged him away amid the cries of the crowd, who'd gone back to shouting, though this time their bellows were half aimed at the prisoner and half directed toward the emperor. Kento was among them, red in the face as he decried the lack of justice from his seat. Amaya's expression was unreadable.

Kaori sighed, trudging back to his throne with his eyes closed. He wanted the crowd gone, but knew it would be quite some time before the attendants managed to clear them away. Doubt plucked at his poorly masked plea for time. When he slumped into his chair, Kaori turned to Taigen, who was still stricken pale in the face.

"Did I do the right thing, Taigen?" he asked.

Taigen stammered. "I cannot tell you, Kaori," he said, staring back at his friend. It was shock that he wore, Kaori realized. "I cannot advise you at all when it comes to this man, I'm afraid. He's my father."

CHAPTER SEVEN
AS THE SUN FOLLOWS THE MOON

Ira

When the soldiers returned from Red Cliff, they brought word of their victory. Most of them had not been made privy to the abilities of the weapon they carried, and their shock was as great as that of the villagers who'd fallen victim to the damages—though among the troops this shock elicited awe and admiration rather than terror and death. Word spread of Fogosombre's new power, his ability to level vast areas with one swift strike. Who now could stand in his way?

For Ira, these discussions of power meant something else entirely.

Fogosombre celebrated his achievement the same way he always did: through relentless, savage lovemaking. He wielded his member like an adolescent boy, always poking her at odd, often inappropriate times of day. It was up to whoever else was in the room to extricate themselves.

The throes of triumph were the only times in which Ira found that she completely tolerated her husband. He was less inclined to carry out his frustrations on her. She could almost convince herself she loved him.

Inadvertently, she found she had more patience with Fernão as well. Though she loved their son more than she'd loved any other human being, she regretted her temper when dealing with him. If only children didn't wear so much on one's temperament. She understood his senses of rationale and pragmatism were still developing, but she wondered how long it would be before he became a son who earned the family name with pride instead of obligation. Yet, amid her period of content, Ira found herself able to overlook some of Fernão's missteps. His youth, after all, had yet to wane.

In the evening, he came to her in her chambers after having scraped his knee while exploring the castle passageways. Ira reprimanded him, but she tended to the mild injury, calling for her servant to bring water to wash the blood and dirt away. Once clean, you could barely tell the scrape was there. He'd had much worse injuries in swordplay lessons.

"Perhaps if you simply walked the passageways instead of sprinting down them as if chased by an Azinheira crane, you wouldn't have fallen." She ran a hand over his wiry black hair. The boy nodded, though she doubted he'd take her words to heart. The day he started listening to her would be the day she knew he'd matured.

"There was a bird trapped in the halls. I was trying to get it outside," he said.

"Oh, so you *were* being chased by a crane."

Fernão giggled. "No, it was a small bird. I had it in my hands." He cupped his palms to show her.

"And what became of this bird when you fell?"

"I suppose she found her way out," he said. Then added, "I hope."

Ira frowned, thinking that if a bird flying about the corridors had got in her way, she'd have killed it without question. The departure of the boy's softness would be another sign of his maturity. You didn't gain nor keep power through kindness. This truth she knew well.

How could Fernão be so tenderhearted? If she didn't know better, she'd have never guessed he was the son of the king.

The door burst open. In walked Fogosombre, his chest out and steps wide. She knew immediately what was on his mind before he'd said a word. Fernão knew too and stood to flee the room. Fogosombre patted the boy on the shoulder as he strode past, grunting with approval.

The door shut behind him.

"What did the boy need?" Fogosombre asked, though Ira knew he wasn't interested.

"He fell while he was running. I cleaned the cut."

"You cleaned the cut? Why didn't he have one of the servants do it?"

"I'm his mother."

"And there are others who can serve him. Besides, he shouldn't need his cuts cleaned," Fogosombre said, itching to begin. "Perhaps I will make you a mother again. More sons make for a stronger legacy."

"Perhaps you should," Ira said, not opposed to the idea but placing little weight in her husband's words. She had once imaged herself mother to a brood of three or four offspring, but bearing

Fernão alone had been an ordeal. Try as they might, she and Fogosombre had never managed another successful birth. In her most introspective moments, Ira bemoaned the loss of this unrealized vision of the future. Fernão would never be half the conqueror Fogosombre was. Faron would fall apart if and when he ascended the throne. Even if there was little love left between Ira and the king, his ability to amass power was undeniable.

The giant man crossed the distance between them in two strides. He lifted her into the air like a dishcloth and laid her on the bed, undoing the front of his trousers with his other hand as he did so. He lifted the hem of her dress above her waist.

The door flew open. Fogosombre continued his advances, used to people leaving once they realized he was in the midst of fornication.

"Your Highness, we have divined something of great importance," Vida said.

"We have," Morta agreed. "You'll want to know immediately."

A flash of annoyance crossed Fogosombre's face, which was inches from Ira's. At once, she hoped whatever news the Fates had would dissuade his arousal. When he was enraged, his lovemaking provided no enjoyment.

Fogosombre stood. "I'm fucking my wife. It cannot wait until I'm finished?"

"No, my king."

"Not a minute longer."

Sighing, the king backed away from the bed and Ira sat up, relieved.

"This had better be important, then," he said. "Get on with it."

The Fates scrambled, their tittering making Ira grit her teeth. She thought about leaving, but stayed, partly because she too was curious about what could be so important, and partly because her husband was blocking her way out.

"It appears—" Vida began.

"—the dust has shown—" Morta continued.

"—that the queen of Kailon—"

"—Yiscel Baquiran—"

"—has opened her lands to refugees from the Red Cliffs—"

"—and other survivors of disciplinary events."

Fogosombre's outrage could've ignited the room. He grabbed the nearest item—a carved, wooden chair—and hurled it across the room where it shattered against the wall. Far from wanting to leave, Ira made certain not to move. The period of Fogosombre's triumphant content was at an end. How short it had been. "That cunt. That insolent bitch. How dare she involve herself in my kingdom? A misguided alignment with rebellious swine trying to usurp my throne? That vile whore."

Ira could practically see the smoke rising from his head. She marveled at the boldness of the island monarch. Either this Yiscel Baquiran was incredibly vain, or she'd no idea who she was dealing with. Her tiny nation could not hope to hold its own against the might of Faron.

"Do you know where they're being kept?" Fogosombre asked.

"There are many islands in Kailon."

"But the five largest are the most populated."

"Medinilla seems most likely."

"Its villages have the most room for growth."

"She will want them close though."

"Yes, she will want to keep an eye on them."

"She will put them on the northern side."

"The Port of Pauwe."

Fogosombre ran a hand over his face, scraping his fingernails across the black scars on his throat. For a brief moment, it appeared the scars writhed in response, but that had to be a trick of the light. Ira could see the machinations of his mind plotting, working out the various scenarios and determining which unfolded to his greatest advantage. She could feel the Fates holding their breaths, probably relieved on some level that he hadn't become more violent. Though he never hurt *them*, his tirades could still be frightening.

Finally, Fogosombre brought his fingertips together as if praying. When he spoke, it was in his deepest voice. One he reserved for his most dangerous of schemes. "This can't go unchallenged," he said. "If Yiscel Baquiran wants to circumvent my authority, then she will feel my wrath."

"What do you mean to do?" Ira breathed, despite her desire to remain invisible.

Fogosombre paced to the hearth, in which the last remnants of fire had dimmed to embers. His bulky frame cast a shadow over the entire room, nearly blocking the light from view. "I will show her my power. I will show her what it means to oppose me. I have enough Shadow Fire to deliver one strong message. We will wipe the northern side of Medinilla off the map."

"That would be an act of war," Ira said. She kept her expression devoid of emotion. Did her husband really mean to start an all-out war with a foreign land? She knew he wouldn't stand for the insult to his power, but she'd expected him to confront the queen and take back his people.

"Have they not already declared war?" he said. "Did they not already assert their intentions the moment they set foot on our land?"

"And what if they retaliate?"

Fogosombre laughed—a grim, humorless sound that echoed his disregard for consequences. "Then we will kill them all. Kailon is so small that I've never contemplated their presence before today. If they seek to put themselves in my path, then they have a death wish I am only too eager to fulfill.

"We are going to the Quartz Basilica," he said suddenly, rounding on Ira. The statement was unexpected—rarely did he leave Ciro—but she held her tongue. "After the recent success, I want the mines to double their efforts."

He moved away from the fire, his boots thudding on the stone floor. "Prepare yourself for travel. We will leave in the morning."

"One thing remains," Vida said as the king made leave.

"Another vision we had," Morta said.

"Just get on with it," Ira complained. All eyes turned to her, but she'd had entirely enough for one evening. At the drop of a hat, she was going to be dragged halfway across the kingdom to satisfy Fogosombre's whims. The Fates' relentless mysticism had pulled her nerves to their extent.

Vida frowned. "You cannot hurry the Fates."

"Divine knowledge comes at its own pace," Morta said.

Ira rolled her eyes and crossed her arms over her chest.

They turned back to Fogosombre, Vida launching back into her mystic tone. "We have seen a warning written in the dust."

"An abysmal warning," Morta said.

"*Where shadow and shadow meet...*" Vida intoned.

"*Death will follow.*"

Fogosombre frowned. "What do you mean by this?"

"We are not given all the answers," Vida said.

"We will ponder the warning further and disclose our findings when the dust has settled." Morta waved her hands in the air, enacting a rain of falling dust. Ira might have found this comical were she not so annoyed.

Fogosombre found no humor in their antics. "I am the one and only shadow," he said, "and death does my bidding."

Arsenio

Spring surged forth across the city, manifesting in colors of every form imaginable. Though the transition had likely taken weeks, Arsenio didn't notice until he looked up one day and found that everything around him thrived. The branches of the deciduous trees filled with brilliant green leaves, and every time the wind picked up, he could hear them quaking. The palace gardens blossomed at once, as if boasting to each other their reds and oranges and blues. Kaori had explained to Arsenio the fascination with Tatsu Garden, and now that the white blooms formed a canopy of clouds above the pathways, he understood. At Kingfisher Palace, humans and nature formed a partnership—like artful equals.

The weather warmed as well. It seemed Black Tide Cove experienced a similar climate to Corva sum Rio, though it was maybe a few degrees warmer. Invigorated by the pleasantness of the outdoors, Arsenio and Kaori took to spending their time together in the palace grounds. Kaori showed Arsenio Kuriku Garden, where they lingered on many an afternoon, most of the time alone but sometimes with Sugi.

Arsenio came to like her, though they didn't always understand each other. Arsenio had learned enough Nokaran that he rarely had to ask Kaori for translations, but there was more to language than words. His appreciation for Kaori's friend and advisor was heightened by the fact that she was the only member of his circle to acknowledge him without pause. When it came to Amaya, Kento, or even Taigen, they always took a moment to recompose themselves once they spotted Arsenio. Sugi greeted him like a friend. Sometimes she and Kaori exchanged words he couldn't hear which made Kaori smile and blush, and Arsenio wondered if they talked about him.

That he caused such discord between Kaori and his other advisors wasn't lost on Arsenio. At times when he was left to his own devices, he wondered whether it wouldn't be better for him to simply leave, to exit the palace grounds and find his own way back to Faron. But every time the notion started to entice him, he would push it away. He couldn't bring himself to go. Never had he felt so utterly connected to someone outside his family. And even then, his connection to the emperor was different. Arsenio loved his family—not to mention his twin, Mariana, who he prayed every night had found safety on Kailon—but these were fated connections. Kaori, he loved, because his sun rose and fell with the emperor's smile. The melodies of the world rang true when he laughed. And when he held Kaori—well, Arsenio could not imagine a greater source of peace and comfort.

He couldn't leave. Not when it'd do nothing but harm them both and resolve none of the issues that plagued them. Kaori would still be attracted to members of the same sex. He had confessed that although his attraction to Arsenio had awakened this truth about his desires, he'd already known this was the case. Whether he'd be forced to take a female spouse was beyond their control, even if Arsenio departed.

Arsenio also couldn't imagine returning home having failed. In fact, whenever he pondered his own happiness with the man he loved, guilt tugged at the back of his mind. His original decision to stay and chip away at Kaori's refusal to involve Nokara wasn't forgotten, but he couldn't deny it had been dragged to the wayside. He'd fallen in love, but his time with Kaori was time stolen from his kin.

Arsenio was left staring into his dark room at night, clinging to Kaori's back as he lay sleeping beside him. He was left wondering when his precarious bliss would have to end, and whether he'd be ready to face the world when it did.

~

One morning, Kaori led Arsenio down to Kuriku Garden before the day's counseling session in the throne room. Hidden by the vines and bushes, they kissed hungrily. Arsenio ran his thumb along Kaori's jaw, feeling the rough texture of the hair poking through the skin.

Before they could become too intertwined however, he heard footsteps coming up the path. The two men sprang apart, straightening their clothes and their tousled hair.

Around the bend emerged not one, but all four advisors. Amaya led the way, a dark cloud hovering over her. They were silent until they reached Kaori. Amaya bowed courteously to Arsenio, who returned the gesture. He looked to Sugi, but even she seemed too grave to show her usual amicable demeanor.

Amaya spoke first. "Your friend should leave," she said.

Kaori sidestepped toward him. "He may stay."

Amaya pursed her lips for the briefest of moments. "I mean neither of you any dishonor, Your Grace. This is a matter of the throne."

"I can leave—" Arsenio began, but Kaori stood firm.

"Please. Stay."

Seeming to think the argument not worth their time, Amaya sighed and pulled a rolled note from her sleeve. "A sparrow arrived this morning. An *eastern* sparrow."

Arsenio's feet became rooted to the spot. He couldn't leave now even if he wanted to. A sparrow from the east? Did that mean Faron? His home? Or maybe they considered Kailon the east as well, which could mean it pertained to his sister.

As Kaori unrolled the message, Arsenio tried to peek over his shoulder at what was written, but his view was obstructed. The longer the emperor took to read, the thicker the air became. Even Kento had shifted, eager to know what word arrived from foreign lands. If it was a Nokari sparrow, they wouldn't have cared so much, but Arsenio couldn't imagine this sort of correspondence was common.

Finally, Kaori lowered the piece of paper. "The woman who writes is a resistance fighter in Faron. She pleads the same case as Arsenio, asking for our help in their desperate situation."

Kento turned away, frustrated. "Was it not enough to send a messenger? Now they must harass us with sparrows?"

"I don't think she's certain that Arsenio ever made it here," Kaori said, reviewing the letter.

Arsenio felt a stab of guilt. He'd failed to send word of his arrival to the Red Cliffs. He'd told himself it was because he had nothing to report, when in reality, he feared Galina would demand he put more pressure on Kaori. "Who is writing?" he asked.

"A woman named Galina Sagrado."

Then it was the same woman who'd sent him and his sister across the Great Ocean.

"Why is she sending a sparrow now?" Taigen asked.

"There's been an attack," Kaori informed them. Arsenio's stomach churned. "According to her, Fogosombre unleashed a power she's never witnessed before. A magic fire that destroyed half her city."

"Now they've got *magic* fires sprouting up," Kento grumbled.

"What can we do?" Kaori asked, concern marking his gaze.

"Nothing. We must maintain our stance," Kento said.

Kaori turned to Amaya. She seemed flustered. "It's a terrible situation to be in, but I can't say I disagree with him."

"What if we merely condemn the king's actions?" Taigen asked, stepping forward. For once, Arsenio felt a stirring of affection for him, glad to hear that someone was speaking up in Faron's favor. "What if we sent a sparrow to this Fogosombre? Let him know that his actions are not condoned by our throne."

"And then what?" Kento asked. "Have him laugh in our faces? That is no threat, it's stupidity."

"We could send ships," Taigen said, "keep them offshore. Show that we're serious."

"Nokari lives sent are Nokari lives endangered."

"But the people of Faron are dying," Arsenio said.

Amaya had no response but to close her eyes. Given how Kaori had described her, Arsenio knew her heart was breaking. She cared too much for human life to go about this so coldly. They needed to emphasize how many lives were at risk, how many families Fogosombre had destroyed. Then, perhaps she'd break. If that were the case, the number of advisors in opposition would shrink to the minority. Arsenio tried to catch Sugi's eye. He wished she'd be more vocal, but she'd confided in him once that as the only advisor not from the palace, she often felt out of place in their discussions.

Kento lowered his voice, drawing near to Kaori. Arsenio didn't know every word the man said, but he understood enough to piece together his message. "If you send your own people into a foreign conflict, if you take fathers and mothers and sons and daughters away from their homes, distrust in your leadership will deepen. Look at your prisoner! At Takahiro! He found someone to infiltrate the palace and *murder* a high-ranking member of the empress' inner circle! The seeds of dissatisfaction have already been sown. If the troops you send die in a struggle that doesn't concern us, that will only be seen as another strike against you. We'll have the beginnings of our own rebellion on our hands."

Kento's eyes flickered to Arsenio.

That appeared to be the final straw. Arsenio watched Kaori's confidence collapse. Sensing his chance slipping away, Arsenio spoke. His words were stilted, but he was determined to speak Nokaran. "Please. How can you say this?"

Not one of them seemed to be able to look him in the eye except Kento, whose hard stare lacked the willingness to budge.

"I have told you of my struggle. I have told you what Fogosombre did to my family, to my village. Now you see what he continues to do. He has power, he has numbers, and now he has new weapons. Are you so afraid of conflict?"

He could hear the desperation in his own voice.

"Perhaps if your people did as he asked, their lives would not feel so threatened?" Kento said.

"You know that's not how this works," Arsenio said, aware that his tone bordered on disrespectful. He looked to each of the others in turn, begging them to look him in the eye and say they couldn't help him. "What will you do when the blood of thousands haunts your dreams? Sugi? Taigen? Amaya?" he said to each, his mouth dry. Tears welled in his eyes. "Kaori?"

"I...I don't know," Kaori whispered.

Arsenio's heart broke.

As the tears spilled over, he rushed past the five, leaving them staring after his retreating form. The pain inside was overwhelming, and the last thing he wanted was to be around any of them at this moment. How could they stand there with that plea for help, discussing whether or not sending aid was the right decision? How could they cast aside the fate of hundreds of thousands without so much as a moment to reflect upon the fact that these were lives? Real, human lives.

And Kaori. The name brought a renewed sadness. Kaori wanted to send help, Arsenio was sure of it, but he let everyone else tell him what to do. Never once did he stand for his own beliefs. He refused to make decisions for himself, and Kento seized on that weakness at every chance.

Fogosombre had destroyed Red Cliff. The idea terrified Arsenio. Galina had said she'd be waiting there with the survivors from Corva sum Rio, and it was up to him and his sister to find help. Now, that help was far too late. They had failed her. *He* had failed his people.

Arsenio found himself in the entrance hall of the palace, the grand pillars rising to the painted ceiling above. All this grandeur. All this wasteful opulence celebrating a throne that lacked empathy for its neighbors.

He sighed, dragging his arm across his eyes to wipe away the remaining tears. He looked down at his borrowed clothing, embroidered silks befitting royalty. An idea struck him as suddenly as lightning. His sadness and frustration were quelled by a sense of renewed purpose. If they would not vote to help his cause, then it was up to him to affect change on his own.

~

Reaching the dungeons was easier than Arsenio expected. He found stairs leading into the bowels of Kingfisher, and once the ornate décor disappeared in favor of harsh stone and rusting lanterns, he knew he'd chosen correctly. The passageway opened unto a square room. Solid wooden doors lined the walls, guarded on either side by sentries. Arsenio couldn't see their faces through their armor, but he knew they saw him. He walked out into the center of the room, standing tall and doing his best to appear confident.

"I seek the prisoner Takahiro," he announced, hoping his regal dress would be authority enough to convince them.

To his relief, a guard to his left spoke. "This way, sir."

The pair guarding the door undid several latches barricading entry before one removed a key from an inside pocket. They slid it into the keyhole, and Arsenio heard the lock click. The passage beyond opened to a chorus of creaking, a long dark corridor lined with barred cells. In the dim light, he could see dust floating down upon the cool, damp air. Would one of the guards accompany him? Or would he go alone?

Arsenio's question was answered when one of the guards handed him a glowing lantern. He passed through the doors and neither sentry followed. With a deep, resounding thud, the door closed behind him, completing the empty silence.

Cell by cell he crept down the length of the dungeon. Most of the small square enclosures were empty; a few housed the forgotten remains of prisoners long since dead. Arsenio shuddered to think how spending the last of his days cooped up in darkness like this would feel. Few visitors. Poor treatment. And little to no hope of seeing the sun rising in the sky again. He pitied the prisoner already, though he'd yet to meet the man.

In one cell, Arsenio found a cowering figured huddled against the far corner. They muttered to themselves and paid no attention to Arsenio when he called out Takahiro's name. Unsettled, Arsenio decided to move one.

Then a voice emerged from the shadows four cells down.

"You are looking for me?"

Arsenio raised the torch in front of him, watching as two hands slid between the bars.

"Takahiro?" Arsenio asked, voice shaking.

"I'd hope so. Otherwise, I've lost my mind far more quickly than I should have."

Leaving the huddled figure, Arsenio hurried along the row of cells to where the hands rested. Inside, he found a solid man with graying hair squatting against the iron bars. He observed Arsenio unflinchingly, eyes filled with curiosity. This was the man sowing seeds of dissatisfaction throughout the empire?

"Where are you from?" Takahiro asked. "Your accent is foreign… you are obviously not Nokari."

"I'm from Faron. Across the Great Ocean."

Arsenio willed his thrashing heart to quiet its temper. The dim lighting played tricks on him, and more than once Arsenio thought he saw shadows moving down the corridor toward him. But when he looked, the long passage was empty, at least to the point where his flame lost its battle with the darkness.

"May I know your name?" Takahiro asked. His tone bordered on insolent, as if Arsenio were wasting his time. Arsenio shook himself out of his stupor.

"Arsenio," he said.

"And why is Arsenio from across the Great Ocean visiting my cell?"

"You're the man who hired the assassin to kill the empress's advisor? One who was capable of avoiding the palace guard?"

"Not just *an* advisor to Empress Mai—her *head* advisor."

Even better. Arsenio cleared his throat as the man frowned, intrigued by his inquiry.

"How would I find this assassin?" Arsenio asked, careful to keep his tone even.

Takahiro gripped the iron bars, bringing his face in close. "I don't know. I'm not aware of how one finds the Jade Dagger."

"Impossible. You just told me you hired them."

"Yes, but she is mysterious, she is elusive. In the months since I found her, she might've changed all her methods of contact."

Arsenio ground his teeth in frustration. "Well, how did you last contact her?"

"I don't remember," Takahiro said defiantly.

"Please, don't play games with me, Takahiro," Arsenio said. Why was everyone so infuriating? He squatted down to the prisoner's level, the glow evenly lighting the man's weary features.

"Why would I tell you these things?" Takahiro hissed. "Do you take me for a fool? You think I'm simply going to tell you how to find her so that when your guards fail to capture her she'll come after me?"

He barked a harsh, mirthless laugh.

"I don't serve the throne," Arsenio said. "I don't seek justice for the man you had killed. I don't even know his name."

"You expect me to believe that when you are dressed in palace silks?" Takahiro gestured to the expensive robes which minutes ago were the very thing that helped Arsenio get into the dungeon. "Those are practically the emperor's robes. In fact, they might be. He's just a boy like you. Playing with power far beyond his abilities."

"I assure you," Arsenio said, fighting the lump in his throat at the mention of Kaori, "I do not serve the emperor."

"Then why are you dressed in his robes?" Takahiro asked.

Having no desire to fabricate elaborate lies, Arsenio told him. He didn't explain everything—he left out much of his journey across the Great Ocean and his love for Kaori—and in some places he didn't have enough mastery of Nokaran to translate, but he recounted everything he could. He spoke of the attack on his village, Galina sending him for help, and being attacked in Black Tide Cove. He recounted waking up in the palace under the care of the emperor, and how he'd pleaded for his people but been denied. Takahiro listened without interruption, his face an unreadable mask. By the time he was done, Arsenio sat against the bars of the cell opposite Takahiro's, watching for the man's reaction.

Takahiro considered his words, stroking the hair which had grown around his lower jaw. There was something faintly familiar about his features that Arsenio couldn't quite place, but he swept the idea from his mind. It was unimportant.

"Your story has moved me," Takahiro said finally, looking into Arsenio's eyes. "I believe you."

"Then you will help me," Arsenio said, excitement flaring within him.

"I will," Takahiro said. "Despite my better judgment, or maybe just to spite the throne. Listen close, and do everything I say. I hope you haven't played me for a fool, Arsenio, or this will bring about a terrible fate for me, though it doesn't appear my situation can get much worse." He gestured to the damp cell around him.

Arsenio got to his knees and crept closer to the prisoner, eager to absorb the instructions. He felt a mixture of nervousness and relief at having finally found someone willing to help him. His mind told him not to consider the outcome yet, to focus his attention on Takahiro. This was most important. He could be selfish later. Right now, saving his people was the priority.

Takahiro massaged his temples as if sorting out details in his mind.

You will have to leave the man you love, the selfish part of Arsenio's mind whispered to him.

"Tell me," he said to Takahiro, feeling a tear run from the corner of his eye.

"Very well, then," Takahiro began. "First, you must travel south to the village of Komorebi."

Emilio

The feeling was akin to having a tooth fall out: one minute there was solid bone, and the next, nothing but a vacant spot beside warm, gummy tissue. The only difference was that this occurred repeatedly over his entire body. Emilio had to tell himself to breathe while the pieces of himself disappeared and his world became obscured by a dense gray fog. Then his vision cleared, and he was taken aback.

He was standing on the shore, the sun gaining altitude behind him. Waves rushed onto the beach, their cool spray washing over Emilio. He felt his heart ache for home. The vision was so real. How could the witch woman tell him it was only a mirage? He could *feel* his boots sinking into the sand.

He found her standing beside him. Her dress shifted in the breeze, though maybe not as much as it should have, as if the wind couldn't quite touch the fabric. Her eyes scanned the beach, brow dipped in concentration.

"How do you know where to begin?" Emilio asked.

"That comes with being a member of the Holy Order," she replied. "As we enter the Graylife, I see images. Flashes of events. And I must home in on one of importance."

"If you don't know the person, how can you tell what's important?"

"The images come layered with emotions. I make my best guess."

She spotted what she was looking for. Emilio's stomach clenched with nerves. He simultaneously suffered the need to look and dreaded what he'd see. In the end, the former won, and he spun to follow the witch woman across the sand.

A boy squatted on the beach a dozen meters away. He drew in the sand with a twig, blissfully ignorant of the pair watching him. He wore a chestnut vest, his dark hair windswept across his forehead. Seeing his brother alive again, Emilio's eyes swam with hot tears. Involuntarily, he let out a gasp of anguish and made to rush forward and embrace the boy, but the witch woman grabbed him by the arm and held him back.

"Remember," she said, her voice soft, "we cannot interfere or we could change the sequence of events. We want the truth."

"Davi," Emilio moaned, his throat thick. He reached out with the arm the witch woman did not hold, but he didn't pull away from her.

"It's your brother's silhouette only, not him," she whispered.

Emilio fell to his knees. The witch woman's grip of restraint became one of comfort. Together, they watched the lonely boy of twelve play by himself on the shore, drawing in the sand and throwing rocks out into the water. He sang as he did so, content.

At this moment, the Emilio in Davi's Graylife was probably nearing Old Mandibula. He was about to learn of Afonso's Light, involuntarily welcomed into the fold by Vittorio. If only Emilio had known then that his brother and father would be dead by the time they returned home, he would've begged his mother not to go. If nothing else he could have said a final goodbye, told his papai and Davi how much he loved them. He could've begged for them to come too. If Davi was too young to know about the rebellion, he could've spent the day exploring the city with their father. Anything to keep them away from the house.

"What was he like, your brother?" the witch asked.

"He was adventurous and filled with curiosity. Always asking questions, always wanting to know more," Emilio said, watching as his brother made the same serious expression every time he flung a stick over the waves. He knew that expression well. It had never made him more sentimental than it did now. "He was known to pull a lighthearted prank every so often—it made him laugh. But, to be honest, he was the more responsible of us. I would disappear into my head, lose focus all the time, and he would cover my chores without complaint so that I wouldn't be punished. He'd never say anything about it afterward, didn't hold it over my head. I never thanked him properly."

Guilt poisoned his well of grief. Emilio couldn't decide which feeling was worse.

"He would've grown into a kindhearted man," the witch woman said. She helped Emilio to his feet.

The sun had reached its zenith and Davi stood, throwing the last stick in his hand out into the sea. He turned and headed inland, wiping sand and dirt from his clothes.

"Come," the witch woman said, "we must follow him."

They trailed after Davi, moving up the shore to the shallow bluffs. With some difficulty—especially on the part of the witch woman, who was in a long dress after all—they climbed the slope, then hurried to catch up with the young boy. His pace was modest, evidence that he felt no hurry to be anywhere. With each bend in the path, Emilio tensed further. Where would it happen? Had Davi made it all the way back to the house first, or had he been intercepted on the way home? The assassin might be near him now, watching his progress through the foliage. The thought made Emilio squirm. Perhaps they should be looking for the killer instead. If they could figure out the assassin's identity first, they wouldn't have to stick around to watch the terrible deed unfold.

Emilio began scanning the surrounding area, but nobody seemed to be stalking his brother. Not as far as he could tell.

At the olive tree with the curling branch, they met with the road, the witch woman following close enough to Davi that a bystander might've thought they were traveling together, were she visible to the folk in Davi's Graylife. The hem of her dress gathered dust, only just long enough to sweep across the path underfoot.

Emilio continued his quick search. Any bush might conceal the assassin, any tree, any boulder. But his efforts were useless. Either they were skilled enough to avoid even the gaze of a phantom observer or they weren't hidden along the path.

Finally, the house came into view.

Emilio's heart drummed a crescendo in his ear, his steady pace became a pounding march toward his brother's impending doom. Could he really let Davi walk to his death like this? He didn't think he'd have the stomach to stand by while the boy was struck down before him. He thought about the way he and his mother had discovered the two: their blood strewn across the dining room, the floor painted scarlet.

Yet, Davi continued his approach, not a worry in his step. No signs that he sensed any danger at all.

And then, from inside the house, there was a yell. A sharp cry of surprise cut short and followed by silence.

Davi froze.

Don't go, Emilio thought, but the boy sprinted away.

Emilio and the witch woman darted forth, struggling to keep up with Davi as he crossed the distance between them and the house, his boots crunching on the gravel. Emilio's pulse pounded in his ears, his breath lost to the wind whipping past his face. He chased his brother, a thousand warnings forming on his tongue. He couldn't interfere—they needed the assassin's identity. This wasn't really his brother, only a distillation of his soul. But how much of his brother was his soul?

Am I really going to let Davi die again?

The boy threw himself against the front door, bursting into the house. Emilio and the witch woman slipped inside.

"Papai?" Davi called out.

Be quiet!

The house creaked around them. The dark wood allowed for too many shadows. Davi's head swiveled, listening for signs of movement. He felt his trouser pockets, but he carried no knife.

The smallest whisper of noise came from down the hall on the left. The door to the dining room was ajar.

Don't go in there, Emilio thought. His father had to be behind that door, likely having already met his fate. Emilio had debated whether he could stand to see his brother dead again, but he hadn't realized he'd be seeing his father as well. His stomach lurched and he took an involuntary step back. He couldn't do this. No, he wouldn't force himself to watch. Not both of them.

Davi started off down the hall, taking careful steps now .Ready, it seemed, to flee at any moment. The floor creaked beneath his feet, the house warning him to run away, it wasn't too late to turn back.

Another step.

"No," Emilio whispered. He shook his head. How did he leave this place? He didn't care any longer who'd murdered his family. He could live without knowing—what good would that knowledge bring? It couldn't revive his father and brother. It wouldn't grant him peace. No matter what he might fantasize, he wasn't likely to find the murderer and exact revenge; they'd be a namely supporter of the Benevolent Leader. He wanted to go back to his own life and his own time. He didn't want to watch his brother and father die.

"Take me home," he groaned.

As Davi crossed in front of the staircase, a figure descended from above. The shadows clung to them, every move they made enshrouded by an impossible darkness that defied light. Terror came like a stab to Emilio's chest. His brother didn't see the intruder, didn't notice as they crept to the ground floor as silent as a spider.

"Davi!" Emilio cried, darting forward. Again, the witch woman stopped him, grabbing a fistful of his shirt in her hand.

"We mustn't," she said.

"He's going to die!"

"Emilio, he's already dead!"

The longer he concentrated on the assassin, the clearer they became. It was a thin woman with pitch-black hair tied at the back of her head. She wore a black tunic. Every time she moved, Emilio lost her again, as though his eyes had to readjust to seeing her.

And Davi still hadn't noticed.

Emilio tugged at the witch woman's grasp.

"You have to let me go," he pleaded. "I have to save him."

"He is beyond saving."

"He's right there."

"That is but his Graylife."

The assassin drew a dagger from her belt. It shone green in the darkness, like no steel blade Emilio had ever encountered. She raised it above her head, ready to strike. Never once making a sound. Davi was less than two paces from the door, hand outstretched to push it open.

Emilio gave a hard yank and ripped himself from the witch woman's grasp. She screamed at him, but he no longer understood her. He threw himself forward, sprinting across the front room toward the hallway, but he was off balance after breaking her hold. Emilio's shoulder collided with the wall just as he cried out again, "Davi! Behind you!"

This time, the boy must've heard. He turned.

For a fraction of a second, their eyes met, and his younger brother recognized him. His lips parted, confused. His gaze full of surprise.

Then the dagger swept across his neck.

Davi let out a choked gasp as blood sprayed out of him. He brought a hand to his neck, but he could not stem the flow. The shock never left him. His voiceless lips mouthed one word, "Emilio."

Emilio was screaming. His cries tore through his throat as he sank to the ground, pleading for the vision to cease. He no longer had control over his body. He wasn't aware of his screams, nor that he clawed at the ground, spilling his own blood on the house as he ripped the nail of his right index finger in two.

The next thing he knew, the queer sensation of disappearing had begun again, though even that wasn't enough to mask the pain he felt inside. Moments later, he was on the stone floor of the observation cell. The witch woman was at his side, holding him tight as his screams turned steadily into sobs.

~

It was nearly half an hour before she could get him to calm down. Emilio knew she was trying everything she could, but each time he started to regain some semblance of composure, he would see the gory scene unfold again and the tears would resume. How could he have let this happen?

Eventually, the shock receded and Emilio found himself sitting against the curved wall of the observatory, his legs stretched out. Collected as always, the witch woman stood opposite him. She'd let down her scarf to reveal dark hair with streaks of gray. Her hazel eyes complemented her olive-toned skin.

They didn't say anything to each other now. Emilio thought that perhaps she was waiting for him to signal when he was ready to converse. After all, he was much more disturbed by the vision than she, obviously. If Graylives were sometimes used to solve murders as she'd said—much the way they'd just done—then he wondered how many times she'd witnessed similar scenes. How else could she remain so calm under such strenuous circumstances? Were they all as bloody? Or had she simply found a way to emotionally detach herself? That seemed a terrible price to pay for knowledge. Emilio vowed that even if he witnessed a thousand such events happening to a thousand people, he would never grow numb to the sight of their blood. A life was a life.

He cleared his throat. He didn't feel much like talking, but he knew it was inevitable.

"There it was," he said, rubbing one wrist with the other hand.

"Yes," she said simply.

"I don't know what good it did."

"We know who the assassin was now," the witch woman said. He could see some triumph in her eyes, though she did her best to mask it for his sake.

"How do we know that?" he asked, confused.

"The weapon." The witch woman held up a clenched fist as if grasping a handle. "She's known as the Jade Dagger."

"The Jade Dagger?" Emilio asked.

"Yes," the witch woman said. Between them, on its pedestal, the box containing the Graylife glowed with a soft white luminescence. She stepped around it to his side of the room. "She's a master assassin—a legend of sorts—from a western empire known as Nokara. She's hard to find, and requires steep payment, but she never fails to get her target. According to the rumors, she can melt through walls like a ghost—though I think that's more myth than reality—and you only know she's struck because she takes a trinket from each hit. Didn't you notice the blade she carried? I've never seen one like it before. Jade steel with a stone handle. Either it's her, or someone trying to be her."

"But then…that means she was hired. Why would someone send a skilled assassin like the Jade Dagger to kill my family?" Emilio asked. He'd been certain one of Fogosombre's supporters had done the deed, someone who'd known about his parents' connections to the rebellion, certainly not a hired hand from overseas.

He looked up into the witch woman's eyes. She sighed and knelt to the ground beside him, looking for the first time as if she was nervous or afraid.

"It was foretold to Fogosombre that your father had the power to destroy him."

"What? Papai—"

"I believe the king must've hired the Jade Dagger to kill him."

"But why would he need someone so skilled?"

The witch woman's gaze unfocused.

"Fogosombre's hubris is incomparable. If he thought someone had the power to destroy him, he would've assumed them to be very dangerous. He must've selected her because he considered her the best." She was talking more to herself now than to Emilio, making connections in her mind at a rapid pace that made very little sense to him.

"My father didn't have anything to kill Fogosombre with."

"I don't think it worked," she mumbled. "And that's why he attacked the other village when he discovered you and your mother had moved to Corva sum Rio. He must've found out that it wasn't your *father* who had the power to destroy him, but something your father *had*."

"What are you talking about? Who moved where? What village was attacked?"

"And they stole your body to figure out what that *something* was. I hope to Deus they didn't find it."

"What are you talking about?" Emilio asked, getting angry now. If he was involved in more things than he knew, then she needed to start explaining to him what was happening. His head spun, trying to make sense of her words, though without context they came off as frightful, incoherent ranting. "How do you know so much about Fogosombre?"

Her gaze snapped back to his, a terrified understanding on her face.

"He holds influence over many things," she said in a dark tone. "Emilio, I'm sorry to have pulled you so far off course."

"Tell me what is happening!"

"My name is Jacinta. I—"

A silver-white fog appeared, materializing out of the air beside the witch woman. The both of them turned to face it, held in suspense as it thickened, and then began to dissipate. Underneath, there was a young woman roughly Emilio's age. She exuded a frantic energy, hopping on the spot as if disoriented—the same way Emilio had felt when he first transitioned to the beach in Davi's Graylife. She had auburn hair that fell just past her chin and round, frightened eyes.

When she spotted the witch woman, she leapt forward and grasped her by the shoulders.

"Jacinta!" she exclaimed.

The witch woman recoiled in disbelief. "Helena? How did you—"

"Fogosombre!" the young woman rasped. "He's here! He's at the basilica! I saw him arrive with the queen. They're here! You have to come quick."

The witch woman exchanged a glance with Emilio as though she meant to apologize, as though she wished she hadn't dragged him through that entire experience with his brother, as if she wished he wasn't witnessing this interaction now.

Both women vanished into a cloud of silver-white fog, which dissipated into thin air. Emilio sat, mouth agape, feeling gravity's strength increase on his body tenfold. He refused to believe the reasoning that slowly trickled into his brain, but the more it took hold, the harder he found it was to deny.

He was in another Graylife. That had to be true. You couldn't appear and disappear in that manner otherwise. But he hadn't entered this one willingly—not that he could remember—which could only mean that it...was *his*.

Emilio rolled forward onto his knees and retched, his insides spilling out of him as his body attempted to physically expunge his terror. His sick splattered across the stone.

No, he hadn't died. He wasn't a Graylife. He was here, now. Alive. Feeling the blood pumping through his veins and the air through his lungs. His heart thrummed in his chest and he felt pain and anguish and grief. He *couldn't* have died.

He couldn't have.

Arsenio

He had to wait at the foot of the steps while Izumi ascended to the emperor's bed chambers to request his admittance. As he waited, Arsenio looked back and forth between the sentries, wondering what kind of training it took to become so resolute and impassive. He hadn't the gall to ask, and wasn't sure they'd answer if he did.

Izumi returned after a few moments to usher him up the steps. In all his months at Kingfisher Palace, he'd never once set foot inside the emperor's chambers. Kaori always came to him. Entering now, Arsenio was astounded by its splendor, the way it unfolded around him. He didn't spot Kaori right away, his attention consumed by his grand surroundings.

The emperor stood waiting for him by a plush sofa. He wore his usual elegant robes, the fabric made warm by the candlelight. Whereas the regal dress was meant to emphasize his power and prosperity, Arsenio thought it accentuated how thin and unimposing this man—just barely out of boyhood—really was. His short black hair was neatly kept. Every ring and necklace, his neck, his jaw, his eyes, were all just as they'd ever been. And yet, the sight of him filled Arsenio with an incredible sorrow. His heart beat fast, hating every second for ticking away from him.

"Thank you, Izumi," Kaori said. "I believe that will be all for the evening."

The servant bowed low and Kaori bowed in return. Then she left, her steps retreating quickly down the stairs.

For a stretch of arduous moments, they stared at each other from across the room. Arsenio didn't know what to say. Didn't know where to begin. He felt incredibly awkward. Not because he was standing before Kaori, but because he had so many sentiments built up inside him and none of the words to get them out.

"*Anaguro, mitsuane*," Kaori said, breaking the silence.

"I've heard that said so many times. I never learned what it meant."

"*Your pain, my sorrow*. It's a poetic apology." Kaori looked every inch as apologetic as was humanly possible, but Arsenio wasn't here for apologies. He didn't want to give Kaori the chance to dissuade him from what he was about to do. "If I didn't think it would—"

But Arsenio had crossed the distance between them. He planted his lips firmly on the emperor's and ran his fingers through Kaori's hair. He had to memorize this mouth, the shapes it made, the way it tasted. He wanted to embed the texture of Kaori's hair on his fingertips, to know exactly how it felt to hold the back of his head and pull him in.

Once he'd overcome the surprise, Kaori reciprocated. He slid his hands around Arsenio. The smell of the soaps Kaori cleaned himself with—floral and bright—encompassed Arsenio and he breathed in gladly. Kaori gripped fistfuls of Arsenio's shirt, the silk fabric at its limits.

They were against one of the bookshelves, the narrow boards running across Arsenio's spine. *More*, he thought. And then *more* again. They had to keep going, further and further into intimacy. He wanted every part of Kaori. Every space he'd been denied. He slid his hands beneath the robe and pulled it down over the emperor's shoulders, baring the light cotton shirt underneath. He removed the sash at Kaori's waist, and the robe fell away completely. Kaori didn't stop the advances this time. He undressed Arsenio, though in his eagerness he fumbled.

Between kisses, Arsenio pulled the shirt up over Kaori's head and removed the last of his undergarments. For the first time, the man stood naked before him, stripped of the embroidered silks and the jewelry, the pretense and presentation. His skin was smooth, paler than the parts of him that saw the sun. Arsenio could observe every transition, from arm to shoulder, to torso, to hip, and thigh. No part of him was hidden. He stood straight, almost a head shorter than Arsenio, a subtle sinew to his surprising confidence. A beautiful poetry to his form.

Arsenio removed the last of his own clothing and stood naked as well. Every barrier had crumbled. Nothing lay between them but air and inhibitions—and how little of that was left.

"I love you," Arsenio said.

"I love you," Kaori said.

Arsenio closed the distance between them. He pressed his body against the emperor's, the tantalizing sensation of skin against bare skin sending a surge of desire through his core. When Kaori had pulled away from him the other night, the shock of unrelieved tension had nearly brought Arsenio to his knees, but there was no chance of that happening now. Kaori's arousal was as plain as his and there was no hesitation in the other man's hungry groping. Arsenio seized his lover by the waist and carried him out of the study. Gently, he lowered Kaori onto the bed, but the emperor sat back up, reaching to a shelf behind the four-poster to withdraw a small bottle like the one they'd found in the market.

"Lubricating oil?" Arsenio asked. "Did you know?"

Kaori smiled shyly. "I just wanted to be ready."

"And are you ready?"

"I want nothing else."

Inexperienced, a fleeting hesitation crossed Arsenio's mind, but his desire swept caution away. He knelt between Kaori's thighs, leaning in for another kiss. Lip to lip. Chest to chest. Hips grinding together.

"I have loved you since the first night you appeared in the infirmary, blushing with excitement," Arsenio said, entangling his fingers in Kaori's dark hair. A knot formed in his throat, but he forced the words through. "I have loved you since my name crossed your tongue. I have loved you since I stepped foot upon the black shore."

Kaori tilted his head back, eyes closed. As Arsenio ran his lips along his neck, Kaori whispered, "You are my night sky and my endless ocean. I will love you so long as the sun follows the moon across the heavens."

Then he opened the bottle.

Arsenio willed himself to breathe steadily, keeping his gaze locked on Kaori's eyes. Wanting to memorize the way they looked loving him. The passion in them. The heat. The strength. He shuddered with anticipation, his need building as the seconds ticked by. Candlelight cast the shadow of his broad shoulders over the young man on the bed.

Finally, Kaori reached out and pulled Arsenio toward him for another kiss, nervous but ready. He looked into Arsenio's eyes, his gaze conveying all that words would fail to encompass.

Then he gasped, the smallest whimper escaping his lips as he took Arsenio in, and Arsenio found Paradise.

My night sky and my endless ocean.

"You're crying," Kaori said, when he'd opened his eyes again.

A droplet fell from Arsenio's cheek onto Kaori's chest. He hadn't realized he was crying.

"It's nothing," Arsenio said. He pressed deeper. Kaori winced.

"Am I hurting you?"

"No," Kaori replied.

"Should I—"

"Please, don't stop," Kaori whispered, his plea so fragile. Almost as if he knew what was to come. He grabbed Arsenio's shoulders and pulled him closer, kissing away the tears that clung to his cheeks. He ran a hand down Arsenio's spine, applying pressure on his lower back, urging him to move inside him again. Arsenio obliged and they sank deep into a rhythmic trance. He held to every part of Kaori he could—waist, chest, shoulders, and hair. Hoping this paradise, this ebullience, never had to end.

~

Arsenio lay facing Kaori, his hand across his stomach. The last vestiges of euphoria pumped through his veins. He was spent, but enraptured and melancholic all at the same time. Sweat coated his skin and sleep tugged at his consciousness, but he lay awake, marveling at the existence of such pleasure. The feel of their intimacy, the sounds they had made would stay with him. Perhaps forever.

Because it was not to last.

So long as the sun follows the moon across the heavens, Kaori had promised. Arsenio believed him, and hoped that it was true.

He slid himself closer to Kaori's side, and turned his head toward him with a gentle hand.

"I never want to leave these bed chambers," Kaori said, still lost in his own euphoria.

"You're alright then?"

"The happiest I've ever been."

Arsenio smiled a bereaved smile.

"I wish the same," he said. "I..."

He let the words drift away, unable to finish his thought.

To his surprise, Kaori stood. He crossed in front of the bed, his naked form a silhouette in the dim light through the open balcony. He tiptoed to the study and returned with something held behind his back. When he'd slid back into the bed, he pulled the instrument out with apparent delight.

"My shinobue," Arsenio said, recognizing the flute.

"Yes, when I was teaching you a few weeks ago, you left it with me by accident. I hope it's alright that I held on to it."

"Of course," Arsenio said, though it gave him pause. To be honest, the instrument had slipped his mind. He'd no intention to dispose of it, especially since Kaori had given it to him. But what would he do with it? How was he to carry it on his journey? He reached to take it from his lover's hand, but Kaori withdrew it an inch, as if hesitant.

"May I present something to you?" he asked.

Arsenio grinned. "You needn't ask to give me something. Of course."

Kaori blushed. They'd just finished sharing the most intimate of gestures and now sat naked before one another, and yet this gift was what made him self-conscious. Arsenio shook his head. He adored the boyish timidity.

The emperor lifted the instrument to his mouth and began to play.

Arsenio wanted to laugh at first—not because the playing was poor, but because he was embarrassed to sit on the cushions while Kaori displayed his heart. The nervous urge faded quickly, however, swept aside by the unfolding melody.

It began low, a sigh he might exhale at the first signs of a setting sun. The breath was caught by the wind blowing out of the bowing trees and carried up into the clouds. There it mixed with the layers of fuchsia and gold, searching for the prettiest color with which to paint the ocean waves.

The pace quickened. The palace gardens blooming, their puckered buds spreading wide, explosions of joy they couldn't contain within. Every path led to another and another. Each decorated by a vibrancy that rewarded the deliberate patience of the waning season.

But the seasons changed as they always did and the song became high and slow, almost mournful in its tenderness. He'd left the palace altogether, standing somewhere where he and his love enjoyed serenity. The landscape was white, blanketed by untouched snow. And somehow it wasn't cold, but comforting. Radiant. Absolute.

When Kaori held the final note and pulled the shinobue from his chin, Arsenio watched him and wondered how he was ever going to leave without destroying himself. Perhaps that wasn't possible. But if he performed his role, if he did everything he could for the good of his people, perhaps Deus would look kindly upon him and he'd find Kaori again.

"Did you like it?" Kaori asked.

Arsenio could only nod. Words would inevitably fall short of describing the admiration he felt for Kaori's gift to him.

"The last time we slept in our own rooms, I lay awake through the night. I thought how terrible it was to not have you beside me, knowing how it felt to be in your arms. I tossed and turned but nothing helped. I needed you with me." He reached out and traced two fingers along Arsenio's shoulder. "I picked up the shinobue and the song spilled out of me. It was the only way I could feel you here."

Arsenio didn't trust himself to speak.

"I call it "The Snowdrift Melody." You are my rare and beautiful flower. From this moment on, my life will always be intertwined with yours."

Arsenio closed his eyes, hating himself for what he was about to say. The world was cruel for bringing him such happiness only to test his resolve to do the right thing. But if he didn't tell Kaori now, he didn't trust that he ever would.

"I can't stay," Arsenio said. There came no response, and so he opened his eyes to make sure he'd been heard. Kaori stared back at him, perplexed.

He stammered, "Do you wish to return to your bed chamber? I would gladly walk you there."

"No, I mean I can't stay here in Black Tide Cove," Arsenio whispered. He watched as realization hit Kaori, and then, as the happiness drained out of him.

"You can't mean that."

"I do. I can't remain here while my people die. I would never be able to live with myself."

"So, your plan is to leave? How will that help?" Kaori grew desperate, fear in his eyes.

"I have to do what I must, but I cannot get the help I need by staying in the palace. I'm healed now. I'm healthy. I have no further excuses."

"You have me," Kaori said. Tears ran down his face. He sat up on his knees and held both of Arsenio's hands in his own.

"I don't want you to be an excuse."

"I will defy my advisors. I am the emperor. I make the final decisions. If you need my armies, then they are yours."

Arsenio hushed him gently. "Kaori, please. I…I understand what your advisors have said to you. I don't wish for you to harm your people or put yourself in a precarious position just to make me stay."

"But I will. I know it's the right thing and I'm sorry I didn't stand up for that sooner. I have much to learn. I'm not used to being the final word."

"And when they rebuke you and tell you not to follow through, can you promise that you'll hold your ground?" Arsenio asked. He didn't mean for the words to sound harsh, but perhaps that would make this all the easier.

"I…I…"

Arsenio slid forward to embrace Kaori, holding him tight about the shoulders. He wished they weren't naked anymore, wished he didn't feel so exposed as he ignored every warring emotion inside him. He could feel the wet drip of Kaori's tears as they trickled down his back. That Kaori now offered to fight for Faron was enticing. After all, that was what Arsenio had traveled to Nokara to achieve. Yet, he wasn't lying when he said he understood the opinions Kento and Amaya clung to, that entering a military conflict would result in lives lost for Kaori's people, and he had seen the way Kento could bully the emperor into reconsidering his position. That was why he'd shifted his focus to the instructions Takahiro gave him. If he could find the Jade Dagger and she was as skilled at her craft as legend held, then there needn't be so many deaths.

"I don't understand," Kaori said. "How else do you hope to find aid?"

"I spoke to Takahiro in the dungeons."

"Takahiro?" Kaori pulled away, looking confused. Arsenio let him find his way to the answer. "You don't mean—you wish to find the Jade Dagger?"

Arsenio said nothing.

"He told you where she lives?"

Again, he remained silent.

"Then you must tell me so she can answer for her crimes against the throne. We've interrogated him night and day and he refuses to cooperate. What did he say to you?"

Arsenio shook his head. "I need her. I can't let you take her."

Kaori searched his gaze, deciding something for himself. Arsenio hoped this didn't strain their goodbye. He didn't wish to fight with the emperor. Instead, Kaori nodded, saying, "If you're successful, she could help you. I won't press you for her whereabouts. This will be my apology to you."

He deflated again.

"Everything will be fine," Arsenio whispered.

"You're leaving me," Kaori replied. "That is the furthest from 'fine' I can think of."

"But our lives are intertwined, remember?" Arsenio said, trying to ease the pain in both their hearts. "You said so yourself."

"I thought we would be together when I said that."

"I'll come back." Arsenio pulled away enough that they could rest their foreheads against one another. With his thumb, he brushed away the moisture on Kaori's face. "As soon as my people are free, I'll find a way back to you. I promise."

"You shall not go empty-handed," Kaori said. "Stay the night. Please, I beg you. In the morning, I'll let you go. You can take provisions; food and drink. You may also take a Nokari tiger to ride and ease the travel. Perhaps Ajira. She's already familiar with you."

"Are you certain?"

"Yes. It's the least I can do." He kissed Arsenio gently, mournfully. "Will you stay the night, then?"

"I will stay until first light," Arsenio agreed, feeling selfish for doing so but unable to deny himself this one last charity. "Then I must go."

He lowered Kaori back onto the bed, the weight of his body pressing down over the young emperor. They made love again, this time with a greater longing, and Arsenio savored the sensation of being inside him, the sound of Kaori's moans and his own rhythmic grunting. His pulsing desire turned tears to sweat until their skin was coated.

After they had finished, they lay intertwined beneath the blankets, the darkness all around them. When Kaori must've thought Arsenio was asleep, he whispered into the top of Arsenio's hair. Arsenio didn't move, pretending to rest though he heard every word.

"I'll be here when you return. I'll look for you every day as the tide rolls in."

CHAPTER EIGHT
DEVASTATION

Taigen

Minutes before the sixth hour, the guard changed. One by one, they vacated their posts and greeted their replacements. Taigen stood in the antechamber of the emperor's quarters, half hidden by shadows. He caught the report of a departing sentry coming from the lattice corridor.

"The foreign visitor entered the bedchambers and has yet to leave," the guard stated matter-of-factly to his replacement. The two exchanged glances, and Taigen felt a twinge in his stomach. So, Sugi was correct about Kaori's activities. Was his friend so daft that he thought the guards might not talk, or was he simply beyond caring anymore?

Taigen shook his head. He'd thought Kaori was smart enough to know when to stop this foolish rebellion against his unwanted claim to the throne. Taigen's reputation exemplified his advocacy for sexual exploration, but Kaori's infatuation with the foreign man fell squarely beyond the bounds of acceptability. What was worse, Taigen thought of all the years he'd spent sharing bed chambers with Kaori—how often he'd been undressed in front of him. Never once had he thought to cover himself in front of his friend. They were boys together, and then they were men. It shouldn't have been necessary.

If he were to strike at the heart of the matter, however, that wasn't the part that bothered him most. Taigen was used to others appreciating his body and even welcomed the attention—though he'd never paid much mind to the possibility that it could be *male* attention. No, more so than unnatural behavior, betrayal was what bothered him. Betrayal that he'd always been so open with Kaori, and yet Kaori never trusted him enough to reciprocate. Not only in this regard, but in all others as well it would seem.

Taigen wished to seize the next opportunity he could to convey his dissatisfaction with the emperor. If he were to continue being his friend and advisor, then he needed to speak out. His nature wouldn't allow him to remain otherwise.

The door into the antechamber opened and Taigen stood tall, watching from the shadows as Kaori entered the room. Arsenio came with him, wearing not the robes he'd been given at the palace but the clothes he'd been found wearing. The servants had done an astounding job cleaning the shirt and trousers of all signs of dirt and blood. The only red that remained came from the burgundy sash wrapped around his waist.

They held hands, taking no measures to conceal their attachment. Taigen frowned. His friend truly had lost his discretion.

The two departed the chamber through the double doors, their pace deliberate yet reluctant. Each step came with hesitation, an awkward falter or the hovering of a foot. So distracted were they by whatever concerns vexed them that they didn't notice Taigen treading several paces in their wake. He wanted to speak to Kaori alone, but seeing them like this now, he didn't feel right interrupting. Something was amiss. Taigen noticed the bag slung across Arsenio's shoulder.

A travel bag.

Did that mean they were leaving the city? No. Kaori didn't have one. Only Arsenio then?

The way they were always carrying on, half a step from touching noses, Taigen had thought they might never part. Even when Kaori had to fulfill his role as emperor, he always fled back to Arsenio's side the instant he'd completed his duties. They were so often together, he'd marveled at how long it'd taken for the rumors to begin in the first place. Was Kaori sending the man away? Perhaps he'd come to his senses after all.

Or perhaps he means to join him in the near future. To escape.

No. Kaori wouldn't do that. He wouldn't abandon his role or his people. He might not be suited for the crown which had been thrust upon him, but he wasn't one to shuck responsibility, especially not something so critical as the throne. His disappearance would lead to chaos in Nokara.

But if he wasn't leaving, it could only mean the separation was permanent, which meant Kaori *had* to have come to his senses. At this conclusion, Taigen felt relief spread across his chest and maybe some semblance of pride as well. Kaori couldn't keep up the charade for long, and no emperor was going to be seen loving someone of the same sex. He must've realized how inane his actions had become. He would return to being the ruler who served his people.

They went outside, descending the front steps of the palace. Kaori and Arsenio remained so fixated on each other that nothing else existed. A guard kept watch at the top of the steps, but Taigen nodded as he walked past her, keeping one flight behind the two men. Another would meet them at the bottom.

Halfway down, he stopped when he spotted Izumi headed toward them. She led Ajira.

Seeing one of Kaori's beloved pets bewildered Taigen. His friend had inherited Ajira from Empress Mai. She was a symbol of the throne. What was he doing giving her to Arsenio? That was unthinkable.

Yet, as the Nokari tiger drew level with the foreigner, she greeted him as though she understood her purpose and welcomed her fate. She ran her sleek, powerful body across him, circling her new rider protectively. When she came to sit beside him, she turned her head briefly to lock eyes with Taigen.

No one else noticed.

"Thank you," Kaori said to Izumi, who bowed and walked away.

Taigen crept closer, wanting to hear the conversation that followed. Both men remained oblivious to his presence, enough for him to sneak behind the stone pillar closest to them. He peered through the ivy leaves. Kaori's face was visible, and Taigen's illusion shattered.

The pain in Kaori's eyes stripped away any of the pride Taigen had felt. He'd never seen his friend express such hurt and loss. Kaori looked stricken and tired, as if he hadn't slept at all. He appeared diminished.

"I know you won't tell me where you're going," he said to Arsenio. They spoke Nokaran, which Taigen was grateful for. "But should you feel the urge to send a sparrow, you know where to find me."

Arsenio nodded. His right hand stroked Ajira absently, fingers combing her thick fur.

"I'm sorry I couldn't help you."

"Please, don't apologize," Arsenio said. His voice was just as soft as Kaori's, just as joyless. "I wish fate would've been kinder to us both. Under different circumstances, I would've enjoyed a lifetime with you."

"Perhaps we still can, when all this is over."

Taigen couldn't hear a response, but he suspected Arsenio agreed.

"Do you have a means to find your way?" Kaori asked.

"Yes, Takahiro told me how."

The mention of his father's name was another shock to Taigen. How had Takahiro become involved in all this? And why was Arsenio talking to him? These were questions he would have to ask Kaori later. For now, he couldn't tear himself away from Kaori's efforts to keep himself composed. The more Taigen watched, the more his anger thawed, giving way to something else.

Guilt.

"Be safe," Kaori whispered.

"I will do my best," Arsenio said. Then, "I love you."

"I love you too."

They kissed. With the sun rising over the palace walls, in the morning hours of a dying spring, they shared a kiss so powered by passion and pain and grief that it no longer mattered who was watching. This was an expression of pure, undeniable honesty. By the time they pulled away from each other, Taigen found that he was no longer trying to hide behind the pillar. He stood, though neither man turned to acknowledge him.

"I will play your song each time I think of you on the road," Arsenio said as he mounted Ajira. The great tiger stood straight, lifting his feet from the ground. Kaori clung to Arsenio's hand for a moment longer. Then Ajira took off running and Arsenio had to grab hold of her fur. The palace gates opened to let him through. In less than a minute, he was a shrinking silhouette in the distance. By two minutes, he was gone from sight.

Taigen watched him go. When he lowered his gaze to Kaori standing beneath him, he found his friend had turned back for the palace. They locked eyes. Taigen was filled with a sorrow he hadn't foreseen and knew it was only an infinitesimal fraction of what plagued Kaori. The emperor looked away.

"I'm sorry," Taigen said.

Kaori didn't respond. He merely stood at the foot of the stairs, face hidden.

"I didn't understand. I didn't know." Taigen struggled to find words. "You loved him."

"I do."

"I should've accepted that," Taigen said, wondering now if maybe he was the reason for the chasm between them and not the other way around. "You are my truest friend. I should've accepted that. You deserve—"

Kaori shook his head. Crying softly, he mounted the steps and began his ascent. "It doesn't matter what I deserve. Fate is not a balance; our fortunes ebb and flow like the tide."

"Still…"

Kaori drew level with him and then continued upward. Taigen made to join him, but the emperor held up a hand to stop him. "I would request to spend the morning alone, if you please. Let the others know that I'll resume my obligations at midday."

Taigen watched him go, wishing for all the world he knew what to say to ease the sadness in his friend's heart.

~

He had no trouble navigating the crowded corridors. The students cleared a path for him, noticing the color and pattern of his robes. In returning to the Palace Academy for the first time since his appointment, Taigen experienced the most conspicuous example of how his life had changed.

Even the eldest students stepped back to let him pass and bowed their respects. Taigen was tempted to make a snide remark to a handful that he recognized, but he held his tongue. If he were emperor, that might be one thing, but he was representing Kaori's court. Only a few months ago, the impulse would've likely overruled his sense of responsibility, but befriending Sugi had its consequences. She was proving to be more influential than either Amaya or Kento.

Taigen wasn't here to see these students. He had the company of one in mind and he knew where she would be.

He slid the library door shut behind him, the noises of the world beyond falling to a muffled quiet. Inside, the tall shelves were practically deserted. As Taigen moved down the center aisle, his head turning this way and that to check for people among the books, he spotted only one student, a young girl who quickly fled without a word.

Taigen moved on. *She* wouldn't be searching the shelves. She always came here knowing precisely what she sought and would've found it straight away. Climbing the narrow stairs past the first floor, he entered the second level, where clusters of kneeling pillows huddled around a pentagon of low circular tables. Only one person sat in the room. She leaned against the wall by a window, a massive leather-bound tome open on the ground before her.

"Yuri," he said.

The young woman looked up at him. Her long hair was held back by a scarlet ribbon. In doing so, she revealed her large ears and the roundness of her face. Smooth, unblemished skin betrayed her preference for spending hours inside the library rather than out in the palace gardens beneath the oft powerful sun. Despite her intelligence and her immaculate reputation, she sat at the cusp of her twenty-first year. The threat of a life in the military or teaching in the Academy loomed over her.

"Akedi Taigen," she said, rising to her knees and bowing her head.

"Please, Yuri," Taigen said, bringing one of the cushions over and kneeling beside her. "You don't need to be so formal with me."

"You serve in the emperor's inner circle, now," Yuri said. "It's only proper."

"But unnecessary," he said, "and uncomfortable."

Yuri smiled. She never showed her teeth when she did. "You'll grow accustomed to it."

"What are you reading about?"

"Oh, the usual. My latest fascination has been with Kaido era art styles," she said.

Taigen looked down at the open page. How she found the ability to read and retain any information from these monotonous volumes he'd never understand.

"If you're not selected, perhaps you could request a retreat to the Hall of Histories," he said. Asking for a retreat before starting mandatory service was not unheard-of among students. More often than not, they were granted unless the request was ridiculous. "They have all these books and more, as well as stores of artifacts to put faces to the names."

"I've been planning on it," Yuri said. They avoided delving further into the likelihood of her less than desirable destiny, opting, as always, to make their time together brief. "But you didn't come here to ask me about brush strokes."

"No," Taigen said. "I'm afraid not."

"What then?"

"Did you hear that the man who hired the Jade Dagger was captured?"

"Of course. I and everyone else in the city is aware."

Taigen nodded. "Do you know who it was?"

"Do tell."

"Our father."

Taigen paused, letting the information sink in. Yuri stared, eyes unfocused. Her expression was impassive, but he knew this to be her way of masking the turmoil inside. She, like he, hadn't seen their father since their respective selection days. But it didn't mean she didn't remember bits and pieces of their life before. Most students of the Palace Academy did, and sheepishly held on to these tendrils despite knowing they were supposed to relinquish all aspects of their former life.

"Is he being held in the palace?" Yuri asked, quietly.

"Yes," Taigen said.

"Why did he do it?"

Taigen explained, recounting the rant Takahiro had given in the throne room: his loss, his disappointment that his children had never been selected for anything honorable—though he'd been unaware of Taigen's presence—and his blaming of Hinata. At the end of his explanation, Yuri's brow furrowed.

"He doesn't understand that honor can come in many forms." She reached forward and shut the book. "It's not all about ruling over lands and people. It's about serving others in an effective way. If I am to teach or march alongside our country's soldiers, who is he to say this is a waste of a life?"

As Yuri looked at her brother, he could see she'd already come to accept she wouldn't be chosen before her twenty-first year. Unlike most students who held certain prejudices against this fate, she didn't view it with the same distaste. She believed her words. This made him respect her all the more.

Her flare of indignation subsided, and Yuri reached out to touch Taigen's cheek.

"I am happy the emperor chose you to be one of his advisors," she said. "I thought you were too much of a wild tiger to be of any help, but I think the role has taught you many things already."

Taigen didn't try to rebuke her even though he knew only months ago he'd been sharing his bed with escorts almost nightly—and maybe still did every once in a while. Besides, plenty of the nobility partook in such comforts, and so long as they were discrete about it, nobody blinked an eye.

"I thank you for informing me about our father," Yuri said, picking up the tome and holding it to her chest as she stood. The volume practically covered her entire torso. "I'm sure at some point, the gossip-mongers would've brought it to my attention, and I'd rather it had come from you."

"I thought you might feel that way," Taigen replied.

"It's good to see you, brother."

"And you as well."

She bowed her head respectfully again, and when he opened his mouth to protest, she only winked and hurried from the room.

Taigen was left alone, staring at the head of the stairwell down which Yuri had disappeared. He didn't often see his sister. Strictly speaking, they were not supposed to know about their sibling relationship, though Yuri had broken that rule a couple years after Taigen had been chosen for the Palace Academy. That they knew and had forged a light familial bond was further frowned upon. Yet, Taigen couldn't bring himself to leave her alone completely, and neither, it seemed, could she. Perhaps this was the compulsory entanglement the law feared.

Taigen followed after Yuri. She hadn't seemed as interested in their father's imprisonment as he. Perturbed, maybe, but her involvement ended there. She showed no desire to see or speak to him.

Taigen left the library thinking he ought to feel the same.

Mariana

Black water rocked the ship, the bow dipping into the path of the moonbeam reflected on the sea. Mariana stood on the deck feeling a heavy weight pressing down on both her shoulders. She listened to the lapping of the swells against the hull, the creak of the ship as it crested the waves. The salty maritime aroma engulfed her. Yet she felt no peace.

Only an hour ago had they finished unloading the refugees on Mauhele. Three hundred people dumped into a land they didn't know with people they couldn't understand. Several queensfolk had been around to direct the crowd, but despite their efforts there'd nearly been a riot. Families had been separated while offloading, people were hungry for something other than the rice and flatbread they'd brought for the journey. None of them were used to the heat and humidity of the islands. Chaos ensued until, very slowly, the Kailonese were able to gain control. The people were led to their new shelters.

Only when they were all out of the harbor did Mariana trust leaving them. She and her companions had boarded the vessels and pulled away from the shore. Fully stocked again, they sailed around the southern tip of the island—through the inlet between Mauhele and Medinilla—the quickest route to the Great Ocean for the return trip to Red Cliff.

If the strain of delivering her people to a foreign land were not enough, there was the thought of making the trip all over again. How she longed for a bed that didn't rock through the night. She wouldn't say no to food other than the stale bread and rice either, but hers was a small sacrifice to pay in order to bring hope to the survivors of Fogosombre's wrath.

She heard footsteps on the deck and spotted Sunev approaching her in the dim light of the hanging lanterns.

"Always churnin', the water is. But it listen," she said, her dark skin glowing by the moonlight. "Him what learns to speak its language is never lonely."

Mariana smirked. "I'm not lonely."

"The long face, then? You fear the fate of your people."

She nodded. "And I don't know if I'm ready to make the journey back, if I'm being honest."

"A life sailing is one to get used to. Took moons to make me feel home at sea. The sick would have me all the time. When I boarded the *Flaming Virtue*, them used to laugh at me tossin' me supper over the rail always. Then the captain'd had enough."

"Did he stop feeding you?"

Sunev snorted. "No. Him threaten to throw me overboard. Says he's tired of listening to me wretch."

"Were you able to stop?"

"No," Sunev said, laughing a bit. "When we make port in J'taika, me seeks out a medicine woman. When I told her me issue, she says to me she has just the thing. Seen me case a thousand times. For a gold coin she gave me a drop of potion to cure my sick. Solved the problem like that."

She snapped her fingers.

"It fixed your seasickness?"

Sunev nodded. "But here's the thing: me can't say what made the potion, thinking back. Clear, it was. Tasteless, it was. And the more me thinks, I can't be sure wasn't water the medicine woman gave me."

"But I thought it cured your sickness?"

"Either it did, or I did."

"You're not mad if it was a sham?"

Sunev shrugged. She leaned against the banister, gazing out into the sea with the shadow of a fond memory on her lips. "Whether she had me or not, I'll never know. But no matter, me lost the sick and fell in love with the sea. Sometimes learning to name your demons is what needs you. Learn them and banish them. The means don't matter much."

"And you were fine after that?"

"Me woke sometimes missing the land life, but them was dreams that got few and far between."

Mariana pondered Sunev's story. It was the most she'd heard her companion say in one conversation. That Sunev was opening up to her made Mariana happy. It'd been a long time since she'd had a friend other than one of her siblings. She hoped Arsenio was alright. Her heart ached for her twin. It'd been too many moons since they'd been separated. She'd thought about sending a sparrow to Nokara in the hopes of reaching him, but hadn't had the time.

"What's that?" Sunev asked. She faced the other side of the ship now, squinting as she struggled to see.

Mariana followed her gaze. It didn't take more than a glance to know what Sunev meant. At the same time, other crew-mates converged on the deck, staring out across the black water at the display.

"Fire," Mariana breathed.

The unmistakable glow of bright flames stood out against the night. Around them, sailors gasped as they came to the same realization. Something was amiss with this fire though. The more

Mariana stared, the more she realized the color was off. The flames had a violet tint beneath the typical orange glow.

"Where is that?" Mariana asked the nearest Kailonese shipmate.

"That must be Medinilla," the man said, then ran to spread the word.

Then, suddenly, a massive burst of flame rent the night, doubling the fire's reach. It sent billowing clouds of smoke into the air, blotting out the stars above. *What in Deus' name?* Mariana had seen things go up in flames before, but never like that. The fire's speed and reach were incredible. In seconds it seemed like a field or more of the coastline was aflame.

"Bring the ship around," the captain bellowed, hurrying past the spot where Sunev and Mariana stood. She was visibly flustered, but motivated her crew in an instant. "That's Pauwe."

"The ships from the royal fleet dock there for maintenance!" someone shouted.

The rowers rushed to their posts and began steering the ship in an about face. In under five minutes they had reversed course and were headed straight for the flames.

A third burst of fire disrupted the night. Mariana watched it billowing into the sky in a great ball. The explosions weren't natural, to be sure. Something was sending the coastline up in flames. How long could the coastal settlement stand before it was burned to the ground? The villagers…

Mariana and Sunev exchanged a glance, both having had the same realization. The sailor had said Pauwe. That was where Ramil and Nohea lived.

Facing Medinilla now, the ship sailed for the coast, sea spraying as the outriggers brushed the surface of the swells. So much of the shore was aflame that as far away as they were, Mariana could see the harbor buildings awash in orange-violet light. The trees and dense foliage had caught as well, roaring with flickering tongues. Villagers ran along the boardwalks casting great shadows against the walls, swarming as the fire engulfed the buildings. Closer they sailed, wind whipping past Mariana's face. Gaping holes in the streets stared back at her like eyes widened in permanent terror.

She immediately thought of the attack at the Red Cliffs. The mass wreckage should have been impossible. Neither swords, arrows, fire, nor catapults could deliver devastation on that scale.

The captain continued to bellow orders, and the crew scrambled to do as she demanded. Mariana stood by the bow, entranced by the image before her. Some part of her whispered an inquiry that sank in her stomach like a swallowed stone. *Did I bring this upon them?* If this was the work of Fogosombre, then she was responsible for this attack on the people of Kailon. Just as the queen had suggested she would be. But how could Fogosombre know? She'd only just delivered the first refugees to Mauhele.

And why did he attack the wrong island?

Off the starboard side, Mariana caught a brilliant flash of light. She turned and saw a burning ball of violet flame hovering above the sea.

No, not hovering. It was on a ship. They couldn't see the ship in the darkness, but it was there. Waiting for them.

"Douse the lamps!" she cried suddenly, running to the closest, which glowed yellow behind her. In the cacophony aboard the ship, nobody heard her screams. She reached up and turned the knob to shut the dampers, then spun to Sunev, who stood several meters away.

"Sunev!" she screamed. "Sunev! The lamps! Put out the lamps!"

But it was too late. Her eyes wide with horror, she watched as the trebuchet aboard the darkened ship swung the flaming ball.

It soared into the air, fire streaming behind it like the tail of a shooting star. The projectile flew true, slicing through the night with deadly precision. It headed straight for them, and instinct told Mariana it would be like no projectile she'd encountered before.

She sprinted forth, grabbing Sunev by the arm as she went. Her friend followed, not an ounce of resistance in her step. Together, they launched themselves over the banister and off the side of the ship. Hand in hand the two women soared through the blackness, warm wind grabbing tight to them like a comforting embrace.

Then the fire-ball collided with the deck of the ship.

It exploded upon impact. The flare of light blinded Mariana, even though she faced away from it. So loud was the sound that for a moment the world went silent. An immense wave of heat enveloped her, and she was thrown like a rag doll much farther than her jump should've allowed. Before she hit the water, every inch of her body felt pain.

She struck the waves. The rage of the sea swallowed her whole. The world was black.

For several seconds, Mariana couldn't understand which way was up. She spun in the water, bubbles cascading up her skin like reverse raindrops. Everything was black except for a building violet glow behind her. That had to be the surface.

Kicking, Mariana swam as hard as she could for it, the cool water easing the heat on her skin. Some part of her wondered if she'd been burned, but the salt of the sea would've stung much worse.

Or maybe her adrenaline kept the pain at bay.

With a final hard kick, she surfaced. Mariana gasped for breath. Black and white and orange and violet all around. Heat mixed with the cool ocean. She treaded water among burning debris. Voices screamed somewhere in the darkness. Cries of anguish. Cries of fear. To her left, she could see the remains of the Kailonese ship blazing in the night, poised to sink beneath the waves. Where was Sunev? Where was Lenora?

Mariana searched around her, but besides the screams she was alone. She couldn't tell board from body. She'd have to move.

"Sunev!" she called, paddling through the mess. "Lenora!"

She didn't expect they'd reply, nor that she'd be able to hear them if they did, but shouting their names felt better than remaining silent. She came across someone floating face down in the water. Doing her best to stay afloat, Mariana flipped them over.

"Sunev?" she asked. But it wasn't her friend. The woman's head rocked to one side. Dead. Mariana swam on.

This occurred several more times. Most were dead, some paddled away from her in pursuit of someone else. Many of the dead were disfigured past recognition—skin boiled into a blistering mass of inflamed tissue, faces melted and hair burned away. She hoped none of these were Lenora or Sunev, but told herself she'd know if they were.

Her muscles began to ache, the feeling coming back into her legs and arms. She paddled over to a large section of the ship's hull and grabbed on, continuing to scan her surroundings as she did so.

A hand grabbed her shoulder.

"Mari—" Sunev sank below the surface, scrabbling desperately at her friend.

Realizing Sunev couldn't stay up on her own, Mariana dived below the surface and helped bring her back above water. The woman flailed, grunting in pain as Mariana urged her to relax and take hold of the makeshift raft.

"Mari!" Sunev repeated. "Damn explosion—cut me up something bad—me leg is broke."

"Grab on," Mariana said. "Grab on, you'll float."

Sunev complied, wincing as her wounds pained her.

"What devils have they?" she asked.

"I don't know," said Mariana. "I've never seen anything like that before. Lenora?"

Sunev shook her head.

"We need to hide," Mariana said. "Fogosombre's people might come for us."

"Aye." Sunev winced. "I'd hold to that."

They started moving through the water, slowly progressing between the flaming remains. The ship beside them had half sunk now, and the few passengers still conscious onboard made to abandon the vessel. Mariana watched their tiny silhouettes leap into the water, becoming a part of the night as their ship burned. Above the salty smell of the ocean came the odor of burning wood. She was glad it masked any stench of charred flesh. Mariana did most of the kicking to keep their progress; Sunev didn't seem to be able to help much without crying out in pain.

"There!" Sunev shouted suddenly, pointing ahead to their right.

A body lay half on a piece of flotsam and half in the water. Her pale skin stood out, lit by the glow of the fire. She'd been burned on one side, but not as badly as some of the others Mariana had seen. Her head hadn't been disfigured, only discolored.

"Lenora!" Mariana shouted, but their friend didn't answer. Quickly, she altered their course. Lenora lay immobile, bobbing up and down on the sea, eyes closed as if she were sleeping. Mariana prayed to Deus that she was only knocked unconscious.

The journey to her took much longer than she would've guessed, but it was hard to estimate distances in the dark. By the time their raft bumped gently into Lenora's, Mariana was heaving labored breaths and had accidentally swallowed several mouthfuls of seawater, which stung her throat and lips. Sunev slid over to their friend and placed a hand first to Lenora's chest and then beneath her nose.

"She's alive," Sunev announced.

"Thank Deus," Mariana sighed.

Carefully, she drifted over to Sunev, and together the women shifted the unconscious Lenora. Moving her without dropping her into the sea or losing control of their raft was harder than it looked. Once, Lenora's head dipped below the surface and Mariana struggled to bring her back up again without going under herself.

Movement caught her eye.

As she dragged Lenora aboard their chunk of debris, she whipped her gaze around toward the remains of the ship. They'd drifted away from the wreckage while they helped their companion, but they were still close enough to be considered part of the flotsam. Hidden in shadow behind the burning wreckage, moving slowly enough as to not disturb the water, sailed a large black ship. The ominous vessel stalked the ruins like a phantom predator, circling their crippled prey before coming in for the kill.

"We need to leave now," Mariana hissed. Sunev nodded.

Getting to one side of the makeshift raft, they began kicking away from the wreckage, Sunev doing her best not to cry out in pain. They'd yet to see any signs of life aboard the black ship, but Mariana had a feeling the moment they did would mean it was far too late for escape.

Queen Yiscel

The jar hit the floor and fragmented into countless pieces. The scattered shards flew far enough to hit the throne room doors, while Yiscel's scream of frustration echoed beneath the high ceiling.

Locaya dismissed the servant boy, who looked frightened beyond belief, his hands outstretched as if still offering the water jug. He bowed quickly and fled the room.

"My queen," Locaya began.

"I cannot believe it," Yiscel hissed, rounding on her advisor. "How foolish I've been. How naïve! This is the thanks I've earned for helping those fucking women. The gods scorn me."

"You did acknowledge the risk, Your Highness."

"Why do you think I am not cursing *Fogosombre*?" Yiscel said. She threw herself onto the bamboo throne. "How did we not see this attack coming?"

Locaya still held the note from the sparrow in her palm. She unraveled it again, scanning the slip of paper as if she might've missed something written there. "The attack came at night. It was dark. There was only one ship, and it had no lights aboard."

"Something is being miscommunicated," Yiscel said. "They said the entire fucking harbor was nearly destroyed. There must have been more than one ship."

"The note specifically mentions 'one ship.'"

"If it was so dark, maybe they couldn't see the others."

"This may be possible, Your Highness."

"And what of the damage? How many of my people did they kill, tell me? How many perished in this attack?" She waved her arm wide, her anger unmitigated. Yiscel hated knowing so little about something which had such a great effect on her realm. She wanted information, all of it, not simply what could be scribbled on a scrap of paper small enough to tie to a sparrow's leg. The note promised more correspondence to follow, but she hadn't the patience. Perhaps it would be better to sail to Pauwe herself.

"We have no estimate yet, my queen. Another sparrow should be arriving at any moment."

"Tell me, how did Fogosombre find out so quickly? I thought the refugees arrived only yesterday." She slammed her fist on the arm of the throne. "You wish to tell me that accursed fucker had a ship ready to follow us from the Red Cliffs?"

"Again, Your Majesty," Locaya said, her hands clasped together. Yiscel knew she was making the woman repeat herself, but she didn't care. The fire within her burned too bright. "The message didn't say. I don't know if anyone has the answer to that question."

"Someone has the answer. He must have spies," Yiscel said. "I've underestimated his ruthlessness."

"My queen?"

"I made a bold decision, yes, but one that would have prompted a warning first from any rational leader." She kneaded her brow with her knuckles. "I suppose his form of warning was to attack first without question."

"I'm afraid so."

"That Faroni cunt *knew* and didn't adequately emphasize his volatility." Yiscel felt her anger flare again. The face of the Mariana woman came to mind. She and her companions, who had made such a determined effort to get her attention. That it was for a true cause couldn't be denied—Fogosombre had proved his violence—but they'd deliberately muffled how damaging his reaction would be in order to ensure her collaboration. The insolence. "I wish to see her and the two traveling companions."

"They'd already left Mauhele." It was Ilocoy who spoke this time. Yiscel had forgotten the king was still in the throne room. Since the moment they were shaken out of their sleep in the dark hours of morning with the terrible news, he'd been quiet. He lingered now behind her, staring up at the stained-glass window above him while silent tears rolled down his face.

"What do you mean?" Yiscel asked harshly, though the statement was clear.

The king turned away from the window. "One of the refugee ships had already restocked and left last night for their second trip to Faron."

Yiscel looked from her husband to her advisor. "*Shit.* Then they are far away by now."

"Yes, my queen."

"The instant they return, I demand their presence."

"At once, Your Majesty."

The doors to the throne room flew open, sweeping aside several large fragments of the shattered jar. The woman on the other side faltered when she noticed the broken shards and puddle of water. She made careful not to slip.

"A sparrow has arrived for Her Majesty," the woman said, drawing a minute roll of paper from her messenger's sash.

Locaya quickly dismounted the dais to fetch their second batch of news that morning.

"To Her Majesty, Queen Yiscel," Locaya read aloud. "The damage is more drastic than originally estimated. Seventy-seven buildings were obliterated by the explosions. Seven vessels of Her Majesty's royal fleet were tethered in the harbor for maintenance and these were sunk as well as an eighth ship, which had come from the sea to provide assistance during the attack. The tally of dead continues to rise. Our conservative estimate begins at one thousand. Signed, Datu Padilla."

Yiscel sat hunched in the throne, her forehead resting on the palm of her hand. The silence in the throne room fell thick and heavy like the humidity in the island's oppressive sunlight. How she had wished for better news. Although the first time had been an act of spontaneous rage, Queen Yiscel had half a mind to order another boy to bring her water if only to give her another jar to hurl.

"Seven seafaring ships from my fleet were in Pauwe?" she asked in a controlled voice that surprised even herself.

"Yes," Locaya said.

"And the eighth ship she mentions?"

Locaya had no answer, but Ilocoy stood behind his own throne on Yiscel's left, and he spoke with dazed numbness. "This was, perhaps, the ship that was headed back to Faron. No other ship in the fleet was scheduled to sail last night."

"And it was sunk." Yiscel shook her head. The gods were truly testing her resolve. Could anything extend the tragedy of the situation? "Meaning Mariana and her companions went down with it."

"Potentially. Unless they managed to escape," Ilocoy said.

"At least one thousand dead." The queen meditated on this estimation. Not during her entire reign had a single event claimed so many lives. The Kailon Islands were a peaceful nation. This was an act of war. When word spread of the tragedy in Pauwe, the people would demand action, and Yiscel was angry enough to grant it. "We must retaliate."

"Do you think that wise?" Ilocoy asked.

"I think it unavoidable," Yiscel said. She loved her husband, but his unyielding softness became weakness in the face of necessary violence. Not all things could be solved with patience.

"With a third of Her Majesty's fleet destroyed?" Locaya had one eyebrow cocked.

Yiscel pursed her lips. Her advisor was correct. Admitting this enraged Yiscel further. How was she supposed to deal vengeance with a third of her ships at the bottom of the ocean? There were many small vessels, of course, but these were no good in a show of force. If Faron's king could do such damage with one ship, how much could he do with the rest of his military?

Locaya cleared her throat. "Might I make a suggestion?"

"You may."

"Her Majesty could return the refugees to their homeland?"

Yiscel straightened in her throne. She couldn't deny the thought had crossed her mind. "This would be unwise," she said. "Returning the refugees would be a sign of weakness. A sign Faron has power over us. Something we cannot do. Nothing would stop their king from lording this power over us again or worse."

"But it might—"

"I have promised those people sanctuary," Yiscel said loudly, banging her fist on the arm of the throne again. Locaya shut her mouth immediately. "Be they the incentive for the attack or not, shuttling them back and forth like bartering chips is an act of poor faith. That is beneath our great nation."

"Of course, Your Grace."

"What would you have us do, then?" Ilocoy asked.

"We must call upon our allies in Nokara," Queen Yiscel said, standing. She straightened her gown, scanning the faces of all the guards and handmaids who populated the throne room. "This is a grievous attack on Kailon. My heart aches for the dead and for their families. Such brutality cannot be left unaddressed.

"Locaya, fetch me a message scroll. I must send a sparrow to Kingfisher Palace," Yiscel said. Her advisor hurried away to gather the necessary materials. "Let us hope young Emperor Kaori is prepared to uphold the friendship between our two great nations."

~

Yiscel spied Harana's back cresting the waves ahead of the boat. It comforted her to know her friend was close by. The great serpent must've sensed her distress. Though Yiscel had learned much about the mythic properties governing the relationship between a bakusawa and their imprinted human, the true depth of such a connection never ceased to amaze her. If only she had the ability to reciprocate.

Her ship approached the port at Pauwe, which was enshrouded in a fog of ash and smoke. All fires had been put out, but they left in their stead a wasteland of bleak grays. Overhead, dark clouds drifted. She prayed they brought with them rain to clear the air and begin the cycle of regrowth.

Once in the harbor, Queen Yiscel could see the shadows of hundreds of kaicats lingering below the calm surface of the water. They'd probably fled their homes along the shore to avoid death by flame. If only the people of Pauwe had had the same ability.

Several docks were damaged or crowded with half-sunken debris, and so they had to sail along until they reached one they could tether to. The second the ramp was in place, Yiscel disembarked; followed closely by the king and her advisor. They were greeted by the datu, who came jogging down the dock flanked by two individuals. She'd foregone the traditional ornamented gowns of her title in favor of common attire. Had Yiscel never met her before, she might've mistaken her for a peasant.

"Forgive my appearance, my queen," Padilla said. "These clothes are more fitting for a walk through the city. I'm afraid your dress will be ruined by the smoke and ash."

"You've made much progress in only a day," Yiscel said, though she eyed the ruins along the water.

"The dead can't help us recover," Padilla said, "but we are working nonstop. This is why I have joined the efforts."

Medinilla's datu raised her arms to better display her worker's clothing. The queen nodded. "I shall send more help, then."

"Her Majesty is most gracious," Padilla said. "But please, my queen didn't come all this way not to be shown the insult enacted upon her realm."

Padilla led Yiscel and her cohort through the streets of Pauwe. The queen was engulfed by a land of white. A layer of ash blanketed the streets and the roofs of the buildings, interrupted only by the black swathes of scorched stone and wood left behind. She saw the evidence of the explosions, damage that looked nothing like the work of fire and which was too great to be caused simply by impact.

Faces peered out from the buildings which remained standing, but the people didn't emerge from their homes to pay their respects. Fear anchored them to their hiding places. Every reminder of what had happened in Pauwe angered Yiscel. Her pulse was feverish, and by the time they'd reached the datu's home—a substantial dwelling perched on a hillside overlooking the city—Yiscel's hands shook and her jaw was clenched in fury.

More than ever, she was determined to retaliate.

Inside, Yiscel stood at the window. She didn't want Pauwe out of her sight; she didn't want to let a single ounce of her ire ebb.

"It is terrible, no?" Padilla said.

"Unimaginable," Ilocoy said, his voice barely above a whisper.

"So much destruction," Locaya muttered.

Yiscel put her hand on the window sill.

"Do you know why this happened?" the datu asked.

Yiscel couldn't avoid telling Padilla. She had a right to know, given what she'd survived. So, the queen told her. She described the three foreign women who'd come to her during the Flower Festival. She described the oppression they'd fled and their plea—she emphasized Fogosombre's brutality, not wanting to underplay what had motivated her to agree to the women's request.

"...but even I was not aware that their tyrant of a ruler was capable of this," Yiscel finished, turning away from the bleak scene below her. "Unfortunately, it seems all three women were aboard the vessel that came to your aid."

"Some survived," Padilla said. "They washed ashore the following morning."

"Were any of them foreigners?" Yiscel asked, a flurry of excitement in her chest.

"I'm afraid not," Padilla said.

Yiscel sighed.

One of the datu's servants entered the room. He handed her something small, which Yiscel couldn't see properly, no matter how she craned her neck to look.

"We've found something of interest," Padilla said. She faced them all and held the object to the light. It was a small, capped bottle. "We've found this substance at some of the explosion sites—black powder. It's not ash. It's not debris. I believe it to be part of whatever weapon that caused the damage."

Yiscel stepped up to her and held out a quivering hand. Padilla laid the bottle in her palm. The queen turned it over and over, watching the contents inside spill around like coarse black sand.

"Careful," Padilla warned. "I believe fire makes it combust, but I'm not sure what else might cause a reaction."

Black sand. The substance reminded Yiscel of the beaches which gave Black Tide Cove its name, though she knew the sands there didn't contain such tremendous power. Where had Fogosombre amassed this dark substance?

"You have suffered much," Yiscel said, thoughtful. "I thank you for your strong leadership on behalf of the people of Pauwe. I thank you also for showing me what's happened here. Please, rest assured knowing this attack will not go unpunished."

"Your firm hand is appreciated, my queen," Padilla said, bowing her head.

"I would like to keep this sample," Yiscel said.

"If it pleases Your Majesty," Padilla said. "If more is found, I can send a sparrow."

"Please do." Yiscel turned to Locaya and Ilocoy. The queen knew at least her advisor would be satisfied by what she intended. Locaya could be reunited with her husband. "I wish to go to

Mauhele now. Seeing the ruins here has both saddened and angered me."

As expected, Locaya had a brief, conspicuous reaction. The king was more inquisitive.

"What do you intend, my love?" Ilocoy asked.

"I must address the refugees," Yiscel said. The head advisor and the king exchanged a concerned glance, but Yiscel did not pause to allow them to voice any misgivings. There would be time to explore her intentions aboard the boat. She headed for the door, her guards immediately moving to her side. With a brief farewell to the datu, she left the house and began her descent down into the ashen ruins of Pauwe.

Ira

As a sanctuary of the Holy Order, the basilica was ill equipped to house royal guests. The beds were adequate, but the linens coarse and plain. Each mattress was small, though Ira was fortunate enough to have her own bed chamber, since no single dwelling was large enough for the royal couple to share. The luxury of her own room ended there, however. Barren stone walls with minuscule, obfuscatory windows greeted her every morning. Like most of the corridors and chambers, it smelled like mold.

Mostly, the visit bored her. Fogosombre talked endlessly about mining with the master, the elders, and Commander Luctus—one of his famed *Omens* who'd been given control of the soldiers in the mines. How much did they yield per day? Could they yield more? Had they looked in *these* areas? The relentless talk went in circles, never accomplishing much except aggravating her husband. She didn't understand why he felt so pressed for time. Nobody had anything like Shadow Fire.

So she stopped attending these meetings, choosing instead to wander on her own.

Fernão had not been brought along. Fogosombre decided his son would be too much of a distraction. Ira's sneaking suspicion was that he wouldn't find the boy useful until the day he could slay men with a sword. Until then, Fernão would stay behind with his guard and his teachers.

Ira did miss her son, but she worried more about her inability to monitor him from this distance. She imagined him causing more trouble in Braecliff Castle than normal, with nobody around willing to punish him. She imagined Fernão sneaking off to loiter about the prisoner Otohiko, who would fill his mind with dangerous thoughts.

She felt more useless here than in Ciro. At least there she could order around the servants who were satisfyingly afraid of her. Only one servant—a young woman named Helena with auburn hair and wide, round eyes—positively cowered at the sight of her. Ira made a point to seek her out whenever she needed a good bout of release.

On the ninth evening after their arrival, Ira sat at the table in a private chamber off the elders' living quarters. She stared into the bright flame of a candle, arms crossed over her chest. The table was Vida and Morta's—their *divining* stone—which they insisted had to be brought wherever they went. The tabletop was made of solid granite, which had caused quite a few delays to getting to the basilica. The Fates would be aghast to see Ira resting her candle on their precious stone. So she took pleasure in doing so in their absence.

Even as the first days of summer arrived, a chill clung to the mountain air in the evenings. Ira pulled the thick fur coat tight around her shoulders, wondering why Master Tais didn't have the servants build a better fire. She half listened to the conversation between the man and her husband, thinking it might be worth it to seek out the fearful girl to feed the flame.

"...that vein will be completely dug up two days from tomorrow. Forgive me, my king, but they are working as fast as they can."

"Then speed is not my issue," Fogosombre said, leaning against the mantle with his forearm. "We cannot let the source run dry. Find another vein."

"I have no one else to spare. They are all in the mines."

"I find that hard to believe, Tais."

"Please, my king, it's true," Tais pleaded. "Every soldier you've sent is down there."

"Then I shall need to send more."

Tais took a few cautionary steps toward Fogosombre, his arms folded into the sleeves of his white robe. He continued speaking in a low tone that Ira could nonetheless make out perfectly. "Need you so much so soon? Are we expecting...a confrontation?"

Fogosombre looked at the man, his eyebrows drawn into a sharp valley. "Do you question me?"

"No, no!" The Master Magistrata gasped, shaking his head.

"Because if you are, finding a new master of the Quartz Basilica may become necessary. Luctus, would you deal with this man."

The looming commander stepped forward.

"I would never," Tais said, his eyes darting back and forth between Fogosombre's black scars and the broach of the pierced skull on Luctus's chest. Ira smirked privately at the way the magistrata cowered in the presence of these greater men. "I am merely curious—"

"Prudence means preparing for your enemy *before* needing to," Fogosombre said. He stood straight, towering above the Magistrata.

"Of course, very wise, Your Grace."

Fogosombre put a hand on his shoulder, and Tais' knees nearly gave way. "I do not wish to keep you in the dark, however. You have been a great help to my cause, Master Tais, and your cooperation is appreciated."

"My king. *Anything* for you. I am ready and willing."

At that moment, the chamber door opened and in walked Vida and Morta. The queen couldn't stop her fists from clenching.

"Your Majesty!" Vida said. "We feel stirrings in other realms."

"Great stirrings!" Morta said, raising her hands. "Such that must be divined."

They turned toward the divining stone and Vida gasped audibly. Ira cringed, not because the sound startled her but because the woman's hiss annoyed her so.

"You have placed a candle on the divining stone?" Vida squealed.

"A candle!" Morta agonized.

"Calm your titters," Ira said. She grabbed the candle holder and stood, brushing her black hair over her shoulder. "I have spilled none of the wax. Your precious table is unharmed."

Vida ran over to investigate the surface, running her fingers across the granite. "Any blemish *any blemish at all*—could mar the magic and render the divining stone useless."

"*Useless!*"

"It must be pure."

"Alright, alright," Ira said, waving her hand before her face as if their words were smoke easily dispersed. She went to stand beside her husband, who watched the Fates with interest. Upon meeting Fogosombre, she would've never assumed him to be a superstitious man, but the faith he placed in Vida and Morta's revelations couldn't be dismissed. Both women reached into their cloaks and withdrew small gray stones. The four looked on with interest—reluctant interest on Ira's part, though she did find she couldn't look away—as they chanted under their breaths in another language and raised their fists high above their heads. In unison, they threw the stones down upon the table.

As the rocks struck the granite, they burst into a rising cloud of gray dust that went swirling into the air. The flickering light from the hearth played across the cloud. Ira tried to hold to her skepticism, but even she saw that among the gray dust, images appeared.

"As we thought," Vida said.

"There is much to divine," Morta agreed. They encircled the round table, observing the sinking cloud from all angles. Though Ira could see the images, she had no idea what they might be. They looked like suggestions of scenes, the vague outlines of human forms. Was it just the dim light, or did the figures move as she watched them?

"Your shadowed future continues to approach."

"Shadow against shadow as we foretold before."

"Unless you choose your path wisely, the clash will become unavoidable."

"And where shadow and shadow meet..."

They finished in unison. "Death will follow."

The dust settled and the crackle of the flames in the hearth became the only sound in the chamber. Ira looked to Fogosombre as did Master Tais in trembling fear. Fogosombre clasped his hands together at his waist and stepped toward the Fates.

"How quickly does the shadow approach?" he asked.

"We cannot say."

"Only that it is indeed coming."

"And will I know when the choices that decide the shadow's imminence are at hand?" Fogosombre asked, his deep growling voice resonating in Ira's chest.

"The dust has not revealed," Vida said.

The king's brow darkened. "I cannot allow anything to stop me. No human and no shadow. Ruminate on these predictions more—tell me all you can. I will continue to oversee the mining here at the basilica."

Deus, no. Please may we not stay for much longer.

As if on cue, something flew through the chamber's open window. It was a small, excited thing that zipped into the room and flapped in tight circles over their heads: a sparrow, gray and brown with black markings on its head. Each pair of eyes followed its progress, wondering where it would land. The spell should've made it instinctively fly to its intended recipient, but perhaps the sender was not so skilled at sending sparrows, or had done so in a hurry.

Finally, the bird landed on the mantel as close to Ira as it could, and held out its leg in offering to her. Unsure of how she could possibly be the correct recipient, Ira turned blankly to the room, but the others merely waited for her to answer the small creature. With delicate hands, she reached out and unfastened the note around its leg.

The moment the note had been removed, the sparrow darted out through the window.

"Well, what does it say?" Fogosombre asked, impatient.

Ira unraveled the scroll. On it was written only one sentence.

"I have figured it out," she read. "Otohiko."

The shift in atmosphere was instant.

"We must go," Fogosombre said.

"But the mines?" Ira asked, heart hammering. "And it's the middle of the night."

"We cannot wait," he said. He crossed to the door, grabbing the handle in his massive fist. "Tais, have someone fetch our horses and our cart. Luctus, wake our people. We depart within the hour."

They were going to leave now? Outside the world was black. Ira understood the urgency, but surely they could wait until morning. That only minutes ago she'd been begging to leave was not lost on the queen, but the circumstances had changed. If the note the prisoner had sent was true, then everything would be different when they made it back to Ciro. Otohiko had been poring over those books for months, and though she'd known eventually he'd have to make some progress, she'd never actually thought he'd solve the issue.

"Wait!" Vida cried, her crackling voice setting Ira's teeth on edge now more than ever.

"You must send soldiers to move the divining stone!" Morta said.

Fogosombre's head snapped around to face them. He grunted with impatience, chin jutting out dangerously. Ira knew that fire in his eyes, that determination to get his way. She feared it. The black scars along his throat shifted grotesquely in the firelight. With slow, lumbering steps, he left the doorway and walked over to the round granite table. With one hand, he reached out and gripped it by the edge. He lifted the table into the air, turned on his heel once more, and left the chamber.

Ira followed without a word. It appeared they would be leaving the Quartz Basilica tonight whether she wanted to or not.

Kaori

Focusing on reality became his daily frustration. He was wont to drift away, his mind pulled into the realms of possibility. In the span of mere months, Arsenio had altered everything he'd envisioned for his future. The future he'd hoped they'd both be a part of. Now, his errant mind extricated itself from his surroundings at inopportune moments. He would see Arsenio in the wide flower blossoms, a face in the reflection of the water. The absence of Ajira also brought him to mind, and Kaori was helpless to avoid it.

If there was any benefit to Arsenio's leaving, it was that his and Taigen's relationship had repaired somewhat. His friend had quashed his penchant for making sexually suggestive comments regarding Kaori and women. He respected Kaori's feelings for the departed boy. Though he did not actively suggest Kaori pursue other men to fulfill his marriage requirement, he kept from bringing up the subject altogether.

If only Amaya and Kento could do the same. Amaya's relief and Kento's smugness at Arsenio's absence drove a wedge of disdain between the emperor and his two elder advisors. He appreciated their wisdom, but loathed their lectures.

They didn't understand.

Where was Arsenio now? He'd be far away down the coast of Nokara. With Ajira at his side, perhaps he wouldn't be troubled by thieves, but there were other dangers on the road. Wild animals lived in the forests. Weather. Terrain. Had Arsenio done an adequate job rationing the food he'd been provided? Was he lonely at night?

Kaori was lonely at night.

His massive bed felt all the more isolating without Arsenio's warmth beside him, without the ability to run his fingers through the dark auburn hair. He missed the curve of Arsenio's back, the brown eyes locked on his, the man's lips, his smile, his laugh, his voice—the deep whisper, half-asleep.

He missed everything.

He could tell all this to Taigen and Sugi, but they couldn't truly understand.

"...if I may, Your Majesty."

Kaori raised his eyes, pulled into the throne room by the address. He looked around. Everyone assembled had gone silent, staring at him expectantly. On the floor stood a woman. Her rough hands described a lifetime of hard, manual labor. Kaori shifted, feeling guilty that he hadn't been paying attention.

"Ah...um. Yes," he said, clearing his throat.

"You summoned me here, my emperor?" the woman said, prompting his memory.

"Oh!" Kaori suddenly recalled. She'd been summoned to Black Tide Cove from the central farming villages as a representative. Kaori was supposed to pass on news to her, good news that she would then take back to her villages. The meetings had been unceasing the past few days.

"Thank you for coming," Kaori said, now fully composed. "As you know, an unusually dry waning season has plagued

Nokara. Several worried farmers from the central regions have come to the palace, including yourself, with pleas for aid. Your voices have been heard, and the Nokari throne wishes to help you.

"After much discussion, it has been decided by the city's chief builders that we will dig out a canal to divert a portion of the great Jishuan River to flow through the central villages. From this water source, you and your people should be able to provide for the crops."

The woman bowed her head when he'd finished speaking. "Your Majesty is most gracious," she said. "This is remarkable news. The farming villages will be pleased to hear of your plan."

"You are most welcome," Kaori said. "Builders will be sent with the materials within a week."

"Thank you," she replied, bowing again. "Thank you, Your Majesty."

Seeing how well she received the news, Kaori felt satisfaction sweep through his veins. The most positive emotion he'd had in days. He breathed it in like a sweet aroma, and mourned it as it quickly faded.

Then a messenger came through the side door and everything changed again. She walked up to the edge of the dais and Sugi stepped down to meet her. They exchanged hushed whispers while the assembly looked on intrigued. Though he had no context, Sugi's dour expression could only mean that whatever news the messenger brought wasn't positive. He thought immediately of Arsenio—pictured him injured and trapped somewhere dangerous. But he steered his mind from this conclusion. Although it would crush Kaori, this type of news wasn't important enough to the empire to warrant such urgency.

The two women broke off their conversation. The messenger left through the doorway as Sugi mounted the dais again to whisper to Kaori and the huddle of advisors.

"It's from Queen Yiscel of Kailon," Sugi said, her eyes wide. "Medinilla has been attacked."

~

As soon as the door closed behind them, Kaori spun to face his advisors.

"This has gone on long enough," he said. "Arsenio warned us of Fogosombre's tyranny, and now the violence has spread to our allies in Kailon."

"The queen was housing refugees," Kento said, as if this justified the attack.

"And without communication, Fogosombre escalated the situation. He lit Medinilla aflame."

"Was there any report on the extent of the damage?" Amaya asked Sugi.

Sugi shook her head. "No, the message was brief."

"May we hear it in its entirety?" Kento asked.

Sugi hesitated, unaccustomed to the attention, but she was strong willed. "Medinilla has been attacked. We are unable to respond fully to this act of war. Emperor Kaori, I am confident you will uphold the friendship of our nations. Signed, Queen Yiscel Baquiran."

An act of war then. She made no fuss over calling this what it was. And she had made a point to mention the link she and Empress Mai had forged between their two countries. *Uphold the friendship of our nations.*

She'd made her expectations clear.

"Are you considering involvement?" Kento asked.

"Whether we like it or not, we have become involved."

"You cannot ignore the plea for aid," Amaya said.

"We should send rations," Taigen said. "Food and clothing."

"Medicine for the wounded," Amaya added.

"Perhaps we shouldn't jump to giving away what they might not need," Kento said. "Send the queen a sparrow."

"She requested action," Kaori said.

"'Uphold the friendship of our nations' does not mean your immediate presence."

"Nor is it casual enough to warrant a flippant sparrow in response."

"There are many islands full of resources."

"And she denoted their inability to recover."

"If you subject your people—"

"I am only talking about traveling to Banguet."

"Kaori, listen—"

"No, you listen to me." He'd had enough. Kaori felt his airways clearing. The more he talked, the easier it was to breathe. Kento was taken aback by this new commanding tone, but the emperor found this reaction only empowered him more. To his right, Taigen gave him an encouraging nod. "I ignored the plea of a foreigner who came to us asking for help, but I cannot also ignore the cries of our closest ally. If I do, I can only see it straining our relationship with the island nation.

"The fact of the matter is this eastern king has proven himself to be a formidable enemy to all. One of our ally's largest islands was attacked. If they are asking for help, then it must be a grave situation indeed."

"We will help then?" Amaya asked. Kaori was worried that she opposed his decision to engage, but he could tell by her tone and her resolute expression revealed her position on the matter had changed. The attack on Medinilla was too great to brush aside.

"Yes," Kaori answered.

"I wonder if Your Majesty shouldn't take more time to consider the consequences," Kento began. "Think of the Nokari *lives* at stake."

"This is not a vote," Kaori said. "I haven't committed us to war yet, Kento. I have merely stated my intention to be present by Queen Yiscel at this time."

"How do you wish to proceed?" Taigen asked.

Kaori considered this. He could guess what Yiscel would want from him. Nokara's navy was large and powerful, much more so than Kailon's. He would urge against retaliation, but depending on how great the damages were, she might not be willing to discuss alternatives. Kaori thought it wise to bring General Benji Atodako, a famously brilliant military mind, but the emperor knew he'd want more perspectives than that of someone who specialized in plotting battle strategies.

"I will sail with Benji Atodako to Banguet City to meet with Queen Yiscel. Amaya." He turned to his advisor, who looked as though she knew what he was about to ask and willingly accepted the responsibility. "You will come with me. Kento, Taigen, and Sugi—you will remain here and govern Nokara in my place until I return."

The three, who would stay behind, bowed.

"We will honor the spirit of your leadership," Sugi said.

Unable to mute his concern, Kento parted his pursed lips. "You know what will come of this, emperor," he said.

"Enlighten me," Kaori replied.

"The queen will want war against Faron."

Kaori nodded. "Perhaps. But maybe that is necessary for peace."

"I will alert General Benji to prepare for departure," Amaya said.

"We will leave as soon as he's ready," Kaori said.

Sugi stepped forward. "I will send word to Queen Yiscel of your arrival."

"Thank you."

Both women left the room.

"It looks like you have matters well taken care of," Kento said, bowing. He seemed resigned to the decision. "If the emperor needs me, I will be in my chambers."

And then there were only the two left.

"I'm surprised you don't want me with you," Taigen said. His voice betrayed the emotions he held back.

Kaori turned toward the exit and his friend followed. "I thought we were done being formal with each other?"

Taigen smirked. "Alright. Then why the hell aren't you bringing me along? I am a more than adequate combatant. I could be of real use by your side out there. You'll need protection."

"I will have guards," Kaori said.

"Yes, but I am also your closest friend."

They pushed open the door, entering the now empty throne room. Without the throngs of people and constant commotion, the hall felt overly grand and empty. Light from the clear day outside shone through the high windows, pouring down upon the floor in great swaths of white.

"That's why I need you here," Kaori said. "Kento has plenty of knowledge, and he's a strong leader, but he doesn't always agree with my way of seeing things. I trust you and Sugi to represent me while I'm gone."

"And how long will you be gone?" Taigen asked.

"I don't know," Kaori said, truthfully. "As long as I'm needed."

Taigen nodded. "I was wrong."

"About what?"

"When I said you couldn't lead a nation." Taigen placed a hand on Kaori's shoulder and gave him a brotherly squeeze. "It's in you, and I see you becoming more aware of that with each passing day."

Kaori didn't say anything in response. He stood beside Taigen, staring up at the dais. In the center was the golden throne, decorated with embellishments and gems meant to represent the regality of his title. To one side, the smaller throne that would one day be the seat of his spouse, to the other, the seat of his head advisor, Amaya. The remaining four seats were divided on either end, the places for his other advisors, though as of now one of those remained unclaimed. He had so reluctantly accepted this title, and yet his decision to leave left Kaori wondering if he would miss the golden throne.

He was sailing for new tides now.

"If Arsenio sends a sparrow or returns—"

"You will be the first to know," Taigen said with a smile.

Turning on his heel, Kaori led the way down the chamber toward the double doors. His shoes echoed off the marble floor, the room reminding him that life was cyclical and things had a way of returning in one form or another. Echoes and seasons, the rise and fall of the sun, or the ebb and flow of the tide—few things in this world could be considered truly stationary.

Kaori placed both palms against the doors and pushed them open. He would be back. For now, it was time for him to witness what lay beyond his home.

Acknowledgements

A picture is worth a thousand words, and apparently fantasy epics are worth a few hundred thousand. That's enough to leave the mind reeling, but luckily I know a lot of willing souls to help me sift through the mess.

My thanks go first and foremost to my husband, Alex, who watched this story evolve from mad scrambling into the first, coherent draft. He has been its most zealous devotee, its harshest critic, and its greatest advocate.

Thanks to my beta readers who helped smooth all the rough edges of this novel. Your feedback is invaluable, always.

Thanks to JRR Tolkien for writing Lord of the Rings, NK Jemisin for writing The Broken Earth, George RR Martin for writing A Song of Ice and Fire (lots of initials here), and David Mitchell for writing, period.

To the team at Midnight Meadow Publishing, thanks for believing in my series enough to pluck it from obscurity. I'm glad to have found such a fitting home for my world and my characters.

Lastly, to you, the readers, who take my many words and turn them into thousands of pictures. Without you these pages would just be the silly ramblings of an overactive imagination.

ABOUT THE AUTHOR

At nine years old, RD Pires began writing his first novel. Titled *Lost* (this was years before the hit TV show), it awoke in him a passion for storytelling that has yet to wane. Throughout his younger years, he would hone this craft, entering young authors' competitions and sharing his works with friends who would scribble commentary in the margins. When it came time to choose a college major, he was torn between his two loves: penning fiction and roller coaster design. He eventually settled on the latter, and studied Mechanical Engineering at University of California, Davis, though writing was never far from his mind.

Robby has since self-published three separate works, including the novel *A Vast, Untethered Ocean*, the novella *In Death Do Flowers Grow*, and a collection of short fiction entitled *A Sky Littered with Stories*. When he's not writing, he can usually be found cooking, watching horror movies, or traveling the country adding roller coasters to his list of ride credits.

He lives in Northern California with his husband.

Printed in the USA
CPSIA information can be obtained
at www.ICGtesting.com
LVHW091122020724
784485LV00006B/308

9 781956 037371